MAI

YALDING

7/06

29. DEC

1 5

KT-416-075

Books should be returned or renewed by the
last date stamped above.

DIM

WITHDRAWN

Kent
County
Council

00884\DTP\RN\04.05   LIB 7

CHARTER MARK

CUSTOMER SERVICE EXCELLENCE

C152776772

SPECIAL MESSAGE TO READERS

This book is published under the auspices of

THE ULVERSCROFT FOUNDATION

(registered charity No. 264873 UK)

Established in 1972 to provide funds for research, diagnosis and treatment of eye diseases. Examples of contributions made are: —

A Children's Assessment Unit at Moorfield's Hospital, London.

•

Twin operating theatres at the Western Ophthalmic Hospital, London.

•

A Chair of Ophthalmology at the Royal Australian College of Ophthalmologists.

•

The Ulverscroft Children's Eye Unit at the Great Ormond Street Hospital For Sick Children, London.

You can help further the work of the Foundation by making a donation or leaving a legacy. Every contribution, no matter how small, is received with gratitude. Please write for details to:

THE ULVERSCROFT FOUNDATION,
The Green, Bradgate Road, Anstey,
Leicester LE7 7FU, England.
Telephone: (0116) 236 4325

In Australia write to:
THE ULVERSCROFT FOUNDATION,
c/o The Royal Australian and New Zealand
College of Ophthalmologists,
94-98, Chalmers Street, Surry Hills,
N.S.W. 2010, Australia

MURDER IN BURGOS

On holiday in Spain, Moss Coen is mistakenly arrested. He tries to escape from police custody, but in the city of Burgos, birthplace of El Cid, evidence connects him with murder. Unable to converse in Spanish, he then encounters Isabel Hervada Arias who has her reasons for offering help . . . There are other victims, and Moss finds himself a target for the killer whose ruthless ambition has led to more than one kind of crime.

LORETTE FOLEY

MURDER IN BURGOS

Complete and Unabridged

LINFORD
Leicester

First published in Great Britain by
Robert Hale Limited
London

First Linford Edition
published 2006
by arrangement with
Robert Hale Limited
London

Copyright © 1981 by Lorette Foley
All rights reserved

British Library CIP Data

Foley, Lorette
 Murder in Burgos.—Large print ed.—
Linford mystery library
 1. Burgos (Spain)—Fiction
 2. Detective and mystery stories
 3. Large type books
 I. Title
 823.9'14 [F]

ISBN 1–84617–260–8

Published by
F. A. Thorpe (Publishing)
Anstey, Leicestershire

Set by Words & Graphics Ltd.
Anstey, Leicestershire
Printed and bound in Great Britain by
T. J. International Ltd., Padstow, Cornwall

This book is printed on acid-free paper

KENT
ARTS & LIBRARIES

C 1 5 2 7 7 6 7 7 2

1

The man stepped out of the train. It was the *Puerta del Sol*, the Paris express which he had boarded in Madrid, and which now deposited him with his modest luggage at a city in Northern Spain. At ten o'clock on a July evening the station was crowded with returning holiday-makers, many of them French tourists. Only three hours before, he had been in Madrid which had seen the beginning of his own private holiday as distinct from the package tour he had taken from Dublin.

Even that had been quite by chance. Inspector Doody's mother-in-law had died and Mrs Doody wouldn't go away. So Doody had offered to exchange with Coen, who was down for September.

When his secretary was told, she asked where he would spend this holiday and Moss had merely shrugged.

'You should get away somewhere,' she

said, aware of her boss's tired eyes and defeated shoulders, and she hunted around for a daily paper. 'Look, here are last-minute holiday bargains in Sitges or Corfu. Or how about Alicante — one week from Saturday?'

'Spain?' Moss evinced no enthusiasm.

However, that Saturday he was a passenger on a charter flight from Dublin to Alicante.

After three days lying on the beach, he began to revive. He enjoyed the night-life. He went sightseeing in the town. There was a bus-trip to Benidorm, and after that he spent a day at sea, sailing to Calpe. Moss realized he didn't want to return home after only one week. But his hotel was fully booked, as were others near-by. Anyway, perhaps he had rather exhausted the attractions of the Costa Blanca. Why not see Madrid?

He went there by train and experienced a hectic four days, after which he decided to travel north to Burgos en route to the frontier. If the money held out he might even manage a few days in Paris. And to think he hadn't actually wanted to come on this holiday at all!

As Moss now emerged from the brightly-lit station, a small sad-faced man moved across his path, the man's eyes fixed on the suitcase Moss was carrying. It bore no label, and a rather curious dialogue ensued, for the visitor spoke little Spanish. However, having taken charge of the suitcase, the man held it firmly and led the way down the street in the direction of the city centre. They passed through several other streets until the guide finally indicated a tall narrow doorway.

'Pensión Excelsior,' Moss read over the door.

The small man rang the bell, and after a slight delay it was answered by a young girl. She said nothing, but stood aside to allow the two men to enter. She then closed the door and would have turned away but the guide detained her, speaking in a low tone. Moss could not hear what was said.

While he waited, he had leisure to look around and noted solid old-fashioned fittings and a rather shabby carpet. There was a framed certificate from the Turismo, and it seemed Pensión Excelsior was among the *pensiones de tercera*, and its charges were modest.

Moss was pleased. He could stay several days and there would be enough money left for his Paris trip and return journey home.

As the visitor was engaged in making these calculations, a young man emerged from a room at the back of the hall and called impatiently: '*¡Maria!*' The girl turned immediately and moved across the hall to where the caller stood in the shadow of the stairs, but even as she did so a plump elderly man descended from the floor above, and the girl gave a quick glance in his direction and then abruptly turned back to Moss and motioned him to accompany her.

Fitting her slim body behind a desk, she began to deal competently with her new arrival. Moss intimated he would be staying for two or three days, and she took his passport. The elderly man, obviously the proprietor, waited for a few moments and then made his way to the back of the house. Of the young man there was now no sign. Moss tipped the guide, who then left.

Maria touched a bell, and presently a boy appeared from the kitchen regions and made to conduct Moss to his room, the visitor first enquiring if it was possible to have a meal. The girl looked at her watch and shrugged. Then she came out from behind the desk, and her elegant shoes clicked musically as she disappeared down the back corridor. When she returned it was to say a dinner would be served in about twenty minutes.

Ushered into a small very clean room with polished floor-boards and heavy oak furniture, Moss unpacked his few belongings. The room was airless and he went to open the window, only to discover that the room faced a small inner courtyard and was apparently above the kitchen, for a heavy smell of cooking wafted in. He shut the window again.

The atmosphere in the dining-room was rather pleasant nevertheless. Soft music came from the radio, followed later by a news-reader making various announcements few of which Moss could understand. Another guest lingered over the remains of his meal and stared whole-heartedly at the stranger. Presently he left.

Moss was finishing his coffee and deciding he might just as well turn in when the door opened and Maria entered. She looked as if she had expected to find the room empty, and paused when she saw him.

The waiter came in just then and began to lay a place for her at a table near the door. She glanced over to Moss and smiled, rather wearily he thought.

'I finish work now,' she said, 'and have dinner.'

He put down his coffee-cup and rose. 'I was just leaving anyway,' he said.

'Please, no . . . '

By the time the waiter returned with a *tortilla*, Moss was seated at her table, and a rather halting conversation was in progress. He ordered a bottle of wine, and the waiter brought two glasses. She was hesitant at first and cast sideways glances towards the door.

'Señor Perille is not here now,' she said at length, and Moss understood that Perille, the plump gentleman on the stairs, would frown at this informality on the part of a member of his staff.

Indeed, half-way through the meal when the door opened abruptly she looked quite startled, but it was only the waiter to say she was wanted on the telephone.

She returned in more light-hearted mood and brought with her a guide-book of the city which she presented to Moss, and she then described to him some of the places of interest, descriptions as graphic as her halting English and his meagre Spanish would allow.

Only a short time later they set out together to view Burgos by night. They took a taxi to the Plaza Paloma, finally ending the evening in a café under the twinkling lights of the Paseo del Espolón, overlooking the Arlanzón river.

It was the happiest evening of his entire holiday he told Maria later. He must have had a presentiment.

2

The stream of events which ultimately put him in hospital, and that only by what might be called a bit of luck, began (as with so many disasters) in one careless moment.

Next morning, Moss woke abruptly. No sunlight entered his room, yet he was conscious of the house stirring and footsteps on the stairs. He looked at his watch. Six o'clock. Too early to get up.

He closed his eyes once more and into his mind came images of the broad squares and little narrow streets he had seen just a few hours ago, and towering over all the great thirteenth-century cathedral, floodlit by night. The streets would be quiet and empty now in the early morning.

He heaved himself out of bed and began dressing, contemplating with pleasure a day full of leisured activity. An early morning stroll, breakfast in some street café perhaps, then a little sightseeing, after which a return to the Excelsior for lunch; the afternoon and evening to be spent with Maria, whose half-day it was. Altogether a very satisfactory programme.

He shaved carefully, for his beard was dark and the growth a heavy one, as was that of his stiff coarse dark hair. Dressed in jacket and slacks and an open-necked shirt, quietly he left the pension, finding the front door already unlocked. No one was about, although sounds of activity were to be heard in the kitchen.

After walking some distance, he emerged into the Plaza de Vega. The sun was up and illuminated the many turrets of St Mary's Arch, under which he passed. He slowly mounted the hill until he came within sight of the castle grounds, and then turned and viewed the surrounding scene bathed in strong warm sunlight: below and to his left the cathedral of Burgos, and behind him the ruins of the castle which figured largely in the life of the legendary Rodrigo Díaz de Vivar, the Cid Campeador.

9

More people were about now as he walked down to the river, strolling along its banks in the direction of the Isla. Here he found a small café and ate a leisurely and substantial breakfast.

It was while waiting for this meal, savouring the aroma of freshly-ground coffee beans and newly-baked rolls, and listening to the proprietor busily preparing his eggs and bacon, that Moss idly turned over the pages of the guide-book Maria had given him. No tourist (said this book) should omit a visit to the famous monastery of Las Huelgas, only a short bus-ride from the centre of Burgos.

Moss looked at his watch. It was not yet nine o'clock. He had plenty of time. Buses every half-hour, so said the guide-book.

When he had finished his meal, he asked the way to the bus-stop, and the proprietor gave him detailed (and confusing) directions to the Plaza José Antonio.

The city was busy now, and the traffic rushed past as he sauntered on his way, pausing every now and then to investigate some quaint little side-street. In spite of the noise, he found it indescribably restful not to have to do anything in particular; just to follow his mood of the moment. His guide-book bulged with facts, historic names and dates and places, but he did not refer to the book again. He was content to drift along, allowing the city to surprise him with its treasures.

Eventually he came upon the Plaza José Antonio and found a bus standing waiting. Inside were other tourists, mostly French and German. Presently they set off, the bus jolting as it negotiated a few sharp turns before crossing the river, and a short while later they were deposited at their destination, the monastery of Las Huelgas.

Moss waited in the bus until the others had all left and then he got up and made his way out, having to push past a number of people who were boarding the bus to return to the city. Of those in his group, the more enterprising had at once entered the building.

He passed under the Gothic arch in the high stone walls and the great Cistercian abbey confronted him, built in the twelfth century, with its magnificent tower and Romanesque portico. A tourist attraction at any time, in late July there were many visitors. Even as he made to follow his own group into the cloisters, a large number of people emerged jostling and calling to one another in the bright sunlight.

A pity he hadn't been here in the early morning, he thought, as he wandered away to view the monastery at a distance. Afterwards he sat on the grass. The sun became very hot and he took off his jacket.

When Moss walked back to the road, it was to find a bus about to leave. He sprinted forward and got in behind a woman in a black shiny dress. The driver, obviously in a hurry, shouted something, and Moss fumbled for his ticket. The driver did not wait but slammed the door shut and scrambled into his own seat, and the bus then lurched forward and gathered speed.

Moss grinned.

The heat was intense, and beside him the woman in the black dress took out a small black cotton fan which she flicked open to the rattle of the jet beads with which it was fringed, commencing to fan herself rhythmically. As the driver savagely changed gears and the bus rolled, two boys at the front started up a song and some others joined in.

They seemed to be taking a more roundabout route on their return journey, Moss noted, bowling along a broad avenue with new buildings much in evidence. Many of his fellow-travellers were obviously local residents. A number of the women carried large shopping-baskets, and a man just in front held a bicycle wheel between his knees.

Before long, the bus turned off the flat highway and plunged into a series of narrow roads, finally squealing to a halt some fifteen minutes later. Moss looked out of the window. He had no idea where he was.

It occurred to him then that he had quite failed to grasp the significance of the baskets and parcels. Their destination was not the Plaza José Antonio. They were in fact travelling away from Burgos and out into the countryside!

He rose to his feet and made his way to the front of the bus. The man with the wheel was getting out too. The driver had jumped out first and was checking passengers waiting to board the bus.

Moss spoke to him, and the driver waved him back impatiently, but then suddenly appeared to remember he had no ticket. With the limited Spanish at his command, Moss did his best to explain while passengers and intending passengers looked on with interest.

Already harassed, the driver waved his arms expressively. What could one do, he seemed to say? His job was to drive the bus, and a non-comprehending tourist — that was a problem for the Turismo!

It was at this juncture that a small man at the back of the crowd pushed his way forward and announced that he spoke English. An overstatement perhaps; however, driver and tourist greeted him warmly, and the small man did in fact understand what Moss had to say and conveyed this information to the driver who nodded abruptly and immediately shouted:

'*¡Torno de Hilar!*'

'*¿Cúanto se tarda?*' asked the little man.

Whatever the driver's reply, the interpreter seemed to agree for the latter then turned to Moss and with a good deal of effort made him understand that this bus would pass through the village of Torno de Hilar. Later the visitor might board a bus travelling from Torno to Burgos.

Resigned, Moss accepted his fate, but remembering his afternoon date with Maria enquired if it were possible to make a telephone call. At this point, the driver seemed about to lose his reason! However, apparently he told the small man that *he* could do the telephoning if he liked. And the little man agreed quite seriously and got Moss to write down the name and address of the Pensión Excelsior together with his own name, and when Moss took out money to pay for the call it was (indignantly) refused.

Impatiently, the driver waved all his passengers back into the bus, once more flung himself into his seat and with a loud fanfare on the horn the bus pulled away.

Soon they were right out in the countryside. The hot sun blazed down on the road, and on either side were fields of wheat. Harvesting was in progress. Men and women reaping with short-handled scythes; the women sometimes clad in black dresses and with black head-scarves. In quite a few of the villages the communal laundry was spread out to dry on the newly-cut fields. Then they came to a river, and along its banks were groups of women scrubbing busily.

Shortly after one o'clock, the bus pulled up beneath the shade of some trees in the centre of a village with one street and a large church. The driver indicated to Moss that he should get out. When the bus moved on, Moss was left standing in the middle of the road feeling rather at a loss.

After the dust-cloud raised by the bus had settled, he looked around. The unpaved street was a wide one, and on either side were terraced houses built over stone colonnades. At this hour the village

16

was deserted except for one old man who sat on a stone bench under a tree, and several mules and carts which were lined up in the shade.

Moss's first impression of Torno de Hilar was of surprise that two buses actually passed this spot. It seemed to him incredible that any motorised transport did so. He had the feeling that he might well have stepped back into another century. He went and sat on the bench beside the old man.

'*¡Buenos días!*' said the old one and gave Moss close scrutiny.

Moss answered his greeting in kind, and the old man became alert.

'*¿Un americano?*' he queried.

Moss conveyed the fact that he was Irish, and the old man's eyes crinkled up with amusement. He laughed softly.

He pulled at an ancient pipe, and Moss took out his own and lit it. Silence reigned until the old man's thought processes had time to formulate several questions which he then put to the newcomer. Moss understood little of this, but in reply he managed to get across the

17

story of misdirection and of waiting for the bus back to Burgos.

The man agreed there would be a bus, later.

After a while Moss enquired if the village had a bar or *posada*. For an answer, the old man rose up stiffly and waved a hand in the direction of the other side of the road. He led the way under one of the colonnades, and they entered a small low-ceilinged room with wooden tables and rough wooden benches lining the walls. A number of men were sitting around, and all eyes turned to view the stranger. Two men who had been playing cards halted their game, and the old man greeted one of these and a rapid conversation followed, ending in a call to a person in the room beyond.

A bottle of wine was produced for which Moss paid and then invited the company to join him. His hunger was assuaged with several dry and rather tasteless rolls, the only food which the bar had to offer. He was beginning to enjoy himself, nevertheless. For one thing, the wine was very good. He reflected that he had probably been sold the most expensive bottle the little bar possessed. 'The stranger' would provide a topic of conversation long after his departure, so good-humouredly he answered their questions — as many as he could understand.

Some small boys appeared and clustered round the open door of the bar. As time went on, their numbers seemed to grow, so that the doorway became crowded, and Moss could even see some women in the background.

Through this gathering more men entered and sat down on the wooden benches, talking in groups, but at the same time keeping a close watch on the movements of the visitor. Moss bore this scrutiny with no outward signs of disquiet; all the same he began to think about the bus and hoped he would not have to wait very much longer.

He got up and moved towards the door, and the crowd made room for him, admitting him to the street and then closing in behind. They meant him no harm, he knew. This being the siesta hour, his arrival had created a diversion. At the same time, with his long experience of crowds, the actual numbers made him a little uneasy.

However, when he reached the street it was to discover the presence of two members of the Guardia Civil who stood in the shade of the trees and appeared to be also waiting for the bus, and sure enough a dust-cloud began to appear at the far end of the village and the incoming bus slowly made its way towards him.

Moss verified that it was travelling to Burgos. The driver did not get out, but was approached by one of the *Benemerita* who held him in conversation. The other guardia turned to Moss who was waiting to board the bus. The policeman asked Moss for his name and was he going to Burgos? Rather surprised, Moss gave the information and the man nodded as though satisfied.

The driver of the bus and the first guardia continued their conversation and Moss wished they would hurry up and open the door. Perhaps they were waiting for more members of the Guardia Civil to arrive. However, finally the two policemen moved back, and the driver started up the engine. The bus began to move, its passenger door still closed, and Moss gave a warning shout. After his long wait, imagine being stuck in this place, possibly until the next day!

When he saw the driver make no move to halt, Moss turned sharply to the two policemen, and at that moment discovered that he was in the act of being handcuffed to one of them. And then he was being led, half-dragged, from the hot street and pushed under the colonnades, as the crowd stood back and watched.

3

The small population of Torno de Hilar being a fairly law-abiding one, the jail (if it could be so called) was not much used. The local guardia were not resident in the village but had their headquarters some fifteen kilometres down the road.

About the only amenity which the two rooms possessed was a telephone, and Moss repeatedly urged its use to substantiate his claim to be a perfectly ordinary tourist. He made the point that his passport, which was at the pension, would give all relevant details. He informed them that he was himself a police officer, and finally he asked to telephone to the Irish consulate in Madrid.

To all of this they paid no heed, and eventually he concluded it had been their job to make the arrest but until further instructions arrived nothing would be done. His very first question had been to ask what he was accused of, but like the others it remained unanswered.

They searched him and took his watch and personal effects. The handcuffs were removed, and he was locked in the inner of the two rooms: a low-ceilinged narrow rectangle with no window — ventilation and light coming from an iron grille in the door. Taking up most of the floor-space was an iron bed covered with a thin mattress. There was an unpleasant smell, and old scars in his mind returned to haunt him now.

He sat on the bed and tried to figure out what the whole thing could be about. Mistaken identity was the most likely explanation. In that event, isolated as he was, proving himself innocent of whatever he was supposed to have done might turn out to be a lengthy process. All the more so as he was holed up in this out-of-the-way place. Had he been arrested in Madrid, for example, contacts might be made and wheels set in motion, whereas in his present situation there seemed little prospect of early liberty.

Standing at the door of his cell and

looking through the grille, he endeavoured to assess the two members of the guardia — 'the pair' as they were known in Spain. One was around his own age or a bit older, forty perhaps, a short thickset individual whom the other guardia had addressed respectfully as *cabo*. *Cabo* meant corporal. The other was a raw recruit, Moss judged, a young lad whose name was Lamas and whose responsibilities seemed to sit rather uneasily on his youthful shoulders. His eyes would return to stare at the prisoner as though Moss had landed from another planet.

There was a clock in the room but it had stopped and no one apparently thought to set it going again. Their prisoner duly secured, the *cabo* commenced filling in a long form in duplicate, a labour which he accomplished slowly and in silence. Lamas, having been instructed to mount guard, did so by staring intently at the grille until Moss, tiring of this scrutiny, lay down on the bed. To continue his observation Lamas then advanced to the door, but a sharp command from his superior ordered him to stand clear of it.

His clerical duties at an end, the *cabo* also approached the grille, looked into the cell at the now recumbent Moss, issued a series of orders to his subordinate, and then went outside.

After the departure of the elder guardia, Lamas several times came to gaze at his seemingly docile prisoner, apparently in the belief that if he neglected to keep a close watch the Irishman would somehow manage to escape. During one of these inspections, Moss brought up the subject of food — a subject never long absent from his thoughts.

'When do we get the next meal?' he said.

Lamas glanced at him dubiously, but made no response. However, when the question had been repeated several times, the young guardia muttered something about '*arroz*'. This did not sound very encouraging, but *arroz*, rice, is usually taken to mean a *paella*.

As things turned out, Moss never saw any food, but that was not the fault of

Lamas or of the other guardia but of events which overtook all three of them, beginning with a telephone call.

At the sound of the phone ringing, Moss quietly rose up and stood beside the cell door. He noted that Lamas, who was regarding the instrument with something like dismay, allowed it to ring for twenty or thirty seconds before answering.

The prisoner's expectancy that this call might possibly herald his release did not survive the opening sentences.

'Yes, it is Lamas,' the young guardia said carefully.

A mumble, which Moss could not hear, was followed by a query: 'But how shall I leave?'

Whatever the reply, Lamas said at once: 'It is as you say, Corporal Martinez.' He glanced over his shoulder to where Moss stood looking through the grille. 'I shall be several minutes only,' he added.

With that Lamas replaced the receiver, stared hard at Moss, and then taking up a bunch of keys from the desk went out into the street, locking the door behind him.

Moss was left to his own reflections which were not very pleasant ones. What on earth did they suppose him to have done? The position in which he found himself was physically intolerable to him and growing worse as the hours went by. To be shut in, deprived of freedom, brought back memories of his adolescence when he had been placed in an institution, as an orphan. It was a period of his life which he had never been able to put behind him, and old sensations of anger, frustration and fear were even now overmastering him, try as he would to reason with them. And if he became really desperate, what might be the end of that? Up until now he had always managed to be in control, to hold on tight and quell an irrational panic. But he knew this self-control could not possibly survive a lengthy spell under present conditions.

The sound of a key turning in the jail door roused him, and he went over to the grille. There were other sounds too, culminating in the noisy arrival of

Martinez and Lamas with another prisoner between them. This man Moss recognized as one of the card-players he had met in the bar earlier in the day. In Moss's present frame of mind, to see someone else shouting and raving did much to restore his own sanity.

It said something about Corporal Martinez that this last arrest had been accomplished almost single-handed (for Lamas was not of much help) and with only the loss of the corporal's black patent-leather hat, for the prisoner was not only taller and very much broader, he was also more than a little drunk and quite mean. The man was shouting and cursing and hitting out in all directions, but Martinez somehow managed to propel his charge inside the door of the jail, at the same time instructing Lamas to open the cell. What they were proposing to do with Moss the Irishman did not know, but the situation had obvious possibilities.

In the event, he was not called upon to put any plan into action. What happened was this: the cell door opened outwards, and as Lamas opened the door the young guardia was of necessity behind it. As he drew back to allow Corporal Martinez to thrust his prisoner inside, the prisoner gave the door one kick causing it to spring back against the wall and pinning the unfortunate Lamas in that position.

Having summarily dealt with one of the *Benemerita*, the drunk lashed out blindly at Martinez, and the next thing there was a mêlée on the floor of the jail with Martinez going down under the sheer wild strength of his prisoner. Moss left the cell, and Lamas extricated his thin lanky form from behind the cell door and the two of them made an attempt to catch hold of the wild one, but before they could do anything the unprotected head of the burly corporal met the stone floor with an unmerciful crack.

Amparo Martinez, *cabo primero de la Guardia Civil*, lay where he had fallen, and to the experienced Moss it did not look as if he would stir for some time, or possibly indeed ever again.

In that moment, Moss was aware that his own position had deteriorated suddenly. It was one thing to be arrested in error, quite another to be involved in a brawl in which a member of the police was seriously injured or worse.

Lamas, dazed, stared at the body on the floor while the drunken man, rather sobered, pursued an erratic but speedy course towards the street and freedom.

Moss could have followed, for Lamas seemed to be in a state of shock and made no move. However, abruptly the Irishman turned and stooped down to examine the prone figure.

'*¿Muerto?*'

It was the first word Lamas had spoken.

Moss shook his head. The fellow looked as if he had a fairly thick skull. He might or might not have a fracture. Anyhow the pulse was there, irregular but not too weak, and a shallow breath could be detected.

'*Traiga un médico,*' Moss said, and summoning up another few words from a meagre vocabulary, added drily: '*y un sacerdote.*'

Lamas crossed himself and, his eyes still fixed on the corporal lying on the floor, slowly moved over to the telephone.

4

Three minutes later Maurice Coen had reached the outskirts of Torno de Hilar, walking as fast as he could.

A few men followed, shouting at him, but they stood off and made no attempt to get in his way. He did not run, but walked very briskly. Once away from the village he would try to locate some form of transport, but for the moment he thought it advisable to avoid the roads.

So he struck out across the fields, the dry stubble making the going very hard underfoot. For the most part, the ground was flat and there were few trees, so that he feared being spotted from a distance. Already dusk, visibility was deteriorating.

Presently the ground fell away slightly, and when Moss looked back Torno de Hilar had disappeared from view. As yet, there was no pursuit.

On his right were some store-houses, caves in the side of the low hill, and it occurred to him he might find shelter in one of them. But he dismissed that idea. He must try for either Burgos or Madrid.

In Madrid was the consul and very probably access to a lawyer. Burgos held his papers, his belongings, his real identity. From Burgos, he might even make it to the frontier.

Without warning, a tall house loomed up out of the dusk and his first thought was to make a detour. He moved away, but not before he had been spotted. A dog barked, and a voice hailed him.

Moss stood still. A man was coming from the direction of the house, a small elderly man with a brown dog. The man hailed him again, and Moss felt compelled to respond.

The man spoke courteously and enquired who he was, while the dog came forward and sniffed suspiciously. There was no help for it now, thought Moss. As soon as he spoke, the man would know him for a foreigner. He might just as well be open about it.

So he explained in careful Spanish how he had taken the wrong bus, had subsequently wandered around the countryside, and was now trying to find his way back to Burgos, that night if at all possible.

At once the man showed concern. That such a thing should happen — and to a visitor! He was French, was he?

Moss thought it better to agree, hoping the fellow was not a fluent French speaker, for he seemed an educated man. However, the questioner continued to speak Spanish, so Moss found it unnecessary to claim to be a Celtic-speaking Breton!

With something of a flourish, the other made himself known as don Santiago Mosquera Blanco, and Moss replied as plain M. Leconte, a native of Orleans. This was accepted without question, and Moss went on to enquire the distance which now separated him from Burgos and how he might best travel there.

They had been walking towards the house, and Mosquera stopped to consider. There was the railway, of course, he pointed out. A distance of some ten kilometres — more, eleven or twelve kilometres to the actual station. He himself would be privileged to direct the visitor to the road which led eventually to a level-crossing. If then he would but follow the railway southwards, he would come upon the station at some two or three kilometres distance.

This was unexpected, and Moss was quite profuse in his thanks, and the elderly man accepted these very well indeed, and when they came to the beginning of the road across the fields — an unsurfaced path, rough underfoot — their leave-taking was accompanied by many expressions of civility on the part of the Spaniard, who bowed before turning to resume his evening stroll, the dog trotting sedately beside him.

For the first time Moss Coen was beginning to believe he might actually make it. He had had luck, and if the same luck held at the station . . . The tiredness left him and he began to put on speed. If he did reach the station he hoped he would not have to wait too long for a train. Spanish trains ran none too frequently, in his experience.

It was two hours later when he reached the level-crossing. He had passed quite a number of houses on the rough track, but no one had stopped him. However, now as the ground sloped down to the railway-line, he made an unpleasant discovery. The crossing was guarded.

There was no barrier. The sentry-box stood beside the opening.

Moss dropped to his knees. Unfortunately there was little cover about. Cautiously he moved back. There was no sign of life, no sounds at all except for the tiny noises made by insects in the fields around him and the occasional faint twitter of a bird in the distance. What should he do? The sentry-box looked to be deserted.

How long he crouched there he could not have said, but his mind was made up for him by a new sound heard from a long way off. It was a small vibration rather than an actual noise. As he listened, he became more and more certain it was the sound of an approaching train.

He craned forward to try and see and

then dropped back again quickly. Whoever was in the sentry-box had heard the sound also and had come out and was now walking up and down outside. Presently, this sentry crossed the line and stood looking up the road opposite, his back turned to Moss.

The latter seized the chance and ran forward silently, ready to drop the instant the sentry should turn, but when this man did move it was to look in the direction of the oncoming train, and Moss reached the shelter of the hut, and still the man had not seen him.

The noise of the train grew louder, and then Moss could see it — still a long way off — its lights winking in the distance. It appeared to be quite a long train, travelling rather slowly.

Moss began to make a plan. A lot would depend on the behaviour of the sentry. If he stayed where he was, the train passing over the level-crossing would obscure his view of Moss's activities on this side. The sentry was moving now. What would he do?

Moss shifted his position in the shadow

of the hut, flattening himself up against its side, as he waited. He could hear footsteps. The man was coming back.

The rumble of the train grew nearer and he could no longer hear the sentry's movements. Cautiously, Moss slid round to the back of the hut. There was no sign of the other man; the sentry must have taken up his position at the door.

Was the train actually going to stop? It was certainly travelling very slowly indeed, and Moss could see its lighted windows. As well as being a long train, it had the appearance of being a full one. Should he once board it, that would be to his advantage!

The engine passed over the level-crossing with no diminution of speed, and a second engine followed. Behind were an assortment of coaches: an old-fashioned but rather opulent sleeping-car; a number of fairly modern firsts and seconds and, finally, two third-class indestructible relics of the past.

Moss knew his luck had held.

As the penultimate carriage rattled over the crossing, he was out from behind the back of the hut and running towards the line. From behind him, a shout went up and his legs moved faster as he sprinted forward. The final carriage came level with the running man, and as it passed him he caught hold of its iron rail and swung himself up and over the top, landing on the rear platform.

The sentry was left behind in the middle of the crossing.

5

The train was certainly crowded. As it picked up speed again, Moss made a move to get off the platform. The central door was locked, but men inside who had viewed Moss's sudden arrival now directed him to the ordinary exit door (with no lock). Moss swung himself up on the rail, and one man held the door open while another pulled the Irishman to safety.

Where he was now standing was a small compartment separating the rear platform from the main section of the carriage. There were no seats, and a group of three men sat on the floor while a fourth leaned out of the far window. The door by which Moss had entered constantly swung to and fro (it opened inwards and the catch was broken) revealing the darkened countryside which they passed in the night. To keep it shut, Moss placed his back against it before squatting on the floor.

The other men did not seem too surprised at his sudden arrival although they regarded him with more attention when they heard him speak.

French, was he?

Moss decided there was no harm in answering in the affirmative, and again this was accepted without question. The question he most wanted to ask was where they were going, but to ask that might give rise to some suspicion. Entrance to the wooden seating-area of the carriage was by a door at right angles to the one against which he now sat, but Moss discovered it to be blocked by luggage and the bodies of a number of people asleep on the floor inside. The men with him watched as he made an attempt to enter and smiled and shrugged when he failed. One of them generously proffered a half-empty bottle of wine, and Moss gratefully took a few mouthfuls and handed back the bottle.

'How far is it to the next station?' he asked, and again met with shrugging shoulders. They had no idea. The next station was Bocina, it was generally agreed, but as Moss had never heard of the place he was no wiser.

He wondered what he should do. If the sentry reported the incident at the crossing, and if the police tied this in with the events at Torno de Hilar (as eventually they must) then there was every likelihood the train would be searched. A lot would depend on how rapid were their communications. For the moment, at any rate, he would do better to stay where he was and keep a careful watch for any signs of police activity.

About thirty minutes later, the train pulled into a country station and a small number of people got out, two of them from the inner compartment of Moss's carriage. In order for these passengers to leave, those persons sleeping on the floor had to rise up and open the inner door, and Moss seized his opportunity to slip inside before the door could shut again.

The compartment in which he now found himself was so crowded it was almost impossible to make any progress through it. Travellers fortunate enough to have obtained seats lay stretched out, feet dangling in the aisle. Other travellers lay on the floor between the seats and heads-to-feet along the aisle itself. The luggage-racks were crammed with parcels, boxes, luggage of all kinds, and in between the bodies on the floor were stacked the owners' suitcases, baskets and a wide variety of personal belongings, food and cooking implements.

Moss despaired of finding anywhere to sit (or even to stand) until a kind-hearted woman with a baby on her lap and four other small children around her somehow made room for him, and he sat down gratefully in their midst. The heat was suffocating, and the baby cried fretfully until the woman began to nurse it. After a while the child fell asleep at her breast, and the woman herself dozed off.

To make room, Moss took one of the other children into his arms and a third child lay on top of his knees. On reflection, he was quite pleased with this arrangement. It would take a sharp-eyed policeman to spot him in the midst of this domestic scene. Presently, he too dozed.

After a long interval, he became aware that the train had stopped again, and he glanced out of the window. Being in the last carriage, he could not see the nameboard, and not until the train was leaving the station did he discover that he was at Estepar. Surely he recognized it — on his journey northwards from Madrid had he not passed through Estepar? The last stop before Burgos!

Twenty minutes later he had reached his destination. Through the window, Moss gazed anxiously up and down the platform but saw no evidence of police. On his previous arrival in Burgos there had been no ticket barrier; the tickets having been inspected earlier on the train. Now he was in a local train for which Burgos seemed to be the terminus. Everyone was getting out.

The woman with the children had many parcels and bags, and he offered to carry some of these, an offer which the harassed woman was only too glad to accept. Shouldering a large parcel which effectively hid one side of his face, and with a number of bags dangling from the same hand, while the other hand clasped that of the second-youngest, Moss made his exit at the rear of a most innocent-looking little procession.

It was seven o'clock in the morning. By the time he arrived at the Pensión Excelsior, some of the staff would be about. He could imagine Maria's face as he recounted his adventures!

However, the first thing to do was to ring Madrid and get them on the job. He spared a thought for the unfortunate Martinez and hoped for both their sakes that the fellow was still breathing.

He parted from the little family at the door of their home, with many thanks for his kind help, the woman said! Then the weary traveller lost no time in making for the Excelsior. Even as he crossed the road, he could see the door standing ajar and señnor Perille already at his desk.

Moss ran up the steps and entered the hall. Perille looked up.

'But you have returned!' he said in English, and he sounded very surprised, even upset.

'I was unavoidably detained,' Moss

replied grimly. 'What I need now is a hot bath, a large breakfast and first of all an urgent telephone call to Madrid. I must phone my consulate — will you get me the number please?'

'Certainly, if you wish it. If you will wait in this room,' Perille indicated a small anteroom, off the hall, 'I shall have breakfast sent into you, and you may take your call. There are no telephones in any of the other rooms.'

Breakfast took precedence over a bath, Moss decided. Perille was certainly being very decent. This impression was confirmed when in a few minutes the proprietor himself carried in a tray bearing a large pot of coffee and a plate of rolls and butter. Having set a place for breakfast, Perille excused himself and said he would attend to the visitor's telephone call.

Eagerly Moss pulled up a chair and began to tackle the meal, drinking several cups of coffee in quick succession. He was still eating, in fact, when the door opened once more, and he turned sharply thinking it might be Maria.

A stout, elderly man entered followed by another, younger man. They were not in uniform, but Moss was not deceived. He rose to his feet.

'We shall ask you some questions,' the elder of the two said in heavily-accented English. 'Please seat yourself.' He indicated the litter of breakfast things, and added with some irony: 'While you were at Torno, they did not offer you food?'

Moss made no response, and the other shrugged. 'That is not my affair. But you will be required to answer in the case.'

Moss said nothing. He was intent on summing up the fat little man opposite. Sixty to seventy, he thought, although with Spaniards it was difficult to be certain. Men aged more quickly. Still, not a day under sixty, and the skin was dry and tightly stretched over the temples. The beautifully-manicured hand was wrinkled even though fat. While not at all familiar with the structure of the Spanish police force, Moss knew enough, he thought, to discount the presence of a member of this age-group among the homicide division.

Martinez, then, must still be alive.

Moss wondered what they intended to charge him with. No harm in asking that question, anyway.

'I will answer at the proper time,' he said formally, 'but first I must know of what it is I am accused.'

The Spaniard thumped the table with his hand. 'You have considered as to have no idea?'

'None whatever,' replied Moss firmly. He wondered if he would have done better to sit it out at Torno de Hilar.

'I insist on speaking to the Irish consul,' he said.

The stout party, who had been addressed by his colleague as señor Urgoiti, rank unspecified, did not reply but instead began to question Moss about his journey, his itinerary in Spain, his arrival in Burgos.

To all of this Moss responded easily. Nor did he see any reason to conceal the details of the trip which had brought him to Torno. He even took a certain relish in recounting the early part of his experiences there. It was only when Urgoiti

48

began to probe about the confrontation at the jail that Moss repeated his request to telephone Madrid.

'You shall come with us,' Urgoiti said.

'Do I have a choice?' queried Moss, and Urgoiti permitted himself the suggestion of a smile, as though conscious of an absurdity.

6

The cold of the room struck Moss unpleasantly. In his own line of business he was used to experiencing a similar chill, although he had never grown accustomed to it. Now his resistance was at a low ebb. He was standing at a table, and he gripped the edge with hands that were not quite steady.

Maria was dead, of course. And had seen the approach of death if he understood her expression correctly. That in spite of the fact that the head was at a curious and unnatural angle, and the eyes decently closed.

'How did it happen?' he asked idiotically of the man by his side.

Urgoiti, who had been steadfastly regarding him, made a soft noise in the throat.

'You do not know?'

Moss raised his eyes, eyes of a peculiarly vivid blue, and they held

Urgoiti's pale-brown ones, bistred and flecked with red.

'No,' he answered baldly. He was finding it difficult to concentrate. Pictures flashed before his mind and, as quickly, disappeared again. Martinez no longer worried him. Neither did the consul's office loom in his thoughts. He needed a lawyer.

'You met this girl at the Excelsior?' Urgoiti persisted, 'and had you been seeing her before then?'

'No.'

'Spoken to her on the telephone?'

'I tell you, no.'

'It has occurred to us to enquire if you shall have reserved a room in advance, and have telephoned from Madrid?'

'I didn't. When I stepped off the train here, I was accosted by a man who carried my luggage to the Excelsior. Perille will confirm this, for he saw the two of us enter together.'

'I will tell you that we have found this man. His name is Taibo. He is to be found at his place of business, that is to say the railway station. It is his understanding that you were asking information, and he obtained for you the pension here. We are in agreement?'

'If you like,' growled Moss, ruffling up his coarse dark hair, and then making an effort to smooth it again. 'You still haven't told me . . . '

'Notwithstanding, it is I who wish that you shall tell me!' Urgoiti emphasized his point by thumping a small fat hand on the table, palm downwards and fingers spread out and turned upwards.

'I am innocent of the death of this girl,' Moss said very earnestly, and saw at once that he had made a correct impression. Urgoiti was regarding him with attention.

'As yet, we are accusing you of nothing,' he said, but he made a slight inclination forward.

Unwillingly Moss gazed once more at the disjointed neck and the body that in life had been Maria. Already there was some post mortem staining.

'There was a fall?' It was not so much a question as a plain statement of fact.

Urgoiti looked at him strangely. 'You express no shock at this event?' the

Spaniard asked with more than a touch of irony.

'As a police officer?' Moss gave a shrug.

This time he was sure he gained ground. Urgoiti made no comment. If only he, Moss Coen, knew the language. Not necessarily the vernacular, but that expression of Spanish thought and ideas. Or ideals. Imperious, but with an ornate (almost baroque) courtesy to equals.

For a man who normally conversed in grunts and nods, this might be difficult of achievement, but danger will sharpen the wits. Moss remembered again that kindly old gentleman outside Torno de Hilar, and made some effort to imitate don Santiago Mosquera Blanco.

'The deceased lady was an employee at the pension,' Moss began in what he hoped were unemotional tones. 'She gave me a guide-book of the city, and offered to act as a guide to several places of interest.'

'We are able to prove,' Urgoiti said, thumping his hand on the table in what was apparently a characteristic gesture, 'we will have the evidence which says that you left the Excelsior with Maria Guzman at twenty minutes to midnight. Afterwards at two o'clock you have come back together and again entered the pension. A member of the staff says he opened the door. Only four hours later, her body is found. Do you now say you have known nothing of her death?'

'Nothing whatever,' Moss replied firmly.

Urgoiti spread out his two hands this time, and Moss noticed that the little finger of the right hand was missing.

'Then tell me, señor Coen, why if you are unaware of anything bad happening to this girl, why are you leaving the pension at six in the morning. And without breakfast, that is a strange act surely!'

'It was pleasant to walk about the quiet streets,' Moss answered simply. 'The city looked very beautiful in the early morning. And afterwards I breakfasted near the Isla Promenade. The café proprietor went to some trouble to prepare a substantial meal at that hour. He will no doubt remember.'

'And if he does, what is that? There is the matter of what is happening at the pension before your precipitate leaving at the same time as the body is being found.'

'It is very cold here,' Moss said. In fact he had begun to shiver. Shock or fear, he wondered?

To his surprise, Urgoiti said without hesitation: 'I will agree with you. To stay here is not necessary.' The Spaniard led the way down a long corridor and opened a door on the left. Their escort obediently trooped in after them and the door was shut.

This room faced the street and was bathed in warm sunlight, and as if in response, Urgoiti became rather more expansive. Perhaps in the hope of gaining an admission from the prisoner, the wary Moss considered. Anyhow, whatever Urgoiti's intentions, he indicated a chair for Moss and took the one opposite for himself, lying back and joining his small fat fingers together over a protuberant stomach.

The man's hair was almost non-existent, and in its place one or two brown marks had appeared. Retirement age had surely come and gone, leaving

Urgoiti still at his post. That argued very considerable success at the job and a determination to stick with it. With the probable addition of an influential friend or relative in the background.

'How did she die?' Moss asked.

Urgoiti swung round and regarded him closely. 'That is what I wish that you shall tell me!'

'I have told you the truth. I know nothing of her death. When last I saw Maria, she was standing in the hallway of the Excelsior and speaking to the young lad who opened the door to us. Why don't you ask him? He saw me go up to my room.'

Urgoiti pounced. 'The boy says so. Notwithstanding, he says also that later he passes the room of the señorita Guzman and he hears voices — the voice of the señorita and that of a man. He says that man is you — and also, I will tell you,' Urgoiti pressed on as Moss began to speak, 'also, the body of Maria Guzman was found outside the door of the kitchen in the courtyard below her room. She was already dead. And our evidence will prove

56

that she was dead before she fell from the window of her room.

'When she is discovered, the whole house wakes. Afterwards you are not there. The boy is questioned. He tells what has happened in the night. We search for you. And you have fled to Torno.'

'Believe me,' Moss said with force, 'no one in their right mind would ever *flee* to Torno de Hilar!'

'I make free to inform you,' Urgoiti went on unheeding, 'that your guilt is indicated by the evidence we are receiving here. And also I shall tell you that the attack on Corporal Martinez is a matter of the most serious kind, and you will have many charges to answer.'

At the mention of the corporal (he presumed still living) Moss experienced surprise. That his initial arrest had been as a result of the circumstantial evidence connecting him with Maria's death was now clear. Since then, however, other evidence must have indicated a doubt at least, for if they intended to charge him with murder at this juncture they would hardly have introduced the subject of Martinez. That is, of course, provided the burly Martinez hadn't died. Moss fervently hoped not.

The fact that they brought the matter up showed their indecision. They could hold him on a charge connected with the events in Torno. Or . . . That he was a foreigner was against him, but that they knew him to be a member of that foreign country's police force stood to his favour.

Urgoiti actually said: 'You are implicated here in two crimes of the gravest matter.'

'You will forgive me,' replied Moss in a high-handed tone, 'but I am most certainly not *implicated* as you put it. I have had the misfortune to stay in a house where a girl is found dead, and in the course of a day's sightseeing to be summarily arrested and to find myself in a prison where an assault takes place. That I had any hand, act or part in either, I most *emphatically* deny,' and the thump Moss gave the chair beside him was a far more aggressive gesture than Urgoiti's.

One of the men near the door made a sudden move forward, but Urgoiti waved him back, while continuing to speak.

'For the present,' Urgoiti said, 'we shall be glad if you will have the kindness to remain with us here in Burgos. Not at the Excelsior. Perille does not find it convenient. We will arrange for you another hotel. The Hostal Esperanza will be of use for your purpose, I think,' he added slyly.

Moss tried not to show his relief. For this mercy, however temporary, much thanks! However there was the matter of finance. He had better raise the subject.

'Much as I dislike to have to mention anything so sordid as money, may I remind you that the Guardia at Torno saw fit to leave me without any.'

'That shall be attended to in other circumstances. Your passport we will retain. I should caution you that any further attempt to evade us, my dear señor Coen, and you will be held in police custody. We are being most liberal to you here.'

'Not without good reason, I imagine,' said Moss, and his eyes caught and held those of Urgoiti in a look of grim understanding.

7

When he saw his new domicile, Moss reflected he was extremely lucky not to be lodged in a Spanish cell. The Hostal Esperanza was all marble floors and exotic plants with mirrors on every wall, and also the food was very good.

If there was a snag, it was the cost, which would he felt sure ultimately have to be borne by Moss Coen and which promised to dig a deep hole in his next few months' salary cheques. Philosophically, he supposed he would be thankful just to receive the said cheques, in the event that he would be able to return home to his job in the Garda Siochana.

All rooms in the Esperanza had private telephone, shower, and a balcony overlooking the Avenida del Cid. Gazing out on this balcony, he had conducted a somewhat one-sided telephone conversation with an official of the consulate, a conversation bringing little joy to either.

And, as a matter of urgency, had been advised to seek legal representation.

Following on that, he had been directed to the office of one señor Lorenzo Doldan, who spoke excellent English, and who listened to his story expressing neither surprise nor dismay, but nevertheless with a rather grave face.

For his own part Moss found it hard to reconcile his difficult (not to say dangerous) situation with his present life-style. He lived in a luxurious vacuum which might at any moment dissolve into very harsh reality.

No one hindered his comings and goings, but he knew well that his second self lived in the Esperanza's foyer and followed him wherever he went. From the point of view of police duty, facilities at the Esperanza were excellent. No doubt the reason the hotel had been chosen.

At first he tried to avoid thinking about the dead girl, but over and over again the image would come into his mind of the shattered corpse with its twisted head, and in memory he saw again the twinkling lights of the Paseo del Espolón, and Maria, glass in hand, her elbows on the table.

Who and what motive could have brought her to this death? The police had uncovered enough to rule out suicide. Dead women don't throw themselves from windows.

Moss remembered his own waking at six. He had heard footsteps. Ordinary footsteps, surely some members of the staff beginning their day's work. A great pity he was no longer staying at the Excelsior. There were questions he wanted to ask.

At the Hostal Esperanza, balconies were furnished with plastic-topped tables and tubular steel chairs. The sun blazed down, but some shade was afforded by the adjoining building and also by the overhanging balcony of the floor above. Moss covered the hot tubular steel with a towel, and then sat at the table. He searched in his memory for every detail he could think of about his arrival at the pension three nights ago, and how Maria had opened the door, and each little subsequent action.

It was then he remembered the man who had spoken to the girl in the hallway of the Excelsior. He had left at about the time Taibo had gone out. Of course, this man might be another employee. But Moss did not think so. There had been something in the way Maria responded to the summons and then broke off the conversation at the appearance of the proprietor, Perille.

In retrospect, that little scene suggested an assignation later. Yet Maria had spent the evening with Moss. Had she previously arranged to meet the other man?

If this fellow actually worked at the Excelsior, he might have seen her return with Moss, and in a fit of jealous rage have gone to her room and in an ensuing violent quarrel have killed her. Afterwards trying to hide the crime by tipping the body out of the window.

This scenario would certainly cover all the known facts. However, it was surprising that it had apparently been accomplished with so little noise. That argued quite a different kind of killer. There was the evidence of the boy who heard (he said) a second voice in the room. That voice had not been Moss Coen's.

The first thing to do was to find Taibo and discover if Taibo knew the man who had spoken to Maria. Even if he didn't actually know him, Taibo might be able to identify the man again.

Moss also remembered the phone call Maria had received while they were at dinner, and how her mood had brightened afterwards. Possible of course that the caller was simply making a reservation. He wondered who it was had first answered the telephone. The waiter, for example, might remember something about the caller.

Unfortunately for Moss Coen, once he began making enquiries the police would know of it. And if he went to the railway station to try to contact Taibo, they would probably believe he was going to make a bolt for it, and arrest him again.

The Excelsior seemed to be the best bet. His suitcase had been neatly packed up, and when the police delivered it to his new place of residence Moss found it contained the Excelsior's bill for a modest fifteen hundred pesetas.

None of his personal effects had as yet arrived from Torno de Hilar, but he had been handed a warrant for the amount of money he had had on him, not counting travellers' cheques. His first act had been to cash the warrant, so he was in funds again.

He decided he would take a stroll in the direction of the Excelsior, proffer the bill together with payment and enquire for those members of the staff with whom he desired to leave a tip.

There was no trouble about it. His shadow of course went with him, but made no attempt to interfere. Perille had gone out, and the new desk-clerk, a very young man, receipted the bill and stamped it with an official stamp before returning it with something of a flourish. With Moss's request to speak to the waiter, the young man at once complied.

The waiter seemed rather surprised at the summons and gave Moss an odd look, but the main difficulty was one of language, not of hostility. The man must know Moss to be a suspect, so without further preamble the Irishman launched into a prepared speech about having to clear his name of this suspicion. The waiter's brow lifted, and a large tip changed hands.

The only trouble was that while Moss had carefully thought out and translated his questions beforehand, he was not fully able to understand the answers! Indeed, he envied his shadow in this regard. The man had entered the pension and was standing a little distance away, but still within earshot.

Questioned about the phone call, the waiter said, yes, he remembered answering the telephone as señor Perille had gone out and the señorita Guzman *que descanso en la paz del Señor* had been at dinner, which he had served to her for the last time, not knowing what was to happen only a few hours later.

No, he had not heard anything, which was not surprising as he did not stay in the hotel, having a wife and three children with whom he lived on the outskirts of the city. The first he had known about

66

what was happening was at midday when he arrived to begin work and found the police everywhere.

He gave a kind of nod in the direction of the man in the background.

Moss's eyes followed the waiter's glance, but the third man made no move. 'What of this person who telephoned?' Moss asked.

There was little the waiter could tell him, beyond the undoubted fact that the caller was a man. Questioned as to whether the voice sounded similar to that of the man seen speaking to Maria in the hall, the waiter only vaguely remembered having seen the latter, and he seemed to recall that the man had spoken in a low tone. How long the man had stayed in the building, the waiter could not say. He did not think the man had ever been to the Excelsior before. Not in the recent past anyway. The waiter felt he would have remembered. The man's teeth were rather unusual, he thought.

Unfortunately, Moss couldn't remember much about the man's teeth. The fellow had been standing in the shadow of the stairs, and Moss had only a fleeting recollection of height and weight. About Maria's own age, he would have said.

Finally, Moss broached the subject of the sad-faced guide, Taibo. Now the waiter knew Taibo, though not at all well, he was careful to point out. Taibo's status was obviously very inferior.

Where might he be found at this time of day, Moss enquired? It was now a little after five o'clock, and the waiter gave it as his opinion that Taibo might be discovered in one of the small cafés near the railway station, before working on through the evening. Burgos being on the main lines to both Madrid and Lisbon, there were many trains to be met.

There did not seem to be much more the waiter could tell. However, it occurred to Moss that here was a field where the lawyer, Doldan, might obtain further information. He asked the waiter's name.

'Camino,' the waiter responded with a look of complete understanding, 'Luciano Camino,' he said again, and he found a piece of paper and wrote it down and also his home address.

'Did you get that?' Moss asked of no one in particular as he passed his shadow in the hall. A curious sound came from the man's throat, but he said nothing.

Taibo, when found, was at a café in Santa Dorotea. He looked as sad and dejected as ever, a forlorn and huddled figure sitting over a black coffee and with a cigarette dangling from his thin pinched lips. The café-bar Molinar had few patrons at that hour, and Taibo looked up as he saw Moss approach.

His glance also embraced the man following, and from the side of Taibo's mouth came a rapid stream of words, none of which Moss could understand. The third party paid no attention, but sat down at the next table.

'Won't you join us?' Moss asked hospitably in English, convinced that his shadow must be fluent in that language.

The man did not answer, but instead ordered a coffee, nor did he appear to notice Taibo's continuing expression of distrust.

Moss distracted the porter's attention

by asking what he would have to drink, and when this question had been answered, ordered *a coñac* for each. Taibo looked at the clock and said he would soon have to leave. There would be a train arriving from Madrid.

At once, Moss opened up the subject of the man who had spoken to Maria as Moss and Taibo had waited in the hall of the Excelsior. Had Taibo ever seen this man before? A man with unusual teeth, Moss stressed.

Taibo sipped his *coñac* with deliberation, while Moss again went through the details of their arrival together at the Excelsior, and of the man's cry of 'Maria!'

'Do you remember this man?' he asked.

Taibo said he hadn't noticed the man particularly, and Moss then enquired if Taibo had noticed the man's teeth, but apparently the man hadn't been speaking when Taibo saw him, so the porter could neither confirm nor deny the waiter's observation, he said.

However, the Irishman had the feeling the sad-faced little man could say more if he chose to. Perhaps the presence of the law was discouraging. In the end, Moss gave it up (for the moment, anyway).

Taibo left to meet the train, and in a leisurely fashion Moss returned to his new hotel, stopping at an *estanco* and purchasing a cheap pipe and some tobacco of a local brand, a combination which tasted foully when he first lighted up. He wondered what the police were doing with his pipe and his wallet of special mixture.

After a while he managed to forget the acrid taste. He must certainly have a further interview with Luciano Camino, the waiter. It might be possible to get a more exact description of the 'very unusual' teeth. It was the only lead he had.

8

The dining-room of the Hostal Esperanza had a decor of olive-green and gold. Along the length of one wall were patio doors which opened onto the Esperanza's (heated) pool. These were hung with fine mesh curtains, and in the evenings closed off with heavy drapes of olive-green shot with gold. The floor was marble-effect tiles, and the walls alternate marble and mirror, with gilt fittings and cut-glass shaded lights.

It was not a room in which Moss Coen felt particularly at home, but the Esperanza's good food made him reluctant to dine elsewhere.

On his first evening at the hotel he had been offered a table in an obscure corner flanked on one side by the cutlery table and on the other by two service doors. He did not quarrel with this position, but it was one, he reflected, more suited to the person detailed to keep an eye on him, and the following evening he was amused at being offered a 'better' table.

Saying nothing, Moss allowed himself to be led across the crowded room to a central table occupied already by a rather lovely and expensively-dressed girl.

Not a man who normally gave much thought to his appearance, Moss suddenly became aware of his crumpled slacks and well-worn jacket.

The señorita had obviously just begun to eat and looked up in surprise at being asked if she would mind etc., as there were few vacant places.

Resisting the temptation to say 'I feel sure there is a table near the door' Moss turned around and saw that his own table had been taken by a party of four. Perhaps the police did not care for the rattle of forks and spoons!

Anyhow the girl made no protest, other than to indicate with a slight smile that he should remove her evening-wrap from the chair before he sat down. When he did so, she thanked him gravely and resumed her meal.

The waiter brought a menu, and Moss

then entered into a serious discussion. When decisions had been taken and the waiter had left, Moss found his companion regarding him enquiringly.

'You are on holiday here?' she asked in Spanish, and he said that he was.

But for the perfection of her accent and its native ring, he might have believed her to be a visitor also. Her hair, a natural pale-blonde, framed a small oval rather grave face, and the eyes of a delicate egg-shell blue were fringed with very fine lashes.

She wore a simple black evening-dress. Even Moss Coen who had been educated at a school where the social graces were unheard of, even he was aware it had never seen the inside of a dress shop.

As he consumed cold soup followed by *calamares en su tinta* and a steak, he wondered a little about his companion.

She was very young, not more than twenty he would have said. She wore no ornament, except for a pair of tiny diamond earrings. Even at a seaside resort, a young Spanish girl of this type was not too often seen unescorted. Here, in Burgos, it was even more unusual.

But then he reflected (he was glad of anything which took his mind off his own problems) how much did he really know of Spanish customs? One thing though, under the stress of the last few days he was rapidly acquiring a very much better Spanish vocabulary.

When it came to the dessert, after consultation with the waiter he ordered a local dish made with ground almonds, and the girl said she would have it also. With its arrival, she then asked:

'You are English, perhaps?'

'Irish,' he said, and at once her eyes crinkled up and she laughed.

'I was in Ireland some years ago,' she replied, speaking English with only a slight accent. 'As a student, I spent two summers in Dublin. Do you know it well?'

'Very well,' he answered, also smiling, and she was at once aware of the extraordinary blue eyes. 'I live there,' he added.

She began to speak about various places she had visited, mostly restaurants where the students used to congregate in the afternoons.

'It was a pleasant time,' she concluded, and at once he was struck by a note in her voice. Pleasure seemed to be associated only with the past.

In spite of himself, Moss smiled. Youth was like that. Three or four years — at twenty that might seem to belong to another age. At thirty-seven, he was conscious only that four years ago he had been in the same job, occupying the same office, doing the same work. However, he reflected soberly that a change might now be imminent.

'When I was in Dublin,' she was saying, 'I stayed with an Irish family in Mount Merrion. That is outside the city, but not far away. Each day we would take the bus to the city and also we went many times to Dun Laoghaire.' The girl pronounced the last name with care, and Moss said at once: 'I see you have not forgotten, but I suppose these visits of yours were not too long ago.'

'It seems rather a long time ago now,' and her mouth held a wry twist.

There was no mistaking this mood of gravity, and Moss cast his eye over the black dress. Perhaps it was significant. As if to confirm his supposition, the lady appeared to withdraw into her own sombre thoughts, and a long silence intervened.

In an effort to reopen the conversation, her companion at length said: 'I should have introduced myself. My name is Maurice Coen. Most of my friends call me Moss.'

'Coen?' she asked, at once interested. 'That is not an Irish name, is it?'

He smiled. 'Oh, there are quite a few Coens in Ireland, particularly west of the Shannon. Though it is generally held,' he added with a grin, 'that I resemble my mother's family who were from the borders of Cork and Tipperary.'

'Were?'

He laughed outright. 'Why I speak of them in the past tense, I don't really know. Unless it is because I hardly ever see them. There are numbers of them in quite a few places around the world — Britain, America, Australia. A large family, they tended to scatter.'

'You are one of a large family also?'

'No. My parents died before there was much time to have any more.' Moss spoke lightly, but his hands moved restlessly on the table.

'My father and mother are living,' the girl replied seriously, 'and I have three brothers also.'

Moss had been wrong then. There appeared to be no evidence of a funeral aftermath. Curious, though, that he should have had the feeling . . .

He gave himself a mental shake. This was reaction following on the events of the last two days. His mind was running at top speed, as it did when he was in the middle of a case. Only here he had few facts to grapple with, and there was no outlet for increased brain-power, hampered in addition by his inability to converse freely.

However, as the tongue became silent, the eyes penetrated deeper, and Moss found himself perceptive to human signals which normally he would not see or would choose to ignore.

'I am Isabel — ' the girl was saying — 'Isabel Hervada Arias.'

'I'll bet you are,' Moss thought, while making a polite response. This lady, buttressed about with family, wealth and position, had no need of Moss Coen to interest himself in her concerns. Particularly since he (the fool) was up to his neck in trouble anyway.

Almost in response to these thoughts, he saw the young man who was approaching their table. A slim, dark-haired young man of slightly more than average height, he looked rather strangely at Moss but smiled at Isabel and engaged her in conversation.

She appeared surprised, and Moss fancied there was just a trace of embarrassment in her rejoinders. After a few moments she turned towards Moss and said: 'Let me introduce you. Felipe, this is señor Maurice Coen, who is on holiday here from Ireland.'

The young man bowed punctiliously, not seeming to notice the Irishman's doubtful clothes, though he himself was impeccably clad. His name, it appeared, was Felipe Serna.

After this exchange, the young man asked Isabel something, speaking rapidly in Spanish so that Moss did not catch what was said. Isabel nodded, and Felipe picked up her wrap and placed it around her shoulders.

She got up, and Moss rose also. 'I shall leave you now,' she said in English, and gave him her hand in defiance of local custom. His own square fist closed round it for a moment.

'This meeting has been a great pleasure,' he said.

'Until tomorrow then,' she replied gravely, and went away on the arm of her escort.

9

What was *that* all about, Moss wondered? Apparently the message picked up by his antennae was the correct one. The lady had something on her mind. There had been a definite plea in her 'until tomorrow then'.

But how did she know he would be there tomorrow? Unless she herself was staying at this hotel, and had made enquiries.

The table incident then had nothing to do with the police. It had been of her own making. But why? Hardly because of his nationality. Irish people were thin on the ground in Burgos. Why should this girl wish to consult one?

No satisfactory answers could be given to these questions, but one query he could and did settle. The desk-clerk, when asked to convey a message to Miss Hervada Arias, wrote it down at once, regretted that the señorita had just this minute left the hotel, and said he would give it to her on her return.

Moss murmured something about being sorry not to have been able to greet her on arrival, and the desk-clerk replied that the lady had in fact enquired for him when registering, but had left no message.

How *very* odd, thought Moss as he came away. This girl could scarcely be concerned in the affairs of Martinez; neither did a connection with Maria Guzman seem likely. Why was Isabel anxious to see him? He wished he could find out more about her.

In one of those curious coincidences which sometimes happen, later that night he did. While at the *estanco* he had purchased local newspapers and a news magazine in order to search for anything in print concerning the death of Maria. However, apart from brief notices which said that a young girl had fallen from a hotel bedroom window, he could find no other references to her death, nor was there any mention of police involvement. The news magazine he discovered to be useless anyway as it was a monthly affair and had in fact been issued in June.

With nothing better to do, he leafed through its pages. And there it was. A picture with the caption: '*En la foto, la señorita Hervada Arias y su prometido.*' There was no doubt at all about the identity of the engaged couple. The man was Felipe Serna.

Why had Isabel, who wore no ring, introduced her fiancé simply as a friend? There did not seem to be any kind of quarrel. The pair appeared perfectly friendly. On the other hand, they certainly did not appear to be engaged. And in this country an engagement was taken rather seriously, or so Moss understood.

Next morning he got up early, and feeling he could not endure another meal under police scrutiny ordered breakfast to be served in his room. He sat out on the balcony in the early morning sun and watched Burgos travel to work.

When breakfast arrived, on the tray beside his coffee and rolls was a note from the hand of Miss Hervada Arias accepting his kind invitation to lunch but suggesting instead of the hotel restaurant an alternative venue in the street of San Pedro Cardeña.

Moss looked at the note for a long time. Miss Hervada might be an enigma, but her charm was undeniable. He finished the meal; he did not phone through to the desk-clerk but instead went in search of notepaper and envelopes and wrote a formal reply. This he handed in as he left the hotel, together with a (by Moss's standards) substantial tip, reflecting that if correspondence was to be conducted in this way, the man would certainly earn it.

The note he left unsealed. To save time and effort on the part of the police.

Luciano Camino, waiter at the Pensión Excelsior, had not yet left for work when Moss called at his home. The Irishman arrived in a taxi which he retained to carry him on to his next appointment. Camino seemed surprised at such an early visit. Nevertheless, Moss was welcomed.

'My house is your house,' the waiter said in Spanish, as he led the way into cramped living-quarters, where the señora de Camino, equally hospitable, made coffee for the visitor.

Moss was touched by this warmth. Even making allowances for Camino's habit of professional deference, together with expectations of a financial nature, there remained a residue that was genuinely friendly. The world of smash-and-grab is a cold one, and Moss had suffered from early exposure.

As the señora de Camino spoke no English, and Luciano's English vocabulary consisted of words and phrases picked up in the course of his employment, conversation was slow. Moss mentioned again the man who had been standing by the stairs in the Pensión Excelsior and who had spoken to Maria on the evening before her death.

'I have told you,' Camino answered in Spanish, 'I see nothing unusual. There was a man. He speaks to the señorita Guzman. They are together for some time. I am coming and going and still they are speaking.'

'Can't you tell me any more? He

seemed to me to be a fairly young man, well-built. Do you remember?'

Camino at once agreed. Now that he thought about it carefully, he would say also that the man was not a small man nor a very thin man. And the head! Camino became quite excited. He was remembering the head. In the past he had remembered only the teeth. Now he was seeing the whole head, the face of the man señor Coen wished to question. And what he, Camino, would say was this: it was a face with brown eyes and the hair was brown, and the shape of the face was like that of a horse!

'When he opens his mouth, you mean?'

'That is so. The señor understands. It is the mouth, the teeth. They are like the teeth of the horse.'

In the borderland of Moss Coen's brain there rose some half-forgotten fable of an ancient king having horse's ears, and of a harp which revealed this terrible secret! Angrily almost, he shook off the frisson. Back home, there might be quite a number of horse-faced Irishmen, but a horse-faced Spaniard could scarcely pass unnoticed. The lawyer, Doldan, would know best how to make use of this valuable information.

Moss asked again about the telephone call Maria had received. Camino had said it was made by a man also. Could the waiter remember anything about the man's voice? Was this second man soft-spoken, for instance, or did he speak in harsh tones?

Camino seemed to hesitate. Then he said slowly: 'The man spoke pleasantly, I remember. He asked to speak with the señorita Guzman, and when I said I would fetch her he thanked me politely. It was a cultured voice, I think.'

'The police asked you the same questions, no doubt?'

'The police!' Camino shrugged eloquently.

'Would you have any objection to answering questions put to you by my lawyer?'

Camino looked a little dubious, and Moss hastened to add that any expense involved would of course be reimbursed. He wrote out Doldan's address and handed it to the waiter together with a sum on account, and they parted with renewed offers of hospitality on the part of the Caminos, offers not meant to be taken too literally, but nevertheless intended to speed the departing guest in a spirit of kindly goodwill.

However, goodwill was totally lacking when Moss stepped into his waiting taxi.

'*Calle San Pedro Cardeña*,' he said to the driver, not appearing to notice the figure already occupying the rear seat, and discovering that it was in fact Urgoiti.

'I have been waiting,' said that gentleman.

'You wanted to speak to Camino, perhaps?' Moss replied. 'He has some useful information, certainly.'

Urgoiti looked up sharply. 'I make free to tell you that the intention of the police is not that you be allowed to travel everywhere.'

'I have not travelled anywhere without your knowledge, of that I am sure,' Moss said with a slight smile.

'Notwithstanding, you have interested yourself in various activities,' Urgoiti continued without heeding. 'You have been speaking to the porter, Taibo. What have you been saying there?'

'I have no doubt every word I said to Taibo is by now typed up and sitting on your desk.'

Urgoiti gave a sardonic smile. 'Is it that you have also visited the *Comisaría*?' He growled with sudden ferocity: 'If you shall come again, it may be we shall keep you there.'

Moss felt it prudent to remain silent, and in another change of tone, Urgoiti continued: 'There is a curious coincidence in this case. It may be that you are aware of it? No? I find that difficult of comprehension, and I will tell you that you are here in a position that is not good.'

'Thanks for the tip,' Moss replied grimly. 'I'll work at it.'

'You will not interfere with the work of the police!' Urgoiti slapped his open palm on the top of the passenger seat. 'You are the person most nearly implicated in this crime. Instead of the confines of a prison cell, we let you now reside at the Hostal

Esperanza, *lujo* . . . '

'You are paying for all that luxury for me?' Moss asked ironically.

Urgoiti gave what could only be described as a roar! 'Pay! Is it your impression that the police shall pay for suspected persons to be accommodated as the very rich?' He slapped his palm two or three times on the seat.

'Oh, I'm not complaining,' Moss hastened to say. 'I only wondered, that's all.'

'Your kind, I know it well,' Urgoiti replied with some feeling.

'You must try to understand my position,' the Irishman said more soberly. 'To have suspicion wrongfully attached to me, that is what I fear. Even if nothing is proved, there is my career. My reputation demands that I clear myself totally of any charge in connection with the affair.'

This was not how Moss Coen normally spoke, nor was he so greatly concerned about his future position in the Garda Siochana but, as he had previously observed, it was the language Urgoiti understood and the latter responded to it.

'That I comprehend,' he said. 'We

also are anxious there shall not be a mistake. But I shall tell you that by the evidence which we are receiving from all sides you are implicated. Opportunity is there, and also there is a possibility of motive. We shall await developments. If you are innocent, that shall be proved. If your guilt is indicated, then you will have charges to answer. Now return to the Esperanza, and have gratitude you are permitted to stay there for a time.'

'I'm so sorry,' Moss said with a grimace, 'I have to meet a girl for lunch. You know her name, of course.'

Urgoiti did not answer at once, and sat looking at Moss with an expression which the Irishman did not understand.

'I am an old man,' Urgoiti said unexpectedly, and indicated that he was getting out of the taxi. His legs were stiff, and the driver ran round and held the door open while the little man slowly emerged.

'I should not let this continue,' he said to Moss, and in a sudden gesture gripped him by the arm. 'You will exercise care,' he said.

10

The lunch in the calle San Pedro Cardeña turned out to be not at a café or restaurant but in a first-floor private apartment.

Moss was admitted by an elderly woman, tall and gaunt, who conducted him to a sparsely-furnished but brightly-polished room, whose floor-boards creaked under his tread and the window of which gave an uninterrupted view of the railway.

His first reaction was one of surprise. This was not a milieu in which he would have imagined Isabel Hervada Arias. When she came in, apologising for her late arrival, and he saw her with the woman who addressed her as Isabel, he guessed the elderly person to be some pensioned family retainer. Almost at once, his guess was confirmed.

'Benita,' said the young girl in Spanish as she pulled the woman forward and linked arms with her, 'you remember when I went away to Ireland one summer?'

The woman shot her a swift glance. 'I remember,' she answered somewhat dourly.

'This is a friend of mine from that country, señor Coen.'

The woman nodded respectfully, but still with an air of almost distrust. A table had been laid in the centre of the cool peaceful room, and they sat down while Benita left them.

Taking himself in hand, Moss said: 'It was kind of you to invite me. I thought we might have lunch together at the Esperanza, but this is more pleasant.'

She smiled. 'I hope you will like it. I wish to speak to you about something which concerns me. The Esperanza is always so crowded, it is difficult to speak.'

This gave Moss the opening for his next sentence. 'You must forgive me,' he said, 'last evening when I met Felipe Serna I was unaware of your engagement.'

She gave a sharp exclamation: 'Who told you that?'

He did his best to look surprised. 'Your picture was in a magazine I was reading.'

'It was in all the papers,' she said with a sigh. 'Felipe has been very good, very kind. It was my family really. I have known Felipe since I can remember. We were good friends and there was an 'arrangement' in the family, but I put it off for a long time. Only my mother kept saying that now I was twenty-three and almost all my friends were married. Then Felipe and I became engaged.'

She was older than he had guessed, Moss reflected. 'I don't know much about Spanish customs,' he said, 'but I thought engagements were rather serious affairs in this country.'

Isabel nodded, her delicate blue eyes clouding over. 'That is true. My family could not understand. And Felipe, he says he hopes we will marry.'

Moss did his best to sound polite. He wondered that she should unburden herself to him. Benita was surely the ideal confidente.

He roused himself suddenly. He was sitting down to a very pleasant meal, served in peaceful and charming surroundings, and with a most attractive companion, when he might have been still cooped up in the little two-roomed jail at Torno de Hilar or instead detained here in Burgos. He should at least show appreciation of the good things while they lasted.

He began to converse with his companion, asking Isabel about her work and interests, a desultory conversation until a chance remark in praise of the very good wine served by Benita led to the subject of the vineyards owned by Isabel's mother, Pilar Arias.

'Are the vineyards close to Burgos?' Moss asked.

'They are near to Logroño,' she said.

Logroño is the centre of a famous wine-growing district, Moss was aware.

'Is that far from here?' He trusted he did not sound too hopelessly ignorant. However, Isabel was delighted to tell him all about the vineyards, about twenty kilometres from Logroño.

'Logroño is on the Ebro, isn't it?'

'Yes, the land all about is very fertile,

and on either side of the river the scenery is very beautiful also. There is the ancient city of Calahorra; you should visit it. If you will come, we shall be pleased if you will stay with us.'

Whatever he had expected, it was not this. The thought which rose unbidden was of Urgoiti receiving the news that his prime suspect had gone to Logroño! That picture was so gratifying, Moss was almost tempted to accept.

Isabel raised her delicately-coloured blue eyes to his, and once again he marvelled at the serenity of that small oval face, and his pulse-rate increased.

It was ridiculous, of course. It was an illusion, a summer mirage. Probably fortunately for him. If her heart could remain untouched by years of devotion on the part of the handsome Serna, it was unlikely that Moss . . . He had a feeling too, for which he found it difficult to discover the cause, but the effect was one of unease. For her or of her, he would have been unable to say, an unease which may well have existed only in the imagination of Maurice Coen. All nonsense, probably!

Isabel was telling him that he must not think her invitation a mere politeness. Her parents' house was large, and there were often guests staying. He would find pleasant company, or if he wished to occupy himself exploring the surrounding countryside, he might do whatever pleased him best.

'Do you know who I am?' he asked abruptly.

He had meant this as a rhetorical question, prior to explaining (part of) his present dilemma, and why her family might find him an unwelcome guest. Instead he became aware of her quick intake of breath and the convulsive heave of her small breasts.

He was surprised, and his eyes asked a question. She coloured a little and then said quietly: 'I know.'

'Know what?' he demanded.

'That is what I shall tell you. It is the reason I wished you to come here, so that I might speak with you privately.'

Benita had brought two cups of coffee and had gone out shutting the door.

Isabel rose to her feet and began to

97

move about the room. At length she broke the silence, saying: 'You will find this a little strange, I think.'

He cocked an eyebrow: 'You are not by any chance some relation of Corporal Martinez, are you?' He knew very well that she was not.

Isabel gave a nervous laugh: 'Who is this Martinez?'

'He is, or was — I am not sure which — a member of the Guardia.'

She was puzzled and shook her head, saying: 'I have never heard of this man . . . ' She stopped. 'Why do you ask me that?'

'I suppose because he is on my mind a good deal.' In fact he had instructed Doldan to make discreet enquiries.

'I should very much like to know whether he is in fact still with us, as they say.'

She looked rather unhappy.

'Tell me,' he said, 'what is it?'

The girl still hesitated, for once unsure. Then all of a sudden, she spoke very quickly: 'I will tell you. The death at the Pensión Excelsior on Thursday — Maria

Guzman — I knew her.'

Moss was surprised at the connection.

'Maria lived close to your family home in Logroño, perhaps?' he asked.

'No.' As if conscious of a bald negative, Isabel went on: 'She was a friend from when we were at school together.'

'Oh, I see.' This, Moss could understand. Even he who had been educated compulsorily and gratuitously by the State, even he had an old school-friend, a fellow who never stayed out of trouble, but whose claim on Moss's friendship stemming from an incident which happened a good twenty years earlier had so far kept him clear of absolute disaster.

Isabel ceased her wanderings around the room and came to rest near the window which looked out on the railway-lines.

'Why do you come to me?' Moss asked.

'Because you were there.'

This simple statement gave him a jolt, and he regarded her with new eyes.

'How did you know that?'

She looked at him for a moment and smiled an enigmatic smile. 'I will tell you,' she said. 'When I read of Maria's death, I came to Burgos and went to the pension to make enquiries. The police were already there and would tell me very little. Afterwards, I went to see her mother, who told me the police had asked questions about a man Maria had been seen with on the morning of her death. Your name was mentioned and the police wanted to know if Maria had ever spoken to you. The mother could tell them nothing, but she did say to me that she believed you were arrested.'

Isabel continued: 'Yesterday, I returned to the pension and spoke to the maid who packed up your things. She told me they had been sent to the Esperanza, so it did not seem to me that you were arrested at all! And so it was quite easy for me to find you.'

'I don't know why you specially wanted to. I hadn't anything to do with Maria's death, if that's what you intended to ask me!'

But was it? If Isabel were speaking the truth, it must mean she had set out to interview a possible murderer and with no more protection than Benita. And here she was poised and cool, asking questions without appearing to give credence to the doubt which prompted them. In a calm voice she expressed herself quite sure Moss was not in any way involved in Maria's death.

Moss longed to say: 'I wish the police were as sure.' He said nothing.

'How did Maria seem to you when you met her?' Isabel asked simply. 'I presume what the police said was true, and that you and she . . . '

Isabel hesitated, and Moss finished the sentence: ' . . . went to see the sights?'

'You were together anyway,' Isabel went on hurriedly. 'Did Maria seem anxious or afraid?'

'You must remember,' Moss replied, getting up and coming over to the window, 'that I had never met her before. Therefore it is difficult for me to say. While we were having dinner together in the pension, Maria did seem a little anxious, yes, but I think it was in case the proprietor should walk in unexpectedly. When we went out on the town she was

laughing, enjoying herself. You are thinking it might possibly be suicide?'

Moss had no intention of adding that
the police totally discounted this theory.

'It is very terrible that, yes, but less
terrible than to think a person deliberately killed her. And for what reason
would they do so?'

The Irishman said nothing. Through
his mind passed a whole series of reasons
which in his line of work he had to deal
with on an everyday basis. Looking down
on that calm detached countenance, he
found he did not care to mention any of
them.

Isabel, too, was silent for a time before
asking:

'Did you see the body?'

'Yes,' he answered baldly.

She hurried into her next question.
'Was there evidence of . . . I mean what
actually happened to her?'

'There were some injuries.' Moss
ruthlessly thrust from him the sudden
vision of the twisted body.

'Because she fell?'

'The window of her room opened out

to an inner courtyard, and Maria was found lying just outside the kitchen two floors down.'

'In that case, someone must have heard her fall. Did she not cry out?'

'I myself heard nothing,' Moss admitted, 'and I slept in a room overlooking the same courtyard.'

'You heard nothing at all?'

'I was aware of certain noises in the house, but they were noises one would expect to hear in the early morning. Footsteps on the stairs and some activity in the kitchen.'

'You said Maria was found outside the kitchen door?'

Moss regarded Isabel for a moment before replying: 'I know that. Unfortunately for me, it seems someone on the staff found the body just at the precise moment that I stepped out of the pension. In the eyes of the police, a most suspicious circumstance.'

'The police — they suspect *you*?'

The incredulity in her voice pleased him enormously. 'They do indeed,' he answered almost cheerfully, 'and were it not for some other circumstance of which I am aware but don't know what it *is*, if you follow me, if it were not for that I'd have been arrested.'

'The police have evidence against some other person, is that what you mean?' Her body was tense.

'If so, they haven't told me about it,' he responded easily. 'Maybe they will one of these days. Tell me,' he added abruptly, sitting on one of the wooden chairs, 'you said you had spoken to Maria's mother. I'd like to interview that woman myself — where does she live?'

Isabel said, after a slight pause: 'When I went to see the mother, she was crying. We did not speak too long. The señora de Guzman did not know anything of Maria's life apart from that her daughter lived and worked at the pension and would visit her sometimes in the evenings on a free day.' There was silence, then: 'I did not see Maria for some years,' Isabel finally said.

'Still, there might be *something*, you never know,' and Moss sounded wistful.

'The mother doesn't speak English, I suppose?'

Isabel smiled at that. 'I do not think so. Señora de Guzman lives in an apartment house close by the Casa de Miranda. I will accompany you there, if you wish to see her.'

'That will be very nice,' Moss replied. He was aware that Isabel did not wish him to see Maria's mother alone.

11

The cathedral was fairly crowded, and in a chapel to the right of the main entrance Mass was being celebrated with a Sunday evening attendance which included Moss Coen. So much at peace with the world was he that he patiently endured a fifteen-minute sermon, delivered at some speed and scarcely a word of which he understood, and forbore to remonstrate with the lady next to him who rattled her black fan ceaselessly in his ear. (The evening was hot and sultry.)

Afterwards he explored the art treasures of the Gothic cathedral, three centuries in construction; the famous *escalera dorada*, golden staircase; the Sarmental and Coroneria doorways; the porch known as La Pellejería.

An enquiry produced the information that the bodies of the Cid and of his wife, Jimena, lay buried beneath the transept. The evening sun striking against the stained-glass windows flooded the nave with light, and when Moss had turned away from viewing the magnificence of the tombs of the Constables of Castile, he discovered a small group of people gathered in the vestry, while a notice on the vestry door proclaimed the availability of an English, French or Italian-speaking guide.

The group was a mixed one, the main body being part of an American tour group, whose two coaches were parked outside. In due course the guide arrived, and after consultation with the leader of the tour group, the former led the way having gathered the Americans around him. Moss tagged along too.

Much of what they now viewed Moss had already seen for himself, and he was content to let his attention wander and close his ears to the succession of names and dates flowing from the lips of the gentlemen whose business it was to tell all.

It was while standing under the rose window between the ornamented fifteenth-century twin towers of Juan de Colonia that Moss saw Taibo.

For once the little porter appeared quite cheerful, and looking up at that moment he saw Moss and gave a sign of recognition. The Irishman would have spoken, but just then the tour group which had spread out to view the centre nave now closed in behind their guide who indicated he would lead the way out to the cloisters. The party hastened forward, sweeping Moss along with them, and when he looked again Taibo had disappeared.

Once inside the cloisters, Moss forgot all about Taibo. Stained-glass enclosed three sides of the quadrangle from the cloister garden, the latter visible from the fourth side and open to the street beyond. In the pale evening sun, the whole was filled with kaleidoscopic rich glowing colour.

Moss failed to notice that the remainder of the group had disappeared through a doorway, leaving only one other man apparently given up to contemplation like himself. This man made no move to follow the others, but remained behind, impassive.

The Irishman came back to reality with a jolt. Urgoiti still had him on the hook. He imagined again Urgoiti's expression if he, Moss Coen, should decamp to Logroño. It was a thought which continued to gratify. And why not accept the invitation, whatever the risk? Whether or not he went to Logroño, Moss might well be arrested again anyway.

He admitted to himself that he was more than curious to see the Hervada Arias home. Before he left, he had still to interview Maria's mother, and also he had better see Doldan. Moss had arranged to visit Mrs Guzman later that evening. Doldan he would probably find at the lawyer's office early next morning.

So why not go? The more he thought about it, the better pleased he was. Moss even remembered the ancient city of Calahorra. If he stayed free long enough, he could send Urgoiti a postcard!

He glanced at the man near him. On a sudden mad impulse he took out his notebook and wrote a brief message which he then tore out and placed in an envelope thoughtfully supplied by the

Hostal Esperanza. Before parting with it, Moss gazed at the superscription for some moments, and then carefully placed the envelope beneath one of the windows. Grinning broadly, he walked towards the door.

This led to the sacristy, and to the wonders displayed; many old and beautiful chalices and ciboria, silver reliquaries covered in semi-precious stones, cloth-of-gold vestments magnificently embroidered.

Finally, gazing at the frescoes which looked down on him from seven hundred years, Moss left his current problems to take care of themselves.

12

The interview with the señora de Guzman was all it had promised to be. By prior arrangement Isabel was there to introduce and interpret.

The widow lived in a small apartment not far from the Casa de Miranda; the latter containing the eleventh-century gold and enamel altar-piece of Santo Domingo de Silos. However, no gold or enamel was visible in the tiny dwelling-place of Maria Guzman's mother, whose name in spite of her tight lips, was Generosa.

The woman's attitude of antagonism towards Moss the Irishman could understand, for what woman would not show fear and distrust of a man suspected of having killed her daughter. What Moss found less easy to fathom was Generosa's overt dislike of Isabel, which even customary Spanish politeness failed to mask. Unless it should be that the mother was angry with Isabel for having brought him to the house.

Isabel had described Maria as a school-friend, and mothers often regarded with almost maternal affection their children's first friends, particularly when they met those friends again later in life. So what was it? Was Mrs Guzman jealous of the wealth displayed by Isabel whose way of life seemed totally remote from this mean little room?

There were other queries too. How was it that Isabel had attended the same school as Maria and, in the intervening years, how closely had their friendship been maintained? According to Isabel, the girls had not met for some years.

These were not matters Moss could openly speculate upon, at least not for the present anyway, so when they had all seated themselves on uncomfortable and insecure chairs, he began with a formal expression of sympathy to the mother in her bereavement. This Isabel translated faithfully, but it produced no softening on the part of the elder person. Moss felt, rather than saw, a defence mechanism come into operation.

'You have already been asked many questions by the police, I am sure,' was his opening remark.

'Yes.'

Moss sighed. 'They will no doubt have asked the kind of life she led, what men friends she had, whether anyone had reason to kill her?'

Before Isabel could complete the translation, Generosa answered with a touch of defiance: 'She was a good girl.'

How many times had Moss heard that. Of course there were times when it was true.

He decided on a blunt approach: 'The police have evidence that shortly before your daughter fell from the window, a man was with her and was heard to speak to her.'

'You are that man!'

'If so, I should not be here with you now. The police would have arrested me. It is because they know I had nothing to do with Maria's death that they let me go free.'

As Moss said this, mentally he was

looking over his shoulder. He trusted Urgoiti would not contradict him. Almost in spite of herself, the woman was impressed. Her eyes seemed to bore into his, trying to read his thoughts, which even had she been able to, she could not have understood.

'Tell me about Maria,' Moss continued patiently, settling himself into his chair (an unwise move, for it jerked ominously under his weight). 'How long was she at work in her present job, for example?'

'Three years.'

'She was happy there?'

The woman shrugged. 'She did not complain. Señor Perille was sometimes upset when little things went wrong. Maria said he would have preferred to employ a man in her position.'

'Oh? Why was that?'

'He is of the old-fashioned type. But Maria was very proficient. She had many diplomas.' Pride was strong in Generosa's voice.

Here then was perhaps the answer to Moss's query about schooling. A brilliant pupil might win a burse or a scholarship to an expensive school. Odd, though, that such talent should have been content to accept employment in Perille's guest-house, one of the *pensiones de tercera*, third-class.

Looking around at the painfully-neat and clean little room with its meagre furniture and absence of comfort, Moss supposed that the position of cashier at the Pensión Excelsior was not without prestige of a kind. And free lodging must also be taken into account. And meals.

'Was your daughter friendly with any member of the staff of the Excelsior? I mean,' added Moss, 'any male member of the staff?'

'Not at all,' the señora de Guzman waved her arms expressively. 'Cooks, waiters, porters! What should Maria have to do with those?'

'What indeed?' murmured Moss, half to himself. From his brief encounter with Maria, he was aware that she held herself aloof from any members of the staff present on that occasion.

However, that did not entirely rule out the possibility . . . The person with the

115

easiest access to Maria's room at the Excelsior *would* be a member of the staff. And the boy who acted as night-porter had heard voices. Or so he said. Or so Urgoiti *said* that he had said.

In any case, Doldan's forthcoming examination of the waiter might throw some light on that subject. No need to labour the point here. Moss was treading his way so very delicately, being careful to give no offence, that the reaction to his next question took him off guard.

It was a routine query. He asked if Maria had had a previous job prior to working for Perille.

Into the stifled silence which followed his question, Generosa eventually dropped a blank 'yes'. It was not so much the apprehension clearly visible on the older woman's face; Isabel's strained look prompted him to ask of the latter: 'Did Maria perhaps work for your family at Logroño?'

'Oh, no.' Isabel's negative carried conviction, and Moss's ears registered also a note of relief.

Generosa's tight little mouth, which looked as if a smile would break it in pieces, opened briefly to say:

'Maria worked for a large company.'

'Did she?' This accorded better with the new picture of Maria, the girl with the diplomas. It opened up certain possibilities, and altogether it sounded more promising than the history so far related of Maria's domicile at the Pensión Excelsior.

Mentally busy, Moss forgot to be cautious, and asked abruptly: 'Why did she leave?'

Generosa's thin pinched face screwed itself up as though to ward off a blow. Isabel's countenance, on the other hand, gave nothing away. It was she who replied when it became apparent Generosa was going to remain silent.

'Maria went to work for a large firm when she left school,' Isabel said. 'As the señora de Guzman has told you, Maria had many qualifications, and was soon promoted.' Those delicately-coloured blue eyes seemed to consider thoughtfully, and to be unaware of the venom in the face of the woman who watched her. 'In the end, she had what you would call a nervous collapse. She became ill. When she recovered she went to work for señor Perille, a job of less responsibility.'

This was said in English, and the mother was silent, not understanding. Isabel had scarcely finished speaking when the older woman broke into a tirade against her. The younger woman ceased to translate, but Moss understood a good deal of what was said, phrases like: 'Oh, that I have lived to suffer as I do! It is nothing to you. Why should you care? Maria is dead, and you are alive. Why do you sit there? It is because of *you* that she died!'

Moss looked at Isabel in wonder, for the girl showed no signs of emotion. As the woman's bitter attack continued and became more incoherent, Isabel finally rose and made as if to depart. Then she turned to the older woman and spoke in Spanish, very quietly, so that Moss caught only the last sentence: 'It was not my fault.'

The mother began to weep, her anger turning into tears of pity for her loss.

Gazing at Generosa's sobbing figure in

an apparent mixture of compassion and distaste, Isabel said: 'It was this way the last time also. You will not be able to ask her anything further, and she has told you all she knows.'

Accepting the futility of a longer stay, Moss allowed himself to be escorted from the room. But he was far from accepting the word of his guide that the mother had nothing further to tell him.

13

The gold-and-white telephone which the Hostal Esperanza provided for each guest trilled discreetly, and Moss's dark head emerged from under the sheet and his stubby fingers clasped hold of the receiver and dragged it down to his ear.

'Huh?' he said sleepily.

A torrent of official Spanish flowed in response. Moss muttered a 'no entiendo' and slid under the sheet again. His hand released the phone, and the receiver came to rest on top of his head. He dozed off.

Slow-spoken English in a deep rumbling voice prodded him awake once more.

He could hear the voice saying: ' . . . to me. You shall have that facility.'

Where had he heard that voice? *Urgoiti!* What time was it anyway?

He reached for the light-switch, while the voice rumbled on without ceasing. Ignoring sounds of speech, Moss looked

120

at the digital clock and discovered it was 4 a.m.

He picked up the receiver and listened.

'Notwithstanding,' the voice was saying (characteristically), 'we shall be pleased if you will now attend at the *Comisaría*, where questions remain to be resolved.'

'And I will have many questions to answer!' Moss exploded. 'Listen, I've answered all your damn questions, and I'll give you the name of my *grandmother* if it'll keep you happy, but does it have to be at four in the morning!'

'But how shall it be of assistance to me to know the name of your grandmother? My dear señor Coen, I make free to tell you that your reply is not at all reasonable.'

'I'm tired,' Moss said wearily.

'So you are tired!' Urgoiti's voice was soft but held a note of savagery. 'You are in bed and you wish to sleep? I shall make known to you the fact that I have not slept. Not this night, not last night. I, Luis Urgoiti, *I* am tired.'

'In this job there are always late nights,' Moss mumbled unkindly. He roused himself. 'However, in case it may somehow have escaped your attention, may I remind you that I am on holiday, my well-earned vacation from bodies-laid-out-on-slabs.'

A thump in the background betrayed Urgoiti's anger. But still his voice was soft: 'For your stay among us we obtained for you a nice hotel. We shall have given you the facility for your holiday, but it seems to us that you are not considering to remain in the hotel. You visit Camino at the pension as well as also his apartment. Then you are speaking to the señora de Guzman, and also . . . '

Urgoiti broke off and then his voice could be heard in a rapid undertone: '¿Como? Qué dice usted? Repitalo, por favor.' An interval, during which Moss could hear other voices. It seemed to him that some important news had come in and the informant was being asked to wait. The rumble grew louder again, and then continued in English: 'You will attend to me, señor Coen. We shall expect you without delay. A car will be sent and you shall accompany my men.'

So this was it. In a way, pretty decent of the old Spaniard. Urgoiti could simply have issued an order to have Moss picked up.

'You have understood me?' the old man was saying.

'Oh, I think so,' Moss replied. 'Shall I have time to shave?'

From the depths of Urgoiti's throat a curious sound emerged. 'We are here in a murder case.' A pause. 'My men will wait.'

'Right.'

By the time they hammered on the door Moss had not only shaved but had packed up his things. No point in adding to an already large hotel bill. Moss wrote a hurried note saying he had been unexpectedly called away and could be contacted through the *Comisaría del distrito*. This he addressed to the manager and handed it to the night-porter together with a brief note to Isabel.

The latter gave a watered-down version of his current predicament, and regretted he might reluctantly be compelled to decline her kind invitation to stay at

Logroño. He even had time to telephone to Madrid, and leave a message.

Urgoiti was in the car which waited outside the hotel. That was the first inkling Moss had that things were not as he supposed.

As the car sped away, the elder man said peevishly: 'You go to this person, you speak to yet another one, seldom you are at rest. All the time we shall have followed you. We are aware of much that you have been saying.'

'There's no crime in that.'

'Is it that you are purposefully not understanding? The matter of Domenech Taibo, is that not a crime?'

'Taibo?'

'Why do you stare? Did I myself not speak with you on the telephone and did I not say to you *clearly* . . . '

'I wasn't listening. Half-asleep, I'm afraid. What's this about Taibo?'

'*But he is dead!*'

'How?' Even as Moss made this laconic rejoinder, he knew the answer. 'It was not accidental?'

'It was considered as to have that

appearance. Taibo was found on the line near the railway station. It was a crossing he made many times, without authorization, and it seems to us that a train shall have passed by and señor Taibo shall have had the misfortune to . . . ' Urgoiti left the sentence unfinished.

Moss noticed that in death Taibo had become *señor* Taibo. He was beginning to discover a liking for the old man.

'You mean he was dead before the train struck?'

'What I shall tell you is that there *was* no train,' and Urgoiti waved his hands, the four remaining fingers of the right hand all the more noticeable. 'Taibo was seen outside the station at twenty minutes to midnight. The express to Vigo was departing to Venta de Baños, and he had no client, so say my informants. Next, the body of Domenech Taibo is being found on the line *a las dos y veinte.*'

Moss wondered what this had to do with him. During the period in question, he had been leading a blameless life under surveillance at the Esperanza. 'How was the body found?' he asked.

'We are making enquiries from all sides,' Urgoiti replied, as the car sped on. 'It is discovered that with the Barcelona express there was delay.'

'Yes?'

'Notwithstanding that it is due at Burgos before one o'clock, on this occasion it is stopped at Astorga and does not arrive until *after* Taibo's body is found.'

'Bad luck for someone?'

'It is as you say,' Urgoiti nodded graciously.

'You are treating it as murder?'

'We have little doubt.'

'Some local or domestic feud?'

'But you, my dear señor Coen,' Urgoiti's gestures were positively baroque, 'you have had the experience to speak to Taibo. You ask him questions about a man he has seen with Maria Guzman. What did he say to you?'

'As if you didn't know quite well,' Moss thought to himself. He replied, nevertheless: 'Taibo would say very little. It seems he saw nothing unusual.'

'So Taibo says to us also. Notwithstanding, it is our belief that he was possessed of information.'

'Which he was in the process of trading?' Moss was remembering again Taibo's face in the crowd at the door of the cathedral. The little man had looked very pleased with himself, the poor devil. The price of his silence was probably only a few thousand pesetas, and for that he had paid very dear.

'Your description accords well,' Urgoiti was saying.

'Does it indeed?' Moss thought. However, on the credit side his *bona fides* seemed to be in a fair way of being accepted at last, and the vision of a prison cell was, thankfully, receding.

They pulled up at the station. Taibo's body had obviously had to be moved fairly quickly, and as a temporary measure was now located in a shed at one end of the platform.

'How was he found?' Moss repeated.

'A passenger, Urgoiti replied, 'is waiting for the train which does not arrive. It is held up at Astorga. Others are waiting also, but this man is walking towards the line and he sees something, he does not know what. He fears the train will come at any moment. It is long overdue. The alarm is given, and the body of Taibo is then found.'

The shed (used to store workmen's tools) had been hastily converted, with two rough tables placed together and the whole covered in plastic sheeting.

The small limp body of Domenech Taibo lay stretched upon this makeshift bier. Under the glare of the imported lights, the head injuries were very noticeable.

The shed was already full to overflowing when the latest official party arrived. In its narrow confines, technical experts were completing preliminary work prior to removal of the body.

But there was no doubt about who was in charge. Urgoiti's rotund little figure stumped into the circle of light, as others left space for him. The soft felt hat, which he wore with a brim so wide as to shade his face, cast a shadow over the corpse. He removed the hat and handed it to the detective at his side.

Turning suddenly to Moss, Urgoiti asked him in English: 'When is it you are last speaking to Taibo?'

'I *saw* him yesterday evening, but we did not speak.'

'Where is this happening?'

Moss related the incident and his own interpretation of it. Out of the corner of his mouth, Urgoiti began translating for the benefit of the man behind him, and this man took notes.

'At what time did you see Taibo?' Urgoiti persisted.

'Around seven.'

Moss was gratified to discover his shadow had missed seeing Taibo. But of course yesterday evening Domenech Taibo was just a face in the crowd. Ten hours had brought tragic, if brief, notoriety.

They left the shed and walked along the platform. Barriers had been erected, and intending passengers were being shut up in the station's main hall until such times as their trains arrived. On Urgoiti's approach a uniformed guard slid aside one of the barriers, and several men conducted them to a railed-off section of the line.

Floodlights revealed members of the forensic department on hands and knees beside the track. A long and heavily-laden broad-gauge Pyrenean express rolled ponderously over the rails, and Moss had his face seared by a sudden blast of heat from the great diesel monsters which pulled her.

Under a sign which warned '*prohibido el paso*' and impervious to noise and heat alike, Urgoiti made his way to the centre of operations. The old man turned and indicated to Moss that the latter should take a closer look.

In fact, there was very little to see. The stains which were being examined by the technical staff might well be of human blood, but to the naked eye they were impossible of identification in the midst of oil and dirt.

An outline had been drawn of the position in which the body was found, lying to one side of the track as though flung aside upon impact with a passing train.

Moss had doubts. 'Taibo could not have been killed in the way this seems to suggest?'

'I shall tell you again. There are no trains passing. We have a witness, most reliable,' (Police? Moss wondered) 'and this man says Taibo is standing outside the station after the train to Venta de Baños is departing at twenty minutes before midnight.'

'And between then and two-twenty there were no trains at all? Even in or around the station itself — no movement of engines, shunting of empty coaches or trucks?'

'Shunting?'

Moss Coen's Spanish, although much improved, was unequal to the strain of translating 'to shunt'.

He shrugged, and Urgoiti did likewise.

'It is as I have said,' the latter repeated, 'nothing is happening here, nothing.'

'In that case, remembering the way Maria died, isn't there a certain similarity — of *method*, I mean?'

'I will agree with you,' Urgoiti said.

14

When Maurice Coen arrived at his lawyer's office, Doldan was engaged with another client. The narrow confines of the dark-panelled waiting-room with its legal text-books in glass-fronted cases, and framed diplomas and certificates all in the name of Lorenzo Doldan, reflected a conservative attitude on the part of that gentleman, who must have been under some pressure to have accepted Moss as a client.

However, the Irishman was conscious that changes had taken place since his last visit. For one thing, he was once again able to smoke his own pipe; his personal effects and travellers' cheques had been returned to him at his hotel.

Having retrieved his early-morning correspondence, Moss telephoned Isabel and arranged a meeting for lunch. In view of Taibo's demise, he didn't want to go away just yet. Another call to Madrid cancelled the information relayed earlier.

When he finally saw Doldan, he discovered that the lawyer had good news also.

'We have made enquiries,' Doldan said cheerfully, 'and discovered that Corporal Martinez is receiving treatment in hospital. The medical opinion is concussion and the man has been ill, but he is now recovering.'

'I am delighted to hear that,' Moss replied with some feeling. He went on to detail events of the past twenty-four hours.

Doldan listened, and then said abruptly: 'It would seem that your position is in any case greatly improved.'

'Have you ever met Urgoiti?'

'I know him, a little,' and the lawyer gave a brief wintry smile.

Moss asked if anything had been heard from Camino, and the answer was no. He shrugged and said that perhaps it was a bit soon.

'The waiter's information could be very helpful,' Moss added, 'for he can identify the man who was with Maria in the hallway of the Excelsior. Of course, we may not find this man, and even if we do, his presence there may have been quite innocent. But it's about the only real lead we have.'

'You have mentioned this to the police?'

'No.'

'Is that wise?'

'Well, they've had the opportunity to question Camino for themselves. Presumably what I know they *now* know. Also, I found difficulty in understanding everything the waiter said, so when he comes to see you, get him to go over the whole incident in as much detail as possible. As well as that, Camino may be able to tell you something about the kind of life Maria led, and what sort of person she was.'

The lawyer made a few notes. 'I will question this man as you suggest.'

'If Camino fails to contact you let me know tomorrow and I'll bring him along myself. He may be reluctant to become 'involved' any further.' Moss paused, and then went on: 'Another person I should like you to interview is Maria's mother.'

'But I understood from you that this had already been done?'

His client scowled. 'Oh yes, I was taken there,' the Irishman replied with a touch of bitterness, 'and in fact I had an interpreter.' Moss ruffled up his coarse dark hair and then smoothed it into a semblance of order. Doldan did not speak.

'Maria worked for Perille for three years,' Moss continued, 'and before that she was employed with a large firm here in Burgos. I want you to find out the name of this company and the reason why she left what appears to have been an important position. The subject came up during my interview with the mother, and I tell you that woman looked like death! *Something* happened there, something which caused Maria to have a nervous breakdown. Mrs Guzman doesn't want me to know.' Moss could have added that Miss Hervada Arias was similarly uncommunicative, but he refrained.

Doldan looked rather surprised, but he said at once: 'If the firm is located in

Burgos this information will not be difficult to obtain.'

The lawyer's smooth grey hair was carefully brushed back from his narrow forehead. His well-tailored light grey suit subtly compensated for a certain lack of width underneath. However, the face was not that of a man solely devoted to prudence. There was, thought Moss, evidence of the odd flash of something else, even if ten years or more separated each reckless act.

Doldan now said: 'You will forgive me, but is this enquiry necessary? The police will make every effort to discover in the life and work of the murdered girl a motive for the killing. And they are more easily able to do this investigation. In so far as suspicion has rested upon you, it was necessary to supply evidence of motive and opportunity for a third party, whereas now . . . ' Doldan's gaze fixed upon his client. 'Perhaps you will relate to me the events surrounding the death of this,' he coughed, 'Domenech Taibo.'

The day was not yet hot, and Doldan's severely functional window was open just a little. Abruptly, the Irishman rose and pushed it wide, standing in the current of warm air and watching the small boys who were playing down at the river-bank. The hand which had tightened on the catch relaxed its grip, even as the lawyer watched him.

'The circumstances were unpleasant?'

For a moment Moss did not answer. Then he turned and said briefly: 'Not more than usual. The position of the body on the tracks — combined with injuries to the head; the frontal bone was fractured and the parietal badly crushed — would suggest that he was walking along the track and received a glancing blow from a passing train. The right arm and shoulder showed bruising.'

'And did this not in fact happen?'

'In the first place, Taibo made his living in and around the station, and had done so as long as anyone can remember. Even an animal living close by a railway will come to know when to expect a train. Constantly coming and going, Taibo was almost a time-table in himself. In addition, the police are satisfied no movement of rolling-stock took place during the time of the supposed 'accident'. A train which was due didn't come in until *after* the body had been found.'

'There is a connection between this affair and the Guzman killing?'

'One view is that Taibo had information and was engaged in extracting the price of silence.'

'And was, in consequence, removed?'

'The police seem to be working along these lines. On the night of my arrival at the Excelsior Taibo insisted on having a private conversation with Maria. He may have been asking for a tip from the house, or it may have been something quite different. And almost certainly Taibo saw the horse-faced man described by Camino, although he afterwards said he couldn't remember. At the time I felt he could have remembered a good deal if he wanted to.' Moss's pipe had gone out and he tapped it gently over Doldan's ash-tray. 'A fact which does support the police view is the similarity of the killings — a blow struck, and the body afterwards placed so as to look like suicide or accident.'

'You take this view also?'

'Well, I should,' Moss replied, lighting his pipe afresh and sitting down in a more relaxed attitude. 'If Maria Guzman's murderer killed Domenech Taibo then *I* am not that murderer, for the police have kept a round-the-clock check on my movements ever since I arrived back in Burgos.'

Doldan's thin smile was almost cordial.

15

Isabel's car was parked outside the hotel and she sat in it, waiting for him. His apologies were brushed aside.

'What has happened? Are you again in trouble with the police?'

She opened the door for him, and he slid down into the seat beside her. The car was a sports model, a red two-seater fastback.

'It is nothing,' Moss replied, as the engine burst into life.

'Tell me what it is!'

For once that tranquil face showed signs of strong emotion, and the vehemence of her tone took him by surprise.

'A porter at the railway station, Taibo, was killed last night. The police wanted me to see the body.'

Her own body lost its tension, and she said after a slight pause: 'What has this man to do with you?'

'I met him on a few occasions. On the

night I first arrived in Burgos, it was he who brought me to the Excelsior.'

She shrugged. 'It seems very strange that you should be sent for, you who met him only casually. Has this man no relatives or friends?'

'For all I know, he may well have. It's just that the police seem to have got it into their heads that if a death takes place here in the city then I must be involved, so they rush to interview me!'

'But you are joking?'

'A little,' he admitted with a smile. While they had been speaking, the car had left the hotel grounds and was now caught up in a stream of traffic. It was close on noon. 'Until this morning, it was no joke,' he added ruefully.

Her face asked a question.

'Well, you see,' he explained, 'the police had been keeping a careful eye on me, and knew all my movements. So when this last thing happened they were aware I could not be responsible.'

'You tell me this man was killed,' she repeated slowly. 'What you are saying is that he was murdered?'

'The police believe so.'

'And they know you cannot have had anything to do with this matter?'

'Yes.'

They were going through an intersection at this time, and she gave her attention to the road ahead. Presently she said: 'Why should anyone think you would do this thing?'

Moss expected this question and had carefully considered his answer. 'Taibo knew Maria Guzman,' he said.

The car, designed with sharp cornering in mind, nevertheless made an awkward turn to cross a narrow bridge. Isabel was wearing a blue flowered dress of cotton material, edged in a blue which matched her eyes. A simple outfit which gave emphasis to her skin and colouring. Small silver ear-rings studded her ears.

Regarding her from under his thick lashes, Moss was aware that this mild exterior masked some primitive force. He was not always aware of its presence, but each time it obtruded into his consciousness it caused renewed surprise. The small hand which rested so lightly on the wheel, the expensively-shod foot which pressed the accelerator, the very car, all bore witness to a life-style remote from his.

After a long pause Isabel said: 'Working at the pension, Maria must have known many of the porters.'

The car was speeding along an open stretch of road. Moss decided on a more direct approach. 'The police think Taibo was killed in the same way as Maria, and for that and other reasons they believe the crimes are linked.'

Her answer was accompanied by a shrug of the shoulders. 'The police, what are they doing? They know very little, I think.'

There was no mistaking the scorn in her voice. Here was a reaction with which Moss was familiar. His professional anger died as he remembered she was ignorant of his own membership of a police force. Abruptly, he said: 'Have you met Luis Urgoiti?'

In spite of her poise, he knew that some emotion moved her, emotion which was not, he would have said, sorrow for the dead Maria, and which appeared to him to stem from anxiety rather than a great hurt.

'Who is this man, Urgoiti?' Isabel asked.

'He is the police officer in charge of the investigation into Maria's death, and also now that of Taibo.'

'I do not know him,' she replied with finality.

All the while the red car had sped on, taking them through fertile land, where heavily-laden fruit trees marched with the road.

'Where are we going?' he asked suddenly.

She smiled at last. 'I have kidnapped you,' she replied gaily, 'and we shall go out into the countryside to have lunch. The heat and noise of Burgos at midday!'

Moss did not quarrel with this arrangement, beyond wishing for the meal to be served fairly soon. Every now and then they came upon a small stream and four or five houses clustered together in a village, and at any of these places he would have been pleased for them to pull in. Isabel, however, had other ideas.

'We shall go to Santo Domingo,' she said, 'and we shall find lunch waiting for us at an ancient *posada*. Frequently, on the way to Logroño, I stop there for a meal.'

Moss had little idea of the whereabouts of this spot, and felt it prudent to mention that he must return to Burgos later in the day.

The highway was a good one, and they reached Santo Domingo around one o'clock. Its full name, Isabel explained, was Santo Domingo de la Calzada; the last part referring to the road or 'way' to Santiago, along which pilgrims trod during the Middle Ages. Santo Domingo de la Calzada was a resting-place on this journey to the tomb of St James the Apostle, a journey which led across Northern Spain to the shrine of Santiago de Compostela.

Moss absorbed this information as they left the car and made their way into the cool shade of a vinery under which tables were set out for the visitors. The market town, with its twelfth-century cathedral, attracted a number of tourists.

It was at once apparent that Isabel was well-known. A young couple seated at a table called out a greeting, and the proprietor hastened to direct them to a very pleasant table.

The food, when it came, was good; a *tortilla* filled with chopped ham and onion, a *cocido* of mutton, potatoes and vegetables, and in addition one of the famous Rioja wines of the district.

During the meal conversation flagged. Moss, as always, tended to concentrate on what was set before him, particularly if he was enjoying it. In present company, though, he could easily have been stimulated into making pleasant conversation, but Isabel, too, seemed to have much to occupy her thoughts.

It was while they were lingering over the remains of their meal that she asked if his holiday would last much longer. He told her the story of his trip so far, and how his originally-intended two- or three-day stay in Burgos had lengthened into nearly a week, and now looked as if it could last several weeks.

'You do not have to return home?'

'Oh, I do, but until this morning I wasn't free to go anywhere. In fact, I was bluntly told I was lucky not to be in a cell. Now it seems things have changed a bit. Naturally I'd prefer to have this whole affair cleared up before I return home. I don't want to go through life with a kind of 'grey area' hanging over my sojourn in Burgos.'

'The police may never find out who killed Maria, or why.'

'Do you think so? Luis Urgoiti looks to me the type of old fellow who never lets go. I'm a police officer myself, you see.'

He wanted badly to see what her reaction would be, and was surprised at her calm reception of this news. She asked a few questions about his work, seemingly in a spirit of mere politeness and without apparent real interest.

Being now more than ever determined to go to Logroño, where he could expect to learn more of Isabel, as they walked together across to the car Moss said: 'I think I shall visit the city of Calahorra!'

She turned to him at once, her quiet

mood changed in an instant.

'You will come?' she exclaimed. 'We will be delighted to have you stay with us. When shall you come? I myself leave Burgos tomorrow. Shall we travel together?'

With no more than a mental reservation caused by the thought of Urgoiti, Moss agreed.

16

In response to a summons from Doldan, Moss went round to his office that evening.

'I am glad you were able to come,' was Doldan's greeting, 'I must go away tomorrow and shall not return for several days. We have obtained some information.'

'Camino?'

'No, it is the firm which employed Maria Guzman. Your interpretation of the mother's reaction has proved correct. There was something.'

'What is it?'

'I will tell you as I myself discovered. As soon as the name of the firm was mentioned, I remembered the trial.' The lawyer indicated a comfortable chair for Moss, and himself sifted through the heap of papers on his desk. Moss noticed that Doldan's appearance had altered since the previous visit. It was not only the shirt-sleeves; his facial expression was entirely different. He was now like a cat that has found a mouse in a long-vacant mouse-hole.

'As the mother told you, Valdivia Commercial is a large company. It seems that when Maria Guzman left her school she was first employed in this firm as a junior clerk. The following year, she was appointed to a more senior position, and later the same year became assistant cashier in their salaries office.'

Moss let out a sigh. 'Cashier?'

Doldan nodded vigorously. 'Yes, yes, you find that interesting.'

'This is a matter concerning money?'

'Six hundred thousand pesetas.'

'Fraud?'

'The money was stolen and was never recovered.'

'And what part did Maria Guzman play in all of this?'

'I will tell you.' Doldan sat down and collected several of the papers, which he sorted and held under his hand. 'I shall describe to you what I learned from an official of the firm, and what I have put together from the records of the trial.'

Moss grinned, and an incredible smile of delight spread over the lawyer's face. He jumped up from the desk and opened one of his solid oak presses. From it he extracted several bottles and two glasses. He looked at the bottles, and again at his client.

'Anís?' he queried.

Moss nodded, and the lawyer carefully poured the liqueur. Once more seated, and taking tiny sips of his drink, Doldan continued:

'In the firm of Valdivia Commercial, members of the staff whose salaries are below a certain figure are paid weekly in cash. This money is collected each week from the bank and delivered to the cashier's office by the two security guards the firm employs. During the week I speak about, the head of the salaries section was absent on holidays, and his assistant, Maria Guzman, took his place.'

'Ah,' was all Moss said.

'The cash was duly delivered and was checked and signed for by the acting cashier. This took place on a Friday morning, and the money was placed in a safe to which only the cashier and two other members of the staff had access. These other persons were the chief accountant, who had been with the firm for over thirty years, and the office manager, who was about to retire and who had joined the firm when he was only fourteen.'

'And Maria Guzman had been there for only two or three years. Not a pleasant position to be in. I'm not surprised she had a nervous breakdown afterwards.' Moss cocked his head to one side. 'I'm assuming, of course, that Miss Guzman did not make off with the six hundred thousand pesetas?'

'She was not the accused.'

'But her evidence at the trial helped to convict the guilty party? I take it there *was* a conviction.'

'Yes.' Doldan looked rather put out. 'I have here the history of the events as they occurred,' he said, and Moss waved an apologetic hand.

'Please continue.'

Amicable relations restored, the story

unfolded. Office hours were from eight-thirty until one o'clock, and from three until seven. During the hours of siesta the main door was not locked, but one of the security men remained on duty in the entrance hall. Individual offices were locked by their occupants, who were responsible for the keys. Executive members of the staff might remain at work if they wished.

On the Friday of the week in question several members of the staff were due to begin their holidays, and this resulted in extra work preparing larger-than-usual wage-packets. In the cashier's office one or two people were already on holidays, and temporary staff had been taken on to help out.

They were behind schedule, and by lunch-time Maria was expressing concern. She herself had a lunch appointment, but she was reluctant to allow the work to remain over, as even when her section had finished making up the wages there were the figures to balance. For this whole operation, the normal deadline was one o'clock.

There seemed no help for it but to cancel her lunch-date and continue working. On the point of telephoning her regrets, she was stopped by another member of the staff who offered to take her place and remain behind instead.

After some initial hesitation, Maria finally agreed, and it was arranged that her assistant would stay until two-thirty, by which time Maria would have returned from lunch.

Afterwards of course, she was strongly criticised for having taken this action, particularly as the person to whom she entrusted the keys had been with the firm for less than three weeks! And in fact, as it transpired, she herself was delayed and did not return to the office until a quarter to three.

On arrival, Maria found her office door shut but not locked, her assistant having already left. Anxious about what he might have done with the keys of the safe, she rang the porter's office but could get no answer. After some delay she managed to contact the security guard who said he remembered the person in question leaving the building at around two-thirty. Maria concluded that her assistant had taken the keys with him, having first locked up the safe. It was not until four o'clock came, and her assistant had not returned, that Maria became uneasy.

'At the trial,' Doldan continued, 'it was pointed out that the door of Maria's office was unlocked and the room unoccupied for at least ten minutes.'

'The objection to that is,' Moss replied, 'that unless the combination of the safe was known, a person finding the door of the office unlocked would not be able to get their hands on the money unless they forced open the safe, and if anything had been tampered with Miss Guzman would surely have raised the alarm when she first returned.'

'I will agree with you but for one other fact: the assistant did not know the combination of the safe and merely relocked the inner safe door.'

Moss shrugged, but his eyes grew thoughtful. 'I suppose we can take the next bit as read,' he said. 'An agitated Miss Guzman, agonizing and prolonged absence of the assistant, and finally an interview with the management and then the police.'

'You have read the situation correctly, my dear señor Coen. But I must tell you that the assistant *did* return, at four-thirty, by which time the office manager had been summoned and had opened the safe revealing the loss of the money. When confronted with the empty safe and asked to account for the missing cash, the assistant stated that all was in order prior to his departure. He had, he said, carefully made up the remaining wage-packets and had then placed these in the safe along with the others. He did not know the combination, but had locked the safe's inner steel door, afterwards depositing the keys in Miss Guzman's desk-drawer. He said he supposed that he should have waited until the cashier had returned to the office, but as he had not had anything to eat since early morning he was very hungry. The cashier had promised to be back by two-thirty. He waited an extra five minutes and then left.'

'The keys were in the desk-drawer?'

'No. It is doubtful if they ever were. Maria Guzman said that after she had contacted the security guard who saw her assistant leave the building, it occurred to her that the keys might have been left in her desk and she searched thoroughly. She found no keys.'

'And what, if anything, had the helpful assistant to say to that?'

'The man insisted that what he had said was the truth, and that any reasonable person might have acted as he had done.'

'The reaction of an innocent person, possibly?'

Doldan's dark eyes regarded his client shrewdly. 'At the trial,' the lawyer admitted, 'the investigating judge upheld that interpretation, and cast doubts upon the quality of the evidence against the accused.'

'And what was this evidence?'

'The keys were recovered. They were found in refuse collected from this man's home.'

Moss raised his thick eyebrows. 'I'm

not surprised the judge had doubts. A very amateur thief, apparently.'

'That is indicated. An unexpected opportunity presents itself, and the man takes it.'

'Foolish fellow,' Moss remarked briefly. 'By the way, you didn't tell me the man's name.'

Doldan's face relaxed into a mildly humorous expression. 'His name is Angel,' he said.

17

'Well, what happened next? This man was convicted, you said?'

Doldan had now arrived at what was to him the most interesting part — the trial. 'The accused, Angel Baldomir, confessed to having taken the money. Before the case concluded, he admitted the offence and asked for clemency.'

'Despite the fact that the investigating judge was not satisfied?'

'My dear señor Coen, you are wise to make that point,' Doldan beamed his approval. 'Indeed very wise.' ('At any moment,' thought Moss, 'he'll offer to take me into the partnership!')

'The young man had legal advice, good advice no doubt. I was not myself involved in the case in any way . . . ' Doldan's unfinished sentence left the unmistakable impression that his advice would have been quite different. 'There was of course risk,' he added, taking the lawyer's detached view, 'the sentence might have been severe. As it was, Baldomir's family repaid the money and he was sent to prison for three years.'

'Three years!' Moss echoed.

'Not a long sentence,' Doldan agreed, and was about to add something, when Moss said: 'But that means he is now free. He has been released?'

Doldan shrugged. 'No doubt Baldomir is once again at liberty.'

The lawyer's disinterest stung Moss. 'Well then,' the latter retorted, placing his empty glass on the floor and getting up and pacing round the room, 'this man has been set free *recently*. Let us suppose that the investigating judge was on the right track, and that this Angel never took the money. For some reason — bad legal advice, his own fear that the evidence against him was too strong, pressure from his family perhaps; whatever the reasons for his confession, suppose Angel Baldomir has spent three years in prison for something he didn't do?'

Doldan was surprised at the vehemence of his client. 'What you suggest would be regrettable . . . ' His mild voice broke off as Moss intervened.

'That would mean, of course, that another person took the money. Only one other person is a likely suspect, a person who it turns out has been killed within a short time of this man's release!'

Doldan's mild expression disappeared and he came up out of his chair in one continuous movement.

'What you are saying is . . . '

'I'm saying that from what you've told me, Maria Guzman was alone in that office for ten, possibly fifteen, minutes. Possibly even longer. The security guard remembered that Baldomir left the building at around two-thirty. Was the guard also able to say when Maria arrived?'

'The question was asked, but the man could not recall.'

'The problem is, how did she get rid of the money? I presume the building was searched straight away.'

Fascinated by this new view of the case, Doldan slowly sat down again and began a search through his papers. 'Not immediately, I think,' he said, after a look at the trial transcript.

'By the way,' Moss added, frowning suddenly as a thought occurred to him, 'six hundred thousand pesetas would add up to some bulk. A good proportion of it must have been in notes of small denominations?'

'Yes, yes, that is true, although over half the money was in notes of one thousand pesetas, but there was in addition ten thousand in coin.'

'Coin?' Moss asked blankly.

Doldan was delighted to be able to provide further information. 'I have here the figures,' he said.

Moss said nothing but stared blankly at the list. 'None of this was recovered?'

'None. The police believed they should trace part of the money stolen, for the notes of one thousand pesetas were unused and the bank retained a record, but nothing was ever found.'

'Miss Guzman wise after the event, or Mr Baldomir in prison and unable to spend the cash! Anyone taking that lot out must have had a container. Did either carry a brief-case?'

'Maria Guzman had such a case. Baldomir, being merely a temporary clerk, was not entrusted with office papers.'

'Well, I suppose a plastic bag would have done just as well, or any container. Did anything come out about that at the trial?'

'Naturally it was necessary to prove that Baldomir had the opportunity to take the money away with him, and in fact the security guard remembered that he had been carrying a large parcel. Baldomir, in his first statement, said that this had contained books, and other members of the staff confirmed that he had brought the parcel to work that morning. No one could be found, however, who remembered seeing the contents, then or later.'

'What about Miss Guzman?'

'She admitted that during the lunch-break she had been shopping in company with the friend with whom she had lunch, and that this had delayed her return to the office. When, panic-stricken, she remembered the time, the friend drove her back to the office.'

'Male or female friend?'

Doldan smiled. 'Male.'

'So Maria drives up to the office door and enters with parcels or bags, apparently unnoticed by anyone. How did the security guard miss seeing her?'

'He went off duty at a quarter to three.'

'Why was that?'

'The porter came on duty at that time. He was in the building, but had not yet taken up his position at his desk in the hall.'

'So there was a gap of five minutes or longer. Maria said she rang the porter's office but could get no reply. What was to prevent her from stepping out of the office and returning a little later. If she was spotted on the return journey, she could say she had just returned from lunch. What about the friend? Did the man confirm her story of arriving at the office at a quarter to three?'

'He did.' Doldan seemed rather amused. 'He did not have to give evidence at the trial, of course. A man of what you would call 'good family' the impression of the police was that he very much regretted his name should be linked with this affair, and as soon as possible afterwards severed his connection with the señorita Guzman.'

Moss turned to Doldan with a sudden query: 'What sort of family has Angel Baldomir? Was it a parent who paid the money, or did the family pass round the hat or something?'

'There is not any official information on the subject. Unofficially it is believed the money was repaid by the father-in-law.'

'Baldomir has a wife?'

'He is not married. Forgive me, the relationship is what you would call,' he coughed, 'stepfather.'

'And who is this generous stepfather ready to hand over a large sum of money for a son not his own?'

Doldan coughed again. 'When the name was mentioned, I understood why it was that Angel Baldomir, though only a temporary employee, was appointed to work in the office of the cashier, and also the reason why he was entrusted with the keys. In spite of the firm's later denunciation of her decision to do this, at the time Maria Guzman must have believed it involved no risk.'

'Some local big name, obviously?'

'As you say. Don Julio Meyer is well known, besides having been elected to the Cortes.'

'What?'

'He has been elected Procurador — a member of the parliament. He is an influential person, known to many people.'

'Can't have been pleasant for this man to have a relative in prison, even a stepson.'

'That is undoubtedly correct. But,' said Doldan in a sudden flash of candour, 'if we should all be held responsible for the actions of our relatives, which of us should escape censure?'

18

The wooden-framed and creaking windows opened out onto some steps leading to a patio. In the early-morning sun were flowers and shrubs and a climbing rose tree.

Beyond, in a peaceful garden, in the still dry air, hung rows of sheets edged with the most wonderful lace and embroidery.

As Moss listened, the sounds of human voices reached his ears, and two women crossed the patio, carrying between them a basket filled with laundry, and singing as they went.

Lying where he was and not remembering anything, and not caring, he absorbed the tranquillity of this scene, until with a sudden jerk memory returned. He had driven to Logroño with Isabel the night before.

When leaving Burgos, he had telephoned Urgoiti. At first Urgoiti was reticent. Less so, though, when Moss mentioned his proposed trip to the Hervada Arias estates.

'You are busy, busy,' Urgoiti grumbled. 'We shall inform ourselves of matters necessary to the case. It seems to us that we shall have soon a favourable outcome. We do not recommend that you continue with your enquiry.'

'But I have simply accepted a very kind invitation!' Moss argued.

'I know the señorita Isabel,' Urgoiti said waspishly, 'I see *fotos* in the newspapers. She is what you shall call a socialite.'

Urgoiti's pronunciation of the last word threw Moss off guard, but the old man continued to behave in a rather extraordinary way over the Irishman's proposed trip. 'We have here your passport,' he growled.

'If the police at Logroño ask me, I shall of course refer them to you.'

'You are pleased to make a joke,' Urgoiti sounded really angry. 'I have already warned you . . . '

'Of what?'

There was a long silence. 'If you shall become a danger. Understand me. We have not here one death and then another. You wish to discover certain matters. It may be that you will be successful. In that case, I must know at once when you shall have found these things. In that way only shall you go to Logroño. You will agree with me to do this?'

Moss solemnly agreed.

He and Isabel were rather late arriving at their destination, which meant that Moss was introduced to the rest of the family at dinner. Señor Hervada was away on business, but his young sons, Carlos, a tall elegantly-dressed young man, and fifteen-year-old Ramón were there together with their mother. Isabel's previous assurance that Moss would not be the only guest was borne out by the arrival of two friends of the señora de Hervada.

One of the advantages of their late arrival was that Isabel said they had better not take the time to change, as she herself was exhausted and absolutely starving and she was sure that he must be too.

Whether or not this was actually the case, Moss was conscious of what had prompted these remarks: the lady being by now undoubtedly aware that he possessed one suit only. (His jacket and slacks had been to the cleaners, and although improved in appearance, neither could be said to have recovered from their sojourn in Torno and its surrounding district.)

And in spite of polite efforts made by his hostess to include him in the orbit of her smiles, Moss was conscious of tension between mother and daughter, of which he felt (partly correctly) that he might possibly be the cause.

However, it seemed that the night brought counsel, or perhaps merely an exchange of information; anyhow, at breakfast the atmosphere felt rather more cordial. Attired in the newly-cleaned jacket and slacks, he no longer looked out of place but only a little shabby.

A riding party was due to set out after breakfast, and Moss was invited along. His protests that it was years since he had been on a horse, and in any case he had no riding-outfit, were impatiently brushed aside, and he was led into an enclosed stable-yard.

As he had said, it was a long time since Maurice Coen had sat astride a horse, nor did the animal he had once ridden bear any relationship to the descendants of Arab horseflesh now parading in front of him. Sister and brothers claimed their respective mounts, while the groom looked at Moss and seemed to weigh up the latter's bulky frame.

Carlos said something very rapidly, and the groom scratched his head and reluctantly, it seemed to Moss, gave instructions for a horse to be taken out of one of the bigger loose-boxes. As Moss watched the animal being led forth, his heart sank.

A dark-brown gelding, the horse towered over his stable companions.

'An interesting animal, that,' Moss said, surveying his mount with a critical look, assumed to mask his growing anxiety.

'He will carry you forever,' Isabel laughed as she matched his look with an apologetic shrug. 'My father bought

Salmonte,' she added, 'but now he does not always have the time to ride the horse.'

When the animal had been saddled, Moss was assisted to mount. His first sensation was of height; the ground looked far away; the second sensation was of motion, for as Moss gathered the reins together and straightened in the saddle, the horse began an unchecked movement towards the gate.

The stirrups had not been adjusted and were in fact too short, and the groom was waiting to perform this task. Moss tightened his grip on the reins and pulled. Salmonte lengthened his stride, and horse and rider passed under the arched gateway. On such an animal might Rodrigo Díaz de Vivar have ridden out, but the present twentieth-century rider was only too aware of his inability to communicate with his mount, or indeed to have effective control over the animal's movements, to have leisure to reflect upon possible riders of the past.

Isabel, whose natural lithe grace matched that of her horse, and who wore a perfectly-fitting brown velvet riding-jacket over her white silk blouse and fawn breeches, now cantered up to draw level with Moss.

'But you ride Salmonte beautifully!' she exclaimed.

After that, he knew he must not fall off, although he was too preoccupied with the actual task of remaining in the saddle to give consideration to the reasons for this new determination. Salmonte was not a frisky animal, but the big horse had a formidable stride, and conscious of a novice rider's ineffectual efforts to hold him in check strove to lengthen it. While not appearing to move particularly fast, Moss steadily drew ahead.

They cantered along a broad path which had a hard dry surface and was fairly level. To right and left were orchards, while the gentle slopes visible in the distance were planted with row upon row of vines.

They came to a fork in the path, one side of which led uphill, and with the idea of checking the progress of his mount, Moss made an effort to turn the animal in that direction. Unfortunately, Salmonte was determined to take the downhill path!

The horse shook off the attempted opposition (nearly unseating Moss in the process) before galloping down the hill.

An hour later, Isabel's jesting remark: 'He will carry you forever' had proved to be nothing less than the truth. Salmonte was untiring. This, thought Moss, is seeing the Spanish countryside with a difference. All around was evidence of viticulture, and in places where the vine was not planted olive trees flourished, and there were orchards in abundance.

In due course, the path led to a minor road, and though the rider was apprehensive of motor traffic (in fact he met none at all) even the most primitive of roads will lead to a village where, hopefully, Salmonte might be induced to slow down if not actually come to a halt. Isabel, Carlos and Ramón had long since been left behind.

Presently they came to a river, guarded by a fortified bridge. The bridge was an ancient one and the tower a twelfth- or thirteenth-century structure. Moss, when he saw it, was not concerned with its antiquity but with the realization that, in crossing the river, the horse would have to pass through the narrow entrance to the tower, in former times closed by a portcullis.

As they cantered up to the bridge, Moss was relieved to find their pace had slackened, and when Salmonte became aware of the obstacle in his path, he slowed to a trot.

The portcullis was no longer in existence, but the superstructure of the tower cast its shadow over the Roman bridge, the road surface of which was poor. Stepping carefully to avoid loose stones, the animal was induced to halt under the shade of the tower, and Moss slid down from the saddle and leant his weary body against the parapet. Both his legs had cramp.

The scene was one which in other circumstances he would have appreciated. Just across the bridge, a small village nestled in the shadow of the great fortification, and the low red-tiled roofs peeped over the tall grasses of the river-bank. Two men with a donkey-cart were shovelling something, Moss was not sure what, into the back of the cart, while the donkey stood patiently at the river's edge.

The men saw him, of course, and looked in his direction. After a while, they stopped work altogether and gazed intently.

In his weary state, it took Moss a little time to realize that the men's attention was not focused on himself, but on that part of the bridge which was nearer to them. The tower blocked his view of what had attracted their attention and (stupidly, he had to admit afterwards) he continued to watch without thinking of the obvious.

On the far side, where the bridge met the road to the village, a path sloped gently down to the water's edge. As Moss leaned out over the top of the parapet, a dark-brown mass detached itself from the bridge and turned onto the path, ambling down towards the river. Salmonte, going to get himself a drink!

Aware that he was responsible for this valuable piece of horseflesh, Moss hastened under the tower as fast as his cramped limbs would carry him, and met one of the men clambering up to the bridge. As memory returned of his imprisonment at Torno de Hilar, Moss hoped he would not again be arrested, this time as a horse-thief! For the two men obviously knew the horse; the man at the river-bank had gone up to the animal and was now holding the reins, while his companion at the bridge gave the rider careful scrutiny.

Conscious that his attire did not match his expensive mount, Moss expected suspicion, but instead he was met with sheepish smiles. Encouraged, the Irishman waved a vague hand in the direction from which he had come, and indicated that he was a guest of don Francisco Hervada, to whom the horse belonged.

The man who was holding the reins grinned and nodded, muttering something which Moss could not understand, but in any case showing no signs of hostility.

As the two men continued to regard him, waiting for him to speak, their attention was distracted by the sight of another man on horseback crossing the bridge.

At first Moss thought it was Carlos, for the rider was tall and slim, but as horse and rider emerged from under the tower gateway, Moss realized that the man was older. And yet, surely vaguely familiar.

Sitting easily in the saddle, Felipe Serna made his way carefully over the rough surface of the bridge, and then reined in his horse.

'But you are found!' he cried out, as he dismounted and led his horse towards the river, where Moss, the two men, Salmonte and the donkey all stood. Serna spoke rapidly to the two Spaniards, and the man holding the reins replied with many gesticulations and a hand waving in all directions. The gist of the discussion seemed to centre round the friend of señor Hervada, and was it possible he had met with an accident?

Moss broke in to explain that his presence in this spot was due entirely to Salmonte. The problem was now that until the cramps in his legs had eased he would not, indeed *could* not, ride twenty kilometres.

This produced another discussion in which donkey and cart were in danger of becoming involved at one stage, a notion sternly vetoed by Moss. At length, it was decided that Serna would telephone Isabel with news of her guest's whereabouts, and Moss would return at a later hour when horse and rider were rested.

'You live near to this place?' Moss enquired of Felipe. The scheme in connection with the donkey and cart had been a proposal to transport Moss to the Serna home.

'It is not a great distance away,' responded the other. 'I was riding this morning, and I met Isabel. She says you have ridden away alone. They are concerned for your safe return. On the road here, I meet with a man who says he has seen the big horse, but he does not know the rider. And so I discover you.'

This was said with a certain coolness of tone which made Moss think that Isabel's concern for the stranger did not altogether please the man who, until very recently, she had been engaged to marry. Moss was not at all sure of his own feelings towards the lady, but to be even *thought of* as a possible rival by this handsome disdainful young fellow, Moss found surprisingly gratifying.

The two men with the donkey were put in charge of the stranger and directed to lead him to the local *posada* for refreshment for himself and his horse (and themselves also, naturally), and Felipe Serna bade the party '*Adiós*' and mounted his horse and made his way back across the bridge.

After some hesitation on the part of the escort, work was abandoned. The cart was left where it was, and the donkey taken out of the shafts. Then the two men, each leading an animal, and with Moss following, led the procession down the village street.

This tranquil interlude was a prelude to more stirring events.

19

The incident took place on the return journey. Moss left the village at about five o'clock, having parted from his two companions with evidence of good-fellowship on both sides.

Salmonte was led forth by the proprietor of the inn, and Moss stiffly climbed into the saddle once more. The horse needed no urging to take the road homeward. Having carefully stepped over the potholes beneath the tower, Salmonte turned when he came to the road and began to lengthen his stride. Soon they were cantering along at a good pace, and it was not until the road petered out into the rough path which eventually led back to the Hervada home, that Salmonte showed signs of faltering.

The path led uphill, of course, and Moss began to wonder if Salmonte just disliked hills. He urged the horse up the gentle slope, but still Salmonte appeared reluctant. Finally, the horse came to a standstill.

'If only you'd taken it into your head to act like this on the outward journey, we wouldn't be here now,' Moss grumbled. 'Come on, let's get going.' As he spoke, he spurred the horse forward, but Salmonte moved only a few feet.

Was there ever such a tiresome animal! Moss could visualize another search-party having to be dispatched.

'First you wouldn't stop, now you won't go,' Moss accused his mount, laughing to himself in spite of his frustration. If only someone could see him; what could be more idiotic — talking to a horse in a foreign tongue!

He had leisure to view the surrounding scene. The evening sun striking the trees which bordered the path in this spot threw long shadows across the track. The heat of the day was slowly dying, and the birds were singing in the cooler evening air. But it was quiet, so quiet that he heard the steps of the person approaching, although that person must have been a little distance away.

Moss shook up his horse, and Salmonte stepped sideways across the path. The nervous animal communicated fear to the rider, already with a sense of unease. There was another sound, quite close, and one which Moss recognized. Behind the trees, someone with a rifle had removed the safety-lock. What was it Urgoiti had said? 'We have not here one death and then another.'

Moss Coen clapped his stirrups to the horse's flanks, and let out a yell in Salmonte's ear. As a shot rang out, horse and rider took off, the Irishman very nearly unseated by the galvanic leap of his mount. They were ten yards down the path before the second shot missed them. Moss leaned as far forward as he dared, both hands clutching Salmonte's mane.

When it came, the third shot was far away, and Moss guessed he was safe from a bullet. Salmonte was going flat out, and the rider, whose hold on the animal was precarious, was in great danger of being thrown. He slipped first to one side and then the other. Then they came again to the fork in the path and Salmonte blindly plunged to the right. Moss and his mount came apart.

He was lucky in a way. The grapes saved him. The vine grew at the edge of the path, a bush heavy with slowly-ripening fruit. Into this he was flung, smashing his way through its soft branches. But it cushioned his arrival on the ground, so that the fall did him little harm.

Moss lay there and did not attempt to stir for some minutes. He had had a narrow escape. But for Salmonte's long stride, that second shot might not have missed. He could picture the arrival back at the stables of the sweaty horse, and the setting forth of anxious searchers for the rider.

Would Isabel be among them, or was she already out 'looking' for him? It was she who had come upon Felipe Serna and told him that her guest was missing — lost in the surrounding countryside. Later, when Serna would have telephoned her with the news that Moss was found, easy for Isabel to express anxiety and say that she would ride out to meet the visitor on his return.

The shots which had been fired — were they intended to kill or (and this brought Moss up out of his grapevine) was what actually *had* happened the intended outcome all along; the horse startled by shots fired near at hand, and the rider thrown (subsequently to be found with a crushed skull)?

Just another unfortunate 'accident' and with plenty of assorted witnesses to testify to a novice rider's inability to control his mount; Felipe Serna, the men with the donkey, the innkeeper. Moss could picture the supercilious Serna giving evidence of finding the dismounted rider at the bridge, and when Moss remembered how at the time he had been gratified at Serna's little touch of jealousy, a cold chill ran down the Irishman's back. (He was now hurrying towards the house as fast as his bruised legs would carry him.)

What was it that Maria's mother had said to Isabel: 'It is because of you that she died.' And Isabel's curious reply: 'It was not my fault.' To such people, it was never their fault. Whatever posed a threat to their security, their greed or desires or whatever, that threat must be removed, no matter how. No one else's right to exist counted.

What the motive could be Moss could not begin to imagine. Urgoiti knew something. Urgoiti had warned him not to come here.

And as if in response to these thoughts, Moss heard the sounds behind him. They were distant as yet. He began to run. He could now see the lights of the house and the arched gateway to the stables, but both were yet a long way off. The sounds in the rear grew closer.

Then Moss saw two mounted figures emerge from the stable-gate. The hoof-beats behind him were very near. Desperately, frantically, Moss waved. The men at the gate saw him. One was . . . surely, it was Ramón?

The two horsemen cantered out to meet him, even as the other rider drew level and Isabel's cool amused voice fell on his ears: 'Is it possible you have run all the way home?'

20

In addition to his already battered condition, Moss had to endure a certain amount of good-natured chaff over this incident, and although the more adult Carlos expressed concern about the fate of their guest, Ramón openly indulged his wit at the visitor's expense.

Showing no apparent suspicion, Moss described how the horse had been startled by the sounds of someone letting off a rifle in a nearby field. Salmonte had bolted, and Moss had been thrown. Uninjured, the rider picked himself up and had run after the loose horse.

At dinner that evening Moss was seated next to Felipe Serna. The latter refrained from adding to the Irishman's discomfiture and offered certain anecdotes of his own experiences when riding the same animal. When the satire of Ramón threatened to overstep the bounds of what might be considered reasonable,

Serna's acid tongue kept the boy in check.

Isabel was seated opposite but seemed to have little taste for conversation. In his formal and rather stilted way, Felipe made a number of attempts to engage her attention, but she answered in monosyllables. The dignified Spaniard then turned his attention to the visitor and conversed with Moss in English.

There was a curious tensity about Isabel this evening, and her normally soft features appeared fine-drawn. Her whole body seemed taut with . . . suspense was it? Moss noticed that she watched one of the other guests. The attendance being formally clad, Isabel herself wore an evening-dress the colour of pale corn, cut on very simple lines. Again, this simplicity gave her a childish look strongly at variance with her present expression.

As Moss continued to regard her closely, he let his attention focus on the person whom she devoured with her eyes. The man was tall and broad-shouldered, with slightly-receding hair going grey at the temples. In addition, he wore a short dark beard in which there were as yet few grey hairs. He was very much the darling of his hostess, the señora de Hervada, who had long since abandoned Coen with a fixed smile and a nod.

Isabel's stares drew the attention of her former fiancé whose gaze seldom wandered far from her. However, as Felipe seemed to make up his mind to speak to Isabel, the girl without seeing him abruptly turned and walked away.

Moss was surprised when he saw Felipe's look of grave concern. The Spaniard seemed to hesitate. As if conscious of Moss's curiosity, Felipe gave a slight start, and then with a word of apology made to turn away also.

At that moment, Moss heard a voice close to his ear, and discovered that he was wanted on the phone. Only a few people knew where he was; Urgoiti, Doldan and an official of the consul's office, so it was almost certain to be one of these three. It was Doldan.

On the telephone, the lawyer proved irritatingly prudent in speech. It took Moss some time to discover what in fact

Doldan wanted to tell him, and even when they had progressed to that point, the actual information was slow in coming across. It concerned a person, from whom they had obtained information.

'Which one?' Moss asked bluntly.

Very reluctantly Doldan admitted it was the waiter.

The Hervada Arias household contained a number of phones. This one was in a small room close to the dining-area, and in the distance voices could still be heard. Moss pushed the door shut with his foot, and the background noise ceased abruptly.

So Camino had got in touch after all. 'Well, what does he say? Can he identify the man we want?'

'The answer to your question is yes, señor Coen. I know you will be pleased. Previously the waiter was reluctant to speak, but he called to my office today. When he had left, I telephoned you but you were not there. I may tell you the identification is complete.'

'Who is it?'

'In the case we were speaking about, the man who was convicted . . . '

'Baldomir. Camino identifies Baldomir?'

'Yes.' The lawyer sounded shocked at this blunt speaking.

'Identifies him at the Pensión Excelsior, is that it? The brown-eyed, horse-toothed young man who spoke to Maria that evening in the hall has turned out to be our old friend Angel Baldomir?'

'That is correct.'

'No possibility of a mistake?'

'The waiter is very sure. Indeed, the features are so distinctive . . . We obtained a photograph to show to our informant and he says there is no doubt in his mind. And also . . . '

'Yes?'

'There is in addition another matter.'

'Tell me,' Moss said.

'I shall refer to the money which was taken, and the day on which it was stolen.'

Moss gazed blankly in front of him. 'Information about the money has come from Camino? But how can he know anything; he only met Maria after she came to work at the pension?'

'He is a waiter, my dear señor Coen. For the past fifteen years he has been a waiter, and not always at the Excelsior. On the day of the theft, Camino was working in a well-known small restaurant in the city.'

'You mean where Maria had her lunch?'

'Because the trial took place soon afterwards, the waiter has remembered the day.'

'Something happened during the lunch, or is it that Maria told Camino something concerning the money?'

'It was never mentioned between them, he says.'

'Look, can't you speak a little more plainly? Camino saw or heard something which he afterwards connected with Angel Baldomir?'

'Baldomir?' The lawyer seemed surprised. 'Oh, no.'

'Listen,' Moss said roughly, 'I'm coming back to Burgos tomorrow. Ask Camino to come to your office at whatever time's convenient, and leave a message for me at the Esperanza.' He rang off, scarcely waiting for Doldan's reply.

Moss went and found Isabel. Even though he was still chewing over Doldan's news which gave promise of developments, Moss was not blind to the change in Isabel. When he met her now, she looked even more on edge than she had been fifteen minutes earlier. He told her he would be returning to Burgos first thing in the morning.

'You must leave?' she asked almost bitterly. 'Why is this?'

'I have an appointment I must keep.'

'Please do not leave us so soon. Can you not wait another day?' And, as he shook his head, she added with a return of something like her old manner: 'But you have not yet visited the city of Calahorra!'

He looked at her in wonder. She was so lovely. Yet that face was a mask which hid an emotion which he could feel was tearing her to pieces. He was out of his depth, but he now had the sense to know it.

'I have to go back,' he said flatly.

She made no immediate reply, but after a short pause she said: 'I will drive you myself. Will you wait until after lunch?'

His first reaction was to refuse the lift. Then he told himself he was a fool. A refusal would give rise to suspicion. And no 'accident' would be arranged while Isabel herself was known to be with him. 'That'll suit me fine,' he said.

21

In no way was Moss Coen prepared for the later events of that night. On the plea of exhaustion, he retired early. Once away from the other guests, he remembered his promise to Urgoiti. Not that Doldan's information came under that heading, but in view of what the lawyer had said, Moss was not too easy in his mind about Camino. If he, Moss Coen, had understood Doldan correctly (it was perfectly possible of course that he had *not*, but if he had) then Camino might be vulnerable. Remembering Taibo.

He phoned the number Urgoiti had given him, and it rang persistently, but there was no reply. Thirty minutes later, he rang again and still no answer. He took a shower and went to bed.

After three hours of heavy sleep, Moss woke conscious that he had something on his mind. He remembered again about Urgoiti. Serve the old codger right if he broke into his night's rest. Urgoiti had insisted he be told if anything developed. Moss rang the number.

An elderly female voice answered, and Moss gave his name. There was a certain amount of subdued conversation followed by thumping sounds. Urgoiti was at home!

'What is it you are saying to me at this time, señor Coen?'

The well-known voice.

'I apologize if I've disturbed you,' Moss answered with tongue-in-cheek politeness. 'I did phone earlier but there was no reply.'

'Something is happening with you there?'

'I'll tell you when I see you,' Moss said. 'There's something which bothers me,' and he proceeded to tell Urgoiti what Doldan had said.

At the other end of the line Urgoiti almost purred. His annoyance at being woken up at two in the morning vanished entirely. He was even gracious.

'This information you are receiving is good, very good.'

'I'm glad you seem to think so. I didn't quite get the hang of the second part. Admittedly, Doldan told me as little as he possibly could.'

'When you shall return to us in Burgos, we shall have many things to discuss,' Urgoiti answered smoothly. 'Now I shall attend to Camino. *Adiós*.'

Moss put down the receiver and padded back to his room. He was not a man to bother travelling with a pair of slippers, and on rising he had not troubled to put on shoes. The phone extension was in an alcove opposite the door of his room. The wooden floor under his feet led down the corridor to a door which opened on the patio visible from his bedroom.

The door was slightly ajar, and the long net curtains wafted in the gentle breeze.

Footsteps sounded on the tiled surface of the patio, and the shadow of a woman's figure appeared on the wall and then vanished. Intrigued, Moss ambled down to the door and looked out. There was no one there, but he could still hear the footsteps, very faintly.

He opened the door and stepped outside, then crossed the patio, his bare feet silent on the polished tiles. A further flight of steps led to a walled garden, down the centre path of which he could see the hurrying figure. As he watched, she reached the gateway and, turning to the left, disappeared from his sight.

It was Isabel.

Maurice Coen hesitated for just a moment. A man, barefoot and clad in pyjamas, pursuing his hostess at two in the morning is apt to be misunderstood.

But whatever errand took Isabel out into the night, he would not discover it by going back for his clothes.

He silently ran down the path and hoped the going would not get too rough underfoot. He, in turn, reached the gate and flattened himself against the wall before venturing further.

Cautiously, he craned forward. The moon was partly obscured by cloud, but there was sufficient light. He glanced along the direction taken by Isabel, but there was now no sign of her.

The thought that he might be about to

fall into a trap struck Moss unpleasantly. Easy for a person listening to his telephone conversation to afterwards attract his attention and bring him into the open, there to deal with him. So had Taibo been dealt with.

Moss moved away from the wall. He had no wish to become the victim of a supposed loose stone.

Nothing happened, however, and he came to the spot where the path swept round a corner of the garden and led directly to the stables.

Someone was moving inside the stable-yard. The horses were restless, and he could hear a door swinging on its hinges. Then there was a sound of hoofs on the hard-packed earth.

Moss left the shadow of the wall and hid in the shelter of a tree near by. He had not long to wait. Five minutes later Isabel emerged mounted up and leading another horse. She was not in riding-kit but was dressed in sweater and slacks, and the animals were serviceable mounts.

The rider looked all around before turning her horse onto the same path

Moss had taken the previous morning. Once away from the house and its environs, she urged the horses on, and in a short time had disappeared from view.

That, Moss was aware, left *him* with nothing to do but retrace his steps to the house.

For the moment, however, he stayed where he was. The second horse must be to collect another rider. Although why she didn't take the car . . . Shivering in the night air, Moss decided to wait a bit. There was a possibility both riders might return.

Feeling horribly conspicuous, Moss entered the stable-yard. After carefully choosing his spot, he lay concealed in the barn.

The time passed slowly, and he had leisure for reflection. The happenings of the past twenty-four hours provided enough food for thought.

There was Isabel, motive unknown, but with an apparent interest in doing away with her guest — a guest whom she had been at particular pains to lure to this spot. She had traced Moss to the Hostal

Esperanza, arranged an encounter for no other purpose it would appear than to invite him to Logroño, there to have him meet with an 'accident'. Obviously there *must* be a motive ... Perhaps he knew something he didn't realize that he knew. Or even more dangerous, perhaps Isabel believed Moss Coen was in possession of real evidence. But evidence of what? His meeting with Maria Guzman had been so brief, what did anyone imagine he could have learned? And anyway, what the Irishman knew about that whole episode the police knew as well.

Against all of this, there was now positive identification of Baldomir. Horse-faced Baldomir had been in the hall-way of the pension, and he and Maria held a lengthy conversation, watched by Camino, and prior to the arrival of Moss and Taibo.

Now if Maria Guzman took the money and Baldomir had nothing to do with the theft, then he might have been trying to force an admission from her. He might have used threats; might have killed her and afterwards in a panic tipped the body out of the window. Although how a violent quarrel could have been accomplished in virtual *silence* Moss was at a loss to understand. However, leave that for the moment.

Next there was Taibo. The idea was that Taibo had seen somebody — probably the killer entering or leaving the Excelsior in the early hours. When questioned by the police, Taibo had remained silent. But it appeared that he had endeavoured to extract payment for this silence, and the payment had been swift.

That argued a very different type of killer — not a blind savage desire to kill, but a careful arrangement of time and place. The train had let the killer down; the train which had been stopped at Astorga.

Moss listened intently. Wasn't that a sound? How long had he been here? Surely about an hour. The horses were returning.

The sounds of soft hoof-beats ceased for a while, and Moss fancied he heard voices. He was actually out of the barn and running swiftly towards the gate when the noise of the rider's re-entry into the stable-yard caused him to hastily dart back into his place of concealment.

It was Isabel, again leading the two horses. Where was her companion? Had the second person gone into the house? Isabel made no effort to unsaddle either animal, but instead went into the harness-room and presently came out carrying what looked like supplies prepared in advance. There was a roll of bedding, a plastic ground-sheet, and several bags of what looked to be provisions and utensils. Swiftly, she loaded these items onto one of the animals, securing each pack carefully. Then she let both animals drink for a little, and finally led them up and down, obviously waiting for the return of the second person.

He was not very long in coming. She had scarcely been waiting five minutes when he appeared, crossing the stable-yard in long swift strides. She had just turned the horses and was walking towards him, but the pair were not ten feet away from where Moss lay crouched in the barn.

The man was in shadow and his back was to Moss, but Isabel was clearly visible. Hers was not an expressive face, but Moss now saw it register anxiety . . . and something else.

'What did he say?' she asked in Spanish.

'He says the police questioned him. He does not want to know anything. Whatever can be done, he will do. He told me to get out and stay away.'

'Does he know that I . . . ?'

'No.' This was spoken roughly. 'You are not to become involved. It is too dangerous.'

'Nevertheless I will come when it is possible. I will bring whatever is needed.'

The man seemed to hesitate. He was about to mount the second horse, but still he did not go.

Isabel leant against the horse's flank, her face still turned towards Moss. The man was still in shadow. She said: 'No one will know where you are. You will be safe. I will come tomorrow with news.'

The man said nothing but caught her to him, pressing his face down into her pale-gold hair which glinted even in the half-light. Her arms were around his neck and he swung her round, kissing her very quickly. Then he turned abruptly and mounted the saddle, gathering the reins of the other horse into his hands.

He moved off without a word, and horses and rider made little noise on the hard earth. Isabel stood and watched them go before she too crossed the stable-yard and passed under the arched gateway, where she halted for a moment and then walked in the direction of the house.

The man in the barn remained where he was. He would follow the lady back to the house when it was safe to do so. In the meantime Moss Coen had plenty to think about. The face of the man who had ridden away was not one Moss could remember, but he was in no doubt at all about the man's identity. Horse and rider presented the same profile. It was Angel Baldomir.

22

Next morning Moss decided on his course of action. It was of no practical use to return to Burgos. Whatever Camino knew he could tell the police. Moss Coen had the important part of the case under his hands and had better stick close to it.

Over their coffee and rolls, he surprised Isabel by saying he had decided to postpone his departure. 'I should be sorry to go away without having seen the city of Calahorra! I shall go there today.'

Isabel, whose face was pale and drawn, at once seemed anxious to discover the reason for this sudden change of plan. 'But you said you must return to Burgos for an appointment there?'

'It can wait,' Moss shrugged. 'In a few days I must travel back to Dublin, and when shall I ever see Calahorra again?'

Isabel smiled, a wan smile. 'Unfortunately, I shall have to go to Burgos today. I was certain we should travel there together, and return here this evening.'

'There's no need to upset any arrangements on my account. I shall go into Logroño and hire a car to take me to Calahorra. I may stay one night there.' This plan, Moss felt, would give him a certain freedom of manoeuvre. He had no intention of going anywhere as far away as Calahorra.

'It is not necessary to hire a car,' Isabel said, her breath coming unevenly. 'We will find a car for you here.'

The Irishman's reply was cut short by the arrival of Isabel's mother. Of Pilar Arias's desire to be rid of an unwelcome guest, only a small trace showed in her manner. Even at that early hour she was elegantly and beautifully attired, her face expensively cared for and haloed by faultless waves of hair. The effect was in sharp contrast to her daughter's plain dress. Isabel made some excuse and left the room.

Moss lingered in the hope that some chance remark of the mother's might shed light on the activities of the daughter, but just then another guest entered, ruefully admitting he was a late riser.

Pilar smiled, a wide benign smile, and said: 'But you must do exactly as you wish. Everything is to be as you shall like it.'

'You are charming as always, Pilar my dear,' the man replied, kissing her hand.

The señora de Hervada had already turned away from Moss in an attitude of dismissal. Moss did not move. The man facing him was the person so intently regarded by Isabel during dinner the evening before.

And this person's eyes now asked a question of his hostess, looking over her shoulder at Moss standing there. There was a slight shrug, a movement of the shoulder-blades, as the lady reluctantly responded: 'This friend of Isabel is on holiday from Ireland.'

Did Moss imagine it, or was the other man a little taken aback? A tall and well-nourished gentleman who wore his beautifully-made clothes with an air of having worked in them; the rather high-domed and bronzed forehead was set off by receding grey hair, and the sensuous mouth to some extent obscured by the dark beard.

As their hostess made no attempt to complete the introduction, Moss put out his hand and said: 'I am delighted to meet you. My name is Maurice Coen.'

The other man did not look all that delighted, but he responded by clasping the hand firmly and giving his own name. 'I am Julio Meyer,' he said, with some evidence of self-satisfaction.

Moss said something, he didn't quite know what. Julio Meyer! This, obviously, was the man Baldomir had come to visit last night. His stepfather. The phrases overheard by Moss in the barn now took on a new significance. And what was it the lawyer, Doldan, had earlier said: 'Don Julio Meyer is a well-known figure and a member of the parliament.'

The Irishman sat down again and poured himself another cup of coffee. Isabel's mother positively glared at him, but seemed to find his presence inhibiting, and within a short time she left the room. A maid appeared with a further supply of hot coffee and freshly-baked rolls, and Moss opened a conversation with his fellow guest by remarking that he thought it was going to be a very hot day. 'Those of us from northern climates are not used to such heat,' he added, 'but perhaps you have been to Ireland, señor Meyer?'

'One day it may be that I shall go there.'

'Isabel has been telling me she visited Dublin once or twice. Your stepson has been there also?'

This last was a gambit to introduce the subject of Angel, but Meyer's startled look convinced Moss he had inadvertently spoken the truth. 'When they were students together of course,' the Irishman finished smoothly. He was getting on. He was acquiring bits of information. Bits and pieces that fitted together nicely.

Meyer regarded him warily. 'You know my stepson?'

'A little,' Moss answered. 'Of course, Isabel and he . . . '

Meyer nodded and seemed to Moss to relax slightly. 'As you say, they were students together. That was before I knew Angel,' Meyer paused, and then added: 'or his mother.'

Moss interposed: 'But quite recently Isabel became engaged to someone else, an old friend of hers, Felipe Serna. Although I understand that engagement is now ended. At the time it was announced, Angel was still in prison, I suppose?'

Meyer raised a protesting hand. 'That subject I do not wish to discuss. My wife's son is once more at liberty, and whatever he has done in the past is to be forgotten.'

'Forgive me,' Moss said apologetically, 'but did either you or his mother consider the possibility that he might not have taken the money. Until Angel confessed, I understand that the investigating judge himself had doubts . . . '

Meyer raised limpid eyes. 'You show a great interest in this affair. Why should you concern yourself?'

'Isabel is concerned.'

'And has confided in you?'

'Some things she has told me. Others I

211

have guessed. For example, there is a rumour that the money to repay the stolen cash was put up by yourself. A very generous act.'

Julio shook his head impatiently. 'My wife and I had been married for a short time only, and this affair cast a shadow over our lives and our happiness. Whatever I did was to spare my wife further suffering.'

'I wonder if that *was* your motive?' Moss thought, but he allowed the conversation to be led (firmly) into other channels.

Presently the Irishman excused himself and went out to join Isabel who was apparently waiting for him.

'I must leave now,' she said, walking to where her red two-seater was parked in front of the house. 'Ramón will bring your car for you. It is a rather old one I am afraid, but I hope you will not mind. It is not very fast, but it will get you to Calahorra.'

Moss could do nothing but express thanks for all this kindness. Intent on getting away quickly, she slid into the driving-seat, and her car roared into life.

'I shall see you again in a few days,' Isabel cried, and the car sped away down towards the road.

Moss hoped it would not be quite that long.

23

In fact Moss was to see Isabel again later that day. He had duly driven to Logroño with the intention of making it his headquarters for a search of the surrounding countryside. He purchased a good map, and over lunch at an hotel made enquiries about excursions to isolated 'scenic' spots, paying particular reference to any likely place in or near the Hervada Arias demesne.

Afterwards he made a few other purchases — a powerful torch, a dark wool sweater, and in addition several items in case he was forced to prolong his search into the following day.

His expedition got off to a bad start when, having left the city, he was halted by traffic police who told him he was driving too close to the left side of the road. Moss was informed he must pay an on-the-spot fine, and was left poorer by three or four pounds.

Immediately afterwards he abandoned the highway and turned on to a secondary road which led up into the hills, but the hill-road on which he found himself was poorly surfaced, indeed scarcely fit for motor traffic at all. It ended in a small village, and Moss saw a group of men and asked for directions. The car bumped its way over a narrow track to join another, slightly better, road which climbed steadily upwards. This road in turn led to a rough track which divided, and Moss pulled up and consulted his map. The map showed the village from which he had just come, although the track was not marked. The Hervada home was about six kilometres from this spot.

About to move off again, some instinct made Moss halt. Perhaps he had already heard a faint sound. He remained where he was, screened by the trees which shaded the path. The sound grew louder and was presently identified as that of a powerful engine being driven over extremely rough terrain. Less than two hundred metres away, a red car came into view, exposed on the hard grassy slopes thinly populated with sheep. The car slowly mounted the crest of the hill and then disappeared. Although Moss could not positively identify the driver, he was sure it was Isabel.

She could not be returning to the Hervada *hacienda*. The latter was approached by a well-surfaced road. Nor would anyone drive a fast car up this track for choice, or even a short cut.

He had no idea what he was going to find over the top of the hill. Moss found a secluded spot and drove his car in off the track. Then he unloaded his supplies and waited.

When it grew dark, he set out on foot to follow the path to its conclusion. His real difficulties began when he emerged into open ground near the summit. Sheep, aware of his presence, scattered at his approach, and even in the bad places he was reluctant to use his torch.

The weather was fine and dry, the air cool at this height. A gentle breeze rested on his back and helped him upwards. The moon was in its first quarter, and there were few stars.

As Moss came to the crest of the hill,

he crawled along, a yard at a time, and finally lay flat on the stony ground as he pulled himself into a position to reconnoitre the downward slopes.

What he saw gave him new heart. About a hundred yards away, nestling in the side of the hill, was a small ruin. Close by, and silhouetted against the sky, Moss saw the outline of a horse or mule.

The building, with its dome-shaped and corbelled roof, was about the size of a two-roomed cottage. It was in all probability an ancient hermitage, for part of the ruin looked to be the remains of what had once been a small belfry.

Someone had lit a fire.

Moss lay very still while he debated what he should do next. Then he retreated slowly and carefully, made an encircling movement to the left and downwards, and finally approached his target from the rear of the belfry.

The fire had sunk to a dim red glow; sunk to become scarcely visible. Footsteps caused Moss to flatten himself against the hard earth. Someone was emerging from the ruin. Although he did not have a view of the fire the sounds suggested movement in and around its vicinity, and there was a scraping noise, as of utensils.

Under cover of this noise, and using his arms and knees, Moss made progress over the rough surface. He reached the projecting wall of the belfry, where it joined the smaller building, and sank into this cover.

The noises ceased, and then he could hear footsteps retreating. He waited. He fancied the footsteps were beginning again, but a long silence followed. Gently, Moss eased his body forward until he could see the fire. There was no one in sight.

At the last second, conscious of danger, he turned, but not in time to ward off the blow which sent him reeling into the open.

A little yet powerful body descended on him, and a sudden explosion of pain was followed by loss of consciousness.

24

At first the man thought he was in hospital. The light was dim, and he imagined he could distinguish a white-washed ceiling. He was in pain all over, yet he had that detached feeling as if pain might possibly be elsewhere. His head felt extraordinarily large and heavy, and when he tried to move it even a little he wanted to cry out, but no voice uttered.

Realization came slowly. There was something very wrong. He was unable to move any part of his body, and his mind didn't seem to be working any too well either. He could not, at present, remember just who he was.

Which was odd, really, because the face of the man who caused the damage loomed in his nightmares.

When he woke up again the bare whitewashed ceiling was still in place, but now there was light enough to recognize it for what it actually was — the inside of a stone roof. He was lying in a corner, under an unglazed window, and he knew he was Maurice Coen, and he remembered some if not all of the events which had led to his being in this position.

Moss was aware he was at the hermitage. When he saw Angel Baldomir he understood that even in his present beat-up condition the worst was very likely still to come.

Angel's lips opened to reveal his mouthful of large teeth. 'Isabel has left,' he said, as if by way of explanation. He squatted on the floor and regarded his hands, one of which was bandaged. On closer inspection, his face appeared to have suffered also.

At the mention of Isabel's name, Moss Coen's heart beat faster. 'Is she coming back?' he asked.

'She will return,' was the answer.

'Soon?'

'An hour, perhaps two hours.'

Two hours! And to be lying here, helpless as a baby. Moss came to a decision. 'Listen, Angel,' he mumbled, 'you and I might as well understand each other. Maria's death is no longer a mystery to me. I'm beginning to understand the motive. You met Isabel in Dublin, didn't you?'

Angel, who had been frowning over the first part of this speech, was knocked out of his stride.

'Isabel has told you?'

'I made enquiries. About seven years ago, wasn't it?'

'It was the summer of seventy-four,' Angel replied simply. He lowered himself to the ground, stretched out his legs, and propped his back against the wall. From Moss's point of view the situation was no less dangerous.

'I suppose it was the classic case of being rejected by the lady's family,' the Irishman went on in easy conversational tones. 'And then something happened which changed everything. I mean, in your own family. Your widowed mother remarried, and took as her second husband that very respected and highly-thought-of politician, Julio Meyer.'

Angel nodded his head several times,

kneading his hands together and unclasping them. Every time he opened his mouth, Moss was conscious of the square jaw.

'You still have the horse?' Moss asked abruptly, his ears strained for any sounds of arrival.

Angel seemed reluctant to leave the subject under discussion. He waved an impatient hand. 'The mare returns to the Hervada home last night. Isabel sees the animal and wonders what is happening here, and she comes to discover what has gone wrong.'

'She's that kind of girl,' Moss agreed.

'She is always as she was when we first met. We came to Dublin,' Angel went on, 'and there were many of us. Every day we met with the group of students for lectures, tours, visits. From the beginning Isabel and I were together.'

'And after this happy idyll you returned to Burgos and bitter reality?'

Angel looked blank. 'The mother is hostile, but Isabel's father is less so, and their opposition was to be expected in any case. They are possessed of much wealth, whereas I — ' he laughed savagely — 'well, it is as you see. Nothing.'

'The acquisition of Julio Meyer as a relative produced a change in the situation?' Moss knew it had done so, that it was the key to the whole of what had followed.

Angel's teeth came out in a bitter smile, and he raised one knee against his chest and hugged it there. Moss of course was unable even to wiggle his big toe, but he found the conversation satisfying. Time was moving on, though he dared not allow hopeful thoughts, not yet. He speculated upon the reasons why he was still alive. He could find none, unless it had something to do with Angel's injured hand.

'Of course,' Moss took a deep breath, 'there was the affair of the stolen money.'

'Isabel . . . ?' Baldomir cried, and Moss could hear the hurt in his throat.

'No, no,' Moss mumbled. His own voice was growing weaker. 'I heard about it from someone else.'

Angel turned round and regarded the figure lying there. 'You have been busy in this matter,' he said.

The phrase reminded Moss of Urgoiti. He wondered how much the old Spaniard knew.

'When I arrived in Burgos I saw you with Maria that first evening,' Moss said. 'Afterwards I was suspected of having killed her. It was necessary to prove that I did not.'

Angel's smile was sardonic. 'I also tried to prove something, but without success.'

'You had nothing to do with the theft of the money, *that* I know,' Moss said at once. This was quite true, and no harm to say it. The effect was astonishing. Angel came out from the wall in one continuous movement, and dropped to his hands and knees.

'How do you know?' he demanded of the recumbent Moss.

Now that the crunch had come, the Irishman could feel exhaustion creeping over him. Mentally, he struggled up and said carefully: 'Isabel has been your concern from the beginning. That was why you went to see Maria?'

'I will tell you,' Angel breathed.

'Thank God,' muttered the man on the floor, and it was a prayer.

All Moss could see was a pair of hot brown eyes and the mouthful of teeth. The dam having been breached, Angel scarcely paused for breath. He knew Maria from when she had been Isabel's friend at school. Maria worked for Valdivia Commercial, and when the firm decided to take on extra staff it was Maria who suggested that he apply.

At that time, his mother and Julio had been married for about three months. When Valdivia asked for details of his family background, Angel mentioned his new stepfather. He was offered a good salary and given a responsible position, working in the same office as Maria.

The job presented no difficulties, and because of the firm's nice treatment of him (entirely on Julio's account) Angel was made aware that his circumstances had changed for the better. Marriage to Isabel was no longer just a dream.

Then came the robbery, and what he had said in the first instance was what had actually happened. He put the money in the safe, locked it, and placed the keys in Maria's desk. Angel supposed that only a few minutes would separate his departure from the office and Maria's return. He knew he should have waited, but he had not had anything to eat since early that morning, and he was starving. All his actions had helped to build evidence against himself. The only alternative to his story was that a person had entered the office, come upon the keys by chance and then used them.

'Not chance, exactly,' Moss said. 'I think the person who used the keys knew a good deal. He had luck, of course. He might have been spotted entering the building, or you might have taken the keys with you. Either would have prevented what followed.'

'How did this person know anything?'

'While they were having lunch together, I believe that Maria told him.' For Moss had placed Doldan's remarks concerning Camino. The waiter had said he was in attendance during the meal. He must have overheard something.

'Who is the man?'

'I don't know,' Moss answered. This was true. He did not *know*. Oh, but he could guess. Only one man had a great overwhelming motive; motive to incriminate Baldomir; to silence Maria and to remove poor little Taibo. When he, Moss Coen, had seen the motive face-to-face and not recognized it then for what it was, he was already another potential victim.

'At the trial,' he said to Baldomir, 'you admitted having taken the money. Why was that?'

Baldomir's brown eyes clouded over, and he sat up and began kneading his hands together. 'I was without hope,' he said. 'No one believed me. My own family would not believe. Julio said he would pay the money, but first I must confess. With the money repaid, he said I should not have to serve a long sentence.'

'You agreed to this?'

'I no longer cared. Everything was lost to me then.'

'Isabel?'

Baldomir's head shook from side to side, as though to drive away pain. 'I knew we could not marry. My own family . . . ' He stopped abruptly. 'Even if I was not in prison, it was finished, ended.'

Moss found he could move his head slightly without feeling the cervical column would come unstuck. The thing he knew was going to happen hadn't happened yet. 'So you came out of prison,' he went on, wondering if he was doing the right thing, 'and then you set about convincing everyone they had got it wrong.'

'Isabel.'

'You wanted to convince Isabel?'

'Yes, yes, yes.' Angel nodded vehemently.

'Why did that matter so much now, when you regarded everything as hopeless three years ago?'

Baldomir slapped a hand on the leg stretched out in front of him. 'It is strange that,' he said, almost as if he were talking to himself. 'I could not understand it. I felt I must see her, speak with her. She must tell me all was not over between us. In those three years, what I had suffered because of her, and now she . . . '

Limping along on two cylinders, Moss's brain managed to grasp this oblique reference and translate it. 'You read in the papers that she had become engaged?'

The velvety-brown eyes looked down into Moss's cold blue ones, and Angel let out a long sigh. 'It was the photograph. Seeing it in the newspaper. I could not let it happen. She and I — we belong together. I went to see her.' There was a pause, and then Baldomir began again: 'At the time I felt an outcast. I remember thinking perhaps she will not even speak to me. And then Isabel told me that her engagement was ended. She had drifted into it, not caring. Just as I had no longer cared. In that one meeting we discovered that we were the same two people who had met at the beginning. Nothing was changed. We were the same. I said I would try to prove it was not I who was the thief. Whatever happened, she said, we would be married.'

'After this you were determined to obtain proof?'

'It is true. While I was in prison, over and over I would ask myself what really happened that day?'

'So you went to see Maria as being the best person to throw light on the subject. What had she to say?'

'I asked her if she thought anyone could have come into the office after I had left it, and I told her very plainly that I knew someone *must* have, or else Maria had taken the money herself, and I was now going to find out the truth.'

Moss could imagine the effect of this statement on Maria. No wonder the girl had been on edge. Obviously she had tried to contact the second person. Later, as a result of this man's telephone call, she had calmed down, and in a carefree mood had gone out with Moss to view Burgos by night. No, Maria had not taken the money, but she knew who it was had the opportunity. A man who, three years earlier, she would have regarded as quite above suspicion. No wonder the cash had never been traced. The person who took it was playing for far higher stakes.

As if in answer to Moss's thoughts, a

flicker of sardonic humour showed in Baldomir's face. 'Your involvement has brought you to this unhappy position. You should have kept away.'

'Unfortunately there were other lives to be considered.'

Angel looked at the man on the ground. 'I do not comprehend you. What other lives?'

'Your own. Finally, I think, Isabel's also.'

Looking up at the primitive expression which marked every feature so close to his, Moss experienced qualms.

'How is Isabel now in danger?' Angel ground out.

'She is not, nor has she ever been,' said another voice.

Moss could not see who was standing in the opening where once the door had been, but he recognized the tone of voice. Slowly Angel turned round and regarded the newcomer.

It was Felipe Serna.

25

For Moss, the most important thing about Felipe Serna was that he carried a gun. In other circumstances that might have ended the matter but not, he imagined, in any situation of which Angel Baldomir was a part.

Since he had regained consciousness, Moss had two aims in view. The first was to survive if at all possible, with the apprehension of a dangerous killer as a secondary consideration. That both these aims might best be served if he managed to become ambulant, Moss admitted, however brief the period for which a fairly upright position could be maintained.

Even as Baldomir moved away from him and stood between Moss and the doorway, Moss was doing his best to unstick himself from the ground, a slow and painful process. He used the wall, against which he lay, to try to shift himself into a sitting position, and discovered, in spite of the agony, that he could move although his legs seemed to be without any power.

Meanwhile Baldomir was advancing on Felipe who, though armed, nevertheless glanced nervously over his shoulder. Angel's face was hidden from Moss, but viewed from the rear the tall lanky Baldomir seemed incapable of being stopped unless Serna put a bullet in him, which Moss would have guessed was not the latter's original intention. The plan was surely to leave Baldomir with a body and a gun to explain to the police. Moss had a fair idea who was supposed to provide the body.

Even as Serna hesitated, a gap opened up between Angel and the man lying against the wall. Felipe's gun wavered and Moss exerted every ounce of strength he had left.

In the time, he managed to shift himself only about six inches, but it was enough. The bullet whined as it struck the wall and ricochetted, narrowly missing Angel's foot as the latter flung himself on the now desperate Serna. As a contest of physical strength, it was of course one-sided, but Serna was in possession of the gun.

Moss knew he could do nothing. The one sudden jerk had left him immobile, in an agony of pain and sweat. Helplessly, he watched the other two roll over and over. There was another report, as Serna fired, but the bullet entered the soft ground outside the hermitage. Angel's fingers closed round the other man's wrist, and Felipe let out a despairing cry as the gun slipped from his grasp.

That was the end of any real fight, although Serna continued to struggle until Baldomir knocked him out. Angel rose up, his breath coming in gasps, his face contorted. He raised his forearm to wipe away the sweat, and glanced over to where Moss lay against the wall.

'You are hit?' he rasped.

'I'm half-dead,' Moss answered in as cool a tone as he could muster.

This remark seemed to throw Angel off balance. He sat down and laughed, until the tears streamed from the brown eyes and made furrows on his sweat-stained face.

He was still laughing when the police arrived.

26

Two men walked together in the hills above Logroño. Although it was a warm afternoon and the autumn sun threw long shadows in front of the trees, Moss was too recently up on his feet again not to have to frequently pause for a rest.

'When I first came here,' he was saying to the older man, 'you seemed to be warning me against Isabel. Did you really suspect her?'

'My dear señor Coen,' Urgoiti was at his most expansive, 'that charming and lovely young girl! It is clear to me that she provides motives for the killings, but never do the police accuse her of complicity in these crimes. *Never*,' he added with force. 'And you, my dear señor Coen, you are well?' he continued. 'We are seeking news of your improvement in health. It is not good that you shall have left hospital so soon.'

'Oh, I'm fine again,' Moss answered

brusquely, walking on ahead. 'I don't suppose Felipe Serna has given you a confession!' he flung at Urgoiti ambling stiffly behind.

'That one,' Urgoiti waved his four-fingered hand in a certain gesture, 'he will not be the one to confess. He has a good lawyer, the best he is able to obtain.'

'Well, you have the evidence that the fellow twice tried to kill *me*. Three times,' Moss amended, remembering the incident of the shots fired on his return from meeting Serna at the bridge.

'He feared your interest in this affair?'

'Perhaps,' Moss answered, slowing his pace to allow Urgoiti to catch up. But it was Isabel's interest in Moss Coen that had done the damage, slight though that interest was. Serna's jealousy had magnified every look, every smile, her very concern for Moss on the back of the horse, Salmonte.

'We have Baldomir and his evidence that Serna attacked you outside the hermitage.'

'And came out and saved me before Serna had time to finish me off, eh? Angel dragged me inside and took care of me, and then Isabel arrived and he sent her to fetch help. In the meantime, Felipe Serna decided to make a second attempt, this time with a gun. It would be rather suspicious if *two* dead bodies were found, so the plan was to kill *me* and leave Angel with a corpse on his hands. That the plan didn't work is largely due to Angel.'

'I am quickly there,' Urgoiti protested. 'We have traced you through your meeting with the traffic police at Logroño, and then comes word from the señorita Isabel of what is happening at the hermitage.'

'I was very pleased to see you,' Moss acknowledged and Urgoiti was smiling again.

'Notwithstanding that there have been many difficulties, all is brought to a conclusion. We have the money!'

'Felipe hid the cash?'

'In a safe-deposit. We find the key and make enquiries. The safe-deposit is discovered and opened. The notes of one thousand pesetas are checked with the numbers from the bank. It is the money taken from Valdivia Commercial.'

'So Angel Baldomir is officially cleared? That will please him enormously.'

'It is strange that Serna who is of a good family and is not in debt should steal this money which he afterwards makes no use of!'

'He took the money hoping, as indeed it turned out, that Baldomir would get the blame.' Moss laughed shortly. 'A prison sentence would terminate any idea of marriage with Isabel. You see,' Moss went on, 'for a long time the Hervada Arias family encouraged Felipe Serna to think of himself as their future son-in-law. He saw their great wealth, and he grew accustomed to the idea that with Isabel as his wife he would one day share in it. The discovery, late in the day, that his beautiful future was threatened by Isabel's preference for an obscure student gave Serna a nasty jolt. However, a little investigation showed Angel to be the son of a widow of meagre resources, and no serious rival. It was the widow's remarriage to Julio Meyer which brought things to a head.'

'Señor Meyer is much esteemed and respected.'

'So I have heard,' Moss answered drily. 'Well, anyway, faced with this challenge, Felipe becomes desperate. He has to do something, and the opportunity presents itself one day when he is lunching with Maria.'

'The waiter, Camino, has given us evidence that the señorita Guzman revealed to Serna much of what was taking place in the office, and how Baldomir remained alone.'

Moss nodded. 'Felipe goes shopping with Maria and manages to delay her return to the office until Baldomir shall have left. He makes some excuse to come up to the office with her — probably carries her parcels — and is not seen by anyone entering the building. After that it's all so easy. During Maria's confused comings and goings searching for the keys, he is able to look for them himself, extract them from her desk and open the safe. It is the work of a few minutes to tip the contents into a bag and pocket the keys. He leaves quietly, unnoticed. No one suspects Serna. Why should they? Maria knows he has been to the office, but in the midst of condemnation from her employers for having given the keys to Angel, she is unlikely to admit the fact. Only in the event that she herself is suspected, for Serna's presence has given her an alibi of sorts. Hence, the planting of the keys for the police to find during a search of Baldomir's home. An overkill which very nearly went wrong, because the trial judge was not convinced. Unexpectedly, Angel Baldomir 'confesses' and Serna's plan has proved effective. His rival in prison, he becomes engaged to Isabel.'

'An engagement which is of short duration,' Urgoiti nodded sagely.

'Hard on Serna after all his effort!' Moss agreed. 'And worse follows. Released from prison, Angel puts pressure on Maria to tell everything which happened on the day of the robbery. She herself never suspected Felipe, I imagine, and she telephones him now to let him know that Angel is being very persistent. Should she tell that Serna was with her in the office that day? We don't know what Felipe told her, but my guess is that later he entered the pension and waited for his chance. He took a great risk, but of course he was fairly desperate. Unfortunately for him, he seems to have been spotted by Taibo. The police come on the scene and Taibo is made aware, if he had not been aware of it before, of the value of his information. He arranges an interview with Serna, an unwise proceeding, and he does not survive it.

'So Felipe comes off clear, and better than that, for Baldomir is actually suspected of killing Maria. From Felipe's point of view, very satisfactory. And then he returns to Logroño where I turn up!'

The two men were now approaching a church, and the ground sloped a little towards the old portico with its carved stone figures. A wedding was taking place and the simple altar was adorned with many flowers.

When the bride entered, Moss had the opportunity of seeing for the first time Francisco Hervada, her father. The bridegroom was escorted by his mother, as is the Spanish custom. Showing no signs of his recent ordeal, *el novio* was smiling broadly, while the mother, a good-natured looking person, acknowledged greetings from friends.

Isabel, very beautiful, her blonde hair set with an antique comb over which a veil of fine silk lace was arranged, wore a long-sleeved dress, the white emphasizing her pale looks. She was composed, but only barely so, and towards the end of the ceremony Moss noticed tears in her eyes. But she managed a tremulous smile, as she put her hand in the arm of her new husband, and his long brown fingers closed over it.

Isabel Carmen Hervada Arias had married Angel Julián Baldomir, as the newspapers would write of it the next day, and it was probable that the name of Moss Coen would appear in these reports, as a *testigo*, a witness on behalf of the bride.

We do hope that you have enjoyed reading this large print book.

Did you know that all of our titles are available for purchase?

We publish a wide range of high quality large print books including:
Romances, Mysteries, Classics General Fiction Non Fiction and Westerns

Special interest titles available in large print are:
The Little Oxford Dictionary Music Book, Song Book Hymn Book, Service Book

Also available from us courtesy of Oxford University Press:
Young Readers' Dictionary (large print edition) Young Readers' Thesaurus (large print edition)

For further information or a free brochure, please contact us at:
**Ulverscroft Large Print Books Ltd., The Green, Bradgate Road, Anstey, Leicester, LE7 7FU, England.
Tel:** (00 44) **0116 236 4325
Fax:** (00 44) **0116 234 0205**

Other titles in the
Linford Mystery Library:

THE CRIMSON RAMBLER

John Russell Fearn

The murder at Darnworth Manor was particularly baffling. Autocratic financier Warner Darnworth had been working alone in his study. The study door was locked on the inside, and the only window was of the non-opening variety. Yet Darnworth had been found slumped over his desk, shot through the head. No weapon was found, either in the room or anywhere else in the manor. To add to the problems of Chief Inspector Gossage and Sergeant Blair, every member of Darnworth's family had good reason to hate him.

ENFORCER

Sydney J. Bounds

When ex-Vietnam veteran Washington T. Diamond quits working as racketeer Leon Greco's 'enforcer', he and his nightclub singer girlfriend Chelsea are drawn into a web of danger. Greco exerts a vicious reprisal, but Diamond receives support from Cave, a police detective, who sets him up as a private investigator. But Cave is only using Diamond as a pawn to bring down Greco's empire. Diamond becomes the bait when Greco takes out a contract on him, and he needs all his jungle experience to stay alive . . .

DECOYS

Richard Hoyt

Introducing herself as a detective working for Coyote, the San Francisco Prostitutes' Union, stunning Pamela Yew walks into the office of private investigator John Denson and tells him a brutal story of four girls who were murdered by their pimp. It seems that the pimp is hiding in Cayuse, Oregon — Denson's home town. All Denson has to do is act as Pamela's decoy by introducing her as his fiancée while she goes about her business. Once he arrives home, though, Denson finds that Pamela Yew is working on a far more deadly game than vengeance . . .

THE MIND OF DR. MORELLE

Ernest Dudley

On the plane from New York to London, Dr. Morelle chances to meet Edwin Gale, a smooth-tongued swindler. Inexplicably, Gale finds himself drawn to the famous psychiatrist-detective, and so begins one of Dr. Morelle's most intriguing cases. Back in London, the Doctor encounters Edwin Gale again, and, as a result, finds himself involved in the dark machinations of Dolores del Robia, who is as evil as she is lovely. When Dolores is found strangled to death, Dr. Morelle must investigate a maelstrom of violence to unmask the murderer . . .

THE BIG GOODBYE

Peter Chambers

When gorgeous Juanita Morales arrived in Monkton City looking for bright lights and glamour, she found herself mixed up in an elaborate racket and finally murder . . . Mark Preston didn't mind so long as women like Dixie Whitton and Sylvia Le Fay kept cropping up. He minded more when a fat man stuck a pistol in his face, and ice-picks in the back became the things to wear. Preston was on thin ice, because Rourke of Homicide was muttering about jail . . . And of course there were still more dames.

DEATH IN DARKNESS

George Douglas

When Detective Sergeant Lee of the Benfield City Police investigates a possible murder, his enquiries centre on the inhabitants of Pycroft Lane and jailbird James Nixon. But Lee is suddenly faced with a bank robbery and the manager is a resident of Pycroft Lane. Then Nixon is found, shot through the head. Lee knows that the key to all three of these events lies in Pycroft Lane, and he finds it with the aid of a woman who is snatched from the brink of death only by an old countryman — and his dog.

LIBRARY & HERITAGE SERVICE

Online Services
www.kingston.g___.uk

THE ROYAL BOROUGH OF
KINGSTON
UPON THAMES

Renew a book (5 times)   _uest a '
Change of address   _ail a '
Library news and upd___   Get y
Search the catal___   Access r_

KT-416-007

and criminology.
___047___ __estselling debut *The*
___ _or king as a TV screenwriter,
and he lives __ ___ ___

ROTATION STOCK

KT 2158629 2

Also by Donato Carrisi

The Whisperer
The Lost Girls of Rome

THE
VANISHED ONES

DONATO CARRISI

Translated by Howard Curtis

ABACUS

First published in Italy in 2013 as *L'Ipotesi del Male* by Longanesi & C.
First published in Great Britain in 2014 by Abacus
This paperback edition published in 2015 by Abacus

1 3 5 7 9 10 8 6 4 2

Copyright © Donato Carrisi 2013
Translation © Howard Curtis 2014

The moral right of the author has been asserted.

*All characters and events in this publication, other than those
clearly in the public domain, are fictitious and any resemblance
to real persons, living or dead, is purely coincidental.*

All rights reserved.
No part of this publication may be reproduced, stored in a
retrieval system, or transmitted, in any form or by any means, without
the prior permission in writing of the publisher, nor be otherwise circulated
in any form of binding or cover other than that in which it is published
and without a similar condition including this condition
being imposed on the subsequent purchaser.

A CIP catalogue record for this book
is available from the British Library.

ISBN 978-0-349-14003-2

Typeset in Horley by M Rules
Printed and bound in Great Britain by
Clays Ltd, St Ives plc

Papers used by Abacus are from well-managed forests
and other responsible sources.

MIX
Paper from
responsible sources
FSC
www.fsc.org   FSC® C104740

Abacus
An imprint of
Little, Brown Book Group
100 Victoria Embankment
London EC4Y 0DY

An Hachette UK Company
www.hachette.co.uk

www.littlebrown.co.uk

THE
VANISHED ONES

Kingston upon Thames Libraries	
KT 2158629 2	
Askews & Holts	16-Jan-2015
AF THR	£7.99
TW	KT00000355

Room 13 of the State Morgue was where the sleepers were kept.

It was on the fourth and lowest level of the basement, like one of the circles of hell, but this was a hell of cold and refrigeration, an area reserved for unidentified corpses. It was rare for anyone to pay it a visit.

Tonight, though, a visitor was on his way down.

The attendant was waiting for him by the lift, looking up at the numbers on the luminous panel that marked the cabin's descent. As he waited, he wondered who the unexpected visitor could be. And, more intriguing, why anyone would come all the way to this distant outpost so alien to anything living.

The last number lit up. There was a moment's pause before the lift door slid open to reveal a man in his forties in a dark blue suit. Then, as happened whenever a stranger set foot down here for the first time, the attendant saw the look of surprise on the man's face as he realised this wasn't a place of white tiles and sterile fluorescent tubes, but of green walls and orange lights.

'The colours prevent panic attacks,' the attendant said in answer to the man's silent question, and handed him a blue gown.

The visitor said nothing. He put on the gown and the two men set off.

'The corpses on this floor are mainly homeless people and illegal immigrants,' the attendant said. 'No ID, no family, so when they kick the bucket they end up down here. They're all in

Rooms one to nine. Rooms ten and eleven are for people who pay their taxes and watch football matches on TV, just like you and me, but suddenly drop dead of a heart attack on the metro one morning. One of the other passengers pretends to help them, instead of which they grab their wallet, and *voilà*, the trick has worked: the man or woman vanishes for ever. Sometimes, though, it's just a question of bureaucracy: a member of staff messes up the paperwork, and the relatives who come in to identify the body are shown another body entirely. It's as if you aren't dead and they're still looking for you.' He was trying to impress his guest, but the man didn't react. 'Then there are the suicide or accident cases: Room twelve. Sometimes the corpse is in such a bad state, you can't believe it was ever a person.' He was not squeamish himself, but was putting the visitor's stomach to the test. 'Anyway, the law requires the same treatment for all of them: they have to stay in the cold chamber for at least eighteen months. Then, if nobody claims or identifies the body, and the police have no intention of reopening the investigation, authorisation is given to dispose of it by cremation.' He had quoted the rules from memory.

At this point, his tone changed, becoming slightly nervous. He was about to touch on the purpose of this nocturnal visit.

'And then there are those in Room thirteen.'

The nameless victims of unsolved murders.

'In cases of murder, the law states that the body constitutes evidence until such time as the identity of the victim has been confirmed. You can't sentence a murderer if you can't prove that the person he murdered actually existed. In the absence of a name, the body is the only proof of that existence. That's why there's no time limit to how long it can be kept. It's one of those odd legal technicalities that lawyers like so much.'

The law stipulated that until such time as the criminal act that had caused the death was defined, the body could neither be destroyed nor be allowed to decompose naturally.

'We call them the sleepers.'

Unknown men, women and children whose killers had not yet been identified. They had been waiting for years for someone to turn up and deliver them from the curse of resembling the living. And, just as in some kind of macabre fairy tale, for that to happen all you needed to do was say the magic word.

Their name.

The room that housed them – Room 13 – was the last one at the far end of the corridor.

They came to a metal door and the attendant fussed with his keys until he found the right one. He opened it, then stood back to let his visitor enter the dark room. As soon as he did so, a row of yellow ceiling lights came on, triggered by sensors. In the middle of the room stood an autopsy table, and the high walls were lined with dozens of drawers.

A steel beehive.

'You have to sign in, it's the rule,' the attendant said, holding out a register. He was starting to grow restless. 'Which one are you interested in?'

At last, the visitor opened his mouth. 'The one that's been here the longest.'

AHF-93-K999.

The attendant knew the number by heart. He savoured in advance the solution to an old mystery. He went immediately to the drawer with the label attached to the handle. It was on the left-hand wall, third from the bottom. He pointed it out to the visitor. 'Of all the bodies down here, that one doesn't even have the most original story. One Saturday afternoon, some kids were playing football in the park. The ball went into the bushes, and that's where they found him. He'd been shot in the head. There

3

was no ID on him, and no keys. His face was still perfectly recognisable, but nobody called the emergency numbers to ask about him, nobody filed a missing persons report. Until they find his killer, which may never happen, the only evidence of the crime is the actual body. That's why the court ruled that it should be kept until the case was solved and justice was done.' He paused for a moment. 'It's been years now, but he's still here.'

The attendant had long wondered what the point was in keeping the evidence for a crime that nobody even remembered. He had always assumed that the world had forgotten the anonymous occupant of Room 13 a long time ago. But the request the visitor now made told him that the secret preserved behind those few inches of steel went way beyond mere identity.

'Open it up. I want to see him.'

AHF-93-K999. That had been his name for years, but maybe things were about to change. The attendant activated the air valve to open the drawer.

The sleeper was about to wake.

Mila

Exhibit 397-H/5

Transcript of recording made at 6.40 a.m. on
21 September ▮▮▮▮

Subject: telephone call to the emergency
number at ▮▮▮▮▮▮▮▮▮. Operator: Officer
Clara Salgado.

Operator: Emergency. Where are you calling
  from?
X: . . .
Operator: I can't hear you, sir. Where are you
  calling from?
X: This is Jes.
Operator: You must give me your full name,
  sir.
X: Jes Belman.
Operator: How old are you, Jes?
X: Ten.
Operator: Where are you calling from?
X: Home.

Operator: Can you give me the address?

X: . . .

Operator: Jes, can you give me the address, please?

X: I live at ███████████████.

Operator: All right. What's happening? You do know this is a police number, don't you? Why are you calling?

X: Yes, I know. They're dead.

Operator: Did you say 'they' are dead, Jes?

X: . . .

Operator: Jes, are you there? Who's dead?

X: Yes. They're all dead.

Operator: This isn't a joke, Jes, is it?

X: No, miss.

Operator: Can you tell me how it happened?

X: Yes.

Operator: Jes, are you still there?

X: Yes.

Operator: Why don't you tell me about it? Take all the time you need.

X: He came last night. We were having dinner.

Operator: Who came?

X: . . .

Operator: Who, Jes?

X: He shot them.

Operator: All right, Jes. I want to help you, but for now you have to help me. OK?

X: OK.

Operator: Are you telling me a man came to your house while you were having dinner and started shooting?

8

X: Yes.

Operator: And then he left and didn't shoot you. You are all right, aren't you?

X: No.

Operator: Do you mean you've been hurt, Jes?

X: No, I mean he didn't leave.

Operator: The man who did the shooting is still there?

X: . . .

Operator: Jes, please answer me.

X: He says you have to come. You have to come now.

Line cut off. End of recording.

1

It was a few minutes to six when the street began coming to life.

The refuse lorries collected the rubbish from the bins that stood in line like toy soldiers outside the houses. Then it was the turn of the street-sweeping vehicle that cleaned the asphalt with revolving brushes. The gardeners' mini-vans soon followed. The lawns and drives were cleared of leaves and weeds, and the hedges pruned to their ideal height. Their task accomplished, they went away, leaving behind a neat, silent, motionless world.

This happy place was ready to greet its happy inhabitants, Mila thought.

It had been a quiet night. Every night was quiet here. At about seven a.m., the houses began languidly to awaken. Behind the windows, fathers, mothers and children could be seen cheerfully preparing for the new day ahead of them.

Another day in a happy life.

Mila sat watching them in her Hyundai at the end of the block. She felt no envy. She knew that if you scratched the gilded surface, something else always emerged. Sometimes the true picture, made up of light and shade, as was only to be expected. At other times, though, there was a black hole. You were overcome by the foul breath of a hungry abyss and, from its depths, you thought you heard someone whispering your name.

Mila Vasquez knew the appeal of darkness only too well. She had been dancing with shadows since the day she was born.

She clicked her fingers, putting pressure on her left index. The fleeting pain gave her the kick she needed to keep concentrating. Soon afterwards, the front doors of the houses started opening, and the occupants began leaving home to face the challenges of the world – which would always be too easy for them, Mila thought.

She saw the Conners leave their house. The father, an attorney, was a slim man of about forty, with slightly greying hair that emphasised his tanned face. He was dressed in an impeccable grey suit. The mother was blonde, and still had the body and face of a young woman. Time would never have any effect on her, Mila was sure of that. Then came the girls. The elder one was already in middle school, the younger one – a cascade of curls – still in kindergarten. They were the image of their parents. If anyone still doubted the theory of evolution, Mila could have dispelled those doubts by showing them the Conners. They were beautiful and perfect and obviously could only live in a happy place like this.

After kissing his wife and daughters goodbye, Attorney Conner got into a blue Audi A6 and drove off to pursue his brilliant career. The woman set off in a green Nissan SUV to drop the girls off at their schools. Once they were gone, Mila got out of her old car, ready to enter the Conners' villa – and their lives. In spite of the heat, she had chosen a tracksuit as a disguise. It was only the first day of autumn, but if she had worn a T-shirt and shorts, her scars would have attracted far more attention. According to the calculations she had made since beginning this surveillance a few days earlier, she only had about forty minutes before Mrs Conner returned home.

Forty minutes to discover if this happy place was hiding a ghost.

The Conners had been her object of study for a few weeks now. It had all started by chance.

Police officers working on missing persons cases can't just sit at their desks and wait for reports to come in. Sometimes those who disappear have no family to report anything at all. Either because they are foreigners, or because they have cut off all their ties, or simply because they don't have anyone in the world.

Mila called them 'the predestined'. People who had a void around them and never imagined they would one day be swallowed up by it. That meant she first had to look for the opportunity, and only then the missing person. She would walk the streets, combing through places of hopelessness, where the shadows dog your every step and never leave you alone. But people could also disappear from a healthy, protected emotional environment.

For example, a child.

Sometimes – in fact, far too often – parents, distracted by their well-tried routine, failed to notice a small but vital change. Someone outside the home might approach their children and they would never know about it. Children tended to feel guilty when they were the object of an adult's attention, because they were torn between two pieces of advice most parents gave their offspring and which were hard to reconcile: to be polite to grown-ups and not to talk to strangers. Whichever they chose, there was always going to be something to hide. But Mila had discovered an excellent way to find out what was going on in a child's life.

Every month she paid a visit to a different school.

She would ask permission to walk around the classrooms when the pupils were not there, and would linger over the drawings on the walls. Their imaginary worlds often concealed elements of real life. They condensed the secret and often unconscious emotions which the child absorbed like a sponge and then poured out again. Mila liked visiting schools. She particularly liked the smell – wax crayons, paper paste, new books, chewing gum. It gave her an odd sense of calm, and made her feel as if nothing could happen to her.

Because for an adult, the safest places are where there are children.

It was during one of these visits that, among dozens of drawings displayed on a wall, Mila had discovered one by the Conners' younger daughter. She had chosen that kindergarten at random at the beginning of the school year, and had gone there during playtime, while the children were all outside. She had lingered in their tiny world, enjoying the sound of their joyous cries in the background.

What had struck her about the Conner girl's drawing was the happy family it depicted. Her mummy, her daddy, her sister and the girl herself on the front lawn of their house on a beautiful sunny day. The four of them were holding hands. Standing apart from the main group, though, was an incongruous element. A fifth character. It immediately gave her an odd pang of anxiety. It seemed to float and had no face.

A ghost, was Mila's first thought.

She was about to let it go, but then searched the wall for more drawings by the girl, and in every one of them there was the same shadowy presence.

It was too specific to be mere chance. Her instinct told her to dig deeper.

She asked the little girl's teacher, who was very helpful and confirmed that this thing with the ghosts had been going on for a while now. In her experience, she said, there was nothing to worry about – that kind of thing was common after a relative or acquaintance had died, it was the youngster's way of coming to terms with their grief. Just to be on the safe side, the teacher had asked Mrs Conner. Although there had been no deaths in the family recently, the little girl had had a nightmare not so long ago, which might have been the cause of everything.

But Mila had learnt from child psychologists that children often depict real people as imaginary characters, and not always negative ones. So although a stranger could become a vampire, he could just as easily be a friendly clown or even Spiderman. Nevertheless, there was always a detail that revealed the figure as human. She recalled the case of Samantha Hernandez, who had drawn the white-bearded man who approached her every day in the park as Father Christmas. Except that in the drawing, as in real life, he had a tattoo on his forearm. But nobody had noticed. And so all that the pervert who would abduct and kill her had needed to do was promise her a present.

In the case of the Conners' little girl, the tell-tale element was repetition.

Mila was convinced that the little girl was scared of something. She had to find out if a real person was involved and, above all, if he or she was harmless.

Following her usual procedure, she hadn't informed the parents. There was no point in scaring them unnecessarily just because of a vague suspicion. She had begun to watch the little Conner girl, to see who she was in contact with outside the house or during the few times when she was out of her parents' sight, at nursery for example, or at dance classes.

She hadn't seen any stranger taking a particular interest in the girl.

Her suspicions were unfounded. That was expected sometimes, and she didn't mind wasting twenty days' work if it ended with her heaving a sigh of relief.

Just to be on the safe side, though, she had also decided to visit the Conners' elder daughter's school. There were no disturbing features in her drawings. In her case, the anomaly was concealed in a composition the teacher had set as homework.

The girl had chosen to write a horror story with a ghost as the main character.

It was quite possible that it was just a figment of the elder girl's imagination, which had then had an effect on the younger sister. Or else it might be proof that it wasn't an imaginary person after all. Maybe the very fact that Mila hadn't seen any suspicious strangers meant that the threat was closer than she had originally thought.

In other words, the threat wasn't a stranger, but someone in the house.

That was why she had decided to go further and have a look inside the Conners' home. She, too, would have to change.

From a hunter of children to a hunter of ghosts.

It was almost eight in the morning. Mila put on a pair of earphones attached to an MP3 player that wasn't even switched on and, trying to look like a jogger, quickly covered the stretch of pavement that separated her from the Conners' drive. Just before she got to the house, she turned right and continued along the side of the building until she reached the back. She tried the back door, then the windows. They were all closed. If she had found anything open, and someone had caught her breaking in, she could have said she had gone in because she had suspected that a burglary was in process. It still wouldn't have looked good, and she would probably have been reprimanded for it, but at least she would have had a better chance of getting away with it. But now, if she forced a lock, she'd be taking a pointless and stupid risk.

She thought again about her reason for being here. You

couldn't explain a gut feeling, all police officers knew that. But in her case, there was always an irresistible urge to cross the line. Even so, she could hardly knock on the Conners' door and say, 'Hi. Something tells me your daughters are in danger because of a ghost that might be a real person.' So, as usual, her feeling of unease got the better of her common sense: she returned to the back door and forced it open.

The air conditioning hit her like a wall. In the kitchen, the breakfast dishes remained unwashed. On the fridge were holiday snaps and school exercises that had received good marks.

Mila took a black plastic case from the pocket of her tracksuit. It contained a miniature camera the size of a button, from which protruded a lead that served as a transmitter. Thanks to WiFi, she would be able to watch what was happening in the house from a distance. She just had to find the best place to put it. She checked her watch, then set off to search the rest of the house. As she didn't have much time, she decided to focus on the room where most of the family activities took place.

In the living room, along with the sofas and the television set, there was a bookcase inlaid with briar. Instead of books, it contained the certificates Conner had received in the course of his legal career or had earned in recognition of his services to the community. He was a highly respected man, a model citizen. On one of the shelves was an ice-skating trophy, awarded to their elder daughter. It struck Mila as a nice idea to share this space for distinctions with another member of the family.

On the mantelpiece was a photograph of the Conners smiling happily, all wearing identical comfy red Christmas sweaters. It was clearly a family tradition. Mila could never have posed for such a picture. Her life was too different. She was too different. She quickly looked away, finding the sight unbearable.

She decided to look upstairs.

In the bedrooms, the beds were unmade, waiting for the return of Mrs Conner, who had given up her own career to devote herself to looking after the house and bringing up her daughters. Mila merely glanced into the girls' rooms. In the parents' room, the wardrobe stood open. She lingered over Mrs Conner's clothes. The life of a happy mother aroused her curiosity. Mila's feelings, her emotions, were blocked inside her, so she was incapable of knowing what it felt like. But she could certainly imagine it.

A husband, two daughters, a house as comfortable and protective as a nest.

Momentarily forgetting the reason for her search, Mila noticed that some of the clothes on the hangers were of different sizes. It was reassuring to think that even beautiful women put on weight. That never happened to her. She was skinny. To judge by the loose-fitting clothes Mrs Conner had used to conceal her extra pounds, she must have found it hard to get her perfect figure back.

Suddenly, Mila realised what she was doing. She had lost control. Instead of hunting for dangers, she herself had become a danger to this family.

The stranger who invades your living space.

She had also lost track of time: Mrs Conner might already be on her way back. So she decided quickly that the ideal place for the miniature camera was the living room.

She found the best location inside the bookcase with the family trophies. Using double-sided tape, she placed the device in such a way that it would be as well hidden as possible among the ornaments. As she was doing this, though, she became aware of a red spot on the right-hand edge of her field of vision, like a flashing light on the wall just above the mantelpiece.

Mila stopped what she was doing, turned, and found herself

looking again at the photograph of the family wearing Christmas sweaters, which she had hurriedly passed over earlier because it had made her feel absurdly jealous. Looking at it more closely now, she realised that there were cracks in the idyllic picture. In particular, there was the silence in Mrs Conner's eyes, like the windows of an uninhabited house. Mr Conner gave the impression that he was forcing himself to look radiant, but the embrace in which he held his wife and daughters didn't convey a sense of security, but rather one of ownership. And there was something else in the picture, although Mila couldn't figure out what it was. Something wrong, hidden in that false happiness of the Conners'. Then she saw it.

The girls were right. There was a ghost among them.

In the background of the photograph, instead of the bookcase filled with awards, there was a door.

2

Where does a ghost normally hide?

In a dark place where it won't be disturbed. An attic. Or, in this case, a cellar. *The thankless task of summoning it has fallen to me*, Mila thought.

She looked down at the wooden floor and only now noticed the scratches, a sign that the bookcase was frequently moved. She moved to the side of the bookcase and looked behind it. There was the door. She slid her fingers into the gap and pulled. The family mementoes jingled, and the bookcase tilted forward dangerously, but Mila finally managed to make an opening wide enough to get through.

As she opened the door, daylight flooded the hidden cave. But Mila had the impression that the darkness inside was attacking her. The door had been lined with soundproofing material, either to keep the noise out, or to keep it in.

Beneath her, a staircase between two rough concrete walls led down to the cellar.

She took her torch from the pocket of her tracksuit and began to descend, her senses alert, her muscles taut and ready for action.

Towards the bottom, the stairs veered to the right, presumably into the main body of the cellar. Reaching the foot of the stairs, Mila found herself in a single large space shrouded in darkness. She trained the torchlight on furniture and other objects that shouldn't have been down here. A changing table, a cot, a playpen. From the latter came a regular, rhythmical sound.

A living sound.

She moved closer, very slowly so as not to wake the creature from its sleep. As befitted a ghost, it was wrapped in a sheet, and had its back to her. There was a little leg sticking out. It showed signs of malnutrition. The lack of light had not helped its growth. The skin was pale. A year old, more or less.

She had to touch it, to make sure it was real.

There was a link between this small creature, Mrs Conner's eating disorders, and her fake smile. She hadn't just put on weight. She had been pregnant.

The little bundle stirred, awakened by the torchlight. The creature turned towards her, hugging a rag doll. Mila thought it was going to burst into tears. But it just looked at her. Then it smiled.

The ghost had huge eyes.

It stretched out its little hands, wanting to be picked up. Mila did just that. The little thing immediately clung to her neck with all its might. It must have sensed she was here to save it. Mila noticed that, even in its deteriorated state, it was clean. It had been cared for: a contradiction between love and hate – between good and evil.

'She likes being picked up.'

The little girl recognised the voice and clapped her hands with joy. Mila turned. Mrs Conner was standing at the foot of the stairs.

'He isn't like other people. He always likes to be in control, and

I try not to let him down. When he found out I was pregnant, he didn't go crazy.' She was talking about her husband, but avoided calling him by his name. 'He never asked me who the father was. Our lives were supposed to be perfect, but I went and spoilt his plans. That's what really bothered him, not the cheating.'

Mila stood there staring at her, not saying a word. She didn't know how to judge her. The woman didn't seem angry, or even surprised to find a stranger here. It was as if she had been expecting it for a long time. Maybe she, too, wanted to be set free.

'I begged him to let me have an abortion, but he wouldn't. He made me keep the pregnancy secret from everyone, and for nine months I assumed he wanted to keep the child. Then one day he showed me how he had converted this cellar, and that's when I understood. Contempt wasn't enough for him. No, he had to punish me.'

Mila felt a knot of anger in her throat.

'He forced me to give birth in the cellar and leave her here. I keep telling him, even now, that we could leave her outside a police station or a hospital – nobody would know. But he won't even answer me any more.'

The little girl was smiling in Mila's arms. Nothing seemed to upset her.

'Sometimes, at night, when he's not here, I take her upstairs and show her her sisters as they sleep. I think they may have been aware of our presence but they probably think it's a dream.'

Or a nightmare, Mila said to herself, remembering the ghost in the drawings and the fairy tale. She decided she had heard enough. She turned to the playpen to grab the rag doll and get out of there as quickly as possible.

'Her name is Na,' the woman said. 'At least that's what she calls her.' She paused. 'What kind of mother would I be if I didn't know the name of my daughter's favourite doll?'

And did you give your daughter a name? Furious as she was, Mila didn't ask. The world outside knew nothing about this little girl. Mila could imagine how things would have ended up if she hadn't arrived.

Nobody looks for a girl who doesn't exist.

The woman saw the disgust in Mila's eyes. 'I know what you're thinking, but we're not murderers. We didn't kill her.'

'That's true,' Mila said. 'You would have waited for her to die.'

3

What kind of mother would I be if I didn't know the name of my daughter's favourite doll?

She had gone over and over that question on her way here in the car. And the answer was always the same.

I'm no better than she is.

Every time that awareness came to the surface, it was like receiving the same wound.

At eleven-forty, she stepped into Limbo.

That was what they called the missing persons bureau at Federal Police Headquarters. It was in the basement of the west wing, as far as possible from the main entrance. That and its name seemed to imply that nobody could care less about the place.

She was greeted by the constant roar of the antiquated air-conditioner, the smell of stale smoke – a legacy of the old days when you could smoke in this building – and the damp that rose from the foundations.

Limbo consisted of a number of rooms, plus a lower floor containing old paper records and a storeroom of exhibits. There were three offices, each containing four desks, except for the one reserved for the captain. The largest room, though, was the first one you came to as you entered.

The Waiting Room.

This was where, for so many, the road ended. As you walked in, you noticed three things. First, the emptiness: in the absence of furniture, echoes could move freely about the space. Second, the feeling of claustrophobia: despite the high ceiling, there were no windows, and the only illumination came from the grey fluorescent lighting. The third thing you noticed was the hundreds of eyes.

The walls were covered in photographs of missing persons.

Men and women. Young and old. Children. It was the children who first hit you. Mila had long wondered why. Then she'd realised that the reason they stood out was because their presence here aroused a niggling feeling of injustice. Children didn't choose to disappear, so it was taken as read that it was an adult who had grabbed them and dragged them into an invisible dimension. But they didn't get any preferential treatment on these walls. Their faces were placed with all the others, following strict chronological order.

All the inhabitants of the wall of silence were equal. There was no distinction of race, religion, sex or age. The photograph was merely the most recent proof of their presence in this life. It might be a snapshot taken at a birthday party or a frame of CCTV footage. They might be smiling without a care, they might not even be aware they were being photographed. Above all, none of them suspected that they were posing for a last picture.

From that point onwards, the world had continued without them. But nobody would abandon them, nobody in Limbo would forget about them.

'They aren't people,' Mila's chief, Steph, would say. 'They're just the subject of our work. And if you can't think like that, you won't last long here. I've been here twenty years.'

But Mila couldn't refer to these people as 'the subject of our work'. In other sections, they would have been called 'victims'. A generic term that simply meant they had been on the receiving end of some kind of crime. Mila's colleagues from outside Limbo had no idea how lucky they were to have that word.

In cases of disappearance, you cannot immediately determine whether the missing person is a victim or has run away of his or her own free will.

Those who worked in Limbo did not really know what they were investigating: kidnapping, murder, runaways. Those who worked in Limbo were not rewarded with justice. They were not motivated by the idea of catching the bad guy. Those who worked in Limbo had to be content with the possibility of finding out the truth. Uncertainty can become an obsession – and not only for those outside whose loved ones have gone missing, those who can't reconcile themselves to their disappearance.

Mila had learnt her lesson well. During her first four years there, she had had a colleague named Eric Vincenti, a quiet, polite man who had once told her that women always dumped him for the same reason. Whenever he took them out to dinner or for a drink, his eyes would wander among the tables and the people passing by. 'My date would be talking to me and I'd get distracted. I'd try to listen but not be able to. One of them told me to stop looking at other women while I was with her.'

Mila recalled Eric Vincenti's faint smile as he told her this. His slightly hoarse, thin voice, the way he nodded. As if he was resigned to the idea and was simply telling her an amusing anecdote. But then he had grown serious.

'I look for them everywhere. I'm always looking for them.'

Those few words had cast an unexpected chill over her that had never left her in the years since.

Eric Vincenti had disappeared one Sunday in March. In his bachelor apartment, the bed was made, his keys lay on the little table in the hall, and his clothes were hanging in the wardrobe. The only photograph they had found showed him with a couple of friends from his past, smiling and proudly showing off a catfish he had just caught. His face had ended up among the others on the east wall.

'He couldn't stand it any more,' was Steph's verdict.

It was the darkness that took him, Mila thought.

As she walked to her own desk, she glanced at Eric Vincenti's. In the two years since he had disappeared, nothing had been moved. It was the last trace left of him.

And so there were now just two people still working in Limbo.

In the other sections of the department, there were so many officers that they had to work packed together like sardines and were expected to live up to the standards of efficiency laid down by their superiors. Not here. Here she and Captain Steph had plenty of room to move about in, and didn't have to account for their methods or guarantee results. Not that any police officer with an ounce of ambition wanted to work here – your hopes for a brilliant career tend to fade when all you have staring at you from the walls are unsolved cases.

Mila, though, had specifically chosen Limbo when, seven years earlier, she had been offered a promotion after the most important case in years. Her superiors were amazed: not many people thought it made any sense to bury yourself in this hole. But Mila had been adamant.

Having taken off the tracksuit she had used as a disguise that morning, she put on her usual clothes – a nondescript sweatshirt, dark jeans and trainers – and sat down at the computer to write up her report on what had happened in the Conners' house. The ghost girl, who didn't yet have a name, had been handed over to social services. Two female psychologists had been taken in a patrol car to pick up her sisters from their schools. Mrs Conner had been arrested and so, as far as Mila knew, had her husband as soon as they had tracked him down at work.

As she waited for her ancient computer to start up, the voice that had followed her around all morning came back.

I'm no better than she is.

She looked up at the door to Steph's room. It was usually kept open, but for some reason it was now closed. She was puzzling about this when the door opened and the captain put his head round it.

'Ah, you're here,' he said. 'Can you come in, please?'

His tone was neutral, but Mila could sense that something was up.

Before she could ask him anything, he vanished again, leaving the door ajar for her. She stood up and walked quickly towards it. As she drew closer, she caught snippets of conversation. There was more than one voice speaking.

No one ever came down to Limbo.

But today, apparently, Steph had company.

4

There must be a serious reason for this visit.

Their colleagues from upstairs steered clear of Limbo, as if there was a curse on it, as if it brought bad luck. It was like a stain on their conscience, something they preferred to forget about. Or perhaps they were all scared of being sucked into the walls of the Waiting Room and remaining trapped there, halfway between life and death. When Mila opened the door, Steph was at his desk. A man sat opposite him, his broad shoulders barely contained within the jacket of his brown suit. He had put on weight, his hairline had receded, and his tie, rather than making him look distinguished, seemed to be choking him, but Mila immediately recognised Klaus Boris's good-natured smile.

He stood up and came to her. 'How are you, Vasquez?' He was about to hug her, but then remembered that Mila didn't like to be touched and dropped his arms awkwardly.

'I'm fine,' she said to defuse the embarrassment. 'You look slimmer.'

Boris let out a booming laugh and gave his prominent belly a pat. 'What can I say? I'm a man of action.'

He's not the old Boris any more, Mila thought. He was married now, with a couple of brats and, as an inspector, was her superior. That was another reason she was sure this wasn't a courtesy call.

'The Judge congratulates you on your discovery this morning.'

The Judge, Mila thought. If the head of the department was taking an interest in the work of an officer from Limbo, that must mean there was something else at the bottom of it. Any missing persons case that could be shown to involve a murder was automatically passed on to Homicide and, if they solved it, they took all the credit.

There would be no medal for Limbo.

The Conner case had followed a similar course. In return, Mila had been given a kind of amnesty for her less than orthodox methods. The Crime Squad had been only too happy to take over the investigation. After all, it was a case of kidnapping, no more and no less.

'The Judge sent you to tell me that? Why not just call me?'

Boris laughed again, but this time the laughter was forced. 'Why don't we make ourselves comfortable?'

Mila glanced at Steph, trying to figure out what was going on, but the captain averted his gaze. It was not for him to speak. Boris sat back down and motioned Mila towards the chair opposite him. But she turned to close the door, then remained standing.

'Come on, Boris, what's going on?' she asked without looking at him. When she finally turned to face him, she saw that a furrow had appeared on his forehead. It was as if the light had imperceptibly dimmed in the room. *Here we are, then*, Mila thought, *the pleasantries are over*.

'What I'm about to say is highly confidential. We're trying to keep it out of the press.'

'Why so cautious?' Steph asked.

'The Judge has ordered a complete blackout. Anyone who

hears about this case will be put on record so that any leak can be traced.'

This wasn't just advice, Mila thought, it was a veiled threat.

'That means that from now on the two of us are on that list,' Steph said. 'Now can you tell us what's behind all this?'

Boris was silent for a moment, then said, 'At six-forty this morning, there was a call to a police station out of town.'

'Where?' Mila asked.

Boris raised his hands. 'Wait till you hear the rest.'

Mila sat down facing him.

Boris rested both his hands in his lap, as if telling the story tired him. 'The call was from a ten-year-old boy named Jes Belman. He said that someone had come into his house at dinner time and started shooting. And that everyone was dead.'

Mila had the impression that the lights in the room had faded even more.

'The address he gave us is a house in the mountains, about twenty-five miles from the nearest built-up area. The owner is Thomas Belman, founder and COE of the pharmaceutical company of the same name.'

'I know it,' Steph said. 'They make my blood pressure pills.'

'Jes is the youngest child. Belman had two others, a boy and a girl: Chris and Lisa.'

The use of the past tense made a red light come on in Mila's mind. *Here comes the painful part*, she thought.

'Aged sixteen and nineteen,' Boris went on. 'Belman's wife's name was Cynthia, she was forty-seven. When the local police went up there to check it out ...' He paused and his eyes darkened with anger. 'Well, there's no point in beating about the bush. The boy was telling the truth. It was a massacre. They were all dead, apart from Jes.'

'Why?' Mila asked, surprised at the distress in her own voice.

'We think the killer may have had a grudge against the head of the family.'

'What makes you think that?' Steph asked with a frown.

'He was killed last.'

The sadistic intention behind that choice was obvious. Thomas Belman must have been aware that his loved ones were dying, and that must have added to his suffering.

'Did the youngest child run away and hide?' Mila asked, trying to appear calm even though that brief account of the crime had shaken her.

Boris gave a brief, incredulous smile. 'The murderer spared him so that he could call us and tell us what happened.'

'You mean the bastard was there during the phone call?' Steph asked.

'He wanted to be sure we'd get it.'

Extreme violence and a desire for attention, Mila thought. Behaviour typical of a particular type of killer: the mass murderer.

Mass murderers were more unpredictable and more lethal than serial killers, even though the media and the general public often confused the two categories. Serial killers left fairly long intervals between their crimes, a mass murderer concentrated his killings into a single well-prepared, coldly executed massacre – like the man who has been fired and who returns to his workplace to kill his colleagues, or the student who turns up at his high school with an assault rifle and shoots down his teachers and classmates as if it were a video game.

Their motive was resentment. Against the government, society, authority, or simply the human race.

The biggest difference between serial killers and mass murderers was that, with luck, you could stop the former – you could have the satisfaction of handcuffing them, looking them in the eye after arresting them, and telling them to their face, 'It's over'. The latter, though, stopped of their own accord once they had reached the required number on their secret list of victims. They reserved a single liberating shot for themselves, fired from the same weapon they had used to carry out their massacre. Or else they deliberately let themselves be shot by the police, in a final act of defiance. But the police were always left feeling they'd arrived too late, because the killer had already achieved their aim.

To take other lives with them to hell.

If there is no perpetrator to arrest and put on trial, his victims vanish with him into oblivion, leaving behind only the anger and emptiness of pointless revenge. In this way, the killer hopes to deprive the police even of the consolation of being able to do something good for those who died.

But that didn't seem to be the case here, Mila thought. If the killer had committed suicide at the end, Boris would have mentioned it.

'He's still out there, though God knows where,' Boris said, reading her mind. 'He's out there, and he's armed. And he may not be finished yet.'

'Do you know who this psychopath is?' Steph asked.

Boris evaded the question. 'We know he approached the house through the woods and left the same way. And we know he used a Bushmaster .223 semi-automatic rifle and a revolver.'

That seemed to be all, but Mila had the feeling something was missing from Boris's story. Something he hadn't yet revealed, something that explained why he had taken the trouble to come down to Limbo.

'The Judge would like you to go and take a look.'

'No.'

Her reply was so immediate, it surprised even her. In a flash,

33

she had seen the four bodies, the walls spattered with blood, the oily red liquid spreading across the floor. She had also smelt it. That stench that seems to recognise you and to tell you with a laugh that one day your death, too, will smell like that.

'No,' she repeated, more resolutely than before. 'I can't do it, I'm sorry.'

'Wait, I don't understand,' Steph said. 'Why does Mila have to go? She's not a criminologist or even a profiler.'

Boris ignored the captain and addressed Mila again. 'The killer has a plan. He may strike again very soon, and more innocent people will die. I know we're asking a lot of you.'

It was seven years since she had last set foot on a crime scene. *You're his. You belong to him. You know that you will like . . .* 'No,' she said a third time, to silence that voice from the darkness.

'I'll explain everything once we're up there. It won't take more than an hour, I promise. We thought—'

Steph laughed scornfully. 'Ever since you walked into this office you've been using the plural. *We* decided, *we* thought. Jesus Christ, we know it was the Judge who thought and decided, and that you're only here to report the Judge's words. So what's this really about?'

Gus Stephanopoulos – to make things easier, everyone had always called him Steph – was a shrewd old officer, so close to retirement now that he didn't care who he insulted. Mila liked him because, even though he seemed always to follow the rules, trying never to tread on anyone's toes, always careful about saying and doing the right thing, his true nature would come out when you least expected it. The look of incredulity that had appeared on Boris's face was something Mila had seen many times before in reaction to one of Steph's remarks.

Steph now turned to Mila with an amused expression. 'Shall I give the inspector a kick up the arse and send him back upstairs?'

Mila didn't reply. She slowly turned to look at Boris. 'You have the perfect crime scene. You can't ask for better. You even have an eyewitness, Belman's son, and I imagine you already have an identikit. Maybe you still haven't quite figured out the motive but you'll find that quite easily: in cases like this, it's usually resentment of some kind. And it doesn't sound as if anyone's missing, so what's all this got to do with us in Limbo? What's it got to do with me?' Mila paused for a moment. 'The reason you're here has something to do with the identity of the killer ...'

She waited for the statement to sink in. Boris, who had been silent all this time, remained impassive.

Steph wouldn't let go. 'You can't identify him, is that it?' It sometimes happened that other sections would ask for their help in putting a name to a face: if they couldn't find the person they were looking for, at least they would have a name. 'You need Mila so that if you don't find him before he kills again, you can blame it on Limbo. We get to do the dirty work, right?'

'Wrong, Captain,' Boris said, breaking his silence. 'We know who he is.'

This threw both Mila and Steph, and neither knew what to say.

'His name is Roger Valin.'

The name immediately set off a stream of data in Mila's head, in no particular order. Bookkeeper. Thirty years old. Sick mother. Obliged to care for her until she died. No other family. No friends. Collected watches as a hobby. Mild-mannered. Invisible. An outsider.

In an instant, Mila's mind ran out of the office and down the corridor to the Waiting Room, stood in front of the left-hand wall and scanned it until she saw him.

Roger Valin. A hollow face, a blank expression. Hair prematurely grey. The only photograph they had managed to find was the one from the badge he used to access his office – light grey suit, striped shirt, green tie.

He had inexplicably vanished into thin air one October morning.

Seventeen years ago.

5

The road hugged the mountain.

As the car climbed, and they left the city with its layer of smog behind them, the landscape had changed. The air had become clearer, and the tall firs took the edge off the lingering post-summer heat.

Outside the window, the sun was playing hide and seek among the branches, casting flickering shadows on the file Mila held open on her lap: the file on Roger Valin. Mila still found it hard to believe that the sad-faced bookkeeper in that photograph in Limbo could have committed such a savage act. As was often the case with mass murderers, he had no history of violence. It had all happened without warning, like a sudden explosion. And it was because Valin had never been in trouble with the law that he had no criminal record.

So how did they know it was him?

When Mila had asked Boris this question, Boris had simply asked her to be patient for just a little longer: she would soon know everything.

He was driving an unmarked saloon. *Why all the caution?* she wondered. The answers that came to mind merely increased her anxiety.

If the reason was really so terrible, she didn't want to know it.

She had spent seven years learning to live with what had happened in the Whisperer case. She still had nightmares, but not at night. In sleep everything vanished. It was in broad daylight that she sometimes experienced sudden fear, felt a presence beside her like a cat instinctively sensing danger. Once she had realised that she could never rid herself of the memories, she had worked out a kind of compromise. It meant imposing a few strict rules on herself. They were her safety net, the line she must never cross. The first of these rules was the most important.

Never utter the monster's name.

But she would have to violate one of the other rules this morning. She had vowed never to see a crime scene again. Mila was afraid of how she would feel when confronted with the signs of violence. *You'll feel what they all feel*, she tried to convince herself. But there was a distant voice inside her telling her the opposite.

You are his. You belong to him. You know you will like—

'Nearly there,' Boris said, silencing the mantra.

Mila nodded, trying to hide her unease. She turned to look out of the window, and her fear rose another notch: two police officers with a speed trap were monitoring the speed of passing cars. It was all a performance. Their real task was to guard the access to the crime scene. As the saloon drove past, the two officers registered them with their eyes. A few yards further on, Boris turned onto a narrow path.

The ground was bumpy and the branches on either side formed a tunnel that seemed about to close in over the car. The woods stretched out to caress them as they passed, as gentle and persuasive as someone concealing an evil intention. But then through the arch of branches they saw a sun-drenched clearing ahead of them. They came out of the shade and unexpectedly found the house right there in front of them.

It was a split-level three-storey building, a combination of the classic local mountain chalet – with sloping roof and exposed logs – and modern design. The raised veranda was surrounded by glass walls.

A rich person's house, Mila immediately thought.

They got out of the car and she looked around. There were four saloons and the forensics van. All the vehicles were unmarked. Quite a deployment of forces.

Two police officers came to greet Boris and update him. She didn't hear what they were saying. She followed them up the stone steps that led to the main entrance, keeping just a few yards behind.

During the car journey, Boris had told her that the owner of the house, Thomas Belman, was a doctor turned businessman who had set up a successful pharmaceuticals company. He was about fifty, and had only ever been married to the same woman, with whom he'd had three children. A man who had known nothing but good luck in his life, but who had died in the worst possible way Mila could imagine: after seeing his whole family wiped out.

'Come on,' Boris urged her.

Mila realised she was lingering in the doorway. In the spacious living room with its large fireplace stood at least twenty colleagues who all turned abruptly to look at her. They had recognised her, and she could guess what they were thinking. It was embarrassing, but her feet stubbornly refused to go any further. She looked down at them. It was as if they belonged to someone else. *If I do this, I can't have any second thoughts. If I take this step, there's no turning back.* The mantra came again, striking fear into her.

You are his. You belong to him. You know you will like . . . what you are about to see, Mila told herself, completing the sentence from memory.

Her left foot moved. She was inside.

There was a sub-category of mass murderer no police officer would ever have wanted to encounter. He was known as a spree killer, and he carried out a number of massacres within a relatively short period of time. That might be the case with Roger Valin. And right now, the passing minutes and hours were not on their side. That was why there was such a sense of anger and powerlessness in the villa. Mila watched her colleagues at work. Remember, there's nothing more they can do for those who died, she told herself.

The hatred that Roger Valin had summoned forth in this house had left an echo behind it, like invisible radiation, which was affecting those who had arrived subsequently.

Without realising it, they were all becoming sick with resentment.

It was almost certainly that same feeling that had motivated the killer himself, feeding his paranoia until he had shouldered an assault rifle whose clear, rhythmic din assuaged the voices in his head that had been hounding him and urging him to take revenge for the wrongs and humiliations he had suffered.

The main event was upstairs, but before she could go up they gave her plastic overshoes, latex gloves and a cap for her hair. While they were getting her ready, Mila saw one of her colleagues hand Boris a mobile phone.

'Yes, she came, she's here,' she heard him say.

She would have bet anything the inspector was talking to the Judge. Despite the nickname, the head of the department had nothing to do with courts or trials. The nickname dated from years earlier, and was intended as a humorous reference to a rather austere expression. Rather than taking it the wrong way, the Judge had accepted it as if it were a title of merit. During the officer's gradual climb through the ranks, the humorous connotations had faded, and now whenever the nickname was uttered it was as a sign of respect mixed with fear. During that unstoppable rise, whoever had first started the joke had had to live with the knowledge that he or she would sooner or later have to pay the consequences. But the Judge showed no resentment: it was better to keep your enemies on tenterhooks.

Mila and the Judge had only met once, four years earlier, when a heart attack had put an end to Terence Mosca's time as head of the department. There had been a lightning visit to Limbo by the new chief, who had said hello to the team and urged them to keep up the good work. Then nothing. Until this morning.

Boris snapped his mobile shut, finished getting ready, then came towards her. 'Ready?'

They entered the small lift that connected the three floors of the house – more of a luxury than a necessity. Boris put in the earphone and, as he waited for radio confirmation that they could go up, turned to her again. 'Thank you for coming.'

But Mila didn't want any more coaxing. 'Tell me what happened last night.'

'They were having dinner at about nine o'clock, at least according to our young witness, Jes. The kitchen is on the first floor, overlooking the veranda at the back. Valin came through the woods, that's why they didn't see him come up the outside steps. The boy said they noticed a man standing outside the French windows, but at first no one could figure out what he was doing there.'

There wasn't any panic at the start, Mila told herself. They simply all stopped talking and turned to look at him. In dangerous situations, the most common reaction isn't fear but disbelief.

'Then Belman got up from the table, opened the French windows and asked the man what he wanted.'

'It was Belman who opened them? Didn't he notice the rifle?'

'Of course he did, but he must have thought he could still control the situation.'

That was typical of certain powerful men, Mila thought. They always thought they had the prerogative of choice. Thomas Belman couldn't accept the possibility that another person might impose other rules on him, especially in his own home. Even if that person was holding a Bushmaster .223 semi-automatic rifle. Like the good businessman he was, Belman had attempted to negotiate, as if he really had something to offer that you couldn't refuse.

But Roger Valin wasn't there to make a deal.

Mila saw Boris raise his hand to his earphone. They were probably giving him the all clear from upstairs. Sure enough, he turned to the row of buttons and pressed the one for the second floor.

'All the boy said on the phone was that Valin started shooting,' he went on as they began their ascent. 'Actually, that's not quite how it happened. There was an argument at first, then he locked Jes in the basement and made the others go upstairs.'

The lift slowed as it reached the floor. Mila took advantage of those few seconds to take a deep breath.

Here we are, she said to herself.

6

The lift doors opened.

Boris and Mila were blinded by the halogen lamps standing on tripods along the corridor – at a crime scene you blacked out the windows or drew the curtains because daylight could be deceptive. Mila remembered that feeling. It was like entering an ice cave. Here, the effect was even stronger because the air conditioning had been turned fully on. But there was a specific reason why the warmth of the September morning shouldn't be allowed to get inside.

The bodies are still here, she said to herself. *They're close.*

The corridor between the rooms was filled with the bustle of the forensics agents, who were roaming the crime scene in their white overalls like silent, highly disciplined aliens. Mila crossed the border between the world of the living and the world of the dead. Behind her, the lift doors closed. Her one escape route had been cut off.

Boris led the way. 'He didn't kill them all at the same time. He separated them, then eliminated them one by one.'

Mila counted four doors on this floor.

'Hello,' Leonard Vross, the pathologist – whom everyone called Chang because of his Asian features – greeted them.

'Hello, Doctor,' Boris said.

'Are you ready to visit the magical world of Roger Valin?' In spite of his somewhat misplaced humour, Chang seemed disturbed by the scene. He gave them a small jar of camphor paste to rub under their nostrils in order to cover up the smells. 'We have four primary scenes on the second floor and a secondary one below. As you can see, we've left no stone unturned.'

The distinction between primary and secondary scenes depended on the method used to execute the crime. Secondary scenes were less important in ascertaining the dynamics of the principal act, but could prove to be vital in reconstructing the motive.

Since Boris hadn't mentioned a secondary scene, Mila wondered what was on the floor below.

Chang led the way to the room that had belonged to Chris, Belman's sixteen-year-old son.

Posters of heavy metal bands on the walls. A few pairs of trainers. A sports bag in a corner. A computer, a plasma TV and a video game console. Draped over the back of a chair was a T-shirt in praise of Satan. But the real devil didn't look anything like the one depicted on the T-shirt. He had manifested himself in that room in the innocuous guise of a bookkeeper.

One of the team was busy measuring the distance between a swivel chair and the body, which lay between sheets soaked with blood.

'The corpse has a large gunshot wound in the abdomen.'

Mila looked at his bloodstained clothes. The boy had bled to death. 'He didn't shoot him in the head or through the heart,' she said. 'He chose the stomach to prolong the agony.'

'Valin wanted to enjoy the show.' Boris pointed to the chair in front of the bed.

'The show wasn't for himself,' Mila corrected him. 'It was for

Belman senior, who could hear his son crying and screaming from his room.' She could imagine this long-drawn-out torment all too well. The victims confined to rooms that had been turned into prison cells, in the very place where they had their happiest memories, listening to what was happening to their own flesh and blood, and trembling with the knowledge that it would soon be their turn to suffer the same treatment.

'Roger Valin was a sadistic bastard,' Chang said. 'Maybe he went from room to room and talked to them. Maybe he wanted to make them think they had a way out. That if they said or did the right thing, they might escape their fate.'

'A kind of trial,' Mila said.

'Or a kind of torture,' Chang replied.

One shot, and Valin had moved on. Just as they now did. The next room was the daughter's. Lisa, nineteen. Pink curtains and wallpaper with purple daisies. Even though she was no longer a child, she hadn't changed her room too much. So dolls and cuddly toys cohabited with make-up bags and lipsticks. School certificates and a photograph showing her in Disneyland, between Pluto and the Little Mermaid, shared the walls with posters of various rock bands.

On the pale carpet, the girl's body lay oddly. Before she was killed, she had managed to break the window in an attempt to escape, but desperate as she had been, she had not had the courage to brave a fifteen-foot jump. She had given up in the vain hope of being spared: her body was in a kneeling position.

'He shot her in the right lung.' Chang pointed to the exit wound in her back.

'Valin didn't have any knives on him, did he?' There was a specific reason Mila asked the question.

'There was no physical contact,' Chang confirmed, reading her mind. 'He kept a distance from his victims at all times.'

It was an important point. The fact that the killer hadn't wanted to get blood on his hands ruled out a psychotic element. A word came to mind that perfectly described what had happened within these walls.

Executions.

They went on to the third room, which was a bathroom. Mrs Belmont lay slumped by the door.

Chang pointed to the window. 'It looks out on the embankment. Unlike the rest of this floor, it's only five or six feet to the ground. She could have jumped. She might have broken a leg, but then again she might not. She could have reached the road, stopped a car and asked for help.'

But Mila knew why she hadn't done that. And the position of the body, next to the door, confirmed it. She imagined that Mrs Belman had stayed there all the time, crying and imploring the killer for mercy or calling out to her children, to let them know their mummy was there. She would never have abandoned them, not even to try and save them. Her maternal instinct had won out over her instinct for survival.

The killer had shown her no pity. He had shot her several times in the legs, again using the rifle. Then why had he also had a revolver with him? Mila couldn't figure that out at all.

'I'm sure you won't be disappointed by the end of this tour, ladies and gentlemen,' Chang said. 'Valin left the best till last.'

7

The master bedroom was at the end of the corridor.

It was currently the exclusive territory of the most senior forensic expert in the department. Krepp's elderly oval face, emerging from the hood of the sterile overalls, was the only recognisable part of him. There were piercings on his nose and eyebrow. Mila was always somewhat startled to see this well-mannered man with the look of a sage covered in tattoos and studs. Krepp's eccentricity, though, was equalled by his talent and expertise.

Everything in the room had been turned upside down. Thomas Belman had clearly tried to free himself from his prison by hurling furniture at the door.

The body lay on the bed, shoulders propped against the padded headboard. The eyes were wide open, and so were the arms, as if waiting to be freed by a bullet. The entry wound was at the level of the heart.

In the room, standing apart from the forensics team, was a man who, like Mila and Boris, was wearing overshoes, gloves and cap in addition to his dark suit. He had small eyes and an aquiline nose. He stood with his hands in his pockets, watching the forensic team at work. It was only when he turned that Mila recognised him.

Gurevich was the same rank as Boris, but everyone knew he was the only officer the Judge trusted blindly. Because of the influence he exercised over the chief, he was considered the *éminence grise* of the department. Although a careerist, he was incorruptible, and so ruthless and intransigent as to deserve his reputation as a bastard. His few qualities had been pushed to such extremes, they had become defects.

Gurevich's presence was the one thing that made Dr Chang uneasy, so he took his leave of them. 'Well, have fun. I have some bodies to remove.'

Boris and Gurevich simply ignored each other. Boris turned to Krepp. 'So has your theory been confirmed?'

Krepp thought for a moment. 'I'd say it has. Let me show you.' He glanced at Mila and raised an eyebrow in greeting: he had never been one to bother overmuch with pleasantries.

Mila noticed that the revolver was on the bed, and found it odd that the killer would have left it behind. Unless that was part of the performance, and Valin actually wanted the police to reconstruct everything that had happened in that room down to the smallest detail.

Krepp had put the revolver into a plastic bag, then placed it back where they had found it, with a label marked with the letter A. Two more labels were attached to a bullet on the bedside table – the latter undamaged when the door had been broken down – and to the corpse's right hand, the fingers of which formed a V for victory sign.

Krepp made one final tour of the room to make sure everything was in its place before he began his reconstruction. 'Right,' he said, adjusting his gloves. 'This is more or less what the scene was like when we arrived. The gun, a Smith & Wesson 686, was lying on the bed. It can fire six shots but two bullets are missing from the cylinder. One of them is in the late Thomas Belman's heart. The other is still there, perfectly intact, on the bedside table.'

They all turned to look at the .357 Magnum bullet on the surface of the table.

'Now I think there's a simple explanation,' Krepp went on. 'Valin wanted to give his host a chance to survive. It was like a game of Russian roulette in reverse. He took one of the bullets out of the barrel – the one that's on this bedside table, in fact – and told Belman to pick a number.'

Mila looked at Belman's hand again. What she had taken for a victory sign actually indicated the choice he had made.

The number two.

'Belman had a one in six chance of escaping death,' Krepp said. 'He was unlucky.'

'Valin also wanted to test Belman's wish to carry on living after his loved ones had died,' Mila said, to everyone's surprise. 'To make him feel as if he could one day take revenge on the man who'd murdered his family. And to drive home to him how precarious his situation was, hovering between life and death. That still doesn't give us the motive for all this . . . '

Inspector Gurevich moved away from the corner where he had been standing and began a slow handclap. 'Good, very good,' he said, approaching the group. 'I'm glad you could come, Officer Vasquez,' he added in a honeyed tone, and stopped clapping.

I didn't think I had a choice, she thought. 'Only doing my duty, sir.'

Maybe Gurevich picked up on the hint of falsity in her voice. He came even closer and Mila could see his face clearly, a face dominated by a nose as thin as a blade. He had already gone bald at the temples, making his bony forehead look like some kind of carapace.

'Tell me, Officer Vasquez, in the light of what you've just said, do you think you could give us a profile of the murderer?'

Mila felt confident after reading through Valin's file during the car ride. 'All his life, Roger Valin looked after his sick mother. She was all he had in the world. The woman had a rare degenerative condition that required constant care. Valin had been hired as a bookkeeper by an auditing firm, so during the day, while he was at work, his mother was looked after by a specialist nurse whose wages ate up practically everything he earned. When his work-mates were questioned after his disappearance, they couldn't give an accurate account of his habits. Some didn't even know his first name. He never talked to anyone, never made friends with anyone, wasn't even included in the Christmas photos.'

'Sounds to me the typical portrait of the psychopath who builds up resentment all his life, and then one day walks into his workplace carrying an AK-47,' Gurevich said.

'I think it might be more complicated than that, sir.'

'Why?'

'We're seeing Valin's life from our point of view. But what seems to us like a wretched life – a man tied down by his mother's illness – is actually quite different.'

'What do you mean?'

'I have no doubt the situation was a burden to him at first, but I think that over time he turned it into a mission. Taking care of his mother became his one purpose in life. In other words, that was his real job. Everything else – the office, relationships with other people – was a bother to him. When his mother died, his world fell to pieces and he felt useless.'

'Why do you think that?'

'I was reading Valin's file on the way here, and I noticed

something that might explain a lot. When his mother died, he stayed in the house and watched over the body for four days. It was the neighbours who noticed the smell and called the fire brigade. Three months after the funeral, he vanished into thin air. He was clearly a person with a limited emotional range, unable to handle grief. In cases like that, the usual outcome isn't murder but suicide.'

'And do you think that's what he'll end up doing, Officer Vasquez?' Gurevich asked provocatively.

'I don't know,' she admitted, embarrassed. Krepp looked at her in tacit solidarity. It was at this point that she understood. 'You already knew the story, didn't you?'

'I admit we haven't been completely open with you,' Gurevich said.

Mila was shaken. Gurevich handed her a transparent folder containing an article from a scientific journal, illustrated by a photograph of Thomas Belman.

'I'll save you the bother of reading it. In a nutshell, it says that Belman's company has long had a patent for the only drug that could guarantee the survival of patients suffering from a rare condition.' Gurevich spoke the words slowly, savouring the moment. 'A wonder drug capable not only of improving the patients' quality of life but of prolonging their lives for several years. The pity of it is that it's very expensive. Guess which rare condition they're talking about.'

Boris now spoke up. 'On his salary, Roger Valin could no longer afford treatment for his mother. He'd spent every penny he had, and when the money ran out he was forced to watch her die.'

That's the root of all his resentment, Mila thought, and she suddenly understood the true meaning of the strange ritual Valin had performed with Belman: the Russian roulette in reverse.

'The missing bullet. He gave his victim a chance to survive – something his mother wasn't given.'

'Precisely,' Boris said. 'And now we need a detailed report on Valin's disappearance, including his psychological profile.'

Mila still didn't understand. 'Why are you asking me? Wouldn't a criminologist be better qualified?'

Gurevich came back into the conversation. 'Who reported Valin's disappearance seventeen years ago?'

He hadn't answered Mila's question, but she responded all the same. 'The company where he worked, after he'd been absent for a week without explanation. He couldn't be reached.'

'When was he last seen?'

'Nobody remembers.'

Gurevich turned to Boris. 'You haven't told her yet, have you?'

'Not yet,' he admitted in a low voice.

Mila stared at them both. 'Told me what?'

8

The place where the prologue to the massacre had been played out was the kitchen.

It was there that Valin had made his entrance, coming from the garden and appearing outside the French windows. But there was another reason why the room had been classified as a 'secondary crime scene'.

It was here that the final act of that long night's drama had taken place.

Gurevich, Boris and Mila went back downstairs. Mila followed her two superiors without asking any more questions, certain that she would soon have all the answers. They descended a wooden staircase into a large room that looked more like a living room than a kitchen. Along one wall, overlooking the garden, were the French windows, which hadn't been blacked out by the forensics team.

No bodies here, Mila thought. But she felt no relief, because she immediately had the feeling that worse was to come.

'What photograph did you use when you were looking for Valin after his disappearance?' Gurevich asked her.

'The one on his security badge from work. He'd only just renewed it.'

'And what did he look like in that picture?'

Mila recalled the photo on the wall in the Waiting Room. 'Grey hair, thin face. He was wearing a pale grey suit, a striped shirt and a green tie.'

'A pale grey suit, a striped shirt and a green tie,' Gurevich repeated slowly.

Mila wondered why the inspector had asked her the question: he should already have been aware of these details.

But instead of explaining, he walked to the middle of the kitchen, where there was a fitted sideboard beneath a big stone hood inlaid with brass. Near it was a solid wooden dining table, on which lay not only the dirty dishes from last night's dinner but also the remnants of another meal.

Breakfast.

Gurevich realised that Mila had noticed this oddity. He came and stood in front of her. 'Have they told you how we managed to identify Roger Valin?'

'Not yet.'

'Just after six, when the sun had risen, Valin freed young Jes from the cellar, brought him up here and made him a breakfast of cornflakes, orange juice and chocolate pancakes.'

Normality in the midst of horror. It was these unexpected deviations that really disturbed Mila. A lull after a storm was usually an omen.

'Valin sat down with the boy and waited for him to finish eating,' Gurevich went on. 'You mentioned that seventeen years ago, he watched over his mother's corpse for four days. Maybe this morning he let Jes live because he wanted him to have the same experience. Be that as it may, it was while the boy was having breakfast that he told him who he was. And to make sure he didn't forget he even made him write it down.'

'Why would he do that?' Mila asked.

Gurevich gestured to her to wait: all would be revealed in due course. 'Jes is a brave little boy, isn't he, Boris?'

'Very brave,' Boris said.

'In spite of all that's happened to him, he stayed calm until not long ago, when he finally broke down in tears. Before that, though, he answered all our questions.'

'When he was shown Valin's photograph – the one where he's wearing a pale grey suit, striped shirt and green tie – he recognised him immediately,' Boris said. Then his face clouded over. 'But when we asked him if he could describe anything else about the man, how he was dressed for instance, he pointed at the photo again and said. "Like that."'

Mila was shaken. 'That's impossible,' she couldn't help saying, remembering the photograph in the Waiting Room.

'I agree,' Gurevich said. 'A man disappears at the age of thirty. Then he turns up again at the age of forty-seven, wearing exactly the same clothes he was wearing seventeen years ago.'

Mila was speechless.

'Where has he been all this time?' Gurevich went on. 'Was he abducted by aliens? He suddenly appeared from out of the woods. Did a spaceship drop him outside the Belmans' front door?'

'And there's something else,' Boris said, pointing to the wall-mounted telephone. 'This morning, Jes used that phone to call the police on Valin's instructions. But according to the records, Valin had previously made another call on it, at about three o'clock in the morning, in the middle of the massacre.'

'The number he called belongs to a twenty-four-hour launderette in the city centre,' Gurevich said. 'It's used mostly by elderly people and immigrants, which is why there's a public phone.'

'There are no staff, nobody's in charge,' Boris said, looking closely at Mila. 'There's only a video surveillance system to discourage vandals and thieves.'

'So then you know who answered the call,' Mila said.

'That's just the point,' Boris replied. 'Nobody did. Valin let it ring for a while, then gave up and didn't try again.'

'That doesn't make sense, does it, Officer Vasquez?' Gurevich said.

Mila knew now why the two inspectors were so worried, but still wasn't sure of her own role in this affair. 'What do you want me to do?'

'We need to know every detail of Valin's past life if we're going to figure out what he'll do next,' Gurevich said. 'Make no mistake, he's got a plan of some kind. Who did he try and call last night? And why did he only try once? Does he have an accomplice? What's his next move? Where's he going with a Bushmaster .223 rifle?'

'And all the answers are linked to one overriding question,' Boris concluded. 'Where has Roger Valin been for the past seventeen years?'

9

The violence of a spree killer is cyclical.

Every cycle lasts about twelve hours and is divided into three stages: calm, incubation and explosion. The first occurs after the initial attack. There is a momentary sense of fulfilment, which is then followed by a new incubatory phase, during which anger becomes mixed with hate. The two feelings act like chemical elements. They are not necessarily harmful in isolation, but when combined they give rise to a highly unstable mixture. At this point, stage three is inevitable. The only possible outcome of the process is death.

But Mila hoped she would be in time.

The natural end to a mass murderer's acts was suicide, and if Valin hadn't killed himself yet, it must mean that he had a plan and that he intended to see it through.

Where would he strike next, and who would his victim be?

The afternoon was fading to evening and the sky was beginning to take on the colours of the dying summer. The Hyundai moved slowly forward as Mila bent over the steering wheel to read the house numbers.

The street was lined on both sides with identical two-storey detached houses with sloping roofs and small front gardens. Only the colours were different –white, beige, green and brown – although all equally faded. A very long time ago young families had lived here, with children playing on the lawn, and a warm, welcoming light behind every window.

Now it was a place for old people.

The white wooden fences that had demarcated the properties had been replaced by metal netting, and the gardens were overgrown and filled with refuse and scrap metal. When she got to number 42, Mila slowed to a halt. On the other side of the street stood the house where Roger Valin had lived.

Seventeen years had passed and the building now belonged to another family, but this was the place where Valin had grown up, the place where he had taken his first steps, played on the lawn, learnt to ride a bicycle. It was through that front door that he had emerged every day, first to go to school, then to work. It was the setting for his routine. And it was also the place where Roger had had to care for his sick mother, waiting long years for the inevitable end.

In her career looking for missing persons, there was one lesson Mila had learnt well. However far we run, home is the place that follows us wherever we go. We can move house often but there is always one we remain attached to. It's as if we belong to it, and not the other way round, as if we were made up of the same materials – earth instead of blood, wood in our joints, bones of concrete.

The one hope Mila clung to, the one thing that might help her track down Roger Valin, was that, despite the anger inside him, despite his deadly intentions, and after all the time he had been away, God alone knew where, the memory of this place would still get the better of him.

She parked the Hyundai by the curb, got out and looked

around. The wind blew through the trees, and every new gust brought the sound of a distant burglar alarm a little closer before it abated and blended in with the background noise. In the garden of the Valins' former residence stood the carcase of a burgundy station wagon without wheels, supported on four stacks of bricks. Inside the house, the new residents could be glimpsed in silhouette. It was unlikely Roger had come any closer than this. To find evidence of that visit, Mila would have to go elsewhere. She looked around and headed for the house opposite.

An elderly lady was taking down washing from a line strung between two posts. With a bundle of clothes in her hands, she started up the steps to the porch. Mila walked quickly towards her, to stop her going indoors.

'Excuse me.'

The woman turned and gave her a suspicious look. Halfway up the path, Mila took out her police badge to set the woman's mind at rest.

'Sorry to bother you, but I need to speak to you.'

'No problem, my dear,' the woman replied with a little smile. She was wearing knee-length terrycloth socks, one of which had slipped down to her ankle, and her dressing gown was stained and worn at the elbows.

'Have you lived here long?'

The woman seemed amused by the question, but then looked about her with a momentary touch of sadness in her eyes. 'Forty years.'

'Then I'm speaking to the right person,' Mila said warmly. She didn't want to scare her by asking straight out if by any chance she'd seen her old neighbour Roger Valin lately – the same Roger Valin who'd been missing for seventeen years. And she suspected that, given her age, the woman might be confused anyway.

'Would you like to come in?'

Mila had been hoping she'd say that. 'All right,' she immediately replied.

The old woman led the way, a troublesome gust of wind ruffling her sparse hair.

Mrs Walcott shuffled in her woollen slippers across the rugs and the worn wooden floor between the heavy furniture filled with all kinds of objects – glass knick-knacks, chipped porcelain, framed photographs of distant lives – carrying a tray with two cups and a teapot. Mila got up from the sofa and helped her to put it down on the coffee table.

'Thank you, dear.'

'You shouldn't have gone to all this trouble.'

'It's a pleasure,' the old woman said, starting to pour. 'I don't get many visitors.'

Mila watched her, wondering if she would be as solitary as this one day. Mrs Walcott's only companion was probably the ginger cat lying curled up in an armchair, which would occasionally half-open its eyes, take a look at the situation, then doze off again.

'Satchmo isn't very sociable with strangers, but he's a good cat.'

Mila waited for the woman to sit down facing her, then picked up her cup of tea and began. 'What I'm about to ask you may seem strange, because it's been such a long time. Do you by any chance remember the Valins, who used to live opposite?' As she pointed in the direction of the house opposite, she saw Mrs Walcott's face cloud over.

'Poor things,' the woman murmured, confirming that she did indeed remember them. 'When my husband Arthur and I bought this house, they'd only recently moved here themselves. They were young, like us, and the neighbourhood was new. It was a nice quiet place to live and bring up children. That's what the estate agent told us and he was right. At least for the first few years. Lots of people moved out here from the city. Mostly office workers and shopkeepers. No factory workers or immigrants.'

Coming as she did from another generation, it was perfectly natural for Mrs Walcott to make such a politically incorrect comment. Mila was bothered by it, but retained her polite demeanour. 'Tell me about the Valins. What kind of people were they?'

'Oh, quite respectable. The wife stayed at home and looked after the house, and the husband had a good job as a sales assistant. She was very beautiful and they seemed happy. We made friends with them immediately. We'd have a barbecue every Sunday, spend public holidays together. Arthur and I hadn't been married long, but they already had a child.'

'Do you remember Roger?'

'How could I forget him? Poor little thing. He could already ride a bicycle at the age of five. He'd ride it up and down the street. Arthur was very fond of the boy, and even built him a tree house. We'd already realised we couldn't have children of our own, but we didn't make a big thing out of it because we didn't want to hurt each other. Arthur was a good man. He'd have made a wonderful father if God had let him.'

Mila nodded. Like many old people, Mrs Walcott had a tendency to drift off at a tangent, and every now and then you had to get her back to the point of the conversation. 'What happened to Roger's parents?'

The woman shook her head. 'Mrs Valin fell seriously ill. The doctors were quite clear from the start that she wouldn't recover. But they also said the Lord wouldn't take her so quickly. She'd have a lot of pain and suffering to endure first. Maybe that's why the husband decided to walk out on the family.'

'Roger's father left them?' Mila hadn't seen that in the file.

'Yes,' Mrs Walcott said in a disapproving tone. 'He remarried and never came back, not even to see how they were getting on. That was when the light started to go out in Roger. He'd been so lively and active before, always had lots of friends, but now Arthur and I saw him becoming more and more isolated. He'd spend hours on his own or with his mother. Such a responsible young man.'

Mrs Walcott sounded genuinely bitter on Roger's behalf. It would probably have been painful for her to learn what a terrible thing he had done the night before.

'My husband felt really sorry for the boy, and angry with his father. Sometimes, I'd hear him call him names. And to think they'd been such good friends. But he'd never say anything bad in front of Roger. Arthur had a special rapport with Roger. He was the only person who could ever get him out of the house.'

'How did he manage that?'

'The watches,' Mrs Walcott said, putting her empty cup down on the tray – Mila realised she had barely touched her own tea. 'Arthur collected watches. He'd buy them in markets or at auctions and spend whole days sitting at the table, taking them to pieces or repairing them. When he retired, I'd have to remind him to eat or go to bed. It was incredible, he'd be surrounded by watches and yet he wouldn't know what time it was.'

'And he shared his passion with Roger,' Mila prompted her, already aware of Valin's hobby.

'He taught him everything he knew about the subject. And the boy went mad for that world of ticking and precision. Arthur said he was really cut out for it.'

Unhappy people were attracted to the infinitely small, Mila thought. They could be out of sight of other people while still having a function in the world, a function as essential as calculating the time. In the end, Roger Valin had simply decided to disappear altogether.

'There's an attic upstairs,' Mrs Walcott said. 'It was going to be the children's room, but of course we never had any. We kept saying we'd rent it out, but then it became Arthur's workshop. He and Roger would shut themselves in up there, and sometimes you wouldn't see them all afternoon. Then my husband fell ill, and almost overnight the boy stopped coming to the house. Arthur would make excuses for him. All teenagers were a bit cold-blooded, he'd say, Roger wasn't doing it out of spite. And besides, he was being forced to watch his mother die, day after day, so he couldn't be expected to be present at the last days of another human being, even if that person was the only friend he had left.' The woman took a crumpled handkerchief from the pocket of her dressing gown and wiped away the tear that had formed in the corner of her eye. Then she rolled it into a ball and laid it in her lap, ready to use again if need be. 'I'm sure Arthur was really upset, though. I think deep down he kept hoping Roger would walk through the door again one day.'

'So you lost touch with him,' Mila said.

'No,' Mrs Walcott said, slightly surprised. 'It was about six months after my husband died. Roger didn't even come to the funeral. Then one morning, completely out of the blue, he turned up on the doorstep and asked if he could go up to the attic and wind the watches. From then on, he got in the habit of coming here on his own.'

Instinctively, Mila raised her eyes. 'Up there?'

'Of course. He'd come back from school and the first thing he'd do would be to see to his mother. Then, if she didn't need anything else, he'd go up to the attic and spend a couple of hours there. He did it even after he'd started his bookkeeping job, but then, one day, I stopped hearing from him.'

Mila realised that she was referring to the time of his disappearance.

'From what you're saying, apart from his mother, you're the person who saw him most often outside work, and yet it wasn't you who reported his disappearance to the authorities. Sorry to ask this, but weren't you surprised when Roger stopped coming round?'

'No, because he'd come and go by himself. The only way to get up to the attic is by an outside staircase, so sometimes we didn't even see each other. He never made any noise, although the odd thing is, I always knew when he was upstairs. I can't explain it. It was just a feeling. I could sense his presence in this house.'

Mila noticed a hint of agitation in the woman's eyes and face. A certain anxiety that she might not be believed, that she might be taken for a crazy old lady. But there was something else. Fear. Mila leant over and placed her hand on hers. 'Mrs Walcott, I want you to tell me the truth. In the last seventeen years, have you ever sensed that Roger was here with you?'

The woman's eyes filled with tears, and her body and lips tensed in an effort to hold them back. Then, as if making up her mind, she nodded emphatically.

'If you don't mind,' Mila said, 'I'd like to take a look around the attic.'

10

The burglar alarm she had heard when she arrived in the neighbourhood was still ringing in the distance.

As she climbed the outside staircase leading to the attic, Mila instinctively put her hand on her gun. She didn't think she would find herself face to face with Roger Valin, but the way Mrs Walcott had reacted to her last question had made an impression. It might just have been the ravings of a lonely old woman, but Mila was convinced that fears were never unfounded.

It was quite possible the house had had a silent, unwelcome visitor. For the second time that day, Mila found herself searching someone else's house. It was only that morning that she'd been in the Conner residence, discovering the ghost girl in the cellar. By the law of probabilities, it was unlikely she would strike it lucky again, but you could never tell.

The attic door was locked, but Mrs Walcott had given her a key. As she tried to open the door, the burglar alarm in the distance seemed to be both warning and mocking her.

Mila leant on the handle and pressed down on it. She had expected a creaking sound, but the door opened with a sigh. The attic stretched in front of her between the sloping ceilings. There was a chest, a stripped bed with a rolled-up mattress at one end, a kitchenette with two gas rings, and a toilet inside a wall cupboard. At the far end of the room, light fell from a dormer window onto a workbench against the wall, on which stood a small cabinet covered in dust. Mila took her hand off her gun and slowly approached, feeling almost as if she was intruding on a private space.

Somebody's lair, she thought.

There was no sign Roger Valin had been here. Everything seemed still, as if it had not been disturbed for years. She sat down at the workbench. There was a vice fixed to the corner of it and a round lamp with a magnifying lens in the middle. Her eyes wandered over the small, neatly arranged tools. She recognised screwdrivers, tweezers, a small knife for opening the cases, a watchmaker's eyeglass, little boxes full of inner parts, a small cushion, a wooden hammer and an oilcan. There were other precision instruments she did not recognise.

If it wasn't for that damned alarm that still hadn't stopped, she would have surrendered to the spell of these silent objects. She looked at the little cabinet in front of her. Inside it, on two levels, Mr Walcott's collection of watches was displayed.

They sat there motionless, in thrall to the one force capable of defeating the power of time: death.

At first sight, there were about fifty of them, both wristwatches and pocket watches. She spotted some Longines, a Tissot, a Revue Thommen with a blue leather strap and a silver-plated case, and a beautiful steel Girard-Perregaux. Mila was no expert but she could see that Mrs Walcott's husband had left her a small fortune in watches, although the woman herself seemed unaware of the fact. All she had to do was sell a few of these items and she could live a more comfortable life. But then Mila had second thoughts. What else could a woman who was alone in the world want? All she needed was the lazy affection of a cat and a myriad memories in the tired form of knick-knacks and old photographs.

Through the dormer window she could see the house opposite. Mila tried to put herself in Roger Valin's mind. *You could see your house from here, so you didn't feel as if you were leaving your mother on her own. But at the same time, sitting here was an opportunity to get away from her. Why did you disappear after she died? Where have you been? And why have you come back? What's the point of your belated revenge? And what are you going to do now?*

The questions mingled with the burglar alarm, becoming ever more oppressive. Why, for the massacre at the Belman house, had Roger Valin put on the same clothes he'd been wearing when he disappeared? Why had he called a launderette that night? Why had no one answered? *Prove to me you were here, Roger. Prove to me that deep down you felt homesick for the world you ran away from and that you wanted to revisit the past, to see your old lair again.*

Suddenly, the alarm stopped, although it continued to echo in Mila's head. It took a while for the silence to fill all the spaces in the attic – and inside her.

That was when she became aware of the ticking.

As regular as a coded message, as insistent as a secret call, it drew Mila's attention, almost as if repeating her name. She opened the cabinet and started searching for the watch that was emitting that obscure signal.

It was an old, rather inexpensive Lanco, with a fake crocodile-skin strap, its case corroded by rust, its glass cracked, and its ivory dial brown with age.

It wasn't unknown for a watch to start working again, thanks to a winding mechanism that had somehow been preserved over the years. But as she took it in her hand, Mila realised this wasn't a case of an object reawakening from its old slumber.

Somebody had wound it recently, because it showed the exact time.

11

'He's been here, there's no doubt about it.'

Mila was sitting in her car outside Mrs Walcott's house. It was just after ten at night: it had taken her that long to reach Boris, who had been tied up in meetings all day, debating whether or not to release the story of the massacre to the press along with the identity of the culprit and his photograph. Boris thought it would serve to isolate Roger Valin and to see if anyone recognised him and helped them to solve, at least partly, the mystery of those seventeen missing years. But Gurevich wouldn't budge. Making the case public, he insisted, would be playing into Valin's hands and might spur him to kill again. In the end, Gurevich had won.

'Excellent work,' Boris said to Mila. 'But we have other priorities now.'

Since the massacre, Roger Valin had vanished without trace. They had no leads. And another night was starting. Whose house would he enter this time? Who would he take out his resentment on?

'The problem is, the motive behind Valin's massacre of the Belmans was real enough, but at the same time there's something random about it. Slaughtering the family of the head of a pharmaceutical company that produces a life-saving but expensive drug doesn't exactly imply a pattern, does it? Who's Valin going to choose next? The chairman of the association for husbands who walk out on sick wives with dependent children?'

Mila understood Boris's frustration.

'Sorry,' he said. 'It's been a hard day. You did really well. I might place Mrs Walcott's house under surveillance, in case our man shows up again.'

Mila turned to look at the house across the street. 'I don't think that'll happen. Valin left us the watch as a kind of sign.'

'Are we sure the old lady didn't restart the watch herself? It's not much of a lead, and I don't see how it's going to help us track down Valin.'

Boris might be right, although Mila was still sure there were other implications. But it was hard to argue for them right now, given the very real risk that Valin would strike again.

'All right, we'll deal with it tomorrow,' Mila said. She started her car and set off for home.

At this time of night, the only place she could find to park her Hyundai was three blocks from her building. Since the sun had gone down, the almost summery temperature that had characterised the day had dropped, and the air was now cold and damp. As Mila was wearing only a T-shirt and jeans, she walked as quickly as she could.

The neighbourhood, built about a hundred years earlier, had recently been discovered by yuppies and famous architects, who were in the process of turning it into the new mecca for style and sophistication. That was happening increasingly often. The city was in a constant state of flux. Only its sins never changed. Neighbourhoods were refurbished and streets were given new names, so that the residents could feel modern and forget that they were leading identical lives to those of their predecessors, repeating the same actions, making the same mistakes.

The predestined victims of predestined executioners.

Maybe, in carrying out that massacre, Valin had been trying to reverse the cycle. Belman was an important man who, like a pagan god, had the power to heal and to grant life, but used that power according to his own whim. What Mila couldn't understand was why Roger had chosen to make the wife and children pay for the sins of the father.

She kept thinking about it as she walked to her building. A little while earlier, she had stopped off to buy a couple of hamburgers from a fast food outlet. She had eaten one, but the other was still in the bag. Coming to an alleyway, she left it on the lid of a dustbin. Then she walked up the steps to the main entrance of the four-storey building. In the time it took her to insert the key in the front door, she saw two dirty hands reach out from the shadows, as she'd expected, and take the precious package of food. That tramp would soon have to abandon the area, too. He didn't fit in with the changing surroundings, as shown on the large billboard that covered the facade of the building being renovated opposite hers, where the fortunate future residents of the neighbourhood were depicted in hyper-realist style.

Mila paused, as she always did, to look at the cheerful pair of giants smiling down at her from the billboard. She found it really hard to envy them.

She closed the door of her apartment behind her, but didn't switch on the light immediately. She was exhausted. She savoured the fact that her thoughts had fallen silent. But it didn't last.

You are his. You belong to him. You know you will like what you are about to see.

It was true. She had felt a familiar sensation, setting foot on a crime scene, coming into direct contact with the traces left by evil. People who watched the news thought they knew, but they had no idea what it really meant to stand there and look at the body of a murder victim. Something strange always happened to police officers. It was a kind of natural process they all went through. At first, you feel disgust. Then you get used to it. Then it becomes a kind of addiction. You start by associating death with fear – fear of being killed, fear of killing, fear of seeing people who have been murdered. But then the idea enters your DNA chain like a virus. In replicating itself, it becomes part of you. Death becomes the one thing that makes you feel alive. This was the legacy left to Mila by the Whisperer case. And not the only part of it.

At last, she reached for the switch, and on the other side of the room a lamp came on. The living room was piled high with books, as were the bedroom, the bathroom, and even the kitchenette. Novels, non-fiction, works of philosophy and history. New and second hand. Some bought in shops, some from market stalls.

She had started accumulating them after Eric Vincenti, her colleague in Limbo, had vanished into thin air. She'd been afraid of ending up like him, devoured by an obsession with missing persons.

I look for them everywhere. I'm always looking for them.

Or else she was afraid of being swallowed up by that same darkness she was trying to explore. In a way, books were a way of staying anchored to life, because they had endings. It didn't matter if those endings were happy or unhappy. Having an ending was a luxury that the stories she dealt with on a daily basis didn't have. And books were also an antidote to silence, because they filled her mind with the words necessary to bridge the gap left by the victims. Above all, they were her escape route. Her own way of disappearing. She would immerse herself in her reading, and everything else – including herself – ceased to exist. In books, she could be anybody she wanted. And that was like being nobody at all.

Every time she walked into her apartment, it was only her books that greeted her.

She walked to the counter separating the living room from the kitchenette, took her gun out of her belt, and put it down next to her badge and her quartz watch. She took off her T-shirt, and as she did so she caught sight of the reflection of her scar-streaked body in one of the windows. She was glad she didn't have curves, or she would have been tempted to dig into them with a razor blade. The wounds she had given herself over the years bore witness to the pain she'd been unable to feel for the victims of other people's wrongdoing. Cutting herself was the only way she knew of reminding herself that she was human after all.

It would soon be the first anniversary of her most recent wound. Although she hadn't promised herself anything, she was trying hard. It was part and parcel of the path to self-improvement she was attempting to follow. Three hundred and sixty-five days without cuts. It was hard to believe. But seeing her reflection in a mirror was still an invitation. Her naked body still tempted her. So she looked away. Before going to ground in the shower, though, she switched on her laptop.

She had an appointment coming up.

12

By now it had become a ritual.

Wearing only her dressing gown, and drying her hair with a towel, Mila lifted the laptop from the table and carried it to the bed. She settled it on her legs, then keyed in a program. She switched off the light and waited for the connection. Somewhere, a twin system responded and a dark window opened on the screen. Mila immediately recognised a sound. It was faint but continuous. It came from out of the darkness, but wasn't hostile.

Breathing.

She listened to it for a while, letting herself be cradled by the calm rhythm of it. After a few seconds, she tapped a command on the keyboard and the black screen was replaced by an image.

A small room lit by a faint green light.

The miniature camera – similar to the one she had nearly placed in the Conners' house – probed the darkness in infrared mode. It was just about possible to make out a wardrobe on the right, a single bed on the left and a soft rug in the middle, strewn with games, posters of cartoon characters and a doll's house.

A little girl lay asleep beneath the blankets.

Mila didn't notice anything untoward. Everything seemed calm. She watched for a little while longer, mesmerised by the serenity of the scene. It was natural to be reminded of another little girl – the ghost child locked in the cellar, whom she had saved a few hours earlier. If she concentrated, she could still feel the girl's weight in her arms as she had carried her away. She felt neither compassion nor tenderness. The only sensation that remained was a tactile memory, a kind of incidental pain that was her punishment for not feeling any empathy. But in a way the encounter with Mrs Conner had marked her.

What kind of mother would I be if I didn't know the name of my daughter's favourite doll?

Something was happening in that little room. Through the open door from the corridor came a distant light, across which a human shadow was soon cast, getting shorter as it approached. It was a woman, although Mila couldn't make out her face. She went to the bed and tucked the little girl in. When she had finished, she leaned against the doorpost and gazed at the sleeping child.

And do you know the name of her favourite doll? Mila wanted to ask the woman on the screen.

Suddenly, though, she felt like an intruder. Instead of closing the connection, she typed a command on the keyboard and another window opened next to the live images, showing Roger Valin's file. She wanted to read it once more before going to sleep. One important point remained unresolved.

The mystery of the call to the launderette.

Why had Valin needed to phone someone? That was what she couldn't understand. And even assuming he had an accomplice, why had nobody answered the call?

It didn't add up. There had to be an explanation. That call didn't make sense, any more than did Valin's decision to wear the same clothes he'd been wearing in that photograph taken seventeen years earlier.

Light grey suit, striped shirt, green tie.

After the massacre, Valin had had breakfast with the Belman boy, taking the opportunity to reveal his identity. He had even made sure Jes wrote his name down on a sheet of paper, so that he wouldn't get it wrong when he passed it on to the police. Above all, he'd wanted the boy to remember his face and how he was dressed.

Gurevich had made a joke about those clothes, saying that maybe Valin had been abducted by aliens seventeen years earlier. But after visiting the Walcott house and seeing the watches, Mila preferred to think of Valin as a time traveller who had passed through a black hole connecting distant periods. Although both theories were equally incredible, the difference between them did suggest a different approach to the investigation. Gurevich, who came from Homicide, was used to concentrating on the present, on the 'here and now', on cause and effect. In Limbo, on the other hand, they dealt with the past.

It was Eric Vincenti who had explained the difference to her. Mila remembered the conversations she had had with him before he, too, had followed the same path as those he sought.

'A murder is instantaneous,' Vincenti would say, 'but in a missing persons case, some time needs to pass. Not just the thirty-six hours the law stipulates before we can start searching, but much longer. A disappearance crystallises when what the person has left behind begins to deteriorate: the electricity company cuts off the supply because of non-payment, the plants on the balcony wilt because there's no one to water them, the clothes in the wardrobe go out of fashion. We have to find the reason for all this decay by going back in time.' Eric Vincenti had a tendency to over-dramatise, but Mila knew that he was basically right.

People start disappearing a long time before they actually disappear.

Kidnapping cases begin when whoever is about to take the victim away first notices them and enters their life as an invisible presence, watching them from a distance. In cases where people run away of their own free will, it begins the day they first get that feeling of unease they can't explain. They feel it grow inside them, like an unsatisfied desire, even though they don't know for what. It's like an itch demanding to be scratched. They know that giving in to the impulse will only make matters worse, but can't help it. The only way to silence it is to heed the call. And follow it into the shadows. That was what must have happened to Roger Valin, and to poor Eric Vincenti.

The reason for a disappearance is in the past, Mila told herself.

She focused again on Valin. There was no letter, no note explaining his action. A mass murderer acts out of hatred, resentment or revenge. A mass murderer expresses himself through his own criminal acts and doesn't care about being understood, she repeated to herself.

What if the clothes, the phone call to the launderette and the watch set to the right time in Mrs Walcott's house were all part of the same message?

The answer was 'time'.

Valin was drawing their attention to the time when he had disappeared.

Mila opened a search engine on her computer. By wearing those clothes, she told herself, Valin was telling us that we have to think as if it was still seventeen years ago. Which meant that when he made that call during the night, he hadn't got the wrong number after all. For him, it was the right number.

Mila found the website of the phone company. There was a section that gave a list of past subscribers. Hoping to find the name and address of the customer that number had been registered to at the time Valin had gone missing, she typed in the number of the launderette and pressed SEARCH.

On the screen, the small hourglass-shaped icon marked the seconds. Mila stared at it, unconsciously biting her lip with impatience. The answer wasn't long in coming. She was right. That number had been active seventeen years ago.

It had belonged to a place called the Chapel of Love, located on the motorway that led to the lake.

Mila immediately searched for a possible new number, only to discover that the Chapel of Love had ceased its activities several years earlier. She stopped to think. What should she do? She could inform Boris right now, or she could wait and tell him tomorrow. This lead might also turn out to be a false one. It might all just be a coincidence.

Once again, she looked at the images of the bedroom where the little girl lay peacefully asleep. She wasn't spying on her, she was protecting her. She thought again about what had happened at the Conners'. *I'm someone who breaks into people's houses and plants hidden cameras*, she told herself. It was only thanks to her recklessness that a ghost child had been released from its prison that morning.

Mila knew there was no way she could wait.

She closed the laptop, got out of bed and got dressed again.

13

The moon was winking out of a clear sky.

The road to the lake was deserted, and not just because it was night. It wasn't any different during the day. This whole area had once been a popular holiday destination. There had been hotels, restaurants, and a fully equipped beach. But about twelve years earlier, an inexplicable disease had struck the fish and animals. The authorities had been unable to pinpoint the cause, although there were those who blamed pollution in the water. There was mass panic, and people stopped visiting the area. Soon afterwards, the problem vanished: the fauna reappeared and the ecosystem regained its balance. But it was too late. The holidaymakers didn't return. The leisure facilities that had welcomed them for generations closed their shutters and began to deteriorate through lack of maintenance. The decline of the area was unstoppable.

The Chapel of Love must have met the same fate.

It was one of those places where people went to get married. It offered a range of lay ceremonies for those who weren't religious but wanted something more than a register office wedding.

As she drove over a speed bump, Mila saw through the

windscreen of her Hyundai the brick arch that served both as an entrance and as a sign, with a pair of hearts in the middle, made out of fluorescent tubes, now extinguished. Above them was a tin Cupid, his expression distorted by the rust that had half eaten his face. He looked like an evil angel guarding a treacherous heaven.

The complex consisted of a series of low buildings surrounding a car park. The largest looked like a post-modern church. The moonlight rescued it from the oblivion of the night but also mercilessly accentuated its desolate state.

Mila parked the car next to the cottage that had served as the reception building. She switched off the engine and got out, to be greeted by the primitive, unwelcoming silence of a world that had learnt to do without the presence of human beings.

The Chapel of Love was situated on a hill overlooking the lake. It wasn't the most scenic location in the area, but from it you could see the abandoned hotels that stood at various points along the shore.

Mila climbed the three steps to the porch of the reception cottage and saw that the door of the office was boarded up. There was no way of moving the boards. Next to the door was a window, also blocked by planks of various sizes, but you could see inside through the cracks. Mila took her torch from the pocket of her leather jacket, moved her face closer to the window and shone the torch inside.

Another face smiled at her.

Mila took a step back. Once she had regained her composure, she realised she was seeing a Cupid similar to the one above the entrance. For a moment, she thought he had abandoned his post in order to scare her off, but it was just a cardboard cut-out. She moved closer again and, apart from her own reflection in the glass, saw a reception desk covered in dust and a display stand for brochures, some of which had fallen on the floor. In full view on one of the walls was a poster with the Chapel of Love logo and the various packages available to customers. According to the text, couples had a choice of how to make their dreams come true. The chapel could be decorated in a number of different styles with evocative, exotic names. You could choose Venice or Paris, or settings inspired by films like *Gone with the Wind* or *Star Wars*. The bottom lines of the poster listed the prices of the various ceremonies, all of which included a free miniature bottle of French champagne.

There was a sudden gust of wind behind Mila, which made her shiver and turn round. The same wind, continuing its course, made one of the doors of the chapel squeak.

Someone seemed to have left it open.

*

Since the moonlight was strong enough to light her way, she switched off the torch. She advanced into the open space between the buildings. Her footsteps crunched on the asphalt, which had crumbled during the long winters. The shadowy wind followed her, dancing between her legs. As she walked, she took out her gun and gripped the handle firmly. The low buildings around her seemed like ruins from some nuclear disaster. The doors and windows were mouths open on shadowy rooms, guarding the darkness of secret worlds, or maybe just the nothingness that fear is made of. Mila kept moving forward, leaving them behind her. From inside, the darkness stared at her progress with black eyes.

She should have called someone, especially Boris. *I'm behaving like one of those women in horror films who seem determined to get themselves killed*, she thought. But she knew the reason. It was just another match in her constant challenge. It was the monster pretending to be asleep inside her that was telling her to keep going. The monster that guided her hand every time she cut her flesh with a blade. The monster she fed with her pain and fear, hoping

81

to assuage its hunger, because if she didn't, she had no idea what it might do to her. Or make her do.

Reaching the entrance to the chapel, she stopped for a moment. Then she walked up the steps that separated her from the doors. She looked in and immediately felt the breath of darkness in her face. She recognised the smell. That's the one positive thing about death: it doesn't hide, it always makes things quite clear to the living. Then she heard the sound. As light as a mass of whispers, but as frenetic as a machine.

She pointed her torch inside, and a heaving swarm of creatures scattered in a second. Some of them, though, paid no attention to her and continued with their task.

The centrepiece of a scene that evoked the Middle Ages was a filthy mattress on which a figure lay strapped down.

Mila fired in the air, and the shot echoed across the square as far as the lake. At last, the rats left the body. Only one hesitated, turning to stare at her for a few moments, its little red eyes filled with hatred of the intruder who had disrupted its meal. Then it, too, vanished into the shadows.

Mila stood looking at the corpse. It was male, of indeterminate age, and was wearing a T-shirt and blue boxer shorts.

The head was enclosed in a plastic bag that had been secured around the throat with insulating tape.

Mila took a step back, lowered the torch, and was just reaching for the mobile phone in her pocket when she saw something glinting on the mattress. The moonlight filtering in behind her had caught something on the dead man's hand. She moved in to take a closer look.

On the fourth finger of the left hand, which the rats had stripped bare of flesh, was a wedding ring.

14

The area was now off limits.

There were barriers across the road, and in order to further deter anyone who might wish to visit the lake, a luminous sign warned of a landslide ahead. For the moment, though, police officers were the only people present in this deserted place.

While waiting for her colleagues to arrive, Mila had sat down on the steps of the fake church to keep guard on the corpse. She had seen dawn trying to force its way above the horizon and flood the valley. The lake had been tinged a fiery red, accentuated even more by the foliage of early autumn.

The pale daylight had mercilessly revealed the full horror of the spectacle behind her. But Mila was surrounded by a strange kind of peace. Exhausted by fatigue and fear, she felt nothing. Without moving from where she was sitting, she had heard the wail of sirens come closer, then seen the flashing lights emerge from the dip at the end of the road and advance towards her like a liberating army.

As soon as the halogen lamps came on to illuminate the crime scene, the horror had disappeared, giving way to cold analysis.

The forensics team had already secured the perimeter and

were collecting exhibits and taking pictures of anything that might constitute evidence. In the choreography centred on a dead body, it was now the pathologist's turn to perform his solo alongside a corps of undertakers.

'All is as it seems, nothing is as it seems,' was Chang's convoluted verdict as he bent over the victim.

While police officers came and went outside, the only people present inside the chapel apart from the technicians were Mila and Gurevich, who didn't seem very pleased with the doctor's pronouncement. 'Could you be more specific?'

Once again, Chang looked at the body lying on the sodden mattress, naked apart from his underwear and the plastic bag over his head. 'Not really.' His answer betrayed the fear the inspector instilled in him.

Chang's indecision irritated Gurevich. 'We need to know the time of death as soon as possible.'

The problem was the rats, which had altered the condition of the body. The hands and feet had suffered most, and were almost completely devoid of flesh, while the armpits and the groin bore the deepest wounds. The havoc the rodents had wrought made it hard to establish the time of death through an external examination, and therefore even harder to pin the responsibility on Roger Valin.

But if this really was Valin's work, Mila thought, it represented a radical change in his modus operandi. It was difficult to see how he could have gone from using a Bushmaster .223, thus avoiding any physical contact with its targets, to what they now had in front of them. That was why everyone was so tense.

Boris came into the chapel, and went and stood in a corner to listen.

Chang was still prevaricating. 'To arrive at a credible theory and find out how long the victim has been here, we need a post-mortem.'

This irritated Gurevich even more. 'I'm not asking for a report. I just want an opinion.'

Chang gave it some thought, like someone who already has an answer in mind but doesn't want to commit himself for fear of making a serious mistake that would subsequently be thrown back in his face. 'I'd say death took place at least twenty-four hours ago.'

There were two implications to this. The lesser of the two was that even if the mystery of the launderette telephone number had been solved earlier, the man with his head in the plastic bag wouldn't have been saved. But the more important consequence was that the killer couldn't have been Roger Valin.

Obviously, this possibility didn't thrill Gurevich. 'Another murderer on our hands.' He shook his head, thinking of what this discovery might lead to. 'All right, let's see who the dead man is.'

At last they were able to proceed with the unveiling of the victim's face. Mila hoped it would help them solve this new mystery.

'I'm about to remove the plastic bag from the head of the corpse,' Chang announced. He changed his latex gloves, fitted a LED frontal lamp to his head, picked up a scalpel and approached the body.

With two fingers, he lifted the edge of that strange shroud away from the face, while with his other hand he made a precise cut in the plastic, starting at the level of the parietal bone.

While the others concentrated on the operation and waited patiently for the outcome, Mila kept staring at the wedding ring on the fourth finger of the victim's left hand. She was thinking of the woman who didn't yet know that she was a widow.

Chang finished his incision below the victim's throat. He put the scalpel down and started delicately removing the strip he had cut.

At last he revealed the victim's face.

'Shit,' was Gurevich's first reaction. It was clear to everyone that he had recognised him.

'It's Randy Philips,' Klaus Boris confirmed. Remembering that he had that morning's paper in his pocket, he took it out and handed it to his colleague. 'Page three.'

Inside was the photograph of a refined-looking man with an arrogant smile. Even though there could be no doubt, Gurevich compared the picture with the face of the corpse, then read out the headline: '"Philips slips up: Judge sentences defendant because his lawyer does not appear in court."'

While Chang completed the examination of the head, Boris turned to his colleagues. 'Randall "Randy" Philips, thirty-six, specialising in domestic violence cases. Usually on the side of the men. His defence strategy was to dig up the worst dirt he could find about the wives and girlfriends. If he couldn't find any, he'd make it up. His speciality was to make the unfortunate women look like trash. It was incredible. Even if the poor woman appeared in court wearing dark glasses to hide her bruises, or was in a wheelchair, Philips could still twist things to make the jury believe she'd asked for it.'

Mila noticed the amused looks exchanged by Chang's men. That boorish male camaraderie reminded her of Randy Philips's appearances on television. His motto had been: 'It's always easy to judge a woman . . . even if it's other women doing the judging.' In most cases he managed to obtain either an acquittal or a considerably reduced sentence for his client. He had earned the nickname 'wife-punisher' as well as the less-than-affectionate 'Randy the Bastard'.

'We may be able to reconstruct what happened,' Chang

announced after his brief examination. 'First he was stunned with an electric weapon, a Taser or a cattle prod.' He pointed to the throat, where there was an obvious if light burn. 'Then he was strapped down and the bag was put over his head. Within a short time, respiratory acidosis led to death.'

This last piece of information was greeted by a moment's silence.

'Was Randy Philips married?'

The unexpected question came from Mila. Everyone turned to look at her, Gurevich with an especially dubious expression.

'I might be wrong,' Boris said, 'but I don't remember his having a wife.'

Without a word, Mila pointed to the left hand of the corpse and the wedding ring she had spotted thanks to that beam of moonlight when she had found the body.

Silence fell again.

It was a kind of retribution.

'Randy forced to marry his own death in a chapel of love, can you believe that?' Chang said ironically as he left the crime scene, making sure he wasn't overheard by Gurevich. Not content with that remark, he went on, 'It's a bit like someone was saying to him: Now you're in a marriage you can't get out of.'

Just like a woman trapped in a dream of love that conceals a nightmare, Mila thought. A woman unable to get a divorce because she has no job, no income, forced to take the abuse because she's less scared of being beaten than of losing everything. A woman who summons up the courage to report her husband's violence but then, thanks to Randy, sees her torturer walk free.

'We'll need to establish if more than one person was involved in the killing,' Gurevich said as Krepp and his team took possession of the place again to complete the work that had been interrupted to make way for the pathologist.

'Just one,' Krepp said dismissively, in his usual cantankerous tone.

'Are you sure?' Boris asked.

'When we arrived and sealed off the scene, I asked my men to check the shoe prints on the chapel floor. It wasn't too difficult, because of all the dust accumulated over the years. Apart from those left by Officer Vasquez, the prints belonged to the victim and to one other person who wore size five shoes.'

'Go on,' Gurevich urged him, his curiosity aroused.

'Outside, we found clear traces of car tyres. We have yet to work out how Philips and the killer got here. I think it would be useful to have the lake dragged.'

The only reason the murderer might have had to get rid of Randy Philips's car, Mila thought, would have been to avoid spoiling the surprise for whoever found the body. Everything had been set up so perfectly, it would have been a pity to ruin it.

'Maybe we should take a closer look at that wedding ring,' Krepp went on.

'If there are any prints on it, you have to find them for me,' Gurevich said.

Krepp muttered something under his breath, then knelt next to the mattress and lifted the corpse's bony hand so gracefully, it looked almost like a romantic gesture. He slipped off the ring and took it to the van parked outside where he had his equipment.

In the open space between the buildings, an officer brought two cups of coffee for Gurevich and Boris. He paid no attention to Mila. Mila kept an appropriate distance from her superiors, but kept her ears open to catch what they were saying.

'Nobody reported Randy missing.'

'No surprise there, if he lived alone. Maybe he didn't go to his office, and didn't keep his secretary informed of his movements. He was involved in many things and obviously had lots of secrets.' Boris made a dispirited gesture. 'But if we rule out Roger Valin – then who killed him?'

Mila had the feeling that there was much more to this than appearances suggested. She would have liked to join in the conversation with her superiors but didn't step forward. It was Gurevich who included her.

'What do you think, Vasquez? Someone abducted Philips and brought him here to kill him. How do you explain that?'

Until now he had made her feel invisible, and yet here he was asking her opinion. She moved closer to the two men. 'I don't think the killer abducted Philips. It would have been too complicated and too risky. I think he tricked him into coming here. Then he stunned him, tied him up and did the rest.'

'Philips was no fool. Why would he come to an isolated place like this?' Gurevich's question didn't sound to Mila like a criticism of what she'd said. He wasn't dismissing her theory – if anything, he was trying to understand it better.

'I can think of several reasons why. The killer may have pretended to have something Philips wanted – maybe some dirt on the wife or partner of one of his clients. Or maybe they already knew each other and Philips had no reason to mistrust him.'

'Go on, Officer Vasquez. Don't be afraid.'

Gurevich clearly sensed that Mila had come to a conclusion but couldn't make up her mind whether to put it to them.

'I think it was a woman.'

Boris's eyebrows went up. 'What makes you think that?'

'Philips thought we were inferior beings, and was convinced he could handle the situation: that's why he was so sure of himself. Plus, only a woman could have had a reason to take her revenge on him.'

'You're thinking this was a revenge killing, just as it was for Valin?' Boris asked.

'I'm not thinking anything yet, it's too soon for that. But I know that this gullibility on the part of Philips and the size of the ring, which is surely more suitable for a woman, do seem to point to that.'

'I've found something,' came Krepp's voice from the forensics van. The three of them went in together.

Krepp was sitting at the counter, examining the wedding ring under a microscope.

'There are no prints,' he announced. 'But there is an interesting inscription on the inside.' He reached out his hand to switch on the monitor connected to the microscope. A magnified image of the ring appeared on the screen. 'It's a date, the date of the wedding, I assume ... 22 September.'

'That's today,' Boris exclaimed.

'Yes, but the engraving's definitely a couple of years old. You can tell by the opaque patina on it.'

'Happy anniversary,' Gurevich said.

'There's something else apart from the date.' Krepp turned the ring under the microscope to reveal another inscription. In this one, the lettering looked very different: it was rougher, more rudimentary, and certainly hadn't been made by an expert. In the furrows, which were almost like scratches, the metal was shinier. 'This was done recently,' Krepp said.

This last discovery seemed to give the inscription a more urgent significance:

h21

Gurevich glanced anxiously at Boris. '22 September, 21 hours. It seems that on top of the two murderers we need to find, we now also have an ultimatum.'

15

No one had any idea what would happen after 21 hours.

In the meantime, though, they had established that Randy Philips had driven to the Chapel of Love in his Mercedes. It had been found at the bottom of the lake, just as Krepp had predicted. That meant the killer must have had his own vehicle, which he had used to get away after the murder.

If they ruled out abduction, they had to figure out why Philips had been so naive as to fall into the trap of going alone to such a deserted place. Mila's intuition that a woman might have been involved had immediately caught on, and many now agreed with her.

A group of police officers was still going through the records in Philips's office, searching for anything that matched the date on the wedding ring.

22 September was the only lead they had amid many – too many – other things they were still in the dark about.

First and foremost, there was the connection between the Belman massacre and the killing in the chapel, a connection discovered only thanks to Mila's brainwave about the old telephone number. There didn't seem to be anything linking the victims, so the only possible link had to be between the perpetrators of the crimes.

During the years when he had been missing, Roger Valin had met someone – a woman? – and together they had hatched a plan for mass murder.

That was the only explanation Mila could come up with as she roamed the corridors of the department like an extra. What had happened, though, wasn't of major importance right now. What mattered was what might be about to happen.

The big emergency now was the ultimatum they'd been given.

As the hours passed, measures were devised to prevent or discourage another murder. Many officers were called back on duty, and shifts were stepped up. It had to be made clear to the killer or killers that the city was well defended, and for that purpose road blocks were set up and the number of patrol cars increased. The regular informants were told to keep their eyes and ears open. The heavy police presence in the city might even persuade some of the underworld bosses to help, if only to get the police off the streets as soon as possible and stop hampering their activities.

To avoid arousing suspicion in the media, a press release had been issued announcing a large-scale operation against organised crime. The newspapers, TV and the internet were now buzzing with attacks on yet another pointless public relations exercise at the taxpayer's expense.

Meanwhile, at Headquarters, there was a succession of more or less restricted meetings aimed at developing a strategy. The top-level ones were chaired by the Judge. There were others all the way down the chain of command. In spite of all she had contributed so far, Mila was soon relegated to the less important ones. She had the distinct impression her role had been deliberately cut down to size, as if they wanted to leave her out of the investigation.

At about five o'clock, she left the upper floors of the department and went back down to Limbo. As evening approached, the fear of what would happen was increasing, but it had been too long since Mila had last slept and she needed to rest if she was going to keep a clear head.

She went to ground in what had once been a storeroom, but which she had equipped with a camp bed for the times she stayed in the office after her shift was over. She took off her trainers and used her leather jacket as a blanket. The cosy little room was completely dark apart from the yellowish light filtering in through the gap under the door. That light was enough to make her feel safe, as if someone out there was watching over her while she was in the dark. Lying on her side with her legs tucked up and her arms crossed, she couldn't get to sleep at first. Then her adrenalin level dropped and her tiredness won out.

'We've got it.'

Mila half-opened her eyes, not sure if she was hearing the words in a dream or in reality. They had been spoken in a calm tone, in order not to startle her. She looked more closely: the door was only slightly ajar, so that the light wouldn't be too blinding. Captain Stephanopoulos was sitting at the foot of the camp bed, cradling a steaming cup in his hands. He held it out to her, but instead of taking it Mila looked at her watch.

'Don't worry, it's nineteen hours. The ultimatum hasn't expired yet.'

Mila sat up and finally accepted the cup of coffee. She blew on it before taking a sip. 'So what is it we've got?'

The search of Philips's office had yielded the desired result. 'A name. Nadia Niverman.'

Even though she had been the first to come up with the theory,

Mila was surprised to hear a woman's name. 'Nadia Niverman,' she repeated, not even noticing she was holding the cup in mid-air.

'She was Eric Vincenti's last missing persons case,' Steph recalled. 'They've just called from upstairs. Apparently, they need you again.'

Mila spent the next ten minutes on the phone with Boris. Before that, she used the computer on Eric Vincenti's desk to email Boris the file on Nadia Niverman's disappearance, which dated back a couple of years.

Nadia Niverman was a thirty-five-year-old housewife, five and a half feet tall, blonde. She was married on 22 September. Three years later, she had separated from her husband because he regularly beat her.

'Don't tell me, her husband was a client of Randy Philips,' Boris said over the phone. 'That's a good motive for revenge.'

Mila couldn't get over it.

'Mila, what's going on? Why the hell are these missing people coming back?'

'I don't know,' was all she said. She didn't understand. It was incomprehensible, and that scared her.

Roger Valin and Nadia Niverman had both gone missing, but their disappearances were separated by many years.

'If they found out about this, the media would call them "the killer couple". Everyone's going crazy here. The Judge has called an emergency meeting.'

'I know. Steph's just gone upstairs.'

'I don't understand why Nadia didn't kill her husband instead of his lawyer,' Boris said. 'Or maybe the ultimatum was for him.'

'Have you warned him?'

'We've taken John Niverman to a safe place. He's getting round-the-clock protection, but you should see how shit-scared he is.'

As in the case of Valin, Nadia's photograph had not been circulated to the media. The big difference between the two cases was that Nadia's disappearance was comparatively recent, so there was more chance of finding out where she had been during her time away.

'Boris, what do you want me to do? Should I come up?'

'No need. We're going to grill the husband to see if there's anything the bastard didn't tell us about his ex-wife at the time she went missing. Then we'll look through her file and see if there was anyone who may have helped her disappear two years ago: an acquaintance, a girlfriend. I'd like you to do the same. Can you check to see if Eric Vincenti left any notes on the case that weren't included in the official report?'

They hung up, and Mila immediately got down to work.

She scrolled through the file on the computer screen. Eric Vincenti had put everything in chronological order. This method was only used in missing persons cases. In homicides, for instance, they always worked backwards, in other words, starting with the victim's death.

Eric Vincenti always took great care in writing his reports. They were like stories.

'It's essential to preserve the emotional impact,' he always said. 'It's the only way to keep the memory alive. Anyone reading the file later should grow to like the missing person.'

According to Vincenti, that way his successor would truly commit himself to search for the truth. Just like he did, Mila thought.

I look for them everywhere. I'm always looking for them.

Mila looked at the photographs included in the file. They

showed the passing of time on Nadia's face, but it was the look in her eyes that aged the most. There was only one thing that could produce such a result.

Mila knew only too well the corrosive effects of pain.

16

Nadia Niverman had been beautiful once. The girl all her male classmates wanted to marry. A champion athlete, outstanding grades, an actress in the school plays. She had continued to excel academically during her years at university, where she studied philosophy. By the age of twenty-four, Nadia was an independent and mature woman. After graduating, she did a Master's degree in journalism, and was hired to work on a part-time basis in the editorial offices of a television company. Her career looked all set to progress. Then one day she met the wrong man.

Compared with her, John Niverman was nothing. He had dropped out of high school, dropped out of the army, and already had one failed marriage under his belt. Having inherited a small but successful haulage company from his father, he had let it go to the dogs.

A destroyer, Mila thought.

Nadia met John at a party. He was tall and handsome, the kind of lovable rogue everyone liked. She fell for him. After a brief engagement, just a couple of months, they married.

Mila could imagine how it had gone after that. Nadia knew from the start that John liked a drink but she was convinced he could handle it, and in time she hoped she'd be able to change him.

That was her biggest mistake.

From what Nadia had told the social workers, the problems started a few months after the wedding. They would argue over unimportant things, just as they had when they were engaged, only now there was something new in their arguments, something Nadia couldn't immediately put her finger on. It was mainly a feeling she got from the way John behaved sometimes. For example, he'd start yelling insults at her and gradually move closer to her, one inch at a time. But then he'd back away at the last minute.

Then, one day, he hit her.

It was a mistake, he said. And she believed him. But she noticed a new glint in his eyes, which she had never seen before. A wicked glint.

Eric Vincenti had obtained a great deal of intimate personal information from reading the complaints Nadia had made to the police over the years, complaints she always withdrew after a few days. Maybe she felt embarrassed that friends and relatives would find out, or maybe she was ashamed to face a trial. Or maybe because when John sobered up he would ask her to forgive him and Nadia would give him a second chance. There had been lots of second chances over the years. You could count them, along with her bruises. At first, they were the kind of bruises you could easily hide with a roll-neck sweater or a liberal amount of foundation. Nadia thought there was no reason to worry as long as there was no blood. Mila knew how it worked for some women: you just have to raise the bar of what you're prepared to tolerate, and you can carry on living as you always did. When you're beaten, you're grateful no bones were broken. And when a bone does get broken, you somehow convince yourself that it could have been worse.

But there was something that hurt more than the beatings. A sense of powerlessness and fear that never left Nadia Niverman. The knowledge that violence was always simmering under the surface and could break out over nothing. She just had to do or say the wrong thing, and John would punish her. She just had to ask one question too many, even a perfectly normal one, like what time he would be back for dinner. Or maybe he would simply find something inappropriate about the way she spoke to him, even in her tone of voice. The most trivial thing could serve as a pretext.

It struck Mila that anyone who hadn't experienced something like that would read this story, wonder why Nadia hadn't run away immediately, and come to the conclusion that, if she was willing to accept such things, then maybe they weren't as bad as all that. But Mila knew the mechanism of domestic violence, in which the roles are clear and unchangeable. It was fear that kept the victim tied to her oppressor, because it produced a paradoxical effect.

In Nadia's wounded psyche, the only person who could protect her from John was John.

There was just one thing over which Nadia had defied her husband. He wanted a child, and she secretly took the pill.

Even though she was convinced that the drunken, half-conscious intercourse John sometimes forced her to have involved no risk, she had kept firmly to her decision. She herself might be prepared to put up with a lot, but she would never force that on another creature.

One morning, though, she came back from the supermarket with a strange sensation in her belly. Her gynaecologist had told her that, even with the pill, there was a tiny chance of getting pregnant. Nadia knew at once that she was expecting a child.

The test confirmed it.

She would have liked to have an abortion, but couldn't convince herself that it was the right thing to do.

She somehow managed to tell John. She was scared that he would immediately lash out at her, but in fact, much to her surprise, he actually grew calmer for a while. There were still arguments after he had been drinking, but no matter how heated they became he didn't hit her. Her pregnant belly had become her armour. She couldn't believe it. She started to feel happy again.

One morning, Nadia was due at the gynaecologist's for a scan. John had offered to take her because it had started to snow. He had that absent, slightly melancholy expression alcoholics have when they have just woken up. He didn't seem angry, though. Nadia put on her coat, took her bag and stood at the top of the steps, ready to put her gloves on. It all happened in an instant. The sudden, violent pressure of hands on her back, the world suddenly disappearing beneath her feet, the feeling that you no longer know what is up and what is down. The first rebound off one of the wooden steps, with her hands instinctively rushing to shield her belly. Another somersault, with more of an impetus than before. The wall coming up to meet her face, the corner of the handrail against her cheekbone, her hands, defeated by centrifugal force, letting go. Another knock, then a third, completely at the mercy of gravity. Her belly cushioning the blow. The fall at last stopping. No pain, no noise, and, worse still, no reaction. Everything seems calm inside, too calm. Nadia remembered John looking down at her from the top of the steps, his face impassive. Then he had turned and walked away, leaving her there.

Mila's lack of empathy prevented Mila from understanding how Nadia had felt. The only emotion she could access was anger. Of course, she felt sorry for the woman, but she feared that she was more like John.

The police couldn't ignore this new incident, with or without an official complaint. What had happened looked too much like attempted murder. They made it clear to Nadia that if she made up a story to exonerate John, saying for example that she had tripped, he would try again. And this time, it wouldn't be the child that died, it would be her.

And so she summoned up the courage. After lodging a complaint, she did everything by the book, even going to stay in a refuge for abused women where he couldn't find her. John was taken into custody, and was refused bail because he had resisted arrest. Nadia's biggest victory wasn't that she had put up with this monster for so many years, but that she obtained a quick separation.

But then Randy Philips came along.

All he had to do was exhibit a pair of high-heeled shoes in court. No witnesses, no other evidence to prove what kind of mother she was. A woman who, during pregnancy, isn't willing to give up a habit even when it might make walking a bit risky on a winter's day with snow on the ground. A woman who doesn't think about the wellbeing of the creature she's carrying inside her.

That day, John was released. And Nadia vanished.

She didn't even take any clothes with her, or any object from her past life, maybe because she wanted people to believe that her ex-husband had done away with her. And indeed it looked for a time as if John was going to be charged. But Randy Philips was able to show that there was no evidence against him. And so Nadia lost that round, too.

Once she had finished reading the file, Mila began thinking. She had to be clear-headed and put aside any feelings of anger she might have. After what she had been through, Nadia didn't deserve to be hunted down like a common criminal. Maybe Valin did. His grief at his mother's death was genuine and understandable, but he could have got over it and moved on. Damn it, he'd had seventeen years to do just that.

The killer couple, as Boris had called them, actually consisted of two very different individuals. At some point in her life as a fugitive – which was how Mila saw a woman who escapes a violent husband – Nadia had met Roger, they had told each other their life stories, and they had discovered they shared the same secret, and maybe the same hatred towards the world. Pooling their resentment, they had created their homicidal little association.

I don't understand why Nadia didn't kill her husband instead of his lawyer, Boris had said on the phone earlier, and had then corrected himself by adding, *Or maybe the ultimatum was for him.*

Mila wasn't sure. If Nadia had really wanted to kill her ex-husband, she would have done things the other way round. What was the point of killing Randy in such a spectacular fashion if it meant that her husband would then be protected by the police? If she had done it the other way round, no one would have suspected she also wanted to kill Philips.

The ultimatum wasn't meant for John Niverman, Mila was sure of that. Boris had said the man was shit-scared. The retribution Nadia had chosen for Philips was the wedding ring and a painful death in a chapel intended for newlyweds. The one for her ex-husband was fear. She didn't want him to have a quick, easy death. She wanted to put him through what she had gone through, to live with the constant threat of danger, to know that at any moment it could be his turn, to experience the unbearable wait for a certain fate.

The telephone on Eric Vincenti's desk rang, startling Mila. She waited a moment before picking up the receiver.

'What are you still doing there?' It was Steph. 'It's past eleven. The ultimatum expired ages ago.'

Mila looked at the clock on the wall. She hadn't noticed the time. 'And?' she asked with trepidation.

'Nothing. Just a couple of men who had a knife fight in a bar, and a man who chose this evening to try and kill his business partner.'

'Have you seen the Judge?'

'We were dismissed a quarter of an hour ago. That's why I'm calling you. I knew you'd still be there. Go home, Vasquez. Is that clear?'

'Yes, Captain.'

17

A thin, cold fog drifted along the streets like a phantom river.

It was almost midnight as Mila went to pick up her Hyundai from the department car park. As she approached it, she noticed it had two flat tyres. She was immediately on the alert: in her head, anything unexpected became a potential danger. A couple of flat tyres might mean that someone wanted to force her to walk and was waiting to attack her further down the street. She immediately dismissed her own paranoia: it was all the fault of the case she was working on. In fact, she only had to look around her to realise that the neighbouring cars had suffered the same treatment. It was obviously the work of hooligans getting their own back on the police. The same thing had happened the month before.

Mila decided to take the metro. She walked to the nearest stop.

The street was deserted, the rubber soles of her shoes moaned on the damp pavement and her footsteps echoed between the buildings. As she reached the entrance to the metro, she was hit by a current of air from a train that was just coming in. She ran down the steps, hoping to make it in time. She inserted her ticket into the barrier but it got stuck. She tried again, to no avail. She heard the train pulling away and decided to give up.

A few moments later, as she stood waiting at the machine for her new ticket, a voice said, 'Have you got something for me?'

Startled, Mila turned abruptly. A boy in a hooded top stood there, his hand held out. Her first instinct was to punch him in the face. But she filled his hand with the change from the machine and watched him walk away looking pleased with himself.

At last, she got through the barrier. She set foot on the escalator – it was the kind that started automatically as soon as someone stepped on it. She got to the platform just as a train was discharging a small group of passengers on the opposite platform. It left a few seconds later, half empty.

Mila looked up at the indicator board. She had four minutes to wait.

She was alone in the station. But that didn't last. She heard a mechanical sound and saw that the escalator had started again. Any time now, another passenger would appear. But Mila didn't see anyone. The steps kept descending like a steel waterfall, with nobody on them. *They're taking too long*, she said to herself. And at that moment, she remembered a lesson she had learnt during the Whisperer case.

The enemy never appears immediately, but first creates a diversion.

Mila put her hand on her gun and turned to the other platform, alert for danger. That was when she saw her.

Facing her on the opposite platform was Nadia Niverman, staring at her with the hollow eyes and timeworn face of someone who has just come back from a long journey. She was wearing a duffle coat that was too large for her and her arms hung wearily at her sides.

They both stood there, motionless, for what seemed like an

eternity. Then Nadia raised her right hand to her face and put a finger to her lips, calling for silence.

Scraps of waste paper rose from the rails, like puppets moved by invisible strings, and performed a brief dance for them. Mila almost didn't notice that the wind stirring them was in fact the precursor of a gust of cold air, but came to her senses when she realised that a train was coming on the other side.

It was near, and would soon interpose itself like a barrier between the two platforms.

'Nadia!' she called out, taking fright when she saw the woman step forward. It was in her heart rather than in her head that she realised she had to do something. Without thinking, she was about to jump onto the rails, intending to ford that invisible river of dust and wind. The train's lights appeared in the tunnel. It was going fast, too fast. She wouldn't make it. 'Wait!' she called to Nadia, who was looking at her without moving a muscle.

The train was some fifty yards away. Mila felt a current of air slap her in the face. 'Please don't!' she found herself pleading as a metallic gallop drowned out her voice.

Nadia smiled, took another step forward and, as the first car started to brake, dropped onto the rails with a grace Mila would never forget. It was as if she was taking flight. The only sound she made was a dull thud, immediately covered by the screeching of the brakes.

Mila was still for a moment, staring at the metal curtain that had come between her and the scene. Then she moved, running up the stairs and across to the other side and down onto the platform where Nadia had been standing only a short time before.

A small knot of people that had got off the train had gathered at the end of the platform near the tunnel. Mila pushed her way through. 'Police,' she said, showing her badge.

The driver was beside himself with anger. 'Fuck – that's the second time this has happened to me this year. Why don't they do it somewhere else?'

Mila looked down at the track. She didn't expect to see blood or human remains. That's how it is, she thought, it always looks as if the train has swallowed the person.

Sure enough, the only thing lying there was a woman's shoe.

For some reason, the image reminded her of her mother, and the time she had tripped while walking Mila to school – a woman who was always so self-controlled, so concerned with her appearance, brought low by a broken heel. Mila remembered her lying there with her hair dishevelled, one shoe missing, a flesh-coloured stocking laddered at the knee, her cool beauty, which always attracted male glances, deflated by the laughter of a passer-by who didn't even stop to help her up. Mila had felt angry with that lout and sorry for her mother – that was the last time she had felt anything in her heart, before the emptiness had arrived.

The memory made her turn to the group of passengers pressing behind her. 'Please step back,' she said. That was when she noticed, standing beyond the group, the boy with the hooded top she had seen earlier. Maybe he had heard the commotion and had run down to take a look, although he had come no closer than the foot of the stairs. But Mila's attention was drawn to the object he was holding, which he was looking at with a puzzled expression.

'Hey, you!' she called.

Startled, the boy turned.

'Drop that,' she ordered, walking towards him.

Scared, he took a step back. Then he held the object out to her. 'I found it here,' he said, pointing at the platform. 'I wasn't trying to steal it, I swear.'

It was a velvet case for a ring.

Mila took it from him. 'Go,' was all she said, and he obeyed. She looked down at the object, immediately connecting it with

Randy Philips's death. But if the wedding ring was on his dead finger, what was inside the case now?

Mila hesitated for a moment, then carefully opened the case, fearful of the secret it would reveal. Although she immediately recognised what she saw, she stared at it uncomprehendingly.

It was a tooth caked with blood. A human tooth.

18

'Trust me, I've seen plenty of mutilated corpses.'

The young sergeant had wondered where the victim's pre-molar had ended up, and why the killer had chosen to take away that particular souvenir.

'Some choose an ear or a finger. Once, under a dealer's bed, we found the head of the junkie he'd murdered a few hours earlier. God alone knows why he decided to take it home with him.'

The anecdote didn't surprise Mila and Boris. If they hadn't shown up, the missing tooth would have ended up as just another of the strange things you tell your colleagues about over lunch. Mila in particular had no desire to listen to macabre stories while, just a mile or two from there, the undertakers were removing Nadia Niverman's body from the tracks over which that damned train had passed.

Fortunately, the young sergeant stopped talking, and the three of them continued on their way past the display rooms of the vast second-hand furniture store – a rustic-style kitchen, then a bedroom in grey gloss, a Victorian-style living room, another kitchen, modern this time. As they walked, Mila thought back over all that had happened that evening, starting with the punctured tyres on her Hyundai: clearly a ploy by Nadia to lure her to the metro station. Before killing herself, the woman had gestured to her to be quiet. Then she had given her that clue. Mila still couldn't get over how easy it had been to locate this new crime scene. All they had had to do was type the word 'tooth' into the department's computer and this strange murder had come up, a murder that had taken place that very morning, around dawn, just as the best minds in the Federal Police had been converging on the Chapel of Love.

'We've found no trace of the killer,' the sergeant said. 'Not a single print, even though there was a lot of blood. It's a professional job, if you ask me.'

The victim was a fifty-five-year-old man of Arab descent named Harash.

'They called him "the undertaker",' the sergeant went on. 'He made his business out of emptying dead people's homes. Whenever anyone kicked the bucket, he'd show up and make the relatives an offer for all his things. He'd buy the whole lot in one go. There are lots of people who live alone. They leave everything to a child or grandchild, who hasn't a clue what to do with the furniture or the appliances. Harash would solve their problem for them, and they couldn't believe they were making money out of all that old stuff. All the undertaker had to do was read the obituaries and sniff out the best deals. But everybody knows he started off by lending money at extortionate rates. Unlike other loan sharks, though, when debtors couldn't pay their instalments, Harash didn't break their bones straight away. Instead, he took their possessions and sold them on, pocketing the income as an advance on the interest.'

Mila looked at the objects around her. They belonged to other times, other lives. Each of them had a story to tell. Who had sat on that sofa? Who had slept in that bed or watched that TV?

They were the leftovers of other people's lives, the wrapping to be recycled after their deaths.

'That's how Harash was able to afford this place,' the sergeant continued, as they walked past yet another anonymous living room. 'After a while, he didn't need to lend money any more. He could be open and upfront about his activities. He'd been lucky, he'd only ever spent a couple of years in prison. He could have gone straight for the rest of his life, but then, on the quiet, he started doing a bit of loan sharking again. As they say, old habits die hard. Harash was greedy, that's for sure, but I think the main reason he did it was for the thrill of dominating the lives of the poor devils who needed his money.'

The sergeant stopped in front of a door with an emergency handle. He pushed it, and the three of them found themselves in a storeroom crammed with furniture of lower quality than that on display. The sergeant led them to the far end of the room, where there was a small office.

'This is where it happened.'

He showed them the spot on the floor where the body had been found. The outline of it was still visible, marked with yellow tape.

'The killer pulled out his teeth one by one with pliers. He was trying to get him to reveal the combination for that.' He pointed to the wall safe. 'It's an old model, with two dials.'

Someone had written, in a crooked hand, a sequence of numbers and letters on the wall in black marker:

6-7-d-5-6-f-8-9-t

Mila and Boris looked at the door of the safe: it was still closed.

'He didn't get all of it,' the sergeant said, reading their

thoughts. 'That mean old bastard was stubborn. He thought he could hold out. The thief got the combination out of him number by number and letter by letter, but Harash croaked before revealing the final part. The pathologist says his fat heart couldn't cope with the strain. Did you know that having a tooth pulled out without an anaesthetic is as painful as being shot?' He shook his head, whether in disbelief or amusement it was hard to say. 'He took out eight teeth. We found seven, and you have the last one. I wonder why he took it away with him ...'

'Because you weren't meant to find out the real reason the killer came here,' Mila said.

'What?' The sergeant didn't understand.

'You were meant to think this was just a burglary that went wrong.' Mila took a pair of latex gloves from the pocket of her jacket, put them on and went to the safe.

'What's she going to do?' the sergeant asked Boris. By way of replying, the inspector gestured to him to just stay there and watch.

Mila started fiddling with the two dials, one with numbers, the other with letters. Looking back and forth between the safe and the wall, she turned them to compose the sequence written in black marker. 'It's not quite correct to say that Harash's killer didn't get the whole combination out of him. It's just that the last part was written somewhere else.'

At the end of the sequence, Mila added h-2-1.

When she pulled the handle towards her, she had confirmation that the engraving inside the wedding ring found on Randy Philips's finger hadn't been an ultimatum.

'Damn,' the sergeant exclaimed.

The inside of the safe was stacked high with banknotes, and there was also a gun. Nothing, though, seemed to have been touched.

'I'll get Krepp over here straight away,' Boris said, excited. 'I want a specialist to turn this place inside out again for prints.'

'The local forensics team did a good job,' the sergeant said, with a touch of irritation at the lack of trust shown by his superior. After all, to him, Mila and Boris weren't colleagues, just two intruders sent by the department to call his methods into question.

'Nothing personal, Sergeant,' Boris replied dismissively. 'Thank your men on our behalf, but we've already wasted a lot of time. Now we need the top people.' He took out his mobile to make the call.

Mila was still examining the inside of the safe. She was disappointed. She had expected to find a decisive clue. *Is this all there is?* She almost hoped to be proved wrong. *It's not possible, I don't believe it.*

Meanwhile, behind her, the argument continued. 'Do whatever you like, but you're making a mistake, sir.' The sergeant was clearly annoyed. 'If you'd listen to me for one minute, I can tell you that the killer—'

'That's just it,' Boris cut in angrily. 'The killer. You keep talking as if there's only one person involved, but it's possible there were two or even three. We can't tell at this stage, can we?'

'No, sir, there was only one,' the sergeant answered in a firm, almost defiant tone.

'How can you be so sure?'

'We have him on video.'

19

The video could turn out to be a turning point.

The sergeant had arranged a screening in his office, enjoying the unexpected popularity he had gained with his latest revelation.

It was just after two in the morning, and Mila was feeling the effects of sleep deprivation and low blood sugar. She had just got herself a bar of chocolate from the vending machine next to the lifts.

'I don't know why, but nothing would surprise me now in this case,' Boris said to her in a low voice as they took their seats in front of the screen.

Mila made no comment.

The sergeant cleared his throat. 'We're almost certain that the killer came into the store through the main door. He may have come late in the day, he may have come in with other customers, and then hid and waited for his moment – that we don't know. What we do know is that he used a side door to get away. As luck would have it, a few yards away there's a pharmacy that has a security camera.'

The local police had promptly confiscated the footage they were about to watch.

The projector was linked to a computer that was being operated by an officer with some IT expertise. 'It all happens fairly quickly,' the sergeant announced. 'So you have to pay attention.'

There was the deserted street, filmed with a wide-angle lens. Cars were parked at the kerb. According to the caption at the top, it was 5.45 in the morning. The image was nothing to write home about, being grainy and sometimes jerky. Mila and Boris waited, not saying a word. Suddenly, a shadowy figure flitted past just below the camera and was gone in an instant.

'That's our man leaving after the murder,' the sergeant said.

'Is that it?' Boris asked.

'Now comes the best part,' the sergeant said, signalling to the officer operating the computer.

The image changed: another street, filmed looking along the length of it. The date and time were the same.

'Once we'd spotted the suspect, we followed him on the other security cameras in the area. That's how we reconstructed his movements: this footage, for instance, comes from a supermarket.'

This time, the killer walked right in front of the camera, and they could clearly see that he was wearing a raincoat and a small hat.

'Unfortunately, his face is hidden by the brim of his hat,' the sergeant said.

The images kept changing: security footage from a cashpoint, from a gym, and from a traffic camera at a junction. On none of them was the suspect's face visible.

'He knows,' Mila said. They all turned to look at her. 'He knows how to avoid being filmed. He's clever.'

'I don't think so,' the sergeant said. 'There are at least forty security cameras in that area. Not all of them are easy to spot. There's no way he could have pulled off something like that.'

'And yet he did,' Mila said, confidently.

They sat staring at the screen, hoping that the killer had made a mistake. After another five minutes of images, the suspect suddenly turned a corner and disappeared.

'What happened?' Boris snapped. He didn't sound at all pleased.

'We lost him,' the sergeant hastened to explain.

'What do you mean, you lost him?'

'I never promised you a face, just proof that he was acting alone.'

'Then why did you make us sit through ten minutes of this stuff?'

The inspector was furious. The sergeant could find nothing to say in reply. He was clearly embarrassed. He signalled to the officer at the computer. 'Now let's watch it in slow motion.'

'I hope for your sake there's something worth seeing this time.'

'Wait,' Mila said. 'Do you have any film from the afternoon before the murder?'

The sergeant couldn't see the connection. 'Yes, we confiscated the footage for the whole day. Why?'

'He knew where the cameras were. He must done a recce.'

'But not necessarily on the day before the murder,' the sergeant said.

An idea was forming in Mila's head. *He wants to be recognised, but not by these amateurs. It's like Roger Valin's clothes or Nadia Niverman's wedding ring. He's putting us to the test. He wanted to be sure the right people were sitting in front of the screen: in this case, those already working on the case. Why?*

'Let's try all the same,' Mila said. 'We may hit it lucky.' Though if she was right – and she was sure she was – it didn't depend on luck.

Boris turned to her. 'If you're right, all we need to see is the footage from one camera. Which one would you suggest?'

'The traffic one: it covers a wider area and the images are sharper.'

The sergeant gave instructions to the officer at the computer and they proceeded.

The same street as before came up on the screen, but in daylight this time, with a constant coming and going of cars and pedestrians.

'Could you fast forward?' Mila asked.

The people and vehicles started moving at a frenetic speed. It was like watching a silent comedy, but nobody felt like laughing. The suspense was tangible. Mila prayed she hadn't made a mistake. It was the only chance they had, but she was aware that she might have got hold of the wrong end of the stick completely.

'There he is!' the sergeant cried triumphantly, pointing at the edge of the screen.

The other officer slowed the images down to normal speed. They saw the man with the little hat walking along the pavement at the edge of the frame, with his head down and his hands in the pockets of his raincoat. He stopped at the crossing, joining other pedestrians who were waiting for the lights to turn green.

You're going to have to look up, Mila said inwardly. *Otherwise, how are you going to spot the camera?* She was urging him. Come on, do it.

The pedestrians started crossing, indicating that the lights had changed. But their man didn't move.

'What's he doing?' the sergeant asked, puzzled.

They kept watching. Mila was beginning to understand. He chose the traffic camera for the same reason we did, she told herself: the angle is wider and the images are sharper. She was sure he was going to show them something.

The suspect crouched down beside a manhole cover to tie his

shoelace. Then he lifted his head and looked straight at the camera. Very calmly, he raised his hand, took off his hat and waved it.

He was greeting them.

'That's not Roger Valin,' Boris said.

'Son of a bitch,' the sergeant cried.

They hadn't recognised him.

There was only one person in that room who knew him: Mila. Not so much because his face was on the wall of the Waiting Room as because for a long time he'd sat at the desk opposite hers, down there in Limbo.

I look for them everywhere. I'm always looking for them.

That was what he'd so often said to her before he disappeared.

Eric Vincenti.

Berish

Exhibit 511-GJ/8

Transcript of the text message sent by the
killer of Victor Moustak – drowned at
███████████████████ on 19 September ██████ –
from the victim's mobile phone:

*The long night has begun. The army of shadows
is already in the city. They are preparing for
his coming, because he will soon be here. The
Wizard, the Enchanter of Souls, the Goodnight
Man: Kairus has more than a thousand names.*

20

Everybody wanted to talk to Simon Berish.

Something about him made people want to open up and reveal their most intimate and personal details. This wasn't a recent discovery. Looking back, he realised it was a talent he'd always had. Like when his teacher had, for some reason, confided in him, and only him, that she was having an affair with the deputy headmaster. Not in so many words, but that was the implication of 'Mr Jordan read your composition when he was at my place the other day, Simon. He says you write really well.'

And once, Wendy, the prettiest girl in the school, had told him, and only him, that she had kissed the girl who sat next to her, adding 'It was *magicocious*' – she had actually invented a word to describe it. But why had she chosen the biggest nerd in the school to reveal it to?

Actually, a few years before Wendy or that teacher, his father had done pretty much the same thing. 'If one day you don't hear my car coming up the drive, don't worry about me, just take care of your mum.' That probably hadn't been the best thing to say to an eight-year-old boy. He hadn't done it to give Simon a sense of responsibility, but rather to take the weight off his own shoulders.

Those memories had suddenly all come flooding back, and now he couldn't stop thinking about them. They weren't particularly sad or unpleasant. But after such a long time, he didn't know what to do with them.

' . . . and Julius was so drunk that he went into the wrong shed and, instead of a cow, there was this great big bull staring at him.' Fontaine laughed heartily at the end of his story, and so did Berish, even though he had lost the thread about halfway through. Fontaine's rustic adventures had taken up the whole of the last half hour. That was a good sign. It meant the farmer was starting to relax.

'How well do you do with oats?' Berish asked.

'I manage to fill up a couple of silos every season. Not bad, I'd say.'

'Good Lord, I didn't realise it was that much. And how will it go this year? I hear the rainfall's been a problem.'

Fontaine shrugged. 'When times are bad, I just tighten my belt a bit, increase the proportion of fallow land, and the following year I sow corn and make up for lost time.'

'I thought it was a continuous cycle these days, I didn't know you still had to let the land lie fallow.' Berish was using what he remembered from his high school agriculture classes. Unfortunately, he had almost exhausted his knowledge. He couldn't afford to lose that connection with Fontaine now: they'd grown quite close in the past hour. He needed to change the subject, though, and he didn't want the transition to seem too abrupt. 'I bet half of what you make goes to the tax people.'

'Oh, yes, those bastards can never keep their hands out of my pockets.'

Taxes. Now there was an excellent topic of conversation. It always worked. It created a sense of complicity, which was just what he needed. He pressed home his advantage. 'There are two people who give me cold shivers whenever I get a call from them: my accountant and my ex-wife.'

They both laughed. In reality, Berish had never been married. But the lie had been a useful way of slipping a forbidden word into the conversation.

Wife.

It was after four in the morning and they still hadn't talked about Fontaine's wife, even though she was the reason they were here, the reason Berish had driven more than forty miles. It struck him that if anyone saw them now, they wouldn't be able to distinguish them from two men who had just met in a bar and were chatting over a beer to pass the time. Except that the location couldn't have been further removed from a bar.

The interview room in this small country police station was narrow and stank of stale nicotine.

Places like this might well be the last remaining public buildings where you could still smoke. Berish had let Fontaine bring in his tobacco and his cigarette papers. His colleagues considered cigarettes a reward. By law, they couldn't stop the suspect from going to the toilet, and they had to provide him with food and drink if he asked for it. So they delayed permission to go to the toilet, or supplied only small bottles of water as warm as piss, but there was always the risk the suspect would lodge a complaint of harassment. Smoking, though, didn't feature on the list of rights, and if the interviewee was unlucky enough to be a heavy smoker, then forcing him to abstain could be a way of putting on the pressure. Berish didn't believe in that. Just as he didn't believe in threats, or in good cop/bad cop tactics. Maybe that was because he himself never needed such tricks, or because in his opinion statements made under pressure weren't always completely reliable. Some police officers made do with them. But Berish believed there could only be one confession, made in one place at one time and that some sins couldn't be admitted in instalments.

Especially unpremeditated murders.

Everything that followed – statements made to the prosecutor or repeated in court for the benefit of the jury – was distorted by the perpetrator's need to negotiate with their own conscience about the crime they'd committed. Because the hard part wasn't having to face the judgement of others, but living night and day for the rest of their life with the thought that they weren't the good person they thought they were.

And so there was only one magic moment when they could really let it all out.

Fontaine was close to his, Berish could sense it. He knew it from the way the farmer reacted to the word 'wife'.

'Women can be a real headache,' Berish said, his tone as casual as possible. But he had opened the door to the ghost of Bernadette Fontaine, who walked into the interview room and sat down silently between them.

It was the fourth time Fontaine had been summoned to give an account of why nobody had seen his wife in nearly a month. No one mentioned the word disappearance, let alone murder, because there was not enough evidence to back up either.

Legally, the correct term for her was 'untraceable'.

This was because Bernadette was in the habit of leaving home every time a man promised to take her away from that stupid husband of hers who smelt of manure. Most of these men were lorry drivers or travelling salesmen who noticed how susceptible she was to flattery and won her over by telling her she was far too pretty and intelligent to stay in this shitty little village. She always fell for it. She'd climb in their lorry or their car but never get further than the first motel they came to. They'd stop there for a few days, the man would have his fun then slap her around a bit and send her back to the fool who had married her. Fontaine would take her back without asking any questions – in fact, without saying a word. That probably made Bernadette despise him all the more, Berish thought. Even if he hit her, it would be a reaction. Instead of which, all she had in her life was this useless man who she knew had never loved her.

Because if you really love someone, then you're also capable of hating them.

Her husband was her jailer. He kept her on a leash, smugly convinced that she'd never find anyone better than him anyway. The mere sight of Fontaine was a reminder every day – every damned second – that even if she was prettier and more intelligent than other women, she didn't deserve anything more out of life than him.

Whenever Bernadette ran away, though, it was never for more than a week at most. This time it had gone on for much longer.

Everyone would have thought she'd finally run off with her latest pickup – an animal feed salesman – but a couple of witnesses said they'd seen her come back to the farm. After that, she hadn't been shopping in the village, nor had she gone to mass on Sunday. So rumours had started circulating that Fontaine had finally got tired of his role as the idiot husband and had done away with her.

The local police had given credence to the gossip because, according to a friend of Bernadette's who had gone to find out why she never returned her calls and had stopped coming round, all her things were still in the house. And when a couple of officers had called by to check it out, her husband had told them that she'd left in the middle of the night with only her pyjamas and a dressing gown. No shoes and no money.

Of course, no one believed that story. But given Bernadette's previous absences, the police had nothing to charge Fontaine with.

If he really had killed her, the easiest way to dispose of the body would have been to bury it in one of his fields.

The police had searched part of the property with dogs but, given how extensive the farm was, it would have taken hundreds of men a couple of months to search it all.

That was why Fontaine had already been summoned to the police station three times. They had grilled him for hours, taking turns. All to no avail. He kept insisting on his version. Each time, they'd had to let him go. For the fourth round of questioning, an expert had been called in from the city. Someone people said was good at his job.

Everybody wanted to talk to Simon Berish.

Berish knew that his colleagues had messed things up. Because the hardest thing to make a man confess isn't that he's committed a murder, it's where he's hidden the body.

That was the reason why, in four per cent of murder cases, the body was never found. Even if he could get Fontaine to admit he had killed his young wife, he was sure he wouldn't get a word out of him about the hiding place of the corpse.

It was quite common, a way for the killer to avoid coming to terms with what he had done. That made confession a compromise: I'll tell you I did it and you let me get the victim out of my life for ever by leaving him or her where he or she is.

Of course, this kind of deal had no basis in law. But Berish knew perfectly well that all the interrogator had to do was foster the culprit's illusions.

'I was married once, and that was once too often,' he joked, preparing the ground. 'Three years of hell, fortunately no children. Though now I have to pay alimony to her and her chihuahua. You've no idea what that dog costs me, and on top of everything else it hates me.'

'I have a couple of mongrels. They're good guard dogs.'

He had changed the subject, which wasn't good, Berish thought. He had to get him back on course. 'I got myself a hovawart years ago.'

'What kind of breed is that?'

'The name means "court guardian". It's a nice big dog with long, light-coloured blond hair.' He wasn't lying. He really did have a hovawart, named Hitch. 'My wife's dog's a pain in the neck. But my father always used to say: when you marry a woman, you're responsible for her and everything she loves.' It wasn't true. His father – the bastard – had run away from his own responsibilities by putting them all on the shoulders of a child of eight. But right now he needed a solid parent capable of imparting nuggets of wisdom.

'My father taught me to work hard,' Fontaine said, his face darkening. 'I am what I am only because that's how he was. I inherited this business and all the sacrifices it involves. It's not an easy life, trust me. Not easy at all.' He had lowered his head and was shaking it slowly, engrossed in his own sadness.

He was withdrawing.

Berish felt the eyes of Bernadette's ghost on him, apparently reproaching him for letting her husband drift further off course. He had to reel him back in quickly or he'd lose him for good. He had to take a chance, but if he didn't get it right it would all be over. If he had understood correctly, Fontaine's father had been just as much of a bastard as his own, so he said, 'It's not our fault we are the way we are. It always depends on who came before us in this fucking world.'

He had introduced an important concept: 'fault'. If Fontaine was the touchy type or if he thought he'd had the best father in the world, he would take offence and this six-hour 'chat' would have been in vain. If, on the other hand, he felt any resentment at having always acted out of weakness, then Berish had just provided him with the opportunity to blame someone else for his own shortcomings.

'My father was strict,' Fontaine said. 'I had to get up at five and get through my chores on the farm before going to school. He expected everything to be done the way he wanted. If I ever made a mistake, then I'd really catch it.'

'I got plenty of slaps from my father, too,' Berish said, to encourage him.

'No, mine used his belt.' Fontaine said this without rancour, in a tone almost of disappointment. 'But he was right. Sometimes, my head was elsewhere. I used to daydream a lot.'

'When I was little, I was always thinking about travelling on spaceships – I loved science fiction comics.'

'I don't even know what I used to think about. I always tried hard to concentrate, but my mind would just wander after a while, and there was nothing I could do about it. Even the teachers said I was slow. But my father wouldn't listen to any excuses, because when you work on a farm you can't afford to be distracted. So every time I did something wrong, he'd teach me a lesson. And I learnt it all right.'

'I'll bet you didn't make any more mistakes after that.'

Fontaine paused for a moment, then said, almost under his breath, 'There's a piece of land near the swamp where nothing's going to grow this year.'

For a moment, Berish wasn't sure he'd actually said it. He didn't reply, letting silence fall between them like a curtain. If it bothered Fontaine, it was up to him to move it aside and show him what was behind it – the rest of that story, terrible as it might be.

'It's probably my fault,' Fontaine went on. 'I used too much herbicide.'

He had put himself and the word 'fault' in the same sentence.

'Will you take me to that piece of land near the swamp?' Berish said calmly. 'I'd really like to see it.'

Fontaine nodded and looked up. There was the hint of a smile on his face. He had put things right. It was exhausting, carrying it all inside you, but at last he was free of it. He didn't have to pretend any more.

Berish turned. Bernadette's ghost had gone.

Within a short time, a line of police cars was speeding across the landscape. Throughout the ride, Fontaine seemed calm. He had earned that serenity, Berish thought. He had done his duty, he had taken care of his wife, and now Bernadette would have a funeral service and a more dignified burial.

Everybody wanted to talk to Simon Berish.

Actually, it would have been more accurate to say that everyone wanted to confess something bad to Simon Berish.

21

Eric Vincenti had kept a copy of *Moby-Dick* in his desk drawer.

Mila found it hard to believe that a man who had found the meaning to his life in Melville's book could be a murderer who had tortured his victim to death by tearing out his teeth.

Moby-Dick, he had said, contained all there was to know about their work. The way Ahab searched for the white whale was just like the way they searched for those who had vanished into an ocean of nothingness. 'There are times, though, when you're not sure which of the two is the real monster in the story, Moby-Dick or Captain Ahab. Why does Ahab insist on looking for something that doesn't want to be found?'

His doubts over the meaning of their work had been summed up in that simple question.

The man who had killed Harash 'the undertaker' was a man of incredible depth, capable of gestures of disarming kindness, like remembering to bring Mila coffee every morning when she was on duty in Limbo. As he worked, he had always kept a little radio on at very low volume, tuned to a station broadcasting only opera, and hummed along to the arias. This was the same Eric Vincenti who, whenever they went to talk to a missing person's parents, always kept a clean handkerchief in his pocket in case they needed to cry. Eric Vincenti, who always offered you mints. Eric Vincenti, who never got angry. Eric Vincenti, the police officer who seemed the least like a police officer of all those she had met.

'Eric used to drink,' Steph said in a low voice. His office had the welcoming silence of a church. 'He was a slave to alcohol.'

'I never realised.'

'Because he wasn't like Nadia's husband, who turned nasty when he had a hangover and took it out on his wife. Eric was what I call a professional alcoholic. People like that can spread a major bender through an entire day without letting it show because they never actually get drunk. He may have seemed like a regular guy, but the dark side always takes its toll in the end. We all wear masks to hide the worst part of ourselves. Eric's mask was the mints.'

Beyond the door of the office, the Crime Squad was removing everything from Vincenti's desk – except his copy of *Moby-Dick*, which had gone missing at the same time he had – hoping to find something that would point them in the direction of the next piece in this intricate puzzle.

So far, they hadn't found any clue to a future crime.

It wasn't in Harash's safe, and it wasn't on his body. This might have been a sign that the whole thing was over, but police officers were distrustful by nature. And they were often right to be that way, Mila thought. She had trusted Eric, for instance, and now she was paying the price.

'Nadia killed herself in front of me in the metro in order to leave me that tooth as a clue ... because I was the only person who could have recognised Eric in that video,' Mila said, with a mixture of bewilderment and bitterness. 'But why Harash? What did a loan shark have to do with Vincenti or his drink habit?'

The motive of personal revenge, which seemed to hold true in the case of Roger Valin and Nadia Niverman, seemed to break down here. In addition, Nadia had chosen to kill herself, whereas both Eric Vincenti and Roger Valin had resurfaced only to then vanish again into thin air. That made things all the more complicated.

'Eric's curse was this place,' Steph said. 'His face was already up there on the wall of the Waiting Room, only he hadn't noticed, and neither had I.' There was a note of regret in his voice now. 'I should have realised that he'd reached breaking point, that he couldn't take the burden of all those unresolved lives any more. Every police officer has to come to terms with his job and all the ugly things it involves. Limbo swallows people and doesn't give them back – at least not the way they were before. It doesn't occur to our colleagues in the department that what they investigate might corrupt them. But the void starts speaking to you one day, and to some it may become attractive. It hands you a clue and convinces you that you can get others. In the meantime, you start to give it part of yourself. But you can't live with the void, you can't make a deal with the void. In the end, you open your door to it, like it's a friend coming to help you. It comes in and starts looting everything.'

'Just like the undertaker,' Mila said.

Steph stopped. He hadn't thought of that. 'Right, just like Harash.' He stared straight ahead of him for a moment, lost in his own thoughts. 'I think Vincenti chose to kill him because he was a parasite who took advantage of the same kind of suffering that usually drives people to disappear.'

Who is the monster, Ahab or Moby-Dick?

The muscles of the captain's face relaxed. 'In all honesty, I can't bring myself to condemn Eric for what he did to that bastard.'

It was a strong statement from Steph, as if he were meeting the darkness halfway. It should have been 'us here, and him there'. But the shadows were always trying to spread, Mila thought, and even officers of the law couldn't resist the temptation to take a look on the other side to see what was there. Basically, everyone needed a white whale to pretend to chase.

Steph rose from his chair and looked at her. 'The meeting's about to start upstairs. But whatever they say about Eric, we won't think any differently of him. The sins of Limbo stay in Limbo.'

Mila nodded. Her gesture was like an absolution.

An emergency briefing session had been called in the department.

The bigwigs were present, along with the section chiefs and the Crime Squad's analysts. There were about fifty people in all. Everything was still top secret.

Mila walked into the room with Captain Stephanopoulos. A mere officer like her wasn't usually allowed to take part in a high-level meeting like this, and she felt out of place. Steph winked at her: they had to stick together because a kind of collective guilt was hanging over Limbo thanks to Eric Vincenti's involvement – they were viewed with suspicion simply because they had worked with him. On top of which, she felt uncomfortable because she was the only woman there.

The most conspicuous absence in that gathering of alpha males was the Judge.

But even without deigning to put in an appearance, the Judge was there in spirit. Mila was convinced that the security camera high up on one of the walls was not as inactive as it looked.

'Gentlemen, if you'll take your seats, we can start,' Boris said, calling to attention all those who had assembled around a small table on which stood two large thermos flasks of hot coffee brought in for the occasion.

Within a few seconds, they had all taken their places.

As the lights were turned down so that they could watch the screen, Mila felt the tingling at the base of her neck which usually meant that something was about to change irreversibly.

That hadn't happened in seven years.

It wasn't necessarily a warning sign. It might just be the darkness that was always inside her rearing its head and claiming its share of attention.

A beam of dusty light crossed the room and struck the screen behind Boris. There, side by side, were the photographs of Roger Valin, Nadia Niverman and Eric Vincenti.

'Six victims in less than forty-eight hours,' Boris said. 'And all we have at the moment on those responsible are questions. Why did these people decide to disappear years ago? Where have they been all this time? Why are they coming back now in order to kill? What's the plan behind this?' He allowed himself a pause for effect. 'As you can see, there are a lot of grey areas, a lot of missing connections. But one thing's for sure: whatever's going on, we'll put a stop to it.'

In police jargon, these words were meant to convey a sense of certainty and determination. But Mila was good at reading body language, and what she picked up here was mainly a feeling of powerlessness and confusion.

When the enemy is beating us, she thought, *our chief concern is not to react but to conceal our weakness*.

But she, too, had been wrong. She had thought Valin and Niverman had met after running away from the world, that they had put together their respective tragedies and resentments and worked out a deadly plan. But the addition of a third protagonist had called the theory of the killer couple into question. The presence of Eric Vincenti was proof that they were dealing with a bigger, more unpredictable phenomenon. That scared her, and she really hoped this meeting would lead to effective countermeasures.

'After much discussion with the Judge, we've decided on a strategy. But in order to put a stop to what's happening, we have first to understand it.' Boris motioned to Gurevich, who now stood up and took his colleague's place in front of the screen.

The first words he uttered were: 'We're dealing with a terrorist organisation.'

*

For a moment, Mila genuinely wondered if she had heard correctly. But then she realised Gurevich was being serious. Terrorism? That was crazy.

'Basically, the nature of these acts is self-evident,' he went on. 'It was the last homicide in the series that opened our eyes. If we rule out resentment as a motive, and given that the connection between the perpetrator and the victim is far from clear, there can be only one explanation.' He looked about the room. 'Subversion.'

An anxious murmur started at the back of the room and rolled forward like a wave. Gurevich put his hands up to silence it.

'Gentlemen, please,' he said. 'The cells of this organisation consist of single individuals, acting apparently out of revenge, but whose true aim is to create panic and destabilise the established order. We know only too well that fear is more powerful than a thousand bombs. These people crave publicity, but we've denied them that by imposing a media blackout.'

This was an absurd version of events, Mila thought. But then police officers were good at stretching reality: when they found themselves with their backs to the wall, rather than admit that they were in difficulty they twisted the facts to make it seem as if they had been just one step behind the enemy all the time.

At this point, the footage from the traffic camera came up on the screen behind Gurevich, showing Eric Vincenti walking along the pavement, stopping at the crossing with other pedestrians, then crouching beside a manhole cover to tie his shoelace before taking off his hat and insolently greeting those watching him.

To Mila, it seemed ridiculous to think of her former colleague as a fanatic fighting against society and its symbols. All the same, she couldn't help thinking how different Eric looked in those images.

'There's no point denying that it's going to be hard to predict the next target,' Gurevich went on, putting his hands together behind his slightly stooped back. 'Let's not forget that the three killers we've had so far had never previously committed any crimes, and so had no record. Roger Valin was identified partly because he revealed his name to the only survivor and partly thanks to a description of the clothes he was wearing, Niverman was identified thanks to the wedding ring on her victim's finger, while Eric Vincenti was recognised by a colleague.'

Mila was grateful he didn't mention her name.

'This supports the theory that we aren't dealing with professional criminals, so we mustn't expect to find a perfect fingerprint, blood or DNA match in our records, now or in the future. But we don't need it. As of now, the anti-terrorism protocol kicks in. Our priority is to track down Roger Valin and Eric Vincenti and find out who their accomplices are, who's backing them, who's hiding them.' He started making a list on the fingers of one hand. 'First: Valin used a Bushmaster .223 rifle to carry out his massacre: where did he get it? A mere bookkeeper doesn't get hold of a toy like that by himself. Second: we need to comb the internet, check out all the extremist websites, see who's been making wild statements, expressing anti-government opinions, even offering practical advice on how to put their crazy plans into action. Third: we need to pull in political activists, arms suppliers, anyone who's theorised in the past, however vaguely, about striking at the established order. We need to hit these people hard. Our motto will be "zero tolerance". One thing's for certain: we'll get the bastards.'

There was spontaneous applause from the audience. It wasn't that they necessarily felt any great conviction. It was actually a measure of their uncertainty: by applauding, they were trying to chase it away. But it was like laying a carpet over a bottomless pit. Mila knew that all those present were afraid of ending up trapped in a case they didn't understand. Gurevich had given them an easy way out and, although there weren't enough elements yet to give credence to his theory, right now her colleagues felt they had no other choice. But the inspector was making a basic mistake: labelling the murderers as 'terrorists' might have been reassuring, but it meant they wouldn't have to bother thinking about what else might be going on.

'If we isolate them and pull the ground away from under their feet, we'll discourage further attacks,' Gurevich concluded, smugly.

Without being aware of it, Mila found herself shaking her head a little too energetically, so much so that she drew the inspector's attention.

'Don't you agree, officer?'

It was only when they all turned to look at her that Mila realised her superior was addressing her. Embarrassment burned through her. 'Yes, sir, but . . . ' she replied tentatively.

'Perhaps you have a suggestion to make, Officer Vasquez.'

'I don't think they're terrorists.' She surprised even herself by saying it out loud, but there was no turning back now. 'Roger Valin was a weak man. Maybe we shouldn't be asking ourselves *how* he's changed in the years he's been missing, but *what* triggered that change in him, what caused him to pick up an assault rifle and carry out a massacre. Frankly, I don't think his revenge has a political motive. There must be a more private, more personal explanation.'

'Actually, I think he's the typical case of the ordinary man who harbours resentment towards a society that doesn't pay any attention to him.'

'As for Nadia,' Mila went on, unperturbed, 'she couldn't even lift a finger against a husband who beat her so badly he almost killed her. I find it hard to imagine her as a terrorist.'

Negative comments were heard from around the room. Boris and Steph were both looking at her with anxious expressions on their faces.

Mila was aware of the hostile murmurs around her, but was determined to keep going. 'And Eric Vincenti was a colleague of mine, a man who devoted his whole life to finding missing persons, and who ended up haunted by them.'

'Are you trying to make us feel sorry for them? Are you trying to tell us they were victims, too?' Gurevich gave her an accusing look. 'I advise you to be very careful about what you say, Officer Vasquez, because there's a serious risk that you'll be misunderstood.'

'I was referring to the fact that, as you yourself said, none of them had criminal records, and that they were people the world had abandoned a long time before they abandoned the world.'

'Precisely the kind of people a subversive organisation would be interested in: people with little or nothing to lose, who are in constant conflict with society and want to pay it back for some of the wrongs done to them. It's obvious someone recruited them, and helped them disappear. They were given a cover and training. Then they were assigned a mission.'

'You're right that there's some kind of purpose,' Mila said, throwing him somewhat. 'But we shouldn't make the mistake of being satisfied with first impressions just because of past experience.' In the room, the grumbling hadn't stopped. Mila looked up, straight into the camera that had been watching the whole meeting in silence from the beginning. 'I say there's definitely a plan behind all this. I say there's no way of predicting the next victim or the next perpetrator.' She was forced to raise her voice to be heard over the hubbub around her. 'I just hope with all my heart that it is terrorism. Because, if it isn't, it's going to be hard to stop.'

23

It had already taken more than an hour to replace the tyres on the Hyundai.

Mila would have liked to go straight home after the meeting. Instead of which, having forgotten all about the unpleasant surprise she'd had earlier, she rediscovered it when she went back to the department car park. It was like living through it all over again, with the addition of the anger she was feeling as a result of the meeting.

So she'd had to call the breakdown truck to take her car to the garage. Now, even as she watched the punctured tyres being replaced, her mind was elsewhere, and her calm was merely apparent.

They hadn't thrown her out of the meeting, but after her intervention the discussion had continued as though she hadn't uttered a word. She had sat back down and waited in silence for the meeting to end, ignored by everyone. That was why she was angry with herself. She had made herself look ridiculous. And she was angry with Eric Vincenti because she felt she had been deceived by someone she respected.

Were you Ahab or Moby-Dick? she wondered. *Neither of them, or maybe both, that's why I never noticed anything.*

A clear motive was lacking for the murder her colleague had committed – if you could call tearing someone's teeth out until they died murder. Mila was troubled by such gratuitous cruelty. And in addition, there was nothing to point the police in the direction of the next murder. That was another reason everyone's nerves were on edge.

There was one thing they were all sure of: this affair was far from over.

So far, the chain of events had been revealed through specific clues, a series of riddles, like a treasure hunt: Valin's clothes, Harash's tooth, the video of Vincenti ... Why would Vincenti have made sure he hadn't left any traces at the scene of the crime, and then practically shown off to the security cameras?

Maybe the solution is so simple, we just can't see it, Mila told herself.

But, instead of concentrating on the next link in the chain, the department was indulging in mad theories. Terrorism? Did they really think all they had to do was give their fear a name?

Shortly afterwards, the Hyundai was returned to her with new tyres. Mila retrieved her sunglasses from the dashboard, and set off for home. It was a beautiful day, with a bright blue sky and only a few clouds to scatter the odd touch of shade.

But as Mila drove, she was seeing more than what was in front of her eyes. The video footage of Eric Vincenti was constantly on a loop inside her head.

She had always been sure Vincenti would return one day. That the darkness would spit him back out like an indigestible morsel, restoring him to Limbo as living proof that it's always possible to come back.

She had imagined Eric walking into the office with a cup of coffee for her, sitting down at his usual desk as if he'd never been away, switching the radio to that station that broadcast only opera, and getting down to work.

Instead of which, she had encountered him in the most unexpected of places.

She would never be able to forget that figure caught by the traffic camera: the man in the raincoat crouching beside the manhole cover to tie his shoelace and then, with a wild, defiant gesture that still made her shudder, removing his hat in greeting.

What was the point of that pantomime? Was it really just so that he would be recognised?

If so, it seemed to substantiate the terrorism theory. But Mila saw something else in those images: her colleague – she still couldn't bring herself to think of him as her ex-colleague – had undergone the baptism of darkness. And that performance for the camera meant one thing above all.

That Eric Vincenti was now dancing with the shadows.

The afternoon sun was already setting behind the houses, flooding the living room of Mila's apartment with golden light, and chasing the dust from the stacks of books as if intent on driving it away. On the other side of the street, the two giants smiled down at the people passing beneath their billboard – even at the tramp pushing a supermarket trolley full of plastic bags and old blankets. Mila would leave some food for him on the dustbin at the end of the alley later. Not a burger this time, maybe some chicken soup.

Feeling calmer now, she moved away from the window, sat down at the laptop and switched it on. Within a few minutes, the software connected to the hidden camera was operational. Once again, the little girl's room that she had under surveillance came up on the screen.

The child was sitting drawing at a little round table, surrounded by a large number of dolls.

I wonder which one is her favourite.

Her long ash-blonde hair was gathered into a ponytail, leaving half her face uncovered. She was holding a coloured pencil and seemed to be concentrating hard on her work – a perfect lady at the age of six, Mila thought. She turned up the volume, but for the moment the only thing coming from the speakers was background noise.

The same woman she had seen a few evenings earlier walked into the frame, carrying a tray. She was over fifty, and still very beautiful. 'Snack time,' she announced.

The girl turned, but then went straight back to her work. 'Just a minute.'

The woman put the tray down on the little table. There was a glass of milk, some biscuits, and a couple of coloured pills. 'Come on, you can finish that later. You must take your vitamins now.'

'I can't,' the girl said, as if she had the most important task in the world to complete.

The woman came closer and took the pencil out of her hand. Stubborn as she was, the girl didn't say anything. *No danger*, Mila thought. *Everything's fine.* Then the child picked up a red-headed doll and hugged it, using it as a kind of barrier, and her little face grew sulky.

What kind of mother would I be if I didn't know the name of my daughter's favourite doll?

'Leave that thing alone,' the woman said. *She doesn't know it*, Mila thought. *Damn, she doesn't know it.*

'She isn't a "thing",' the girl protested.

The woman sighed, gave her the vitamin pills and the glass of milk, and started tidying the table. 'Look at all this mess,' she said.

The girl pretended to tie her shoelace but actually took advantage of the woman's attention being elsewhere to hide the pills in the red-headed doll's dress.

146

Mila couldn't help smiling at the child's slyness. But the smile froze almost immediately on her lips, just as her eyes stopped looking at the screen even though it was right there in front of her. The images had been replaced in her mind with footage from another camera.

Eric Vincenti stopping at the crossing with other pedestrians, waiting for the green light. Eric Vincenti crouching over the manhole cover to tie his shoelace. Eric Vincenti removing his hat in greeting.

No, that isn't it, Mila thought. *He isn't just greeting us. He wants to be recognised, of course . . . but he also wants to attract attention.*

Eric knows what police officers are like, he knows how to drive them crazy. He knew they would indulge in all kinds of complicated speculation rather than admit that they were stumped. The terrorism theory was proof of that.

But the solution is so simple we can't see it, Mila kept telling herself. She replayed every moment of the sequence in her memory, as if in slow motion.

It was the little girl's trick with the vitamins that had given her the idea.

Maybe Eric Vincenti had concealed something for them on that stretch of pavement.

24

The street corner was crowded with pedestrians hurrying home.

On the other side of the road, Mila watched the succession of high-heeled shoes, trainers, moccasins and flip-flops. None of these people were aware that an important clue on which somebody's life or death depended might be right there beneath their feet.

Not wanting to leave anything to chance, she crossed the road. She wanted to perform the same actions she had seen Eric Vincenti perform in that video footage.

First of all, she walked along the pavement with her head down, bumping into other people who weren't looking where they were going, some of whom cursed at her for slowing them down. But Mila kept her eyes peeled on the pavement, examining every inch of it, until she reached the manhole cover beside which Vincenti had crouched before looking up at the camera.

Repeating her colleague's actions, she crouched down and remained there as still as a stone, forcing the stream of pedestrians to step around her, while she looked closely at the cast-iron cover, which bore the city's coat of arms and the name of the foundry that had made it. Details nobody usually lingered over.

An object that everyone stepped on but which barely entered their field of vision.

Mila ran her fingers along the edge until she came across a folded sheet of paper. She attempted to pull it out with her fingertips but it was in too deep. She kept trying, even breaking a fingernail and cutting her finger in the process. At last she did it.

Sucking her finger to stop the bleeding, she stood up again. Without taking her eyes off the paper, and bursting with curiosity, like a child who has found a clue in a treasure hunt before anybody else, she turned the corner into an alley to get away from the other pedestrians. Hands shaking with anticipation, she unfolded the piece of paper.

It was a newspaper cutting.

To be exact, it was a short item about a murder that had taken place on 19 September – the day before Roger Valin's massacre of the Belmans.

It had been judged worthy of inclusion in the local news because of the absurd and cruel method used, although as the victim was only a small-time drug dealer it had been relegated to the bottom of the page.

According to his brother, Victor Moustak hated water. And yet he had drowned. To be precise, he had drowned in a couple of inches of murky liquid. The killer had bound him hand and foot, then plunged his face into the kind of metal bowl normally used for dogs to drink from.

The forensics team had discovered the killer's prints on one of the ropes used to tie Moustak. But no match had been found for them in records, and the perpetrator remained unidentified.

The reporter mentioned another odd aspect of the murder.

Before leaving, the killer had used Moustak's mobile phone to send a text message to the victim's brother – although there was a strong likelihood that the number had been chosen at random from the contact list. The police had chosen not to divulge the contents of that message.

When she had finished reading, Mila noticed something written in pencil at the bottom of the cutting.

P.H.V.

She took her mobile phone out of her pocket and made a call. The captain picked up immediately. 'Stephanopoulos here.'

'The series of killings may have started before the Belman massacre.'

'How do you know?'

'Eric Vincenti left me a clue.'

Steph was silent for a few moments, and Mila guessed that he wasn't alone.

'Can we talk about this later?' he asked.

'I need you to access the department's records on your computer.'

'Give me ten minutes and I'll call you back from my office.'

It was fifteen minutes before Mila's mobile rang.

'What's this all about? You should have called Boris and Gurevich.'

'To corroborate their terrorist plot idea? No way. I'll call them when I have a clearer idea what's going on.'

'Please, Mila,' he said, although he knew he'd never get her to change her mind.

'Don't worry.' She quickly told him about the newspaper article concealed in the manhole and asked him to look up the Victor Moustak case in records. 'I want to know what that text message said.'

Steph took a while to read and summarise the various police reports. When he reached the part about the text message, he laughed.

'What's so funny?'

'Trust me, Mila, you're barking up the wrong tree.'

'Are you going to tell me or not?'

He read it out: '"The long night has begun. The army of shadows is already in the city. They are preparing for his coming, because he will soon be here. The Wizard, the Enchanter of Souls, the Goodnight Man: Kairus has more than a thousand names."'

The army of shadows, Mila thought. It was a perfect definition. 'What's that all about?'

'It's the reason the police haven't breathed a word of this to the press. The whole thing's ridiculous. Listen to me and drop it.'

But Mila had no intention of letting go. 'I want to know more. Then I may well decide to drop it.'

Steph sighed, knowing he was dealing with an immovable object. 'There's someone who can tell you all about this. But before you meet him there are a couple of things you ought to know about him.'

'Such as?'

'He used to be an old-style police officer, the "shoot first and ask questions later" type. But then things changed and he rein-vented himself. He started studying anthropology.'

'Anthropology?' Mila said in surprise.

'He's become the best interrogator in the department.'

'Then why have I never heard of him?'

'That's another aspect of his personality, but you'll find that out for yourself. All this is just to tell you to avoid playing games with him. You'll have to persuade him to cooperate and that won't be easy.'

'What's his name?'

'Simon Berish.'

'Where can I find him?'

'He has breakfast every morning at the café our colleagues all go to in Chinatown.'

'Good. Going back to Victor Moustak, I also need you to check if the killer's fingerprints are in the PHV records. There was a pencilled note on the newspaper cutting.'

'I'll put a request in to Krepp but I won't tell him why I need to know.'

'Thanks.'

'Vasquez . . .'

'Yes?'

'Be careful with Berish.'

'Why?'

'He's a pariah.'

25

The Chinese café was popular with the police.

Police officers, like firefighters, tended to have their favourite spots, which they never changed. The criteria by which they chose them in the first place remained a mystery – it didn't usually depend on the quality of food or the service, or even how close it was to their place of work. It was just as difficult to pinpoint when the choice was made. Who was the first officer to set foot in that particular restaurant or café? Why did others follow? The chosen place became exclusive territory, where other customers – 'civilians' – were a tolerated but not particularly welcome minority. For the owners, it was like manna from heaven: not only did it mean a steady income, it also protected them against thieves, crooked suppliers and other criminals.

As soon as Mila walked in, she was hit by the all-pervasive smell of frying. The loud voices of the uniformed officers who filled the place were equally overpowering. A Chinese waitress greeted her and, realising she was a new customer, immediately informed her that traditional dishes were only served from lunchtime, whereas breakfast was standard international fare. For a moment, Mila was tempted to ask why a Cantonese eatery served bacon and eggs until mid-morning, but she simply thanked the waitress and looked around. It didn't take her long to see what Steph meant when he had described the man she was here to speak to as a pariah.

The other officers were in groups, chatting and joking over their breakfast. Simon Berish was the only one sitting by himself.

Mila made her way between the tables until she reached the last one at the end, which was in a partitioned booth. Berish was wearing a jacket and tie and was engrossed in a newspaper as he sipped his coffee. To his left was a plate with what remained of the bacon and scrambled eggs he had just been eating, as well as half a glass of water with ice and lemon. At his feet, a medium-sized light-coloured dog lay peacefully asleep.

'Excuse me,' Mila said to attract his attention. 'Special Agent Berish?'

He lowered his paper, seeming surprised that he had been spoken to. 'Yes.'

'My name's Mila Vasquez, we're colleagues.'

She held out her hand, but instead of shaking it, he looked at it as if it were a gun pointing at him. Mila realised that all eyes in the room had turned to them, and felt like she had just broken a taboo.

'I'd like to talk to you about one of your old cases,' she said, lowering her hand again, and ignoring her colleagues around them.

Berish didn't ask her to sit down. He left her standing there and looked her up and down with a mistrustful expression. 'Which one?' he asked.

'The Wizard, the Enchanter of Souls, the Goodnight Man. Kairus.'

Berish stiffened.

Mila was feeling more and more uncomfortable. 'It won't take long.'

Berish looked around to make sure no one had heard. 'I don't think it's a good idea.'

'At least tell me why, and I'll leave you alone,' Mila insisted, realising that he would do anything to get rid of her. 'Who is the Wizard, the Enchanter of Souls, the Goodnight Man?'

'A fictitious character,' Berish said in a low voice. 'Someone to keep the Bogeyman and the Loch Ness Monster company. He was created twenty years ago in a mood of widespread hysteria. And the media dredged him up whenever someone went missing. All they had to do to spice up the news was mention one of those names, and the audience figures would rocket. It's like having a navy suit in the wardrobe. You can wear it to a funeral, but it can also come in handy for a wedding.'

'But you believed in him, didn't you?'

'It was a very long time ago, and you were just a child,' Berish said defensively. 'Now if you'll excuse me, I'd like to finish my breakfast.' He went back to his newspaper.

Mila was about to leave. But just then, the uniformed officers at the next table stood up after paying their bill. One of them passed so close to their table that he knocked his hip against the plate Berish had left near the edge, and Berish's tie was spattered with egg. It had been quite deliberate. Even the dog under the table looked up, sensing the tension.

Mila was already dreading the worst, but Berish merely gave the animal a pat, which sent it straight back to sleep, then calmly took a neatly folded handkerchief from his jacket pocket, dipped it in his glass of water and wiped away the bits of food as if nothing had happened. A police officer had shown blatant disrespect to a superior, and in public to boot, and was now not only blithely going on his way but even smiling boastfully at his colleagues.

Mila was just about to intervene when Berish grabbed her wrist.

'Leave it,' he said, without looking at her, and held out his handkerchief.

His gentle tone told her a lot, including the reason he hadn't invited her to sit down at his table. He wasn't being rude, he just wasn't used to having company. In an odd way, Mila understood how he felt. It wasn't empathy, unfortunately, just experience. According to the police code of honour, there weren't many reasons for being made a pariah, but those there were were insurmountable. The most serious were betraying your colleagues and grassing on them. The penalty was equivalent to losing some of your civil rights, but above all it put you in a position of danger. Because it meant that those who by rights should protect you would no longer lift a finger to help you. But Berish seemed to bearing up quite well.

Mila accepted the handkerchief and wiped off the pieces of egg that had landed on her jacket, too.

'Would you like something to eat?' Berish suddenly said. 'It's on me.'

Mila sat down facing him. 'Thanks a lot. I'll have eggs and coffee.'

Berish motioned to a waitress and ordered the eggs and coffee for Mila and an espresso for himself. As they waited to be served, Berish carefully folded the newspaper and leant back against the padded partition. 'Why does someone with a beautiful Hispanic name like yours decide to call herself Mila?'

'How do you know what my real name is?'

'María Elena, right? That's what the diminutive stands for.'

'It's a name that doesn't belong to me, or maybe I don't belong to it.'

Berish took that in, still looking at her closely with his dark eyes. Mila didn't mind. There was a beautiful light in those eyes, and it wasn't unpleasant to be looked at like that. Berish seemed at ease in this situation. His thoughtful demeanour, his sturdy body, the muscles showing through his shirt, made his formal clothes seem like some kind of armour. He hadn't always been the way he was now. Steph had told her that Berish had taken up the study of anthropology. But for the moment, she wasn't interested in what had led him to make such a drastic change.

'So, what can you tell me about Kairus?'

Berish looked at his watch. 'In fifteen minutes, this place will be deserted. So enjoy your breakfast and then I'll answer your questions. Once I've done that, we'll say goodbye and I'll never see you again. Okay?'

'Fine by me.'

Their order arrived. Mila ate her eggs and Berish drank his espresso. Within a short time, as he had predicted, the café had emptied and the waitresses were clearing the tables. The noise that had reigned until a few minutes earlier gave way to the sound of dishes being removed.

Nothing changed for the dog at Berish's feet, which was still fast asleep. Berish, though, started talking again.

'I don't want to know the reason you're here, that doesn't interest me. I put this business aside many years ago. But I'll tell you what I know, even though you could easily have read about it in the relevant file.'

'It was my captain – Stephanopoulos – who suggested I speak with you.'

'Old Steph,' Berish said. 'He was my first chief when I left the academy.'

'I didn't know that. I thought Steph had always worked in Limbo.'

'Oh, no. He was in charge of the Witness Protection Unit.'

'I didn't know we had one.'

'Actually, we don't any more. It was in the days when organised crime was a big problem here and several of the bosses were standing trial. Once the emergency was over, the unit was disbanded and we were all reassigned.' He paused. 'You, though ...'

'What about me?'

Berish looked at her even more closely than before. 'It is you, isn't it?'

'I don't understand.'

'You were involved in the Whisperer case. I remember now.'

'You have a good memory. But if you don't mind, I'd like to keep my ghosts out of it for the time being and talk about yours.' She looked straight at him. 'Tell me about Kairus.'

Berish heaved a deep sigh. It was as if she had opened a door inside him that had long been closed. As Mila had sensed, there were still ghosts stirring behind that door. You could see them taking turns to appear on Berish's face as soon as he began telling his story.

26

The day before the end of the world is usually very ordinary.

People go to work, take the metro, pay their taxes. No one suspects a thing. Why should they? People continue doing what they have always done, on the basis of a simple observation: if today is just like yesterday, then why would tomorrow be any different? That was more or less what Berish was saying, and Mila agreed.

Sometimes the world ends for everyone. Sometimes only for one person.

A man may wake up one morning, not knowing that today is the last day of his life. In some cases, the end is silent, even invisible. It takes shape undisturbed, finally revealing itself in an incongruous detail, or in a formality.

The case of the Goodnight Man, for instance, had begun with a parking ticket.

The windscreen of the car bore a residents' parking permit, but two of the wheels were outside the permitted space. In their zeal, the municipal traffic wardens had spotted the infraction and one ordinary Tuesday morning, a ticket had been placed under the windscreen wiper. The next day, another one was added. And so it went on for the rest of the week, until a sticker was put on

the window, instructing the owner to remove the vehicle immediately. Finally, after nearly three weeks, a municipal breakdown
truck had done the job instead, and the car – a silver-grey Ford –
had ended up in the pound. If the owner wanted it back, he
would have to pay a substantial sum of money. The law stipulated that four months after it had been towed away, the vehicle
would be officially sequestrated. Then the owner was granted
another sixty days to pay before the item was auctioned to cover
the expenses incurred by the council. That deadline, too, had
passed. The auction at which the Ford had been offered for sale
had not attracted any customers, and so the car was sent to be
destroyed. In order to recover its expenses, the council had sent
an official to the unfortunate owner's home to seize his possessions.

That was when they discovered that the man – whose name
was André García, who had no family, who had left the army
because it had been discovered that he was gay, and who had been
living on welfare – had been missing for months.

His letterbox was stuffed with accumulated flyers and
brochures. His utilities had been cut off because he had been in
arrears. His refrigerator had turned into a crypt full of rotting
food.

At the time, journalists had been on the lookout for stories that
showed how politicians squeezed money out of the public in the
most twisted ways, making use of the law and with the full complicity of the bureaucracy.

That was how André García ended up in the newspapers.

The article recounted how that whole mechanism of perse-
cution had been set in motion and how it hadn't occurred to
anyone – until that official showed up – to simply knock at the
man's door and ask him why the hell he didn't just go and move
his damned car a couple of feet. The press had a field day, with

headlines like THE WORLD FORGETS HIM, BUT NOT THE CITY COUNCIL! or GARCÍA, GIVE US BACK OUR MONEY! SAYS THE MAYOR.

In all this, the question nobody had bothered to ask was what had actually happened to poor André. He might have left the city, he might have thrown himself in the river, but if there was nothing to suggest that he had been the victim of a crime, then it was his right to do whatever he wanted with his life. His one great merit was that he had served as an example. And since the public liked being outraged, the media had looked for similar cases where the city council, the banks or the tax authorities had continued to demand money from people who might either be dead and buried, or lying in a coma in hospital after a car crash.

So it was almost a joke when six more cases emerged. Four women and two men, their ages ranging from eighteen to fifty, who had disappeared over a period of a year.

The insomniacs.

'They were ordinary people,' Berish said. 'Just like the waitress who serves us breakfast every morning in our regular café, or the man who washes our car every weekend or cuts our hair once a month. They all lived alone. So do lots of people, you might say. Except that their solitude was different. It clung to them like ivy. It had gradually wrapped itself around them, taking up all the space, completely concealing what lay beneath. They circulated among their fellow human beings with that parasite in their bodies, a parasite that fed not on their blood but on their souls. They weren't invisible. You could interact with them, you could chat to them, exchange smiles as you waited for them to bring your coffee or your bill or your change. You saw them often, but then immediately forgot all about them. It was as if they'd never existed, only to come back to life the next time you saw them, then vanish again. Because they were insignificant, which is a lot worse than being invisible. They were doomed to leave no trace in other people's lives.'

In the course of their existence, they hadn't aroused any interest in those around them. After they disappeared, though, not only did everyone suddenly become aware of them, they even became objects of belated respect.

How could I forget that delivery boy, or the female student who collected unicorns? The retired science teacher or the widow whose three children never visited her? Or the woman with the crippled leg who managed a linen shop, or the department store assistant who spent every Saturday evening at the same bar table, hoping someone would notice her?

Somewhat arbitrarily, the media had linked these seven missing persons. Maybe they had all disappeared for the same reason, or maybe the same person had abducted all of them. The police, as so often, had followed the media's lead, investigating the possibility that a third party might be responsible. There was much debate and many theories. Even though it was never stated openly, the implication in some quarters was that it was all the work of a serial killer.

'It was like a reality show before reality shows existed,' Berish said. 'Those seven missing persons were the stars of the show. Everyone felt entitled to talk about them, to dig around in their lives and judge them. The Federal Police were in the spotlight too, and risked making fools of themselves. The only absentee was the real star: the killer. The presumed killer, obviously, because there were no bodies. Since nobody knew his name, he was given several nicknames. The Magician, because he made people vanish. The Enchanter of Souls, precisely because the bodies were nowhere to be found – that one was a bit on the "dark" side, but was good for circulation. The one that really caught on, though, was the Goodnight Man, because the only concrete thing that emerged from the investigation – the only thing the seven people had in common – was that they all suffered from insomnia and needed pills to get to sleep.'

In the normal run of things, without all that pressure, the Federal Police wouldn't have bothered all that much about a case based on such a tenuous coincidence.

'But so much attention had been created, we couldn't easily drop it. Even though nobody believed there was really a case. It ended the way a lot of people expected. No more insomniacs disappeared, people got tired of the story, and the media followed the public mood and looked elsewhere. It had begun like a farce, with that parking fine for poor García, and ended like a farce: there was no crime and no perpetrator, and that was the last anyone heard of it.'

'Until now,' Mila said.

'I assume that's why you're here,' Berish said. 'But I don't want to know anything about it.'

It was just after ten, and the Chinese café was beginning to fill with new customers, ordinary civilians taking advantage of the absence of men in uniform to demand food and a little attention.

'You've explained how the supposed culprit got those nicknames,' Mila said. 'But what you haven't told me is: why Kairus?'

'Frankly, this is the first time I've heard that name.'

Mila noticed that Berish was carefully avoiding her gaze. Berish might well be the best interrogator in the department, but maybe he wasn't such a good liar. Mila couldn't be sure, though. He had been cooperative and she didn't want to upset him now by accusing him of hiding something. 'I'll get this washed for you,' she said, referring to the handkerchief he had lent her earlier to clean herself up. 'And thanks for breakfast.'

'Don't mention it.'

Mila's mobile made a sound telling her she had received a text message. She read it, then put the mobile back into her pocket, along with the handkerchief, and stood up to leave.

Berish stopped her. 'What did Steph say about me?'

'That you're a pariah, and that I should be careful.'

He nodded. 'Very sensible of him.'

Mila bent down to pat Berish's dog.

'One thing I've been wondering, though. Why would he suggest I talk to you and at the same time put me on my guard against you?'

'You know what happens to someone who shows sympathy for one of the department's pariahs, don't you? It's like an infection.'

'I don't see any reason to be afraid. You seem comfortable enough in this role.'

Berish took in Mila's sarcasm with a smile. 'You see this place? Many years ago, a couple of patrolmen came in through that door at breakfast time and, just as you did, asked for eggs and coffee. The owner, who'd just moved here from China as it happens, had two options: tell them that what they wanted wasn't on the menu and probably lose two customers, or go to the kitchen and beat a few eggs. He chose the second option, and ever since, for three hours a day he's served food that has nothing to do with traditional Cantonese cuisine but that's made his fortune. And that's because he learnt a very important lesson.'

'That the customer is always right?'

'No. That it's easier to adapt a thousand-year-old culture a little than to change a police officer's mind when he asks for bacon and eggs in a fucking Chinese café.'

'If it's any consolation, I don't give a damn what my colleagues think of me.'

'You think this is a game where you score points for acting tough? You're wrong.'

'Is that why you didn't react before when a subordinate showed you disrespect?'

'You probably thought I was a coward, but he wasn't even getting at me,' Berish said, amused. 'When I'm alone at my table, no one dares to bother me. They pretend I'm not here or, at most, they look at me as if I'm a hair in their food: it may be disgusting but you put it aside and carry on eating. What happened this morning was for you. It was you they were trying to warn. The message was quite clear: "Keep away from him or the same thing will happen to you." If I were you, I'd follow their advice.'

Mila was amazed and angry at how blunt he was being. 'Then why do you come here every morning? Steph was sure I'd find you here. Are you a masochist, or what?'

Berish smiled. 'I started coming here when I first joined the police, and it never occurred to me to change. Although to be honest the food is no great shakes, and the smell of frying gets into your clothes. But if I didn't show up, all the people who'd like to see me dead would be proved right.'

Mila had no idea what sin Berish was atoning for, she only knew there was no remedy for it. But as far as the Kairus case was concerned, she had understood one thing. She rested one hand on the table and leant forward so that she loomed over Berish. 'I know why Steph sent me to you. You didn't give up on that case like everyone else, did you? You kept trying to find out the truth about those seven missing persons. That was when you made the mistake that turned you into a pariah. And I think you still haven't given up, even now. You still want to know what happened. Maybe you wish you could forget all about it, but there's a part of you that can't do that, though I don't know why. You pretend you're as detached as a Buddhist monk, but that's just

165

anger turned into silence. The truth is, if you gave up you'd never forgive yourself.'

Berish held her gaze. 'What makes you say that?'

'Because I'd be the same.'

He seemed impressed by her answer. Maybe he was used to other people's harsh and sometimes unfair judgement, but she was the first police officer he'd met who wasn't afraid of the curse surrounding him. 'You'd better forget all about this business. I'm telling you that for your own good. Kairus doesn't exist. The whole thing was a collective hallucination.'

'Do you know what PHV means?' Mila asked abruptly, referring to the pencilled letters at the bottom of the newspaper article left in the manhole by Eric Vincenti.

'What are you getting at?'

'Potential Homicide Victim. There's a special section of records for them in Limbo. It contains prints and blood and DNA samples of missing persons who may have been murdered. We take them off personal effects – a TV remote control, a toothbrush, hair from a comb, a toy. We keep them in case a body needs to be identified.'

'Why are you telling me this?'

'Four days ago, a drug dealer was murdered. To be more precise, he was drowned in two inches of dirty water in a dog bowl. The killer left prints on the ropes he used to tie the victim. But the prints weren't identified.'

'He didn't have a record.'

'He did. Not as a criminal, but as a victim. PHV.' Mila took her mobile out of her pocket and showed it to Berish. 'I got this text five minutes ago. According to forensics, the fingerprints are those of André García, a gay ex-soldier who disappeared twenty years ago.'

Berish turned pale.

'Now, if you like, you can tell me you don't give a damn about what's behind all this.' Mila savoured every second of the silence. 'But it does look like one of the Goodnight Man's supposed victims has returned.'

27

Mila Vasquez knows.

There was no doubt about it. She had walked out of the Chinese café, leaving him alone with her last words echoing in his ears.

Announcing André García's return from the world of shadows.

It wasn't either random or unpredictable. He had returned in order to kill. That jeopardised a lot of things. Things that Simon Berish had, in spite of himself, decided to protect.

Berish sat in his office with his feet on the desk, rocking dangerously on his chair and staring into space, like a mad tightrope walker suspended over his own thoughts.

Hitch was watching him from the corner where he always lay – one of the perks of being a pariah was that you were allowed to bring your dog to the office without anyone objecting.

Outside the room, the department was full of the usual frenzied activity, but none of it ever crossed Berish's threshold, and neither did his colleagues, who kept their distance from him. To him, they were dark shadows fleetingly glimpsed through the frosted glass of his door.

The office was his place of exile.

He always kept it tidy, however, as though expecting visitors. The box files stood in perfect lines on the shelves. On the desk, a stereoscopic lamp, a pen holder, a calendar and a telephone were neatly arranged. And there were two chairs placed an equal distance in front of the desk.

It was routine that had saved him during all these years of forced isolation.

He had built a wall of tried and true habits around himself that made it possible for him to withstand other people's scorn and his own loneliness. After falling down, he'd had to pick himself up and find a new way to be an officer of the law. Having lost everyone's respect, he should have taken the only sensible way out and resigned. But what he'd found hardest to swallow was that he had been condemned without right of appeal. If he'd handed in his badge, he would have kept on his downward path. This way, at least, he had broken the fall.

In spite of the price he had to pay every day, the disrespectful gestures and dirty looks gave him an excuse to keep on fighting.

The first step in the battle was when he had bought his first anthropology book. He had always been a man of action, but now he had decided to tap into a part of himself he had long neglected, and in time it had taken the place of his gun.

His mind had become his weapon.

He had thrown himself body and soul into studying. He hadn't shirked. It may have started as simple curiosity but he had soon seen its potential, how he could apply its lessons to everyday police work.

Anthropology had opened up new horizons, helping him to understand many things about himself and other people.

Of course, everyone in the department thought he had gone mad, spending the hours when he was on duty shut up in his office reading one book after another. But he had nothing else to do anyway. His superiors had stopped assigning him to cases and his colleagues refused to work with him.

They hoped he would just give up and resign.

That was why he had to fill the emptiness of his days some-how. And those books were excellent fillers. At first, it was as if they were written in an incomprehensible language, and more than once he had been tempted to hurl them at the wall. But gradually the meaning of the words had begun to emerge from the pages, like the remains of a lost civilisation breaking the sur-face of the ocean.

His colleagues watched with suspicion as he carried large boxes of books to his office. They couldn't figure out what he was playing at. Actually, Berish himself had no idea where it would all lead. But he was sure he'd find out sooner or later.

It happened when, many years later, he had interrogated a sus-pect. Instead of forcing a confession out of him, he had put himself on the man's level and turned the discussion into a chat. The secret of his success lay in a simple observation.

People don't like talking but they do like being listened to.

Some thought that was an oxymoron. Few people were aware of the difference. Berish was, and from that point on there was no stopping him. Thanks to this particular talent, he had gained a reputation, which hadn't replaced his previous one as a pariah, but was passed on like a masonic secret – the last resort in par-ticularly difficult cases. They called him in when they'd reached a dead end.

And so he had carved a niche for himself, while remaining invisible.

But now Mila Vasquez threatened to drag him out of the zone he had cultivated with such effort over the years. Even though she hadn't said so, Berish had the impression there were others besides André García.

Missing persons who came back in order to kill.

He had noticed a certain heightened tension in the department lately. Of course, no one told him anything, but he was sure something was going on. If Mila had only told him that García's prints had been found on the scene of the murder of a drug dealer, he would of course have been worried, and rightly so.

But she had also mentioned the name Kairus. And that terrified him.

At the Chinese café, he had tried to conceal his surprise, telling Mila Vasquez that it was the first time he'd heard the name. But it wasn't true.

She knows, he repeated to himself. *She knows I lied to her.*

The name Kairus was a detail in the case of seven people who had disappeared twenty years earlier, a detail the Federal Police had preferred not to make public.

It often happened that in the more delicate investigations, a crucial detail would not be divulged, in order to deter potential copycats or to test the accuracy of a witness statement. The decision not to reveal the name Kairus had been dictated by far more serious considerations. That was why only someone who had actually been involved in those events could have known it.

But Stephanopoulos had advised Mila to speak to him. If his old captain had chosen to commit himself to such an extent, that could only mean that there was a crucial new development.

Simon Berish had the unpleasant feeling that a presence that had long been invisible was again manifesting itself.

Maybe he'd been a bit too hasty in dismissing Mila Vasquez.

28

No new murder had been reported in over thirty-six hours.

While everyone in the department waited for the latest move by what they believed to be a terrorist organisation, Mila was increasingly certain that she was on the right track, and for now she had no intention of sharing her findings with her superiors.

It was a risk, but that was part of her nature.

Her conversation with Berish in the Chinese café had opened her eyes. She was sure he hadn't told her the whole truth. Captain Steph had advised her to beware of the man, but had failed to mention that they had worked together in the past, when Berish was fresh out of the academy and Steph ran the Witness Protection Unit.

Mila had formed an opinion anyway. Whatever had happened in his career to make him a pariah, Berish hadn't given up. He hadn't chosen the comforts of alcohol to drown his frustration and resentment, as so many disillusioned officers did. He had adopted a different strategy.

He had changed.

After leaving the café, Mila had gone back to the department. After that meeting in which she had made a fool of herself, Boris and Gurevich hadn't been in touch with her. They were probably far too busy trying to track down Roger Valin and Eric Vincenti.

They didn't know that the chain of crimes was far from over, or that it had started even earlier than they thought, with the death by drowning of a drug dealer on 19 September – the day before Roger Valin slaughtered the Belmans. The method suggested by the sequence of crimes was clear. Mila would find the answers to her questions by going back in time. She needed to look at what had happened twenty years earlier and compare it with what was happening now.

There was an obvious connection between the present and the past.

And the time machine that might help her to find that connection was the Records section on the lower level of Limbo.

Mila descended the staircase into the tomblike darkness. At the foot of the stairs, she reached out and flicked a switch. The fluorescent lights on the low ceiling blinked into life one at a time, revealing a maze of corridors lined with cupboards.

The smell and the coolness and the damp of the basement enveloped her. It was a place far from the world, where daylight was banned and mobile phone signals stopped on the threshold, as if afraid to enter.

Confidently, Mila turned left.

The cupboards she passed were numbered in ascending order, and were glass-fronted so that you could see the contents, objects of various kinds in labelled plastic bags. There were neatly folded and piled articles of clothes, different types of toothbrush, odd shoes – since it was pointless keeping both – pairs of glasses, hats, combs, even cigarette ends. Apart from personal effects and the detritus of everyday life, there were TV remote controls, pillow cases and sheets, cutlery that was still dirty, and telephones.

Anything that might contain organic traces of the missing person was kept along with his or her file.

Officers from Limbo always tried to get hold of objects with which the people they were seeking had been in regular contact, in order to obtain their DNA or just their fingerprints. When there was a well-founded suspicion that they hadn't simply run away, the case would be classified PHV – Potential Homicide Victim.

It was standard procedure when children disappeared, but was also followed when there was anything suggesting a crime of violence.

Every adult citizen of sound mind was free to vanish into thin air if he so wished. 'It isn't our job to force people to come back,' Steph always said. 'We just want to make sure nothing bad happened to them.'

Mila remembered those words every time she set foot in Records.

After walking a short distance, memorised in the course of several visits, she came to a kind of room – actually a square space between the cupboards – which was the heart of the maze.

In the middle was a Formica-topped table, a chair and an old computer.

Before she got down to work, Mila draped her jacket on the back of the chair, emptied the pockets of all the objects weighing it down, and put them on the table. Along with her house and car keys and her mobile was the handkerchief Berish had given her at the Chinese café. She instinctively sniffed it.

It smelt of cologne.

A bit too much, she told herself to dismiss the idea that she actually liked the scent. She put it down with the rest of the things and decided to forget all about it, then went to look for the file on the case of the seven missing insomniacs from twenty years earlier. The records hadn't been computerised until the year after that, so she could only consult this particular file in its paper form.

She found it and carried it back to the table.

As soon as she began looking through it, she realised that it contained only the records relating to the individual missing persons – all classified PHV – and nothing else. No mention of the Wizard, or the Enchanter of Souls, or the Goodnight Man, let alone Kairus. There was just a vague hint that one person might have been behind all the disappearances.

Mila had the impression that the file had been 'cleaned up', that the real results were elsewhere and that the one here was a mirror file – that was what they called those documents that had been marked confidential for reasons of expediency or security.

Except that she had André García.

The ex-soldier with the unpaid fine was like Patient Zero in a pandemic. The origin of everything.

Of the seven people who had disappeared twenty years earlier, he had been the first to go. And of the four killers in the last few days, he had been the first to return.

And to kill, Mila remembered.

That was why there was a lot to be learnt from André García. Just as an epidemiologist goes in search of the initial carrier who triggered the contagion, in order to understand how a disease has developed.

She suddenly had an idea about a possible link between García, Valin, Niverman and Vincenti.

When a person decided to run away, they didn't usually take any luggage, partly because the things they owned would be a constant reminder to them of the life they were trying to escape. If, on the other hand, they did take something with them, then the object – or, rather, the emotional tie it represented – might function as a security rope, allowing them at any moment to retrace their steps all the way home. But it was more frequent to find cases where nothing was premeditated, and they were also the hardest ones to solve.

For some people the only way forward was to completely obliterate all traces of themselves. To track down such people, Limbo trusted to a couple of tricks, and to luck.

The hope was always that the missing person would change his mind or make a mistake, such as use a cashpoint to withdraw money or pay with a credit card. Or that they would try and buy medicines they regularly used. If the individual was a diabetic, for instance, he would need insulin. That was why they always talked to the person's doctor to see if they suffered from any illnesses and why, during the initial search of their home, they would make an inventory of the contents of the medicine cabinet.

It was this latter practice that triggered something in Mila's mind.

First of all, she switched on the old computer in front of her, in order not to have to go back to her desk upstairs. Through it, she accessed Limbo's digital records.

She typed in the names Roger Valin, Nadia Niverman and Eric Vincenti. The relevant files emerged one after the other from the ocean of bytes. As she looked through them, Mila took notes on a pad she kept next to the mouse. When she had finished her search, she reread her notes. The seven missing persons from twenty years ago all took pills to help them sleep – the Goodnight Man, she remembered.

Well, it turned out that Roger Valin kept Halcion at home, prescribed to his sick mother, Nadia Niverman had recently bought a packet of Minias, and Eric Vincenti had a prescription for Rohypnol, although the drug was never found in his apartment.

That meant there was a link with García and the others who went missing twenty years earlier – the insomniacs.

Mila wasn't sure whether to be excited or frightened by this discovery. An old series of disappearances, behind which police at the time had surmised there might be a single perpetrator – a serial killer? – although they had never been able to confirm it. Disappearances that had started for no reason and had also stopped for no reason.

In the light of what she had just found, it seemed they hadn't stopped after all.

Let's say the disappearances of insomniacs stop for a while, Mila thought. Three years go by, people's interest fades, and then it's the turn of Roger Valin, who actually disappeared seventeen years ago. Nobody links his disappearance to the previous ones and things start all over again just as they had before.

'But if these people are coming back, it means they're not dead, so it's wrong to call them victims,' Mila said to the silence.

Equally, the theory that there might be someone behind the disappearances – the Wizard, the Enchanter of Souls, the Goodnight Man – was, at this point, entirely arbitrary.

Except that Berish had a strange reaction when I mentioned the name Kairus, Mila recalled as she switched off the computer prior to going back upstairs. There was something that didn't add up in this reconstruction. A missing piece of the truth. Berish had some vital information on what had happened twenty years earlier but had kept it from her.

Kairus hadn't been just a collective hallucination, she was sure of that.

She gathered her notes and Berish's scented handkerchief from the table and walked back down the long corridors to the stairs to begin the climb back up to the Limbo offices. It was just after nine o'clock.

Mila was so absorbed in thinking about what it might mean if there were indeed a mastermind behind these events that she almost didn't notice that the phone in the pocket of her leather jacket had started vibrating when she was just a few steps from the exit.

She took the phone out and looked at the display screen. She had about ten text messages, all telling her that a particular number had been repeatedly trying to reach her.

It was the number of the department's operations room. There could be only one reason why they would call a Limbo officer, and this sent a shiver up her spine.

When she got to the Waiting Room, she dialled the number. The reply was immediate.

'Officer Vasquez?' came a man's voice.

'Yes,' she said, with a shudder.

'We've been trying to get hold of you all afternoon. We have an alert here.'

Mila knew what those words meant.

When teenagers disappeared, it was often the case that they had run away of their own free will and the matter was quickly and satisfactorily resolved. The young were overfond of technology, and if they had their mobiles with them, it was just a matter of waiting before they could easily be traced.

They usually kept their phones switched off to avoid being contacted – and increase their parents' anxiety. Usually, though, they couldn't hold out for more than twenty-four hours before checking to see if a friend had sent them a text. As soon as they switched their phone back on, even if they didn't make a call or send a message, the SIM card would connect to one of the cells in the area and the police would immediately know exactly where they were.

When they weren't so lucky and the missing teenagers were silent for a long time, the police would ask the phone company not to deactivate the account, because it sometimes happened that a mobile phone or SIM card came back to life after several years. The department's operations room would then monitor the number and wait for a signal.

'There's been a reactivation,' the operator said. 'We've checked, and it isn't a phantom signal, although no calls have been made from the number. The reactivation has definitely been confirmed.'

If there was no mistake, Mila sensed that something was really happening. 'Who is it?' she asked.

'The subscriber's name is Diana Müller.'

Fourteen. Brown hair, dark eyes. Disappeared one February morning on her way to school. According to the records, her mobile had stopped working at 8.18 a.m.

After nine years of silence, her phone had come back to life.

'Have you been able to locate the signal?'

'Of course,' the operator said.

'All right, give me the address.'

29

The phone was an old Nokia.

Diana Müller had found it on a park bench, where somebody must have forgotten it. There was no way to trace the owner. It still worked, but wasn't much of a mobile – the battery only lasted a few hours and the display screen was scratched, presumably from being dropped a lot – and it certainly couldn't compete with the latest generation of smartphones, which didn't even exist when the girl went missing.

But Diana had never owned one before, so it meant a great deal to her.

It was a kind of passport to the grown-up world. Even though it was an old model, she took care of it as if it were new. She even managed to make it look prettier by adding a charm in the shape of a blue angel and a case covered in gold stars. And inside the battery compartment, she had written *Property of Diana Müller* and drawn a little heart with the initials of the boy she liked at school. She thought of that as a kind of magic spell – who knows, maybe one day he might actually call her. The phone she was so proud of would probably not have interested a modern fourteen-year-old. It had no internet access or email or games or apps. You couldn't use it to navigate or even take photographs.

You could only use it to make phone calls or send messages.

'The things you've missed out on, Diana,' Mila said under her breath as she drove towards the address where the mobile had been located. It wasn't far from where she had disappeared, and that troubled her somewhat.

Nine years earlier, a young life seemed to have dissolved into nothingness, carried away on the wind. But Mila believed that the origin of the mystery lay in what that phone, which was now sending a signal from out of the darkness, had represented for Diana.

An obsession.

At an age when a girl might have brought a stray puppy home with her, Diana had come back one day with an old radio she said she had found in the street. It would have been a real shame to just leave it there, she insisted, the owner obviously didn't know what he was doing when he threw it away.

Unlike the mobile, the radio was out of order and beyond repair. But that didn't seem to make a difference to Diana.

In this case, too, her mother had let her keep it, not realising that, from that moment on, she would start bringing home the oddest things – a blanket, a pushchair, glass jars, old magazines – justifying each find with a convincing story.

At first, even though she was aware there was something wrong in her daughter's strange habit, Diana's mother couldn't come up with a good reason to stop her. What she didn't realise was that this fixation was actually a morbid attachment to strange objects, known as disposophobia.

Unlike Diana's mother, Mila knew it was a form of obsessive compulsive disorder. People who suffered from it compulsively hoarded things and were unable to get rid of them.

In Diana's case, it got to the point where her room was filled to the brim with all the things she had collected. Apart from the lack of space, which made it impossible to move freely, there was the matter of hygiene: there was good reason to suspect that Diana's 'treasures', which she claimed to have come across by chance, actually came from rubbish bins.

Her mother realised how bad the situation had become the day the house was overrun by cockroaches. They were everywhere – in the cupboards, on the shelves, under the carpet. They were coming from Diana's room, and when she went to see what was going on, she was horrified to see bags of rubbish she herself had thrown out. For some time now, for no clear reason, her daughter had been bringing them back inside the house, and hiding them in among the rest of her things.

Mila could imagine how disconcerting it must have felt to be confronted with something which, in consumer societies, we usually think we have eliminated from our lives – and therefore from our memories. We throw out leftover food or things we no longer need, confident that they are no longer our concern and that someone else will take care of them. But the very thought that something we have got rid of could suddenly come back to haunt us is as frightening as the idea of someone we thought was dead suddenly coming back to life.

It is incomprehensible and terrifying at the same time – like the unfathomable motives of the insane or the pathological urges of necrophiliacs.

In a panic, Diana's mother decided to throw out all her daughter's stuff. When Diana got back from school, she was faced with a vision of emptiness. A few days later, that emptiness swallowed her up.

Diana's mother was called Chris. Diana had been all she had. Mila recalled the lost look in the woman's eyes. At the time of

Diana's disappearance, Mila hadn't yet started working in Limbo. They had met only later, because Chris would regularly drop by to ask if there was any news. Every time, it meant heartache for them, too.

They would see her standing there in the doorway of the Waiting Room, looking for Diana's photograph to make sure it was still in its place on the wall – as long as it was there, her daughter wouldn't be forgotten. Once she had located it, she would come in, almost on tiptoe, and wait for someone to pay attention to her.

It was usually Eric Vincenti who dealt with her. He would offer her a seat and some tea. Then he would chat to her until he was sure she was ready to go home. Since Eric had disappeared, the task of comforting Chris had fallen to Mila.

Feeling no empathy, it was hard for her to imagine what might be happening in the woman's heart – what kind of suffering she was going through. Mila was good at classifying her own pain: razor blade, burn, bruise. Along with anger and fear, it was the only emotional resource she possessed. Maybe that was why she had never been able to really connect with Diana's mother in the way Vincenti had. All the same, she had understood a lot about her.

For example, Chris wasn't a bad mother. She had raised her daughter, and been strict when she had to, even though there was no man around to provide a father figure. She had put up with Diana's ridiculous obsession because she knew she herself was far from perfect, and that often put her at a disadvantage. Once, she had told Mila that she was sure Diana had been unhappy and secretly hated her, even though she had been such a sweet, gentle child it was hard to imagine her hating anyone.

Chris's big failing was that she liked men.

She had always let them take advantage of her – a kind of

masochism that had led her to make one wrong choice after another.

But it was Diana who had been the real victim of her behaviour.

How many times had the wife of one of her lovers accosted Chris in the supermarket and told her to keep her hands off other women's husbands? And how many times had she been forced to change jobs because her boss had grown tired of his affair with her and fired her? They were constantly obliged to move home, to abandon everything, in order to escape the gossip and malice of those around them.

So when Diana had started her 'collection', she might have been trying to send her mother a message and, at the same time, to mark out a territory that was finally hers. Having no past made up of familiar objects and things to cling to, she took possession of a past other people threw out as rubbish.

But Chris hadn't realised this until it was too late and had treated her daughter as if she were mentally ill. She had once told Mila she was quite sure Diana hadn't run away or even been kidnapped. She was convinced she had killed herself to escape her whore of a mother, because a packet of Rohypnol had gone missing from the house.

Mila braked abruptly, and the engine cut out. She sat there in the middle of the empty street, with a ticking coming from the bonnet and the memory of those words echoing in her head.

A sleeping pill as an element in Diana's disappearance couldn't be a coincidence.

It isn't true, it isn't possible, I don't believe it, she kept telling herself. This time, she ought to inform Boris. She couldn't take the risk by herself.

But you've already gone too far, an inner voice seemed to be telling her. *They'll definitely take you off the case now.*

That signal from a mobile phone that hadn't been used for nine years was an invitation, one meant only for her. Something or someone was waiting for her. Mila switched on the engine again.

She didn't want to miss the appointment.

30

The business district was near the river.

The tall, shiny buildings were mainly offices, and at this time of the evening looked like empty, transparent cathedrals. The office workers had gone, leaving the cleaning staff to manoeuvre floor polishers and carpet shampooers and empty baskets of waste paper.

Mila drove past the first three blocks before finding the side street she was looking for.

She turned left and drove up the street until she came to a sheet metal fence blocking the way. Large signs indicated that works were in progress.

She parked her car, got out and looked around. The address she was looking for was on the other side of that barrier. She called the operations room to ask if Diana's mobile signal was still active and hadn't changed location.

'It's still there,' the operator said.

She hung up and started looking for a gap in the fence. Close to the building on the right, she found a stretch where the bottom of the sheet metal had folded inwards. She bent down and slipped through.

Rising to her full height again, she wiped the dust from her hands and jeans. The building site she now saw in front of her was deserted. She had expected there to be at least a security guard, but no one seemed to be keeping an eye on the place. At the moment, the building under construction only reached ten storeys, but judging by the width of the base was clearly intended to be a lot taller. Next to it was a huge hole, ready for the foundations of another building, a twin of the first, which hadn't been started. Behind were other buildings under construction, intended as satellites of the two main buildings.

In among these smaller constructions was a small redbrick house from the previous century – a last vestige of the old neighbourhood that had been swept away to make room for the skyscrapers. Mila could see the number on the façade. She walked towards it across the open space, past machinery and equipment. Rather than holding her back, the invisible hand of fear urged her forward.

She was moving towards the house, but it seemed like the house was coming to meet her.

The house was two storeys high. The insides of the windows were boarded up with plywood, and there were spray-painted signs warning of the danger of collapse. Surrounded by all this new architecture, the low building stood out like a decaying tooth. It seemed to be in a state of complete neglect.

As Mila approached the heavy front door, she saw there was a sheet of paper stuck to it. It was an expropriation order issued by the council less than three weeks earlier. As approved by the mayor, the house was to be demolished to make room for other buildings, in accordance with the latest development project. The owners were instructed to vacate the building within the next three weeks at the latest.

Mila calculated. To judge by the date of the order, demolition would begin tomorrow.

She tried the door, but it wouldn't budge. She tried forcing the lock, to no avail.

She stepped back, took a running jump at the door, and hit it with her shoulder. Once, twice. It still wouldn't give.

She looked around for something she could use. There was a shovel a few yards away. She fetched it and slid the blade into the crack down the middle of the door. She forced it in a few centimetres, forcing the wood to splinter. Then she leant her whole weight on the handle and pushed, using the shovel as a lever. The wood creaked and started to yield. Mila kept going. Within a few seconds, her forehead was bathed in sweat.

Something inside cracked, and the door fell open.

Mila threw down the shovel and took a step forward. A powerful stench struck her. It was sickly-sweet, like a huge rotting piece of fruit. She couldn't figure out what it was.

The first thing she did was take the torch out of her leather jacket, switch it on and point it straight ahead of her. The beam showed a large, empty room, and a staircase leading upstairs.

She turned to the door she had just taken off its hinges, and noticed that there was a bar on the inside that had kept it shut. It was still in one piece, whereas the iron latches, worn out by rust, had yielded to the pressure of her lever.

Mila listened out once again for the echo, in the hope that it might reveal a presence.

The sound, the smell, the texture of the darkness all created a secret well full of things no longer needed or kept out of sight.

The stench was becoming unbearable. She took out the handkerchief Berish had given her and tied it over her mouth.

It still had the smell of Berish's cologne on it.

She stared into the arrogant darkness. Mila wasn't afraid of it:

she had felt she was a part of it ever since she was a child. But that didn't mean she was brave. It was just that she didn't run away from fear, she needed it. Her dependence on that feeling made her reckless, and she knew it. She should have gone back to her car and called her colleagues in the department. Instead of which, she took out her gun and started slowly up the stairs, to see what awaited her up there.

31

At the top of the stairs there was a door.

That was where the nauseating stench came from. She could smell it through the handkerchief protecting her nose and mouth. Mila reached out to test the resistance of the door but it opened with a simple pressure of the fingers.

She aimed her torch.

Stacks of old newspapers almost reached to the ceiling, which was at least ten feet high. They stood side by side, forming an impassable wall, leaving barely enough space to open the door.

Mila walked into that space, and was wondering how she would get through the barrier when the beam of her torch showed her a gap.

She slipped through it without hesitation.

Beyond the gap was a corridor just wide enough for one person to walk down, like a gorge between two walls of stacked-up material. She began walking along it. Like an animal tamer using his whip to keep a fierce beast at bay, Mila used the torch to ward off the darkness that threatened constantly to attack her.

There were all kinds of things around her.

Plastic containers, empty bottles, tin cans. Scrap iron. Clothes of different styles and colours. A sewing machine from the 1920s. Old leather-bound books and other, more modern ones with colourful covers, although damaged by time. Dolls' heads. Crumpled cigarette packets. Hats. Suitcases. Boxes. An old stereo. Engine parts. A stuffed bird.

It was like a mad junk dealer's storeroom. Or even the belly of a great whale that had collected all kinds of objects on its long journeys by sea.

There was a sense to all this mess, though.

Mila didn't understand it, but she could see it. It was right there in front of her eyes even though she couldn't explain it. It was as if there was a method to it. As if everything had been given its proper place. As if someone had tried, for whatever reason, to bring order to a huge rubbish dump, cataloguing the refuse according to some secret criterion, in which each object had its own role and its own importance.

The answer to what she had in front of her eyes was disposophobia. The disorder Diana Müller had suffered from.

This time, though, she had done everything on a grand scale. A huge warehouse filled to overflowing. A house inside which a maze had been erected.

As she advanced, Mila felt other things under her feet. Things that had fallen off the stacks, which were clearly far from stable. She would have to watch her step.

Reaching the end of the corridor, she realised that the path through the stacks forked. She shone her torch in both directions, and tried to think of a good reason to go one way rather than the other. She decided to turn right, partly because it seemed to lead to the centre of the maze.

It was like the records in Limbo. The remains of thousands of lives seemed to have been crammed in here. The only evidence that all these people who were no longer here had once actually existed.

The army of shadows, Mila remembered. What is this place? Where is Diana Müller's mobile? Where is Diana?

A sudden rustling noise made her stop. Rats. They must be everywhere, like cockroaches. She aimed the beam of light at the floor, and her suspicions were confirmed. It was covered in small pieces of excrement.

She could sense lots of little eyes on her – thousands, maybe. They were watching her from their hiding places, trying to figure out what she was going to do, instinctively wondering if this intruder was a threat or an opportunity for a succulent banquet.

Dismissing that thought, Mila walked more quickly, only to hit her knee on an edge of the protruding wall. She looked up just in time to see a pile of things falling from the top of one of the stacks, about to crush her. She raised her arms to shield herself and a cascade of objects, some hard, some soft, came down on her in a kind of eruption. The torch was knocked out of her hands and the light went off. Her gun fell to the floor, too, letting off a shot that echoed through the cramped space and deafened Mila. She crouched and waited for the avalanche to subside.

At last it stopped, and she was again able, slowly, to open her eyes.

There was a loud ringing in her ears – a single, persistent, penetrating sound. The pain she felt was mixed with fear. Her spine and arms were sore beneath her clothes. Her leather jacket, though, had partly cushioned the blow. Her heart was pounding. She remembered that she had to breathe, and so she tore the handkerchief from her face and, in spite of the stench, managed to get the heartbeat that was tearing her chest apart like a piston to slow down. Her experience of self-harming over the past few years told her that no bones were broken.

She got to her feet and pushed away the objects covering her. The darkness had taken advantage of them to attack her. Then she started digging about in search of the torch.

If there was one thing worse than being crushed to death by an avalanche of refuse, it was surely being trapped in the dark, unable to find the way out.

She finally found the torch. Her hands were shaking as she pressed the button, and when the light didn't come on straight away she almost had a heart attack.

She moved the torch about to see what had happened, and also to look for her gun. She plunged her hand into the mound of objects that had formed beside her, hoping she could touch the weapon with her fingertips. She bent as low as she possibly could, and at last saw it.

It was some three feet away from her, but the things covering it were holding up the wall. If she removed even a single one, the mountain would collapse again.

Damn, she thought.

She put a hand to her mouth, resting the other on her sore hip. She tried to think, which wasn't easy, given the incessant ringing in her ears. She needed to keep moving forward – she would have to come back for the gun. There was no other way. She looked in search of something else she could use as a weapon. She found an iron bar. She grabbed it, weighing up its potential. It would do.

Where there had previously been a wall, that landslide had created a gap. Mila clambered over it, because it was now the only way she could go, and found herself in a parallel corridor.

She proceeded with caution. Every now and again, she spotted something that looked like a swarm of insects, but chose to ignore it. She kept hearing the sound of rats scurrying.

They seemed to be leading her in a particular direction.

With all the twists and turns she had made, she calculated she had covered at least fifty yards. The light beam showed her an obstacle just a few steps ahead. Another wall had collapsed, blocking her way. She was about to turn back when she noticed something protruding from the base of the mound. A long, whitish object. She wanted to be sure she wasn't mistaken, so she went closer.

A shinbone.

It was no hallucination. Mila moved the torch to reveal other parts of a skeleton protruding from the heap. An elbow, the fingers of a hand.

She was in no doubt. Diana Müller.

Mila wondered how long she had been dead. Probably at least a year. *I could have ended up like her,* she thought. If the earlier avalanche hadn't stopped, she might have met the same fate. Trying not to think about it, she managed to get over the obstacle, taking care as she did so not to step on what was left of the body.

Ahead of her, the corridor widened.

When she got there, she realised it was a kind of alcove. On the floor was a mattress covered in dirty blankets and sheets – was that where Diana had slept? There was a table, with tins of foul-smelling food, and various objects such as plastic forks, CDs and toys, which, for some unfathomable reason, had been judged more precious than the rest and so deserved this privileged position.

Amid the chaos, she spotted a charm in the shape of a blue angel. Then she realised it was still attached to Diana's mobile.

Mila put down the iron bar and stuck the torch between her teeth. She picked up the phone and carefully examined the case covered in gold stars.

The display screen was lit up, but there was no record of incoming or outgoing calls.

When she opened the compartment at the back, looking for the final confirmation that this was indeed the missing girl's phone – the words *Property of Diana Müller* and the initials of the classmate she'd had a crush on – she noticed that the battery had recently been replaced. That was to be expected – even Diana had complained the batteries did not last long – or it wouldn't have been able to work non-stop the whole afternoon.

Mila was struck by a terrible realisation. It couldn't have been the woman who was now lying dead not far away who had replaced the battery. Nor was she the one who had switched the mobile back on after nine years.

Mila stiffened, feeling the darkness crowding in around her. She picked up the iron bar and took the torch in her hand again. Slowly turning to get a better idea of her surroundings, she noticed that just behind her was another gap in the maze of rubbish.

Mila made her way towards it. She had to get down on all fours to get through. The hand holding the iron bar trailed on the filthy floor, which was covered in sheets of newspaper. The other held the torch straight in front of her. At last, she reached the end of the tunnel.

There was a second room.

But unlike the first one, everything here was neat and tidy. A real bed stood in the middle, with sheets and blankets. Next to it was a chest of drawers. Candles of different kinds were stacked on a low table. The care with which the room had been organised reminded Mila of the guest room her mother was so proud of.

She got the impression that this house had been a refuge not only to Diana Müller but also to somebody else. Somebody important, worthy of respect. After all, this was an ideal place to vanish from the world.

She was absorbed in these thoughts when she heard the sound of another collapse, somewhere far away in another part of the maze, and she immediately switched off her torch.

Somebody was here.

32

The constant ringing in her ears had stopped her noticing the presence before.

It was only thanks to the noise of that new landslide that she had become aware of it now. Then she saw a light refracted off the ceiling and realised that this other person also had a torch.

He had been spared by the avalanche and was now coming closer.

Having no intention of being trapped with no way out, Mila left what she had christened 'the guest room'. She could go back to the corridor – that way she would at least have an escape route. But since she had to keep her torch switched off in order not to be seen, it would be hard to move around without the risk of causing another landslide.

She had to think of something. She didn't have her gun with her any more, and the iron bar she had found would only prove useful in a hand-to-hand fight. What would happen if the other person had a firearm?

If it's the 'guest', then he'll come straight to his room, she thought. In other words, in her direction. Right now, the only solution, crazy as it might seem, was to go towards him and confront him.

Mila tried to keep calm and apply the rules she had learnt at the academy, which had come in useful during her years of experience in the field. First, you had to study the place in which you found yourself. In the darkness, Mila tried to recall the layout of the building.

She remembered Diana's makeshift bed, and that she had seen some blankets on the mattress. She took one and groped her way back, stepping over the remains of the dead girl.

Maybe there was a way to escape the guest.

But, in order for it to work, she had to find the best spot. There was a stretch along the corridor where it widened to make room for a pillar. Mila decided that it was wide enough. She lay down on the floor and wrapped herself in the foul-smelling blanket.

The plan was to hide and wait for the guest to pass.

When he had, the way would be free for her to reach the exit. In the absence of any alternative, it seemed like a good idea. But she had to be quick about it – whoever the guest was, he was close.

There was enough room for him to walk by her without noticing her. If she was unlucky, and he saw her, Mila would throw off the blanket and confront him with the iron bar. But it was an eventuality she preferred not to consider. *It'll be all right*, she told herself.

She took up her position and listened. The ringing in her ears triggered by the gunshot showed no sign of wearing off – in fact, fear probably made it worse. She had arranged herself under the blanket in such a way as to leave a gap for her eyes and allow her to see what was happening around her, although keeping still severely reduced her field of vision.

She first saw the beam of light searching the end of the tunnel. Even though she couldn't hear the guest's footsteps, muffled as they were by the carpet of rubbish, she knew he must be moving cautiously.

He knows there's an intruder, a little voice kept repeating inside Mila's head. *He knows.*

He was moving closer. She could almost hear him breathing. Then a shadow stopped right in front of her. Through the gap she had left for her eyes, she could see a man's shoes. She held her breath and tried not to make a sound.

Why is he just standing there and not moving?

Time stood still. She felt something enter her belly and spread like a cold wave through her veins. It was fear, the fear she had so often invoked. For a moment, she thought that the ringing in her head was about to drive her crazy.

The shadow turned in her direction. As the beam of light hit her hiding place, she summoned all her strength and came out into the open, brandishing the iron bar. The light blinded her, preventing her from seeing clearly, but she hit out with the bar anyway. It didn't strike anything – she had missed her target. She tried again, and this time grazed him. It was enough to throw him off balance and land him on the floor. He dropped his torch. Once again, darkness took possession of the space.

'Mila!' she heard him yell from the floor. 'Wait!'

Panting, still blindly seeking a target with the iron bar, she caught herself almost screaming, 'Who are you?'

The shadow said nothing.

'Who are you?' she repeated, more firmly this time.

'It's me – Berish.'

The ringing in her ears had prevented her from recognising his voice. 'How did you find me?' she asked, her voice shrill with anxiety.

'I called the department, and they told me you were here.'

'And why did you come?'

'I changed my mind. I realised how serious the situation is, and I decided to help you.'

Mila thought this over for a moment before deciding that the story made sense. 'For fuck's sake, Berish,' she said, lowering the iron bar. 'Get your damned torch. I can't stand being in the dark.'

'Then help me get up.'

Mila was about to reach out to him when someone else came up behind her and took her by the hand. Instinctively, she turned, and as she did so she smelt a familiar scent. She was startled, but didn't react. It was as if everything was happening in slow motion. Whoever it was behind her pulled her to him. Then the gunshots started. They roared through that enclosed corridor but, in the brief flashes they caused, Mila realised that the person who had pulled at her was the real Simon Berish, and the scent that had brought her to her senses was his cologne.

The man lying on the floor had tried to trick her. During that series of instant flashes, she was unable to see the impostor's face because he'd had time to turn and run. She saw him vanish round the first corner, dodging bullets, while the walls of the corridor came crashing down behind him, covering his flight and barring the way to any pursuer.

When the shots ceased, the real Berish turned to her. 'Let's go, now!' he screamed.

He pulled her after him in the darkness for a few yards, then switched on the torch he had brought with him. Mila held tight to his hand, trying to take care where she was stepping. Berish was running now – he seemed to have memorised the route to the exit.

Panic took hold of her, and she felt herself slow down, with that frightening slowness you always felt when running in nightmares. She tried to push forward but she felt as if she was running through an oily liquid, as if the darkness had turned thicker.

Then she recognised the first corridor she had come down. There was the door. So close it seemed unreachable, and the prospect of going through it so wonderful it appeared unreal. She felt the cooler air coming from outside, and it was as if the door was breathing.

They crossed that frontier and started down the stairs. She felt as if the steps were tilting beneath their feet, like the teeth of a creature opening its mouth wide. She heard the insistent bark of a dog that seemed to be calling them from outside the house. They were almost free.

Just before she went out through the front door, Mila had the feeling the redbrick house was closing in on them. She closed her eyes and counted her steps.

Berish came to a halt where his dog was standing. He leant down to pat him. 'Quiet, Hitch. Everything's all right.'

They both caught their breaths. Hitch fell silent. Berish looked at Mila, who was still shaken. She had put her hands over her ears and was grimacing in pain. He decided he ought to explain.

'I found you by calling the department, and they told me you'd come here,' he said in a loud voice, aware that she couldn't hear well.

'Then whoever was pretending to be you knows I went to you and asked for your help.' Mila had a sudden feeling of irritation. 'Who was it?' she asked, pointing towards the house.

But Berish evaded the question. 'Damn it, the place is a *nest*. I'd never seen one before.'

'What are you talking about?'

'A disposophobic's refuge.'

Mila felt disgusted. Diana Müller had shut herself up in that house, rejecting the outside world and preparing a lair for somebody. 'There was a room there. She was expecting a guest.'

Berish took Mila by the shoulders. 'You must tell everyone. Get them here. He's trapped in there, don't you see? He has no way out.'

There was an anxious gleam in Berish's eyes. Without asking any more questions, Mila was about to take the phone and call Boris at the department when Hitch started barking, more loudly than before, to indicate something behind them. Mila and Berish turned to look at the redbrick house.

Grey smoke was emerging from the boarded-up windows. A few seconds later, they exploded in flame.

As the house turned into an inferno, the two officers shielded their faces and quickly moved away, along with Hitch.

When they were at a safe distance, they turned back to look at the fire.

'No, no,' Berish said, his voice sad and powerless.

'Look at me,' Mila said, forcing him to turn to her. 'Who was that man? You knew him.'

Berish lowered his eyes. 'I didn't see his face, but I suppose it was him.'

'Who?'

'Kairus.'

Alice

Exhibit 443-Y/27

Statement of the paramedic on ambulance duty
on the evening of 26 September 2015:

We arrived at the injured party's home just
before midnight. We had already been informed
by radio of his condition and that he was a
member of the police force. When we arrived,
the patient was seen to have widespread third
and fourth degree burns, as well as symptoms
of serious asphyxiation. In spite of this
gravely impaired clinical picture, he was
conscious. As my team prepared to perform the
classical procedure for avoiding potential
complications and at the same time tried to
stabilise his breathing, the subject appeared
very anxious and insisted on communicating
with us. He managed to tear off his oxygen
mask for a few seconds and uttered a number of
incoherent phrases of which we only caught the
words "Please, I don't want to die".
Unfortunately, he died on the way to hospital.

33

Everyone was waiting for the Judge.

The police had taken over the building site, but nobody would say or do anything before the head of the department arrived. It was as if the scene were suspended in time.

The fire had been tamed but the redbrick house had collapsed. In burning, that huge collection of material had produced a toxic cloud which, combined with the light of dawn, had turned the sky a brilliant red.

The effect was both fascinating and deadly, Mila thought as she gazed at it.

Evil things could look beautiful, too. But the firefighters had been forced to evacuate the area.

'Just the kind of publicity we needed,' was Boris's comment.

He was refusing to speak to her. Not only was he angry, Mila was afraid he was disappointed in her. She hadn't kept him informed of her findings. She'd left him out of the loop, hadn't trusted him. Something was irremediably broken in their relationship.

Gurevich was also ignoring her. Mila had called him, not Boris, that night, to avoid arousing the suspicion that she was acting in collusion with her old friend. When reinforcements had arrived, he had listened to what she had to say without batting an eyelid. Mila had reported on the progress of her solitary investigation, from the newspaper cutting found in the manhole to the text message about Kairus to the story of Diana Müller.

The one element she had left out was Simon Berish.

It had been her idea to send him away. She hadn't wanted her superiors to find him there. He had a bad enough reputation as it was without his having to take the blame in a case that wasn't even his. Mila assured him she'd come to see him later and fill him in.

For the past ten minutes, they had been allowed by the firefighters to take off their gas masks. The toxic fumes from the smoking rubble had been neutralised by a jet of foam.

The ringing in Mila's ears had ceased, but she couldn't get the voice of the man in the shadows out of her head.

He had been very clever at luring her into his trap. *He's been watching me*, she thought. *He knows I respond to the call of fear.*

Berish had told her it was Kairus, thereby admitting that he really did exist. But then why had he concealed the truth when they first met?

A black BMW with smoked windows drove through the line of police officers keeping reporters and onlookers away from the area of operations and parked in front of the building under construction. Mila recognised the Judge's car. Gurevich and Boris rushed towards it.

Instead of getting out, the passenger stayed inside and rolled down the window to speak to the two inspectors. Mila was on the other side of the car and was unable to follow the conversation. A few minutes went by. At last, the inspectors stood aside to let the car door open.

A five-inch heel came to rest on the ground made dusty with concrete. A pale blonde mane soon appeared. The suit was predictably black, the make-up perfect even at this time of the morning.

As always, Joanna Shutton, the Judge, was impeccable.

There were many stories about her in the department, none of which had ever gone beyond the level of gossip. All that was known for certain was that she was single and that her private life was a closed book. Most importantly, none of these rumours ever implied anything of a sexual nature. That said a lot about how intimidating she was. Her rise to the post of commander-in-chief had been textbook.

Although she had been the best in her class at the Academy, Joanna Shutton hadn't immediately been given a prestigious role. She may have been promising, but she would have made her male colleagues look bad, in addition to which she was an opinionated pain in the neck. That was why she was only assigned minor cases. Somehow, though, she always managed to shine, thanks to her ability to learn, her commitment, her sense of self-sacrifice. She had even managed to turn the pejorative nickname 'Judge' into a badge of merit.

Journalists had fallen in love with her from the start.

With her mixture of model-girl looks and stern old-school police attitude, she was perfect front-page and TV material. What her superiors had feared – that a sexy-looking blonde would become the image of the federal police – came to pass.

In only two years, after a number of difficult assignments, Joanna Shutton became the youngest inspector in the history of the department. From that point on, her rise to the top post was unstoppable.

She took off her sunglasses and walked confidently into the middle of the scene, her eyes assessing the spectacle of the ruined redbrick house.

'Who can update me?'

She was immediately surrounded by the zealous Gurevich and Boris and the commander of the firefighters. It was the latter who got in first.

'We got the flames under control an hour ago. But then the building caved in. According to your officer, the fire started suddenly. I'm not in any position yet to confirm whether or not it was arson. There was a lot of inflammable material crammed in there, it would only have taken a spark to set it off.'

The Judge pondered his words. 'A spark that, as far as I can see, seems to have waited for years and just happened to choose tonight to set fire to everything.'

Shutton's sarcastic remark fell into the silence like a stone into a pond. They never knew how to react to her, Mila noted. No one was ever sure if she was joking or using irony as a whip to keep them in line.

'Officer Vasquez,' Shutton called without even turning to look at her.

Mila walked up to the little group. The Judge's aura of Chanel wafted over the area, like a sphere of influence into which Mila was also now drawn. 'Yes, ma'am.'

'I'm told you saw a man in there and that he tried to attack you.'

That wasn't quite the way it had happened, but Mila followed the version agreed upon with Berish. 'There was a brief struggle and my torch fell out of my hand. We were left in the dark, but I managed to shoot at him a few times and scare him off.'

'So you didn't wound him.'

'I don't think so.' This time, Mila was telling the truth. 'I just saw him run away. Then I also ran because I was afraid everything would come crashing down on top of me.'

'And you lost your gun, is that right?'

Mila lowered her eyes. It wasn't considered honourable for a police officer to lose their weapon. Since she couldn't reveal that it was Berish who had fired the shots, she had saved herself the trouble of having to admit that she had dropped the gun in a stupid moment of distraction. Not that she came out of it smelling of roses. 'That's correct, Judge.'

In an instant, Shutton lost interest in her and looked around. 'Where's Chang?'

Soon afterwards, the pathologist emerged from the ruins in an asbestos suit and a hard hat. He took off the hat and came and joined them.

'Have you been asking for me?'

'Are there any bodies in there?'

'There were large quantities of chemicals, hydro-carbons and plastic in the place, all of which produce extremely high temperatures when they catch fire. Added to that, the bricks the building was made of acted like a furnace. In conditions like that, any human remains would practically disintegrate.'

'But that man was there,' Mila said almost shrilly, not realising that nobody was accusing her of lying. 'And there was also a skeleton, the skeleton of Diana Müller, who disappeared when she was fourteen and has been missing for nine years.'

'How is it possible that no one ever noticed anything?' the Judge asked.

'The house was part of a joint legacy,' Gurevich said, ignoring Mila. 'According to the company that was supposed to be demolishing it today, nobody lived there. It's odd that no one reported anything to social services in all this time. Look around you: this place isn't exactly out in the sticks. It's the business district, thousands of people pass through here every day.'

True, but after sunset the place is a desert, Mila would have liked to retort. All she did, though, was shake her head in denial.

Boris was the only one who hadn't belittled her, but he was avoiding looking at her. That silence hurt her more than Gurevich's veiled accusations. Joanna Shutton, in the meantime, seemed imperturbable.

'If it happened the way Officer Vasquez says it did,' Gurevich said in a self-important tone, 'then the man who attacked her also started the fire and chose to go up in flames. Why would he do that? It makes no sense.'

The Judge turned back to the commander of the firefighters. 'I assume you've spoken to the company that manages the site.'

'Yes, we called them to get an idea of the layout.'

'Tell me, was there another way into the building apart from the front door?'

The commander thought this over for a moment. 'Well, the sewers run right under the property. It's just possible someone might have found a way of accessing them from inside the building.'

The Judge turned to her male colleagues. 'Now there's a possibility you didn't take into account. Whoever was living in the house may have found a different way to come in and out without being seen. The man who attacked Officer Vasquez could have used it to run away after setting the place on fire.'

Mila took in Shutton's unexpected support. Not that she had any illusions.

The Judge at last looked at her. 'Your colleagues' scepticism, my dear, is due to the fact that you acted without waiting for orders, demonstrating a total lack of respect for the chain of command. Moreover, you've jeopardised this investigation. It's going to be hard to pick up the thread now, since whatever evidence there may have been was destroyed by the fire.'

Mila would have liked to say she was sorry, but it would have sounded like a bad lie. So she stood there silently, with her head bowed, taking it all.

'If you think you're better than us, then just say so. I know your work, I know how good you are. But I would never have expected such behaviour from an experienced police officer.' Shutton turned to the others. 'Leave us alone.'

34

The three men exchanged rapid glances, then walked away.

They may have been in a majority, but with a woman like the Judge males always ended up looking inferior.

When they had gone, Shutton waited a few moments before speaking, as if needing to choose her words with care. 'I'd like to give you a hand, Officer Vasquez.'

Mila, who had been waiting for another reprimand, was taken aback. 'I'm sorry, what did you say?'

'I believe you.'

This was more than support. It sounded like the offer of an alliance.

Shutton started walking and Mila followed her. 'Inspector Gurevich filled me in on my way here. He said you intend to put in your report some references to events that took place twenty years ago.'

'Yes, ma'am.'

'The Wizard, the Enchanter of Souls, the Goodnight Man . . . Is that right?'

'And Kairus.'

'Ah, yes,' the Judge said, coming to a halt. 'There's that other name now, too.'

Mila was convinced that Shutton had heard it before. But it could well be that only a select few were in the know.

'I remember the insomniacs case,' Shutton went on. 'It was the beginning of the end for the Witness Protection Unit. A couple of years later, one of the special agents involved lost his dignity in another sordid affair.'

Mila guessed she was referring to Simon Berish. She didn't ask what had happened, but Shutton told her anyway.

'He took a bribe to help a major underworld informer escape when he should have been watching him.'

Mila couldn't believe that was the reason Berish was considered a pariah, couldn't imagine him as having been corrupt. But she realised that Shutton was dying to tell her the story, and she decided to play along. 'I assume that agent is no longer in the department.'

The Judge turned to look at her. 'Unfortunately, we were never able to find the evidence to nail him.'

'Why are you telling me all this?'

Shutton came right out with it. 'Because I don't want you to go to him for help. Whatever happens, you come only to me. Is that clear?'

'Yes. Do you have anything against my mentioning Kairus in my report?' Mila asked to provoke her.

'Not at all,' the Judge said. Then her tone grew almost conspiratorial. 'But if you want my advice – woman to woman – I wouldn't, if I were you. The case is twenty years old. There's no evidence, no leads, and you're likely to get bogged down. Besides, those nicknames don't mean anything. They were invented by the media to increase the TV ratings and sell more newspapers and magazines. Don't make a fool of yourself by chasing after a comic strip character.'

But Mila couldn't help thinking of the figure she had encountered in the house the previous night. He had been real enough, as much flesh and blood as anyone else. Maybe the circumstances – the nest, the darkness, the fear – had blown him up in her mind, but he was no monster of the imagination.

He existed, and he was real.

'What if I just put in my report that I was attacked by an unknown assailant?'

Shutton smiled. 'Definitely much better.' Then she looked closely at Mila. 'I've been following your progress since the start of the investigation and I think you've done well. I know you've expressed your doubts about the theory that a terrorist organisation might be behind the killings.'

'Yes, and I haven't changed my mind about that.'

'Can I afford to invest in your idea, Officer Vasquez?'

Mila wasn't sure what she meant.

'Gurevich has asked me to take you off the case, but I think you can be useful in other ways.' Shutton motioned to her driver, who immediately got out of the car carrying a brown folder.

The Judge handed it to Mila, who looked at it. It was very slim. 'What is this?'

'I want you to follow a different line of inquiry. I'm sure you'll find something in there to interest you.'

35

The office had always been his refuge, but now it felt more like a cell.

Berish was walking up and down, looking for a way out.

'I didn't hit him,' he said to Hitch, who was lying in his corner, watching his master's restless pacing.

He couldn't forgive himself for what had happened the night before. His hand had shaken in the darkness, and he had missed his target. But then it had been a while since he had last held a gun. The man of action had become a man of the mind, he reminded himself in a mood of self-mockery.

The worst of it was that he hadn't seen the face of the man who had been tormenting him for twenty years. And now he would be plagued with questions yet again.

Kairus is back, he kept telling himself.

Last night, before he left the building site, Mila had told him everything that had happened in the past few days: Roger Valin's massacre of the Belmans, the murders committed by Nadia Niverman and Eric Vincenti. All of them people who, like André García, had vanished then reappeared, but only in order to kill.

As Berish had listened to this account of crimes that had

first been labelled acts of revenge, then of terrorism, an old fear had spread through him and he had felt a lump in his throat, as if all his doubts and anxieties were concentrated there.

What was happening? What was behind this linked sequence of murders?

Every time he felt anxious, it was the thought of Sylvia that calmed him down. The memory permeated the amorphous pall of his anguish like a luminous mirage piercing a blanket of fog. She would come and comfort him with her smile and stroke his hand.

Not a day went by that Berish didn't think of her.

Convinced as he was that he had banished the memory of her to a place inaccessible even to himself, Sylvia always somehow came back, like a cat that always manages to find its way home. He would see her in objects or in a landscape, or she would speak to him through the words of a song.

However brief their relationship might have been, he still loved her.

But no longer in the passionate way he once had – that passion had turned fiercely against him after it was over, calling him to account for what had happened and blaming him for it. Now it was a distant nostalgia. The thought of her, the love, would appear in his heart and he would hold it for a moment in his hands, gaze at it as though it were a gorgeous view, then let it fall again.

The first time they met, he had been struck by her jet-black hair, which she wore in a plait. He would soon learn that when she let it down, it was a sign that she wanted to make love. She wasn't beautiful that day, but he immediately realised that he couldn't live without her.

Three knocks at the door brought him back to reality.

He came to a halt in the middle of the room. Hitch, too, was on the alert.

Nobody ever knocked at the door of his office.

'The man we saw in that house may not have died in the fire. It's possible he got away through the sewers.'

Mila was beside herself. Berish pulled her inside the office, hoping that his colleagues hadn't noticed her. 'Why are you here?'

She was waving a brown folder. 'Shutton told me about you. She was the one who brought up the subject. She advised me – no, warned me – to stay away from you. Now if the head of the department did that, then there must be something to it.'

Berish was taken aback. He couldn't imagine what Shutton might have told Mila. Or rather, he could imagine it only too well. He hoped Mila hadn't been influenced by her. No, he could rule that out – the fact that she'd come here showed that she hadn't been.

'I know you feel safe being the department's pariah,' Mila said, reacting to his silence. 'I get that, but it's all a bit too comfortable now. I want to know everything.'

Berish tried to get her to lower her voice. 'I already told you everything.'

Mila pointed at the door. 'Out there, in the real world, I had to lie for you. I told the head of the department a pack of lies to keep you out of trouble. I think you owe me.'

'I saved your life last night. Isn't that enough?'

'We're both involved now,' Mila said, and put the brown folder down on the desk.

Berish looked at it as if it were a hand grenade ready to explode. 'What's inside?'

'The proof that we were right all along.'

Berish walked behind his desk, sat down, and rested his chin on his folded hands. 'All right. What do you want to know?'

'Everything.'

The case of the seven missing insomniacs twenty years earlier hadn't ended there.

The Federal Police had investigated what possible connection there could be between a homosexual ex-soldier, a delivery boy, a female student, a retired science teacher, a widow, the owner of a linen shop, and a department store assistant.

If they'd been able to find some link between them, they might have been able to discover if and why someone had taken an interest in them and made them disappear. But the only link they had found was the tenuous one that they had all suffered from insomnia.

That could have been mere coincidence, something the media had built up out of all proportion. After all, how many people went missing in the city every day? And how many of them took sleeping pills? But even if the police weren't so sure, the public had liked the macabre idea that someone was responsible.

That was when witnesses started appearing.

'There's always someone who saw or thinks they saw something. In the department, we were trained to spot the people who just wanted to be in the limelight, and we knew how to handle them. First, we'd see if they'd waited too long before coming forward. Then their versions were usually all very similar – that was a classic sign. They'd talk about some suspicious person they'd seen lurking outside one of the missing people's homes. So then we'd give them the identikit test. I don't know why but when it comes to criminals, people always describe more or less the same face, with small eyes and a broad forehead. According to anthropologists, it's a leftover from the evolutionary process – the enemy narrows his eyes when he's aiming at us, and the forehead is the first thing we look out for when trying to spot an adversary hiding in an open space. Whatever the reason, if those two elements recur, you can be pretty sure the identikit is useless.' Berish cleared his throat. 'But one of these witnesses gave us a description that seemed plausible.' He opened a desk drawer and handed Mila a sheet of paper with an identikit picture on it.

Kairus – the man who made people disappear – had an androgynous face.

That was the first thing Mila noticed as she studied it to see if she recognised the face she had glimpsed the night before in the flashes caused by Berish's gunshots. Flat and lacking in perspective as it was, the identikit conveyed the delicacy of the features. They seemed to converge around the black eyes which, like twin spirals, sucked in the surrounding light. The dark hair was like a crown over a bony forehead. The cheekbones were high and the lips full. The dimple in the middle of the chin was a mark of both strength and grace.

As expected, Kairus didn't look like a monster.

'The witness's statement was precise, detailed, and easy to check. Kairus was apparently about forty years old, just under six feet tall, with an athletic build. The witness was so sure about everything because when they met Kairus did something that really stuck in the witness's memory.'

The Goodnight Man had smiled.

'For no reason, as if he simply wanted the witness to remember him. And it worked. That smile created a sense of unease, of anxiety.'

The witness had been placed under police protection, but it hadn't been enough.

'Our star witness vanished into thin air.'

The expression on Berish's face was that of someone who

knows he is dealing with a threat he is unable to comprehend.

'It's like you went to the cinema to see a horror film, and the monster came out of the screen: the fear you bought with your ticket becomes something else, and you don't know what to call it. It's panic, but it's more than that. It's the feeling that there's no way out. The sudden, irreversible realisation that no amount of distance can keep you safe. And that death knows your name.' He ran his fingers through his greying hair. 'We called him and he came: the Goodnight Man was among us. Not only did he have a face, he had even chosen what he wanted to be called.

'Three days after the only person who had seen his face disappeared, a package arrived in the department. It contained a strand of the witness's hair. With it was a note. One word. A name. Kairus.'

He hadn't just come out in the open. He had thrown down the gauntlet to them.

'He seemed to be saying: You've been right so far. It's always been me. You have my identikit and now you also have my name. So find me.'

A heavy air of defeat had hung over the department. The fear had spared no one. Because if that was the level of provocation, then the threat was to everyone, not just the most insignificant of human beings.

'That was the end of it. We didn't hear from Kairus again, and the disappearances stopped. The Goodnight Man's most successful trick was to leave us with a big question mark. He couldn't be called a murderer because there were no bodies. He couldn't be called a kidnapper, because there was no evidence any force had been used in the disappearances. All we had on him and his motives was lots of theories.'

Kairus had committed a crime that had no name. Even if they'd caught him, they wouldn't have known what to charge him with. But the people who had disappeared were still referred to as victims.

'What was the witness's name?'

'Sylvia.'

36

The witness was a woman.

Mila noticed that Berish had hesitated before uttering the name, as if it were an effort for him. 'This Sylvia had already supplied you with a description of Kairus, so why did he make her disappear?'

'To show us what he was capable of doing. And how determined he was to do it.'

'And he succeeded,' Mila concluded bitterly. 'Because, obviously, when the identikit didn't lead you anywhere, you decided to close the case before the failure was too much to bear. Actually, you didn't just close it, you buried it. All I found in Limbo was a cleaned-up file. You justified yourselves by maintaining that the Goodnight Man was just an invention, a kind of urban myth.' Mila was beside herself with anger. 'In fact, he was all too real. We had proof of that last night. There he was, right in front of our eyes.'

Berish still seemed shaken by what had happened in the red-brick house.

'You were working for Steph in the Witness Protection Unit, so it was your job to protect Sylvia, right?' There was disappointment now on Mila's face. 'You and Captain Stephanopoulos were both involved. Who else?'

'Gurevich and Joanna Shutton.'

Mila was taken aback. The Judge? So that was why she'd offered her help earlier. 'With Steph's agreement, you all made a pact to save your careers. The search for those missing persons was called off. None of you gave a damn about them.'

'You're talking to *me* about my career?' Berish gave an ironic laugh. 'And Steph asked to be transferred to Limbo precisely because he didn't want to give up.'

'But you let others drop the case for their own personal interests. You were their accomplice.'

Berish knew the accusation was deserved, but he tried to refute it all the same. 'If I could go back, I'd do exactly the same thing, because Shutton and Gurevich are excellent police officers. I wasn't doing a favour to them, but to the department.'

Mila wondered why Berish was standing up for colleagues who looked on him with such contempt. She remembered what the Judge had told her about the suspicions hovering over Berish that he was corrupt, and for a moment she was struck by the possibility that it might be true.

But she was also starting to understand the reason for the secrecy in which the killings of the past few days – starting with Roger Valin's massacre of the Belmans – had been shrouded. In making sure the news didn't get out, her superiors hadn't been trying to protect the integrity of the investigation, they'd been trying to protect themselves from a scandal concerning what had happened twenty years earlier. 'Does Klaus Boris know?'

'You and your friend are just pawns in this game.'

Mila felt a touch of relief at Berish's words. She couldn't be sure they were the truth, but they comforted her anyway. 'Then why did the Judge give me this file?' She pointed to the brown folder on the table.

'I don't know,' Berish admitted. 'She really should have taken you off the case. But you can never tell with Joanna. She's good at using people.'

'If you read what it says, you'll realise she practically gave me a lead that helped me get at the truth of what you all decided twenty years ago.'

Berish smiled bitterly. 'And you trust her? She probably did it because she knows the story is going to come out anyway. She's just preparing for the worst, believe me.'

Maybe he was right. That was why Mila decided she didn't care if she was dealing with an officer who might once have taken a bribe from a supergrass. 'Why don't you take a look at the file? You never know, you might even decide to give me a hand . . .'

Berish snorted. He looked at Mila, then at the brown folder. Finally, he reached his hand out across the desk, picked up the folder, opened it, and started to read.

Mila watched him as his eyes ran down the single sheet. When he had finished, he put it down.

'If what it says here is true, then it changes everything.'

37

It was a Tuesday at the end of September, but it felt like summer.

The warm air enveloped them like an tight embrace. Hitch kept his head outside the window of the Hyundai, enjoying the artificial breeze created by the forward movement of the car.

Mila kept her eyes on the road as she drove. In the seat beside her, Berish was reading the contents of the brown folder yet again.

He had a coffee stain on his shirt cuff, which he kept trying to hide by pulling down the sleeve of his jacket, almost without realising it. Mila noticed the gesture out of the corner of her eye, and it struck her as endearing. Berish cared about how he looked. It wasn't just about appearances, it was a question of decorum. He reminded her of her father and the care he had taken over polishing his shoes every morning. He'd always said it was important to present yourself well, as a mark of respect towards other people. Berish might not be as old as her father had been when she was a girl, but he had the same kind of old-school manners, and Mila found that reassuring.

'How long is it since you last slept?' he asked her distractedly.

'I'm fine.'

The last twenty-four hours had been one damned thing after another, but now the warmth of the afternoon was having a calming effect on Mila's nerves. The suburb they were passing through was peaceful. The small houses were all different from one another. The people who lived in them were mainly working class. They worked, raised their children, and aspired to nothing more than a quiet life. It was a close-knit community, a place where everyone knew everyone else.

They drove past the Baptist church at the end of the block, a white building with a steeple, surrounded by a large lawn. The sound of joyful hymns could be heard, even though there was a hearse parked outside.

Mila turned just after the church and stopped in front of the third house on the street, which stood in the shade of a tall elm.

They got out of the car, and a blast of hot air hit them and then moved on. In the front garden of the modest, single-storey house were three children – two boys and a girl. They stopped playing to look at the two newcomers. They all had spotty faces.

'Is your mother at home?' Berish asked them, letting Hitch out of the car.

None of the three children replied: they were all far too interested in the dog.

Just then, a woman appeared at the door, with a child of about two in her arms. She looked at them suspiciously for a moment, then smiled when she saw Hitch.

'Hello,' she said.

'Hello,' Berish said, politely. 'Mrs Robertson?'

'Yes, that's me.'

Berish and Mila made their way up the path, dodging a number of toys and a tricycle, and climbed the steps to the porch.

'We're from the Federal Police Department,' Berish said, taking the single sheet of paper out of the brown folder and holding it up between two fingers so that the woman could see it. 'Do you recognise this report?'

'Yes,' Mrs Robertson said, somewhat taken aback. 'But I never heard anything more.'

Berish exchanged a quick glance with Mila, then turned back to the woman. 'May we come in?'

Mila and Berish were sitting in the living room. They had left Hitch out in the garden, playing with Mrs Robertson's older children.

The carpet was strewn with building blocks and jigsaw puzzle pieces. On the dinner table lay a pile of linen waiting to be ironed. A dirty plate was balanced on the arm of one of the armchairs.

'Excuse the mess,' the woman said as she put the child she'd been carrying down in his playpen. 'It's hard to keep up with everything when you have five children to raise.'

She had already explained that the eldest ones weren't at school because they'd come down with German measles. The second youngest – the one who was now in the playpen – was at home today because the kindergarten he attended didn't want the disease to spread. And the youngest of all, who was only three months old, was in the hall, asleep in his cradle.

'Don't worry about it,' Mila said. 'We should apologise for coming here without letting you know first.'

Camilla Robertson was a short, sturdy-looking woman in her early thirties. She had strong arms, short brown hair, a light complexion, pink cheeks and bright blue eyes. Over her yellow blouse, she wore a necklace with a small silver cross. Overall, she gave the impression of a busy but happy mother.

'My husband is Pastor Robertson, from the Baptist Church round the corner,' she said eagerly, sitting down after disposing of the dirty plate on the armchair. 'He's conducting the funeral of one of the brothers in our community, who passed away yesterday. I ought to be with him now.'

'We're very sorry about your friend,' Berish said.

She gave him a sincere smile. 'No need to be sorry. He's in the hands of the Lord now.'

The house was simply furnished. The only decorations were framed family photographs and pictures of Jesus, the Virgin Mary and the Last Supper. Mila didn't think they were there for show. They were clearly the outward signs of a deep religious faith that underlay every aspect of the family's life.

'Can I get you anything?' the woman asked.

'Please don't put yourself to any trouble, Mrs Robertson,' Berish said.

'Camilla,' she corrected him.

'All right . . . Camilla.'

'How about coffee? It won't take a second.'

'To be honest we're in a bit of a hurry,' Berish said, but the woman had already stood up and headed for the kitchen. They were obliged to wait for a few minutes, while the two-year-old in the playpen kept an eye on them. Camilla returned carrying a tray with two steaming cups. She immediately served her guests.

'What can you tell us about that report?' Mila asked, trying to move things along.

Mrs Robertson sat back down on the edge of the armchair and put her hands together between her knees. 'What can I say? It was such a long time ago. Practically another life.'

'You don't need to go into too much detail,' Berish said encouragingly. 'Just tell us what you remember.'

'Let's see . . . I was almost sixteen. I was living with my grandmother in an apartment block near the railway terminal. My mother had left me with her when I was a few months old. She was a drifter and didn't know how to take care of me. And I never knew my father. But I don't bear them a grudge, I've forgiven them.' She made an affectionate face at the child in the playpen, who responded with a toothless smile. 'My grandmother Nora didn't want me, she always said I was a burden to her. She was on welfare because when she was young she'd fractured her hip working in a factory. She kept saying that if it wasn't for me she'd have managed a lot better on that money and it was my fault if she was forced to live a dog's life. She tried putting me in an institution several times but I kept running away and going back to her. God knows why ... Once, when I was eight, I was placed with a family. They were good people and had six other children – some of them with different parents, just like me. They got on well together and were always happy. But I always felt lost, because I couldn't figure out why they gave me their love so selflessly. The woman wasn't a relative of mine, and yet she took care of me: did my washing, made food for me, and so on. I thought I was meant to be grateful somehow, or that they expected me to be. So one night I took off my clothes and got into bed with the husband, just like I'd seen in a film they showed on late-night TV at my grandmother's. He didn't get angry, he was very kind and told me it wasn't right for a little girl to behave like that and I should put my clothes back on. But I could see he was very upset. How was I supposed to know that what I'd tried to do with him was something grown-ups did? Nobody had ever explained it to me. The next day, a social worker came and took me away, and I never saw them again.'

Camilla Robertson had told the story with a lightness that surprised Mila. It was as if she had come to terms with the past and made peace with it, so that she didn't need to hide anything. There was no resentment in her voice, only a touch of sadness.

Berish would have liked her to get to the point, but realised it was best to let her speak.

'I got the first call on my sixteenth birthday. It was two in the afternoon and my grandmother usually slept until six. The phone rang a few times, then stopped, then immediately started again. That's when I picked up the receiver. It was a man wishing me happy birthday. It was strange because no one ever remembered my birthday. I'd only ever had a birthday cake once before, during one of my many stays at the institution, and I'd had to blow out the candles with five children who'd been born around the same time. It was nice, but it was nothing special. So when that man on the phone said he was calling just for me, I felt . . . flattered.'

Mila looked at the photographs of the Robertsons spread about the living room, filled with birthday cakes and smiling faces spattered with whipped cream.

'Did he say who he was?' Berish asked.

'I didn't even ask him. I didn't care. Other people called me "Nora's granddaughter", and whenever Nora needed me she used bad words. So to me the only thing that mattered was that this man knew my name. He wanted to know if I was all right, and asked me questions about my life, for instance if I was going to school, who my friends were, my favourite singer or group. But he also knew quite a lot about me: he knew I liked the colour purple, that whenever I had any pocket money I'd rush to the cinema, that I loved films about animals, and that I wanted to have a dog called Ben.'

'Weren't you surprised that he knew so much about you?' Mila asked.

Camilla Robertson smiled and shook her head. 'I can assure you I was much more impressed by the fact that someone was interested in me.'

'What happened after that?'

'The phone calls became a regular occurrence. He usually called on Saturday afternoons. We'd chat for about twenty minutes, but we talked mainly about me. It was pleasant, and I didn't mind that I had no idea who he was or what he looked like. In fact, it was nice sometimes to think he'd chosen me for this special relationship. He never told me not to tell anyone about our conversations, that's why I never suspected his intentions. He never asked if he could meet me or if I could do anything for him. He was my secret friend.'

'How long did the phone calls continue?' Berish asked.

'About a year, I think, before they stopped. But I still remember the one before last.' She paused. 'His tone of voice was different. He asked me a question he'd never asked before, something like, "Would you like a new life?" Then he explained what he meant by that. If I wanted, I could change my name, move to another city, maybe even have a dog called Ben.'

Mila and Berish exchanged knowing glances.

'He didn't explain how. He just said that if I wanted it, he could make it happen.'

Mila reached out and very slowly, so as not to spoil the atmosphere, put her coffee cup down on the low table.

'It sounded crazy to me. I thought it was a joke. But he was absolutely serious. I told him I was fine, I didn't want another life. Actually, I was only trying to reassure him, because I didn't want him to feel sorry for me. He told me to think it over and give him my answer the following Saturday. When he called a week later, I told him the same thing. He didn't seem angry. We talked about this and that. I didn't know it would be our last conversation. I remember that when the phone didn't ring the week after, I felt more abandoned than I ever had before.' The baby in the cradle started to cry, and Camilla Robertson snapped out of it. 'Excuse me,' she said, getting up and going out into the hall.

Mila turned to Berish and said in a low voice, 'I get the feeling there's a lot she can tell us.'

Berish pointed at the brown folder. 'We still have to talk about this.'

38

Soon afterwards, Camilla Robertson returned, carrying the baby.

She stood there, rocking him in her arms to get him back to sleep. 'He can't stand the heat and, frankly, neither can I. The Lord has given us a long summer this year.'

'Camilla,' Mila said, interrupting her, 'you heard from that man again, didn't you ...?'

'Yes, many years later. I was twenty-five and I wasn't leading what you'd call a righteous life. When I turned eighteen, my grandmother had kicked me out of the house. She said she'd done everything she could for me. She passed away some time later and I pray every day that she is now in Heaven.'

'Being homeless,' Berish said, 'I guess things must have taken a bad turn.'

Camilla looked at him fearlessly. 'Yes, they did. I was scared at first but I was also sure I'd be happy. Only God knew how wrong I was ... My first night on the streets, I was robbed of the small amount of money I had. On the second day, I ended up in Emergency with a cracked rib. Within a week, I'd figured out the only way to survive was to prostitute myself. And a month later

I discovered the secret of being happy in that hell, when I smoked crack for the first time.'

The more Berish looked at that calm, even-tempered woman in front of him, the harder he found it to believe that she was talking about herself.

'I was arrested several times. I was in and out of jail or rehab, but I always went back to the old life. Sometimes I didn't eat for days so that I could buy drugs. I'd take them as payment from clients – the few who still had the courage to go with me, because I was nothing but skin and bones, my hair was falling out, and my teeth were decaying.'

As she spoke, the baby was trying to get at her breast through her blouse. There was a dissonance between the innocent scene they were watching and the scenes the woman was describing.

'I remember one winter's night. It was pouring with rain and there wasn't a soul about, but I had to stay out to make enough money for a dose. I had nowhere to go anyway. I was out of it most of the time, in some kind of parallel dimension. Not only when I was high, but when I was clean, too, because the only survival instinct I had left didn't make me want to eat or sleep, only to get high again. Anyway, that night when it rained, I took shelter in a phone booth. I can't remember how long I stayed there, waiting for the rain to stop. I was soaked to the skin and freezing cold. I tried to warm myself by rubbing my hands all over my body but it didn't work. Just then, the phone rang. I can still remember staring at it for a long time. I couldn't take in what was happening. I let it ring because I didn't have the courage to pick up the receiver. Something inside told me it wasn't a wrong number. That the call was for me.'

Mila waited. She would let the woman take all the time she needed, as if she were back in that phone booth, picking up the receiver just as she had done all those years ago.

'The first thing he said was my name – Camilla. I recognised his voice immediately. Then he asked me how I was and I started crying. You can't imagine how good it feels to cry after you haven't cried for years. Mind you, I'd had my reasons not to cry. That world was a ruthless place, and I couldn't allow myself the weakness of tears, or I'd have died.' Something cracked in the woman's voice. 'Then, for the second time, he asked me that question: "Would you like a new life?" And this time I said yes.'

The baby had fallen asleep in his mother's arms, and the two-year-old was playing quietly in his pen. Outside, the older children were shrieking with joy, running after Hitch. Inside and outside the house, Camilla Robertson was surrounded by all the things that were dearest to her. With commitment and dedication, she had built this little world for herself, as if she had never desired any other.

'Did he tell you how he was going to give you this new life?' Berish asked.

'He gave me very specific instructions. I had to buy some sleeping pills and go the following evening to a hotel, where I would find a room booked in my name.'

That mention of sleeping pills immediately aroused Mila's and Berish's interest. They might actually be close to a solution to the mystery of the insomniacs. But they avoided looking at each other for fear of breaking the flow of Camilla's story.

'I was supposed to lie down on the bed and take a sleeping pill,' she went on. 'Then I'd wake up in a different place and be able to start all over again from scratch.'

Mila made a mental note of these details. She still couldn't believe the story was true. And yet it made a kind of sense. 'And what did you do?' she asked. 'Did you go?'

'Yes. The room really had been booked for me. I went upstairs and opened the door. The place was pretty seedy, but there was nothing that disturbed me or made me think I was in any danger. I took the bottle with the sleeping pills and lay down on the bed without turning down the blanket, and without even taking my clothes off. I remember keeping my hands in my lap, holding the bottle tight, and looking up at the ceiling. I'd been doing drugs for seven years, but at that moment I was scared of taking a sleeping pill. I kept wondering what would happen to me and if I was really ready for a new life.'

'What happened next?' Berish asked.

Camilla Robertson looked at him with tired eyes. 'With a clear-headedness I didn't know I had, I told myself that if I didn't try to get out of this thing by myself, instead of plunging into the void, I was sure to die. Do you understand? For the first time, I realised that, however self-destructive I might be, I really didn't want to die.' She heaved a deep sigh, and the cross she wore around her neck rose at the same time as her chest. 'I got up from the bed and left.'

Berish took Kairus's identikit from his pocket. He unfolded it and held it out to the woman. 'Have you ever seen this man before?'

After a brief hesitation, Camilla Robertson took the piece of paper from Berish and held it away from her, almost as if afraid of it. She stared for a long time at the picture, studying every detail of the face.

Berish and Mila held their breaths.

'No, never seen him in my life.'

The two officers didn't give any indication of how disappointed they were.

'Mrs Robertson,' Mila said, 'we just have a few more questions, if you don't mind. Did you ever receive any more calls?'

'No, never.'

Mila believed her.

'There was no need,' Camilla went on. 'After that experience, I joined a community, and this time I took it seriously. There, I met Pastor Robertson and we got married. As you can see, I did it all by myself.' Her tone was triumphant.

The sin of pride – Berish forgave her with a smile. 'Why did you decide to report these incidents to the police so many years later?'

'Over time, I changed my mind about him. I was no longer sure his intentions were good.'

'What made you think that?' Berish said, genuinely interested to hear her point of view.

'I'm not sure really. When I met my husband and saw how he devoted himself to other people, it made me wonder why someone with good motives would feel the need to hide in the shadows. Plus . . . '

Berish and Mila waited.

'Plus . . . there was something evil . . . .'

Berish pondered her answer. He didn't want to give Camilla the impression she had said something absurd – on the contrary, her words made sense to him.

'One last thing,' Mila said. 'Do you remember the name of the hotel and the number of the room where you went that day?'

'I certainly ought to . . . ' Camilla Robertson looked up at the ceiling as if the memory were there. 'Room 317, Ambrus Hotel.'

39

The Ambrus Hotel was a forgettable place.

It was a narrow building in a row of identical buildings. Six floors, four windows on each one. From it, you could see a railway bridge across which a train passed more or less every three minutes. There was a neon sign on the roof, although it was switched off at this time of day.

Outside, a line of vehicles had formed, and the sound of horns mingled with the house music coming from a car radio. Commuters had to come through this part of town to reach the ring road that led to the middle-class suburbs. But many of them, especially male office workers, would stop off here for a couple of hours. The area was full of red-lit bars, lap dancing clubs and sex shops, all awaiting customers. The flashing signs were an irresistible call to men in search of escape. Pretty girls wearing lots of make-up congregated around the entrance to the metro station.

The role the Ambrus Hotel played in the local economy was fairly obvious.

Mila and Berish walked through a revolving door into a dusty foyer. Thanks to the nearby railway bridge, not much daylight came in, and the yellow wall lights did little to brighten the place, which bathed in a saffron-coloured gloom. The air was heavy with cigarette smoke.

You could still hear the traffic noise outside, but it was muffled now. Distant music seeped through into the room, and Berish thought he recognised an old Edith Piaf record – an aura of doom-laden romanticism to greet the voluntary denizens of this involuntary hell.

A black man in a check jacket and a buttoned-up shirt without a tie sat on a worn leather sofa, staring into space and humming along with the music, one hand propped on a white stick.

Mila and Berish walked past the blind man, following the burgundy-coloured runner that led to the reception desk. There was nobody behind it. They waited.

'Look,' Berish said, pointing to the key rack. Each key was attached to a brass knob with a number engraved on it. 'Room 317 is free.'

The red velvet curtain behind the desk was pushed aside, and a thin man in jeans and a black T-shirt came out. As he did so, the music became momentarily louder. He was the person who'd been listening to Edith Piaf.

'Hi, guys,' he said, stuffing the last piece of a sandwich in his mouth.

'Hi to you,' Berish replied in response to the slightly incongruous greeting.

The man, who was about fifty, wiped his hands with a napkin. The tendons on his arms were taut and covered in faded tattoos. He had grey crew-cut hair, a gold ring in his left earlobe, and a pair of small reading glasses balanced on the tip of his nose. He looked like an aging rock star.

'Do you need a room?' he asked, taking his seat behind the desk and looking down at the register. Clearly, the regulars didn't like the porter to show too much interest in them, so he looked at them as little as possible.

For a moment, Mila and Berish exchanged glances. They had been taken for a couple in search of privacy.

'Yes, please,' she replied, letting him believe what he wanted.

'Do you already know the name you want in the register, or shall I think of one for you?'

'You think of one,' Berish said.

'Do you also want towels?' the porter asked, pointing with his pen at a stack of towels on a laundry trolley.

'No, that's all right,' Mila said. 'Could we have Room 317?'

The man looked up from the register. 'Why?'

'It's our lucky number,' Berish said, leaning across the desk. 'Why, is there a problem?'

'What are you, Satanists, spiritualists, or just nosey parkers?'

Berish looked perplexed.

'Did someone tell you to come here? I don't see any other explanation.'

'Explanation for what?' Mila asked.

'Don't pretend you don't know. If you really want that room, it'll be fifteen per cent extra. Don't try and trick me.'

'We'll pay, no problem,' Berish said to calm him down. 'Now are you going to tell us what's so special about Room 317?'

The man made a reproachful gesture. 'It's stupid, really ... They say someone was murdered there about thirty years ago. Every now and again, someone hears about it and asks for that room to screw in.' He looked from one to the other. 'You aren't into bondage, are you? The other week I had to cut down a man in leather pants who'd asked a whore to hang him by the neck in the wardrobe.'

'Don't worry, we won't cause you any trouble,' Berish reassured him.

'Because these nutters come here in droves. If I ever catch the person who started the rumour about Room 317, I'll show him.' He turned to the key rack and took down the brass knob with the appropriate number. 'Is an hour all right?'

'Perfect,' Berish said. They paid and took the key.

They went up in a creaky, slow-moving wooden lift that was barely large enough for two people. When they got to the third floor, it stopped with a brief jolt.

The doors had to be opened by hand, and Berish pushed aside the grille that separated them from the landing. Having closed it again, they followed the signs to the rooms.

The door they were looking for was the last one at the end of the corridor, next to the goods lift. A varnished black wooden door, like the others, with three numbers in burnished metal.

317.

'What do you think?' Mila asked before Berish slid the key into the lock.

'That having the goods lift so close makes it ideal for getting unconscious people out of the hotel without anyone noticing.'

'So you think the Goodnight Man always used this room to lure his victims?'

'Why wouldn't he? I don't know if there really was a murder here once, but the rumour must have come in useful for Kairus.'

'Of course,' Mila agreed. 'If he'd kept booking the same room, someone might have started to suspect something, even if he was using false names. But thanks to its macabre reputation, Room 317 was already the most popular in the hotel. A perfect choice, I'd say.'

Berish turned the key in the lock and they walked in.

Room 317 looked like a normal hotel room. The walls were covered in dark red paper. There was a wall-to-wall carpet of the

243

same colour, but with big blue flowers – chosen specially so that guests wouldn't notice the stains that would accumulate over the years. A dusty chandelier hung over a brown varnished wooden double bed. The bedspread was burgundy-coloured satin and bore the marks of cigarette burns. There were two bedside tables with grey marble tops and a black telephone on one of them. On the wall above the bed was the still-visible shadow left there over the years by a crucifix that had since been removed. All the windows faced west and looked out onto the street. Some thirty yards away was the railway bridge, with trains rattling across it.

Without explaining what he was looking for, Berish immediately began searching the room.

'Do you really think we'll find clues here to Kairus's motives?' Mila asked.

'Well,' he said, opening the wardrobe and the drawers, 'he'd contact them by phone and gradually win them over with the promise of a new life. It didn't take him long, because he deliberately chose people who had nothing but pain and indifference in their lives. All he had to do was be friendly and pay attention to them as no one else had done. Then, when the time came, he'd tell them to come here with a supply of sleeping pills. Sleep is the state where we're at our most defenceless. And it was in that defenceless state that he'd get them to put themselves in his hands. Do you realise what power of persuasion that took? That's Kairus for you.'

Apart from a row of empty coat hangers, a couple of dusty blankets and an old Bible with a fake leather cover embossed with the hotel's logo, Berish's search proved fruitless. But he didn't give up. His next stop was the bathroom.

The walls were tiled in white, the floor in a black and white chessboard pattern. There was a sink, a toilet, and a bath instead of a shower.

Mila watched from the doorway as Berish took from the mirrored cabinet a half-used bottle of bubble bath and an empty box of condoms. 'You haven't answered my question,' she said. 'Why did the Goodnight Man want those people?'

'He was forming an army. The army of shadows, remember?'

'Yes, but what was the purpose of having them coming back to commit murder?'

Just as Berish was about to answer, a sharp ringing – shrill and unpleasant – echoed through the two rooms. They looked out through the bathroom door into the bedroom.

The black telephone on one of the bedside tables was demanding their attention.

Berish stepped onto the carpet, but Mila was unable to budge from the doorway to the bathroom.

He turned to her and pointed to the phone. 'We have to answer it.'

Mila looked at him as if he had just suggested they jump out of the window together.

Meanwhile, the phone kept calling to them.

It was Mila who finally responded to the call. She walked to the bedside table, but as soon as she put her hand on the receiver, she remembered the question the Goodnight Man had asked his victims.

Would you like a new life?

She was certain those were the words she would hear at the other end of the line. She lifted the receiver and the ringing abruptly stopped. She raised the receiver to her ear and heard nothing but an empty silence that seemed to come from a dark, bottomless well.

Berish threw her a questioning look, and she was about to say something, just to put an end to the oppressive silence. But before the words could emerge from her mouth, she heard music.

It was a classical piece, an old, remote melody.

Mila held out the receiver so that Berish could also hear the music.

This enigmatic message confirmed that they were on the right track. It might also be a clue pointing to the next killing. But what it proved beyond any doubt was that Kairus knew their moves in advance. And that he was watching them.

The line suddenly went dead.

A shudder went through Mila such as she had never experienced before. She looked at Berish and repeated the question she had already asked him twice, in different forms, since they had set foot in Room 317, without getting an answer. This time, she was more direct.

'Berish, what's the army of shadows?'

'I can tell you they aren't terrorists.'

'Then what are they?'

'A cult.'

40

'Have you ever heard of the Hypothesis of Evil?'

Simon Berish's voice echoed through the great library. Mila watched him as she sat at one of the long tables in the reading room, surrounded by old book-filled shelves rising to the ceiling. On the mahogany surface, a number of volumes Berish had taken down from the shelves lay scattered. Now, he was walking up and down impatiently, while Hitch ran about, happy to have so much space to play in.

They were alone.

'No, I haven't,' Mila said in response to Berish's question.

'The first thing to say is that this business has nothing to do with either Satan and his demons or God and his saints.'

'Then what does it have to do with?'

'With the idea of a cult, but not in a religious sense. If it were religious, we'd have had ritualistic killings, full of symbolism and following a similar pattern. Of course, there are many similarities between these killings, but we're more interested in the differences.'

Mila saw a new gleam in Berish's eyes, as if he were experiencing some kind of joyous epiphany. 'Well, we know what they have in common,' she said. 'The killers are all people who disappeared and have come back after a long time away. In the first two cases, the motive is resentment.'

'That's what it looks like,' Berish said, 'but it isn't. Roger Valin exterminates the family of the owner of a pharmaceuticals company because the drug that could have prolonged his mother's life was too expensive? Come on! It doesn't stand up. Nadia Niverman murders her husband's lawyer, but guess what? She doesn't go after her husband.'

'She wanted him to live in fear.'

'Is that why she killed herself afterwards?'

Mila said nothing. The fact was, she hadn't thought of that. John Niverman's torture hadn't lasted long enough.

'So you see, the motive of resentment allegedly triggering acts of revenge is pretty weak in both those killings. But now let's take the other two cases ... Eric Vincenti kills "the undertaker", a money lender he's never had any dealings with.'

'And there's a connection missing in the case of André García, too,' Mila said. 'Why did he pick on a drug dealer? As far as we know, he was never involved with drugs before he disappeared.'

For the first time, she had a clear picture of the inconsistencies in this affair. She had been so intent on trying to refute the terrorism theory that she hadn't bothered to work out one of her own. 'So you're saying these people were killed just because they deserved it?'

'I'm not saying that, either.' Berish rested his hands on the table and leant towards her. 'The answer lies in the Hypothesis of Evil.'

He grabbed one of the books and turned it around so that she could see it properly. It was an old zoology text, and it was open at the chapter on animal ethics.

'There's an anthropological postulate that refers to this subject.'

248

He showed her a picture of a lioness attacking zebra calves. Although it was only a black and white drawing, it was extremely vivid.

'What do you feel when you see this picture?'

'I don't really know,' Mila said. 'Dismay. A sense of injustice, maybe.'

'Good,' Berish said drily, and turned the page.

There was another picture, showing the same lioness feeding her cubs zebra meat.

'Now what do you feel?'

Mila thought for a moment. 'At least it seems justified.'

'That's the point. Is the lioness who kills the zebra calves in order to feed her own cubs good or bad? Of course, the mother zebra will suffer because her offspring are dead, but the only alternative would be for the lioness to watch her own cubs die of starvation. The categories of good and evil get blurred because there aren't any vegetarian lions, are there? In the animal world, where there's no choice, judgement doesn't enter into it. But what about human beings?'

'We've evolved further. It should be easier for us to distinguish between good and bad.'

'The answer, in fact, is in another question. If there were only one man on the planet, would he be good or bad?'

'Neither good nor bad . . . or maybe both.'

'Precisely,' Berish said. 'The two forces aren't a dichotomy, two necessary opposites where good couldn't exist without bad, and vice versa. Good and bad are sometimes the result of convention, but above all they don't exist as absolutes. The Hypothesis of Evil states, "Some people's good always coincides with other people's evil, but the opposite is also true."'

'It's a bit like saying that in doing evil you can also do good, and that in order to do good it's sometimes necessary to do evil.'

Berish nodded, pleased with his new pupil. Mila admired the way he had led her through his argument. She had never thought about it that way. The Hypothesis of Evil summed up to a remarkable degree what she saw on a daily basis as a police officer. But it also explained a lot about her.

It's from darkness that I come, and to darkness that I must, from time to time, return.

As for Berish, his solitude, all those years when he had been marginalised, had left a deep mark on him. It was obvious that he was dying to share the knowledge he had acquired over that long period of time. Mila felt privileged.

'So tell me now,' Berish said, 'how do you transform a victim like Roger Valin, Nadia Niverman, Eric Vincenti or André García into a killer?'

'By convincing them that what they do will improve the lives of other people.'

'Correct,' he said. 'In other words?'

'Valin and Niverman weren't out for revenge. When it came to choosing a target, they chose people they were familiar with. It was experience that drove them, not resentment.'

'The motive was so powerful that Nadia Niverman came to the metro in person to give you that tooth as a clue and then killed herself to avoid being caught, but above all to prove that her faith in the cult was strong enough to make her choose death. Anyone who creates a cult creates a new society, sometimes large, sometimes small, and provides it with a code of conduct and therefore a new ideal of justice.'

'Kairus motivated his followers.'

'He saved them from a miserable existence and indoctrinated them by giving their useless lives a purpose. He made them part of something bigger: a project ... A dealer who exploited other people's unhappiness to sell his drugs, a businessman who could have saved lives but was only interested in profit, a lawyer who should have upheld the law but used deception to get around it, a loan shark who took advantage of his debtors to strip them of everything. The killers' aim wasn't just to punish them for their misdeeds. By eliminating them, they eliminated the problem.'

'It was a mission,' Mila said.

'The Nazis, millenarist sects, Rastafarian extremists, even the Christians during the Crusades used the Hypothesis of Evil to justify their ideas and actions. They talked about "a necessary evil".'

'Seen in that light, Kairus is a guide.'

'Much more than that,' Berish said, his voice turning solemn. 'He's a preacher.'

The echo of these words faded towards the ceiling and, for a moment, silence took possession of the library again.

In the age of the internet, the place was an anachronistic repository of knowledge, apparently as useless as an umbrella in a hurricane. But this was where people would come if a worldwide crash put a sudden end to the digital era, Berish thought for a moment. Then he looked at Hitch. They were separated by millions of years of evolution, and this library was proof of the primacy of human beings.

But humans also have an animal instinct. It's the most vulnerable part of each of us. And that's the part that preachers appeal to, Berish told himself. Then he thought again about the insomniacs.

Kairus helped them to disappear, then transformed them from victims into executioners.

The same fate might have befallen his Sylvia. But for the moment, Berish preferred to dismiss that possibility from his mind.

'There are different categories of so-called "manipulators of consciousness".' He was trying to get to the point in stages. '*Hate mongers*, without appearing to do so, create an evil ideal in the hope that people will decide to follow it: they use false information and spread it in order to incite others to violence. Then there are *revenge seekers*, who impose on an unknown multitude the objective of annihilating their enemy.' Berish leant over Mila's shoulder and showed her another book, this time on anthropology. As he did so, he became aware of her smell. It was a mixture of sweat and deodorant, emanating from her hair and neck. It wasn't unpleasant – quite the contrary, in fact. And this stolen pleasure forced him to ask himself how long it was since he had been so close to a woman. *Too long* was the answer.

'These aren't the only types, are they?' Mila asked, picking up the thread of the conversation.

'No,' Berish said, rising to his full height. 'There is in fact a third one. And that's the one we're concerned with ... The preachers.

'A preacher's principal gift is *mimicry*. And that's a talent Kairus has in spades, given that we haven't been able to find him in twenty years. He enters people's lives, pretending to be their friend. He takes an interest in them, forms a bond with them. That's how he wins them over. His second gift is *discipline*. He's diligent, stubborn, and stays true to his own creed.' Berish moved closer to her, waving his fist to underline his words. 'His will is so solid, his vision so passionate, that he's able to totally dominate his followers. This kind of phenomenon is called a cult because, just as in a religious cult, the members worship their leader and obey him blindly, even though he's not some remote, abstract deity, but a person of flesh and blood.'

Mila stood up from the table, but it was an instinctive movement – she had no idea where to go.

There was fear in that action, but also disorientation, Berish realised. All at once, his own impetus fell away. Maybe he had been so carried away with his explanation that he had said something wrong. Maybe, without realising it, he had been insensitive towards her.

'I can't ... I can't do this again,' Mila muttered to herself, shaking her head.

Berish knew she was thinking of the Whisperer. She had been through a lot because of that case, and now history was repeating itself. There was another invisible enemy – yet another manipulator of consciousness – threatening to invade her life. Before all this talk of the Hypothesis of Evil, of cults and preachers, Mila hadn't thought of Kairus in that light.

But it couldn't only be that. There had to be something else.

He moved closer to her. 'What's the matter?'

'I don't feel up to it, that's all.'

'Why not?' he insisted, instinctively feeling that her reasons went beyond what had happened to her years earlier with the Whisperer. The problem was something connected with her current life. 'You're the best person to hunt down the Goodnight Man. Why do you want to pull out now?'

Mila turned to look at him, and there was fear in her eyes. 'Because I have a daughter.'

41

It wasn't easy, returning home that night.

It was as if she were walking backwards, as if her life were rewinding, taking her back to places she never wanted to go again. Particularly places inside her.

'I can't.' Those were the last words she'd said as she left Berish. And she'd meant them. Tomorrow, she was going to call the Judge and decline the assignment. Berish was disappointed, even though he should have been relieved, seeing that he hadn't wanted her involved at first. Mila was convinced that Berish was trying to gain credit from the Kairus case.

But she wanted nothing to do with it.

Their visit to Room 317 of the Ambrus Hotel, the music they'd heard on the phone, the Hypothesis of Evil . . . she'd had enough.

That was why she was hurrying as she walked the last stretch separating her from her building. The giant couple on the billboard greeted her with their usual fixed smiles. For a moment, she broke away from her thoughts and realised she had contravened her routine.

She hadn't left any food for the tramp who lived in the alley near her building.

She saw him lying on his cardboard bed. He was fast asleep, like a child, beneath a layer of blankets. She went closer, put her hand in her pocket, took out some coins, and was about to drop them at his feet when she recalled what Berish had said about the Hypothesis of Evil. A generous act like this might well soothe the conscience of the person performing it but wasn't necessarily good for the person on the receiving end. The tramp might spend the money on another bottle, thus continuing on his downward path, instead of using it to get himself a hot meal.

But Mila left the coins for him anyway.

After all, he wasn't so different from her. He was constantly struggling against the harshness of the world, like an ascetic or a medieval knight. The stench was his armour, it helped him to keep his enemies at a distance.

She entrusted him to his dreams – or maybe his nightmares. When she got to the front door of her building, she felt a sudden urgency, and looked quickly for her keys. She was tired. She hadn't slept in ages, had hardly thought of sleep in the past few days. She realised that her senses were heightened.

But before she could allow herself to rest, she needed to see her daughter.

She had called her Alice after the main character of her favourite book as a child. An ambiguous, dangerous tale, the story of a parallel, hidden world, like the one she visited every day, a country that normal people never even knew existed.

The lights were off in her apartment, and the computer screen created a luminous halo around her as she lay on her bed in her dressing gown.

Alice was six years old. If her mother had had to choose one adjective to describe her, it would have been 'alert'. She looked at you out of those deep, intense eyes as if she could understand things that should have been a mystery at her age.

But unlike Mila, Alice was very sensitive to other people's feelings. She always knew the right thing to do to comfort someone or show them affection, often in an unconventional or even disconcerting way.

Once, in the park, a little boy had grazed his knee and started to cry. Alice had gone up to him and, without saying a word, had started collecting his tears with her fingers – first the ones that had fallen to the ground, then those on his clothes and finally those on his cheeks – and putting them, one by one, in a handkerchief. The little boy didn't even notice at first, but then had started looking at her in amazement. As she continued, he forgot all about his injury and eventually forgot to cry. When he stopped altogether, she also stopped, smiled at him, and walked away with that treasury of tears. Mila was sure the little boy was left with the feeling he had lost something. What you throw away, I'll pick up – maybe next time he'd think twice before giving way to despair over something so unimportant.

On the computer screen, Mila saw her daughter sleeping in another bed, in another house. She had her back to the hidden camera, but her long hair, which Mila knew was ash blonde, was spread over the pillow.

It's like her father's hair, she said to herself, although there was no need.

Like the Whisperer, that man's name had also been banished from her life. Unable to forget either of them and what they had done to her, she had decided to wipe their names off her lips forever.

There had been a moment during her pregnancy when she really had thought she could get over all that. She had imagined they could live together in peace – she and her daughter. It was a time when she had begun to feel for others again, like a blind woman whose sight has been restored. But it didn't last – only long enough for her to realise that she would never escape evil, that 'far away' would never be far enough for her, and that the darkness could still get to her wherever she was.

After she gave birth, the empathy vanished, and she knew she had been right all along: the fact that for a brief time she had felt human again was all down to the child, not to her. That was why she decided it wouldn't be healthy for Alice to grow up with a mother like her – not completely unable to feel emotions, but incapable of feeling *her* emotions. She was terrified she would never know when her daughter was sad or unhappy, or when she needed her help.

The first few months had been awful. The child would wake up in the middle of the night, crying in her cradle, and Mila would lie there in bed, alert but unable to respond to that desperate call for help. Her state of total emotional alienation made it impossible for her to understand the frail little creature's needs. *She might choke in her sleep just because I wasn't aware she was in pain*, she told herself.

After a few months, she asked Alice's grandmother to look after her.

Ines had been widowed young and had only had one child, Mila. Even though she was no longer young, she had agreed to take care of her granddaughter. Mila would visit them from time to time, usually staying overnight and leaving the following morning.

Any interaction between her and Alice was reduced to a minimum. Mila had actually tried to kiss or stroke her, like any normal mother. But even the child had found those gestures clumsy and stopped demanding them.

Mila had hidden her daughter away.

Not from the rest of the world, but from herself. Putting a

hidden camera in her bedroom to check every now and again that she was all right was just a way of absolving herself of some of the guilt she felt at not being present in her life. Sometimes, though, something would happen that put the clock back, frustrating all her efforts and making her feel inadequate.

You aren't a good mother if you don't know the name of your daughter's favourite doll.

It was the kind of thing people said for effect, but it contained an uncomfortable truth. Ever since she had heard those words spoken by a bad mother, Mila had been obsessed by them.

That was why she now searched the screen. She saw it on the floor, next to the bedside table. The red-headed doll Alice never let out of her sight – it must have slipped out of her arms as she slept.

Mila couldn't remember its name, or maybe she'd never known it. She had to find out before it was too late. She knew it wouldn't make her a better mother, she had far worse shortcomings than that. Yet something inside her urged her to remedy that at least.

As she thought about it, vowing to change, her eyelids grew heavy. She remembered the music she had heard over the phone at the Ambrus Hotel. This time, the gentleness of the melody prevailed over any evil significance it might have. She allowed herself to be cradled by her memory of the notes. Tiredness enveloped her like a warm blanket. The last shreds of consciousness merged into the first rush of sleep.

But as she dozed off, she took one last look at the screen and saw a hand withdraw beneath her daughter's bed.

42

'Come on, answer the damn thing.'

She was driving with her mobile glued to her ear. At the other end, the phone kept ringing but nobody was picking up – the nerve-wracking sound was like a coded signal for despair. Mila stepped on the accelerator.

Her first reaction after fear had gripped her and restored her to consciousness was to get on the phone and contact her mother, all the while getting dressed again and even trying to keep a cool head. She had remembered to take the spare gun she kept in the wardrobe – her regulation pistol had got lost in the fire at Kairus's nest. It was the only thing she could do.

The image of that tapering hand withdrawing into the shadows under Alice's bed was still vivid in her memory. It had only been a second, but Mila was sure of what she had seen.

She couldn't inform her police colleagues. Apart from the fact that she didn't know what to tell them, they wouldn't believe her. And she'd only be wasting precious time.

The Hyundai zoomed through the streets, dodging the cars of night owls who were out in search of sin and adventure. Mila jumped red lights and went past junctions without slowing down, trusting in fate to avoid collisions.

She had never before taken so many risks, even though that was how she usually managed to feel alive. But this was different. Now she understood things she had heard other parents say but had never felt herself. It was what her mother called 'a third eye for looking at the world, the one that pops up between the other two as soon as you give birth.'

That's what a child was. A new sense, completely different from the other five, that gives you an incredibly heightened awareness of everything around you. Suddenly, anything that involves your own flesh and blood concerns you directly.

'If you concentrate,' her mother would say, 'you can tell when Alice is happy or when she's in pain.' But Mila had never experienced that. As she drove like a madwoman, trying to get to her daughter's house as soon as possible, she didn't know if the anxiety growing inside her was what it was like to feel what somebody else was feeling.

What she did know, though, was that if anything bad had happened to her little girl, the pain – that friendly feeling that wiped out all the ugliness of the world – would be unbearable this time.

The residential area on the hill stood apart from the rest of the city, like an alien entity. The houses, too, were separate universes.

That was how Mila had grown up. With her father and mother, just the three of them. Planets with different orbits that rarely crossed.

The car, still not slowing, jolted over the speed bumps, emitting a dull metallic sound. It continued down the long avenue lined with silent gardens and skidded as it neared its destination. The ride ended with a long screech of tyres as the Hyundai mounted the pavement and dug its wheels into the lawn in front of the house.

Mila dropped her mobile on the passenger seat, picked up the gun instead, and got out, barely able to catch her breath.

The windows on both floors of the house were dark.

She ran to the porch, where a white light shone beside the green front door. She pressed hard on the doorbell and then started striking the wood with the palm of her hand. She did not even have a key to the house where she had grown up. The only response she got came from the neighbours' dogs, which began to bark.

It had taken her just a few seconds to forget the rules she had learnt during her training. She hadn't checked the outside of the house to see if there were any signs of forced entry. She'd had no thought for her own safety and had done nothing to avoid exposing herself to retaliation from a possible enemy. And she had broken the most important rule of all, which was that no matter what happened, you had to stay in control.

Getting no response to all her ringing and banging, Mila was about to fire at the lock. Then she came briefly to her senses and remembered that her mother always kept a copy of the key hidden under a pot in the garden. She turned back and began searching. She found it at the third attempt, lifting a pot of begonias.

When at last she got inside, she found the hall shrouded in silence.

'Where are you all?' she cried. 'Answer me!'

She saw a light come on at the top of the stairs, and ran up them two at a time. Her mother was leaning over the banisters, tying the belt of her dressing gown. 'What's going on?' she asked in a sleepy voice. 'Mila, is that you?'

When Mila got to the landing, she dodged her mother, almost

knocking her off balance, and headed straight for Alice's room.

Her heartbeats were like loud footsteps – a huge creature that advanced inside her, like a monster in a fairy tale.

She got to the end of the corridor as lights came on behind her in the house. She reached out in the dark for the switch in Alice's room.

A ceiling light shaped like a bee came on.

Alice was in bed, and Mila grabbed her by the arm, as if the bed had become a horrible creature and she wanted to tear her from its jaws. With her other hand, she pointed her gun. Alice screamed in fright. Taking no notice, Mila kicked the mattress to see what it was hiding.

All she could hear for a few seconds was the sound of her lungs pumping air into her chest. Her ears suddenly popped, as if she were falling from a great height. She breathed, once, twice, and the sounds began to return. The first of them was Alice crying as she struggled in Mila's arms.

The only thing on the floor was a tangle of blankets, soft toys and pillows.

43

Ines was making tea in the kitchen.

Watching as she fiddled with the kettle, Mila felt as if she were reliving a scene from her childhood, when her mother, in the same hair rollers and the same pink dressing gown, would boil a little water for her in the middle of the night – the start of the usual comforting ritual after a bad dream.

'I don't know what came over me,' she said. 'I'm sorry.'

She didn't want to tell her she had hidden a camera in her daughter's room – nobody knew that. And she didn't want Ines to think she didn't trust her. So she lied to her.

'I know I never call at night, but I suddenly felt like checking how Alice was and when you didn't answer the phone, I panicked.'

'You've already said that,' Ines said, turning with a smile. 'You don't need to repeat it. It's my fault – I'm a heavy sleeper, I should have heard the phone ring.'

She had put Alice back to bed, calmed her down and patiently waited for her to get back to sleep, while Mila had stayed out in the corridor, leaning against the wall, head bowed, listening to her mother stand in for her yet again.

She would have liked to tell her daughter that everything was fine, there was no danger, she had made a mistake and nobody was hiding under the bed. The house was quite safe. *I haven't slept for forty-eight hours*, she told herself by way of justification. Her lack of sleep had altered her perception of reality. Plus she now knew there was another manipulator of consciousness to contend with. It had all helped to reawaken in her the fear that the days of the Whisperer had returned.

Ines poured the contents of the kettle into two cups and joined Mila at the table. The warm glow of the low-hanging ceiling light formed a kind of protective bubble around them.

'So how are you?' Ines asked.

'All right,' Mila replied without dwelling on it. She knew Ines would be content with those two words and wouldn't dig any deeper. Her mother had never been happy about her joining the police. She would have preferred a different life for her. Maybe becoming a doctor or an architect. And definitely getting married.

'I've been meaning to talk to you for a while now, Mila.' She sounded worried. 'It's about Alice. The other day at school, she climbed up on the window ledge on the second floor. It took a while to persuade her to come down. She kept saying she didn't want to come down because it wasn't dangerous. In fact, she said it was fun.'

'Oh, that again,' Mila tried to protest. It wasn't the first time they'd talked about it.

'Alice has no sense of danger. You remember that time at the seaside? When she swam so far out and could have drowned? Or that time I looked away for a second and when I looked back she was walking in the middle of the road, with the cars sounding their horns and trying to avoid her.'

'Alice is a perfectly normal child, even the doctors said so.'

'I'd like to get a second opinion. What does a child psychologist know? They don't spend hours with her every day.'

Mila looked down at her cup. 'Neither do I, is that what you meant?'

Ines sighed. 'No, it wasn't. It's just that I've got to know her better than anyone since she came to live with me. I'm not saying there's anything wrong with her, I'm just worried because I can't watch over her all the time.' She reached out and took Mila's hand. 'I know you care about her, and I know what it costs you to be separated from her.'

The weight of her mother's hand was unbearable to Mila. She couldn't stand physical contact, and would have liked to pull her own hand away. But she forced herself not to, even though her skin hurt and she felt a sense of revulsion, as if a reptile were slithering between her fingers. 'What do you suggest?'

Ines took her hand away and looked at her daughter with compassion in her eyes. 'Alice is always asking me about her father. Perhaps you could get her to meet—'

'Don't even say his name,' Mila cut in. 'I don't call him that any more. In fact, I don't call him anything at all.'

'Fair enough, but Alice should at least know what he looks like.'

Mila thought it over for a moment. 'All right. I'll take her to see him tomorrow.'

'I think it's the right thing to do. She's old enough.'

Mila got up from her chair. 'I'll come by in the afternoon.'

'Why not stay here tonight?'

'I can't, I have to get up early for work.'

Ines didn't insist. She knew there was no point. 'Look after yourself,' she said, sounding genuinely worried. With that single recommendation – an expression only mothers can fill with such meaning – she was trying to tell her daughter that she had to change for her own good. Mila would have liked to reply that everything was all right, but the words would have sounded insincere. She simply picked up the gun she had left on the table and walked to the kitchen door. When she got to it, though, she turned to her mother, embarrassed by what she was about to ask.

'Alice's favourite doll is the one with red hair, isn't it?'

'I bought it for her last Christmas,' Ines said by way of confirmation.

'Do you happen to know what she calls it?' she asked almost casually.

'I think she calls it Miss.'

'Miss,' Mila echoed, savouring the name as if it were an achievement. 'I'll be off now. Thanks.'

44

She was sure she would find him at the Chinese café.

But when she walked expectantly into the room brimming with police officers, Simon Berish's table was empty, although the remains of an unfinished breakfast still stood on it.

Mila was about to ask the waitress how long it was since he had left when she spotted Hitch under the chair. Within a short while, she saw his master come out of the toilet, trying to rub coffee stains off his shirt with a napkin. It wasn't difficult to guess what had happened. She heard the usual group of police officers laughing at the back of the room. One of them was the officer who had spattered Berish with eggs and bacon a few days earlier.

Berish returned to his seat and calmly resumed eating. Mila made her way between the chairs and joined him. 'My treat this time,' she said.

Berish was taken aback. 'As it's been a while since I last interacted with my fellow human beings, I'm a little rusty about the correct significance of certain words and gestures. I don't get double-meanings, don't catch nuances, and even have a bit of difficulty with metaphors ... So your offer to buy me breakfast ought to be a way of telling me you want us to work together, am I right?'

She almost smiled at Berish's sarcasm, but stopped herself in time. How did he manage to be so affable after so much humiliation from his colleagues?

'I understand, I'll stop it now,' he said, raising his hands as a sign of surrender.

'Good, now we can get along.' Mila sat down. She ordered something to eat now and a takeaway meal.

Berish wondered who it was for but decided to mind his own business. When the waitress had left, he asked her a question he'd been meaning to ask for a while. 'How come such an able police officer as you, who actually solved the Whisperer case, chose to work in Limbo?'

Mila gave this some thought, even though she already knew the answer. 'This way I don't have to chase after criminals. Instead, I look for their victims.'

'That's a false argument. But it makes sense. In that case, explain to me why they call it Limbo. I've always wondered where the name comes from.'

'Maybe it's because of the photographs on the walls of the Waiting Room. It's as if these people are in a suspended state . . . Living people who don't know they're alive and dead people who can't die.'

Berish took in this explanation, which struck him as reasonable. Those who belonged to the first category went about the world like ghosts – as oblivious of others as others were oblivious of them – just waiting for someone to tell them they were still alive. Those in the second group, though, were wrongly counted among the living because the people still waiting for them couldn't resign themselves to the possibility that they might be dead.

The key word was 'still' – an indefinite extension of time that could only end in either facing the truth or forgetting.

'Are you still of the opinion we shouldn't tell the Judge, or even Gurevich and Boris, that you're involved in my investigation?'

Mila's question brought Berish back down to earth. 'Let them hunt for terrorists,' he said. 'We have a cult to look into.'

'Any ideas how to proceed?'

Berish leant across the table. 'Do you remember the music we heard over the phone at the Ambrus Hotel?' he asked in a low voice.

'Yes, why?'

Berish seemed very pleased with himself. 'I've found out what it is.'

Mila couldn't believe it. 'How did you manage that?'

'I admit I'm no expert on classical music. I went to the conservatory this morning and asked to speak to one of the teachers.' He was a little embarrassed to tell her the rest of the story. 'I hummed him the tune and he recognised it.'

Mila was unable to suppress her amusement.

'I had no choice. But as a reward for my performance, the teacher gave me this . . . ' Berish took a CD out of his pocket.

Stravinsky's *The Firebird*.

'It's a ballet composed in 1910. I think it's a clue to the next murder.'

'I don't see how.'

'In the story of the ballet, the music we heard accompanies the scene where Prince Ivan catches the Firebird.'

Mila made an attempt to figure it out. 'So there are three elements: the capture, the Firebird and the name Ivan. The first one could be a kind of challenge.'

'Only partly correct,' Berish said. 'Kairus isn't in competition with us. He's a preacher, he wants to indoctrinate us. These aren't challenges, they're tests. Every time he sets us a test, he wants us to pass it. The phone call we received in Room 317 was another of his tests. He humiliates us to make us feel inferior, but in a way he's on our side. That's why, even though the puzzles he sets us are complex, the answers are always simple.'

'What's so simple about the image of a firebird?'

'I don't know, but we're going to find out. For now, I'd rather focus on the name Ivan.'

'Do you think it's a clue to the identity of the next victim?'

'Or the next killer ... Think about it. What'd be the point of giving us a name if we didn't have any way of finding out who it belonged to?'

'But how?'

Berish slammed his hand on the table. 'We need to look in the missing persons records for anything connected with the name Ivan.'

'Bearing in mind that we're dealing with a twenty-year period, do you have any idea how many people we're talking about?'

'No, you're the expert.'

'We don't have the time. It's been too long since the last murder. Another of the preacher's disciples must surely be getting ready to strike.'

Berish seemed disappointed. He had really wanted his idea to work.

'We'll have to think of something else,' Mila said, trying to console him. 'Maybe we should start by asking ourselves what the Goodnight Man really wants from us.'

Berish looked up at her. 'At the end of the path of initiation, a revelation awaits us.'

For a moment, Mila stared straight ahead of her. 'I don't know if I'll be able to see this through to the end.'

'I assume that's because of your daughter.'

Mila felt she had already said too much, so she let him think her fears were entirely connected with Alice. *If there's something in the darkness, I always have to take a look*: that was what she should have said, by way of warning. Instead of which, she chose to support his theory, asking him, 'Do you have family, Berish?'

'Never been married, never had children.' He thought of Sylvia and of what might have been if they'd stayed together, but refused to let his most painful memory intrude on the present. 'I'm not risking as much as you are, I realise that. But I also know it's a calculated risk.'

'What do you mean?'

'They're people.'

'You're talking about our enemies.'

'They're vulnerable creatures like the rest of us. Except that we can't see them. But there's an explanation for what they're doing, and it's a rational one. It may seem absurd to us, but as anthropology has taught me, it's sure to be a human reason.'

They pondered that statement in silence. Although they were surrounded by a noisy crowd, they both suddenly felt the chill of solitude. Mila paid for the breakfasts and the waitress brought her the receipt along with the takeaway meal she had ordered.

'So you have a dog, too,' Berish said to break the ice, going against his earlier decision to mind his own business.

'Actually, it's for a tramp who lives near my building.' That was all she said.

But Berish seemed interested. 'Is he a friend of yours?'

'I don't even know his name. Come to think of it, what would be the point of his having a name anyway? For someone who's chosen to be forgotten, a name's quite unnecessary, don't you think?'

There was a sudden gleam in his eyes. 'You may have just

given me an idea about how to use the clue contained in that Stravinsky piece.'

'How?'

'To find a name, we need a man who's never had one.'

45

Berish made the call from a public phone booth.

Mila waited in the car with Hitch, wondering why Berish was being so cautious. When the call was over, and he had replaced the receiver, he even stood there a while longer without moving. Mila still didn't understand. Then he left the booth and paced up and down the pavement, as if waiting for someone.

Twenty minutes went by without anything happening.

Mila was just about to get out of the Hyundai and ask him to explain when he walked back to the booth, where the phone had started ringing. It was only after this second conversation that he came back to the car.

'There are a couple of places we have to go,' he said laconically.

Mila switched on the engine without asking any questions, even though she was starting to get tired of all this. First, they dropped by Berish's building. He didn't ask her up to his apartment and soon came back down again without saying a word. But as he got back in the car, Mila noticed that he had an envelope in the inside pocket of his jacket.

He gave her directions, and half an hour later they reached

an industrial area on the western outskirts of the city – a row of identical warehouses, with heavy goods lorries passing up and down the street. Their destination was a meat processing plant.

They drove into the company car park, and Berish motioned to her to stop and switch off the engine.

There was a loading ramp next to the anonymous white buildings. It was from there that the animals were introduced into the production cycle. A chimney belched out grey smoke that filled the air with an acrid and nauseating smell.

'So who's your friend?' Mila asked, curious and at the same time a little annoyed that Berish still hadn't told her anything.

'He doesn't like questions,' was all he said, as if warning her off.

Mila wasn't sure she could put up with this much longer. She only hoped that this ridiculous veil of secrecy would soon fall.

They sat there in silence. Then a stocky man of about fifty, wearing a white coat and a hard hat, came out through a little door at the back of the plant and walked quickly to the Hyundai with his hands in his pockets.

Berish unlocked the car doors and let him in the back.

'Hello, officer, long time no see,' the little man said.

Hitch barked at him.

'Still got this mutt?'

It was obvious they couldn't stand each other.

Then the man looked at Mila. 'Who's she?'

'Officer Vasquez,' she said irritably. 'Who are *you*?'

Ignoring her, the man turned to Berish again. 'Didn't you tell her I don't like questions?'

'Yes, I did,' Berish said, giving Mila a reproachful look. 'But I haven't yet told her what we're doing here. I thought I'd leave that to you.'

The man seemed to appreciate Berish's thoughtfulness, because this time he addressed Mila directly. 'I don't have a name,' he said. 'My work doesn't exist. What you're about to hear, you're going to have to forget.'

'I still don't know what you do,' Mila replied.

The man was unable to hold back a smile. 'I make people disappear.'

Over the next fifteen minutes, Mila learnt the meaning of those words.

'Let's say you're a wealthy businessman who's having a spot of bother with the law. Someone like me can help you disappear from circulation.'

'You can really do that?' Mila asked, surprised and horrified. 'You help crooks get away with it?'

'Only fraudsters and tax evaders. I have my ethics, too, what did you think?'

Berish intervened. 'Our friend here is a real escape artist. With a computer he can wipe out a person's existence, getting into places the police couldn't begin to approach without a warrant: government records, bank and insurance company databases, and so on.'

'I can wipe out all trace of you and at the same time create a false trail to put any pursuers off the scent. I can buy you an airline ticket to Venezuela, make a credit card purchase for you at the duty free in Hong Kong airport, and finally hire a Piper to Antigua even though by the time it lands the only person on board will be the pilot ... That's how it works: while whoever's after you is off on a wild goose chase, you're already taking it nice and easy, sunbathing on a beach in Belize.'

Mila looked at Berish. 'Is it really possible to do all that?'

He nodded. The implication of this tacit response was that the

Goodnight Man's victims might have taken the same route. Even if you didn't have the financial clout of a company executive, all you needed was the help of someone who knew a lot about computers.

And it was quite likely that Kairus did.

'Remember, there's always a rational explanation,' Berish said, repeating what he had told her an hour earlier.

It was Mila's turn to nod.

'But our escape artist can also do things the other way round,' Berish went on. 'In other words, he can get into the most inaccessible databanks and dig up traces of the man we're looking for.' By way of emphasis, he added, 'These are things you Limbo people can't do.'

It had taken only a few minutes of this conversation for Mila to realise just how inadequate the means she usually had at her disposal really were. From now on, the faces in the Waiting Room would be calling her to account.

Berish turned in his seat and looked at the man without a name. 'So, can you help us?'

As he asked the question, Mila looked in the rear-view mirror and saw Berish slip the envelope he had taken from his apartment into the man's pocket.

They left Hitch to guard the car and followed the man along the corridors of the meat processing plant.

'When we've finished, you can take a nice juicy steak for that wretched animal of yours,' the man said to Berish.

'How come you work here?' Mila couldn't help asking.

This time he didn't take offence. 'I never said I work here.'

'What do you mean?'

'I don't own any computers, mobile phones or credit cards. I don't exist, remember? All those things leave traces. Berish contacts me through a voicemail number that I check once an hour on average. Then I call him back on whatever number he leaves me at the time.'

'Then what are we doing here?' Mila asked, more curious than ever.

'One of the office workers is off sick today, so there's a computer free. We'll use that.'

There was no point asking him how he knew, Mila thought. The man was clearly very good at obtaining information.

They passed several workers but nobody paid any attention to them. The place was too large for people to notice unknown faces.

They came to an office and the man looked about him. Satisfied that there was no one around, he used a skeleton key to get in.

It was a small room with a desk and a couple of filing cabinets. Apart from a few posters of grazing cows, which looked rather macabre in this context, there were family photographs of the person who worked there.

'Don't worry, no one'll come,' the man reassured them. Then he sat down at the computer. 'What do you need?'

'We're looking for a man who disappeared some time in the past twenty years,' Berish said. 'His name was Ivan or something similar.'

'Not much of a lead. Don't you have anything else?'

Berish told him about Stravinsky's ballet *The Firebird*, and the scene of the creature being captured by the prince. 'The person who gave us the clue wants us to follow it up, so it shouldn't be impossible.'

'A challenge,' the man said, clearly pleased. 'Good, I like challenges.'

No, it's a test, Mila thought, tempted to correct him with the same word Berish had used to explain the preacher's intention. But she said nothing, just watched him as he got down to work. In religious silence, he began to key in commands on the keyboard, accessing the digital records of banks, hospitals, newspapers, and even the police. His fingers moved lightly over the keys, as though they knew their way into every place in the cyber-universe. Passwords and encrypted security codes were hacked with enormous ease. All kinds of information came up on the screen: newspaper articles, hospital files, criminal records, bank statements.

Almost an hour went by and Berish hadn't said a word. He paced restlessly about the room, looking through the window from time to time. Mila went up to him. 'How did you two meet?' she asked, indicating the hacker.

'He used to work for the Protection Unit. He helped us hide witnesses from those who didn't want them to talk.'

Mila asked nothing more. She didn't think Berish would share anything else with her. Or more likely, she was the one who didn't want to know the whole truth. Because that image of him handing over the suspect envelope to the hacker was still on her mind. She kept remembering Joanna Shutton's words referring – without naming him – to Berish: 'One of the special agents involved lost his dignity in another sordid affair. He took a bribe to help a major underworld informer to escape when he should have been watching him.'

The hacker's services obviously didn't come cheap. And what was Berish doing with all that cash in his apartment anyway?

The clicking of the keys suddenly stopped. The man without a name was ready to give his answer.

'His name's Michael Ivanovič. He disappeared when he was six years old.'

The same age as Alice, Mila immediately thought. Strange

how children's disappearances particularly affected her since she had had a daughter.

'They always thought he'd been kidnapped,' the hacker went on. 'If we're talking about the same person, he'd be about twenty-six now.'

Mila looked at Berish. 'He went missing at the same time as the insomniacs.'

'If we didn't include him with Kairus's first victims, it must have been because there were no sleeping pills involved.'

Seven people who had vanished into thin air, plus Sylvia made eight. *And now there was a ninth.*

'Where has he been all this time?' Mila asked.

'I couldn't tell you,' the hacker replied. 'What I can tell you for sure is that he suddenly reappeared on the internet a week ago. It's as if he's "virtually" returned.'

'Even without the sleeping pills, it seems like too much of a coincidence, don't you think?' Berish said, enthusiastically. 'I think it's him.'

Mila agreed. 'Now how do we find him?'

'Well, this should help. Ivanovič called a telephone company to activate a mobile phone line, and left his name and surname. Then he made another call to open an online bank account. But the addresses he gave in both cases don't match, which suggests he just wanted to put a message out there in the hope that someone would pick it up. Michael wants you to know who he is, but at the same time he doesn't want to be found.'

Because he has a task to carry out, Mila thought. He has to kill someone.

'What do we do now?' Berish asked.

The hacker smiled. 'I think I may have the answer. From an old medical report when he was a child, it turns out Michael Ivanovič has a rare genetic condition called total *situs inversus*.'

'What does that mean?' Mila asked.

'It means all his organs are reversed,' Berish replied. 'His heart is on the right hand side, his liver's on the left, and so on.'

Mila had never heard of it. 'And how does that help us?'

'Ninety-five per cent of people with *situs inversus* suffer from heart disease,' the hacker said. 'Which means they need frequent medical check-ups.'

Berish seized on this. 'We don't look for his name, we look for his condition. If he's been using a false identity over the years, we can reconstruct his movements through the doctors who've treated him.'

The hacker immediately dampened his enthusiasm. 'That won't be so easy. I haven't found any medical files describing a case of *situs inversus* in a twenty-six-year-old man.'

'How is that possible?' Berish asked.

'Michael Ivanovič may not have been to a hospital in all this time, only to GPs or specialists. They'll take a lot longer to track down.'

'To be honest, we don't have much time.'

The hacker raised his hands. 'Sorry, that's all I can do for now.'

'All right,' Mila said, and turned to Berish. 'It's pointless getting upset. I'm sure if we let him do his work, he'll come up with something on our Michael.'

Berish hoped the same thing. 'All right, let's try. What do we do in the meantime?'

Mila glanced at her watch. 'I have an appointment.'

46

The first time Alice had asked about her father, she was about four.

The question, though, had been on her mind for some time. As so often with children, it had taken other forms, both physical and verbal. Alice had suddenly started including in drawings of her family a figure she had never heard anyone talk about. No one knew when she had become aware that she had another parent. It must have happened when she was talking with her peers, or when she heard Ines mention her husband, Alice's grandfather. If Mila had had a father, why didn't she? However it had come about, the first question she had asked had been a kind of compromise.

'How old is my daddy?'

It was a way of going around the subject without losing sight of the main objective.

Soon afterwards, Alice had returned to it, asking this time about her father's height, as if that were a precious piece of information that could change her life. From then on, it was one question after another. The colour of his eyes, his shoe size, his favourite food.

It was as if Alice was trying to build up an image of her father piece by piece.

It was an exhausting process, one requiring great patience, especially in a child – Mila realised that. Ines had starting hinting that it might be good for father and daughter to meet. Mila kept putting it off, waiting for the right moment, although she wasn't sure how exactly she would know that the right moment had come. When Ines had brought it up again the previous night, Mila had agreed immediately, almost as if they had never talked about it before. After what she had done – bursting into the house like that, causing so much upset – Mila felt she owed Alice. She may not have been a good mother, but she couldn't stop the girl from being a good daughter.

And good daughters go to see their daddies.

Besides, what had happened this week had inevitably taken her back to the days of the Whisperer. Alice's request was no longer so impossible to grant. Maybe fate wanted her to come to terms with the past. Or maybe Alice was trying to tell her that you couldn't ignore the harm that had been done.

Because, without that harm, she wouldn't have been born.

The road climbed into the hills, caressed by the surrounding foliage.

Alice was looking out of the window, and for a moment Mila had the impression she was seeing herself as a little girl in the rear-view mirror. She, too, had liked to steal moments as she travelled at speed. Images rushing past her, of which she caught only fragments. A house, a tree, a woman hanging her washing out to dry.

Mother and daughter had not spoken much on the short ride. Mila had taken the safety seat out of the boot of the Hyundai and put it on the back seat for Alice, then let Ines settle her grand-daughter, making sure her seat belt was fastened and that she had her favourite doll with her.

That day, Ines had made Alice put on a pink cotton dress with straps that left her shoulders bare. She was wearing white train-ers and had a white clip in her hair.

After a few miles, Mila had asked her if she was hot and if she wanted to listen to the radio, but Alice had shaken her head and hugged Miss, the red-headed doll, to her.

'You know where we're going, don't you?'

Alice was still looking out of the window. 'Grandma told me.'

'Are you pleased to be going there?'

'I don't know.'

With that, Alice had put a stop to any desire Mila might have had to continue the conversation. Another mother might have asked why she didn't know. Another mother might even have suggested going back. Maybe another mother would have known what to do. But Mila felt that to Alice she was already her 'other mother', her real mother being Ines.

The grey stone building appeared in the distance.

How many times had she visited in the past seven years? This must be the third time. The first time was nine months after it had happened, but she had been unable to cross the threshold and had run away. The second time, she had got as far as the room and seen him, but hadn't said anything to him. After all, they hadn't spent much time together and had very little in common.

The only night she had spent with him had marked her more deeply than a thousand cuts. The pain she had felt had been dev-astating but also so beautiful, so intense that it couldn't be compared to any kind of love. He had undressed her, revealing the secret of her wounded body, he had covered her scars with kisses, he had entrusted all his despair to her, certain she would make good use of it.

She hadn't been to see him again for at least four years.

A black orderly came out to the car park to greet them. Mila had phoned ahead to warn them of their visit.

'Hello,' the orderly said with a smile. 'We're so glad you've come. He's a lot better today. Come in, he's expecting you.'

This performance was for Alice's benefit, in order not to frighten her. Everything had to look natural.

They went in through the main entrance. There were two private security men behind the desk. They asked Mila if she remembered the procedure for gaining access to the building. She handed over her gun, badge and mobile phone. The security men also checked the red-headed doll. Alice followed this operation with great curiosity and without protesting. Then mother and daughter passed through a metal detector.

'He still gets death threats,' the orderly said, referring to their most important inmate.

They went down a long corridor lined with closed doors. There was a smell of disinfectant. Every now and again, Alice would fall behind her mother and have to run to catch up. At one point, she reached out and touched her mother's hand but then, realising her mistake, immediately withdrew it.

They took a lift to the second floor. More corridors, with rather more animation than downstairs. There were regular sounds coming from the rooms – the repetitive pumping of ventilators, the clinking of heart monitors. The staff here were dressed in white and went about their essential routine in a disciplined way, filling syringes, changing drips, emptying drip bags, or discarding catheters.

Each of these members of staff was assigned a particular

inmate until the time at their disposal ran out. At least that was how a doctor had put it to Mila. 'We're here because at birth these people were granted too many days.' He'd made it sound like some kind of manufacturing error. As if life and death were in a very slow race to see which would give way first.

Except that none of the people lying in these beds had any hope of returning from the journey on which they had embarked.

Dead people who didn't know they were dead, and living people who couldn't die. That was how Mila had described the missing persons in Limbo to Berish. The same phrase could apply to those within these walls.

The orderly stopped outside one of the rooms. 'Would you like to be alone with him?'

'Yes, please,' Mila said.

Mila took a step forward, while Alice stood in the doorway with her feet together, hugging her doll to her.

She stared at the man lying on his back in the bed, his arms protruding from the white sheet folded perfectly over his chest. His hands lay flaccidly on the blankets, palms down. The tube attached to his throat, through which he was breathing, had been covered with gauze – in order not to upset his young visitor, Mila thought.

Alice couldn't take her eyes off her father. Maybe she was trying to find a way to connect what was in front of her with the image of him she had formed in her head.

Mila could have let her think from the start that he was dead. It would have been a lot easier – for herself, too. But, given the way things were, it wouldn't have been the whole truth. It was inevitable that a day would come when she would ask more important questions – questions that went beyond the colour of his eyes or his shoe size. Better to wait, she thought, until she could explain to her that that useless body was the inaccessible prison in which her father's damned soul was confined.

But, fortunately for both of them, there was still time.

Still rooted to the spot, Alice tilted her head for a moment, as if she had become aware of a subtle undertone in the scene – something adults couldn't see. Then she turned to Mila and said simply, 'We can go now.'

47

At the time of Michael Ivanovič's disappearance, it had been common for pictures of missing children to be printed on milk cartons.

It was a simple idea, but potentially a very effective one. Every morning, every family in the country sat at the breakfast table with that face looking at them. Naturally, it became familiar to them and would lead them to report any chance sightings. If the child had been kidnapped, it was a way to make the kidnapper feel that he was being hunted down.

But there was also an unfortunate side effect.

Ideally, the missing children would be adopted by the entire country. They were like the children or grandchildren you worried about and prayed for every night, and everyone looked forward to their being found as they looked forward to the lottery results, confident that there would be a winner.

The problem was that the police – and, along with them, the milk producers – would start to wonder how long the picture should continue to appear on the cartons. Because the more time went by, the less likely a happy ending seemed. Nobody liked having breakfast with the picture of a possibly dead child staring at them. So, from one morning to the next, the photograph would disappear. Nobody ever protested. They preferred to forget.

Michael Ivanovič – affectionately referred to as 'little Michael' – had featured on milk cartons for eighteen months. He was a week past his sixth birthday when he had vanished into thin air. His parents were in the middle of a messy divorce. The media implied that they'd been too busy quarrelling to give their only child the attention he needed. So someone had taken advantage, furtively entering their lives and taking Michael away.

It had happened on a late spring afternoon, in the small park just opposite where his mother worked. Michael was playing on the swing while she was having an argument on a public phone with her soon-to-be ex-husband. She swore to the police that she had hardly ever taken her eyes off her son. In addition, the constant squeak of the swing had reassured her that he was still there.

Except that the wooden seat had kept swinging without Michael being on it.

A thirty-five-year-old plumber was arrested for the child's abduction. His common-law wife had reported him to the police, after finding in their house the green T-shirt with white stripes that the boy was wearing on the day he disappeared. The man's defence was that he had found the T-shirt in a rubbish bin and had decided to keep it because the child was famous now and he liked the idea of owning a 'celebrity souvenir'. In the end, he had been believed and the only charge against him was one of obstructing justice.

Apart from that episode, not a single clue as to Michael Ivanovič's fate had emerged in the past twenty years. Nobody said so, but it was generally believed that he was dead.

As usually happened in such cases, a confidential bulletin had been issued to every forensic pathologist in the country. It contained an anatomical description of the boy to help with identification in case a minor's body was ever found. It also mentioned something that had never been divulged to the press: the fact that Michael Ivanovič suffered from a congenital condition known as *situs inversus*.

When he had finished reading, Berish closed the file. He had printed a copy, downloading it from the Limbo records thanks to the password supplied by Mila.

The Goodnight Man's ninth victim in chronological order, he told himself.

Unfortunately, there were no clues in any of the paperwork as to who Michael Ivanovič's target might be. He had been too young at the time of his disappearance, so it was unlikely that he had chosen his intended victim on the basis of his own experience, as Roger Valin and Nadia Niverman had done. The connection between victim and killer would probably be coincidental, as it had been in the cases of Eric Vincenti and André García.

Yet the fact that this time Kairus had chosen his youngest disciple for the task meant that he wanted the police to do all they could to find him. Why?

'He wants to make us feel inadequate,' Berish thought out loud. 'This time, he has a big target in mind.'

Berish had spent much of the afternoon in his office, waiting for a call from his friend the hacker. When he had finished studying Michael Ivanovič's file, he put it back in the drawer, checked the time, then looked at Hitch, who was lying quietly, uncomplainingly, in his corner. It was after six, and they were both hungry. So he decided to take the dog out for a walk.

He activated the answering machine and set off with Hitch to get something to eat.

There was a stand selling sandwiches and drinks near the main entrance of the department. Hitch loved hot dogs – his master was convinced it was partly because of the name.

They joined the queue with other police officers who, as usual, threw Berish contemptuous looks. For the first time in ages, he actually felt them, as if the armour that had always protected him had grown weaker.

Hitch must have sensed his nervousness, because he raised his head and barked to make sure everything was all right. Berish stroked his muzzle. When he reached the front of the queue, he bought a couple of hot dogs, some tuna sandwiches and a can of Red Bull, and then they both walked briskly away. On the way back, Berish thought about what had just happened. Nothing had changed, and yet it was as if everything had changed. Being in the thick of an investigation again after years of inactivity made him feel alive. After dozens of interrogations in which he had managed to get confessions from murderers and other criminals, he knew he was no worse than they were. But he had always believed that they opened up to him because they recognised some kind of fellow feeling in him.

I don't seem like a police officer, that's why they tell me things.

Now, though, that talent showed itself for what it really was: a prison sentence. And a voice deep in his heart was telling him that the time had come to put an end to his imprisonment.

You've paid enough, Simon. It's time to be a police officer again.

Ruminating on these thoughts, he walked along the corridor towards his office with the packet of sandwiches in one hand and the can of Red Bull in the other, not thinking about needing a hand free to open the door.

In the end, he didn't. It was Hitch who drew his attention to the fact that it was already open.

'Hello, Simon.'

He nearly dropped the can. He had to call on every ounce of self-control at his disposal not to have a heart attack. 'Good God, Steph!'

Captain Stephanopoulos was sitting cross-legged in front of the desk. 'Sorry, I didn't mean to scare you.' Then he clapped his hands to attract Hitch. 'Come here, handsome.'

Hitch went straight to Steph, who took hold of his hairy head and began rubbing it affectionately.

Berish caught his breath, closed the door behind him, and put the hot dogs in Hitch's bowl. 'When you've grown accustomed to being ignored, surprises can be fatal.'

Steph laughed. 'I realise that. But I did knock first, I swear.' Then his expression grew serious. 'I wouldn't have come in and waited for you if I didn't have something important to discuss.'

His eyes fixed on his former superior's face, Berish took his seat on the other side of the desk. 'Would you like one of my sandwiches?' he asked.

'No, thanks. But you go ahead and eat if you want. This won't take long.'

Berish opened the can of Red Bull and took a sip. 'So, what's up?'

'I'll come straight to the point, and I expect an equally straight answer.'

'All right.'

'Are you and Mila Vasquez conducting an unauthorised investigation?'

'Why don't you ask her? Isn't she your officer?'

Steph didn't seem happy with this half-admission. 'I was the one who told her to consult you.'

'I know.'

'What I didn't expect was that the two of you would gang up. Don't you realise this could damage her reputation in the department?'

'I think she can take care of herself.'

'You don't know a fucking thing,' Steph cried, bursting into one of the fits of temper he was prone to. 'Mila is attracted to darkness the way children are attracted to jam. Some really bad things happened to her when she was a child – things you and I couldn't even begin to imagine, thank God. She had two ways to deal with it: give in to fear for the rest of her life, or use it as a resource. Mila gets herself into the riskiest situations because she needs to. Like those war veterans who want to go straight back to the front. Fear of death creates a dependency.'

'I know the type,' Berish cut in. 'But I also know that neither of us will ever be able to dissuade her.'

Steph shook his head in annoyance and looked Berish straight in the eyes. 'You're convinced you're going to get Kairus, aren't you?'

'This time, yes,' Berish said.

'And have you told Mila why you're so keen to settle your score with the Goodnight Man?' He paused. 'Have you told her about you and Sylvia?'

Berish pulled back on his chair. 'No, I haven't,' he said coldly.

'Are you planning to tell her, or don't you think it's important?'

'Why should I tell her?'

Steph slammed his hand down on the desk, startling Hitch. 'Because that's when you started going downhill. You became a son of a bitch, you even screwed up your career and became the pariah of the department. All because of what happened to Sylvia.'

'I should have protected her, instead of which—'

'Instead of which, Kairus took her from you.'

Would you like to have a new life?

The words the Goodnight Man said to his victims over the phone echoed in the room, but only Berish heard them.

Had Sylvia also been to Room 317 of the Ambrus Hotel? Had she also taken the lift to the third floor? Had she seen the dark red wallpaper? Walked on the carpet with the enormous blue flowers? Swallowed the sleeping pill and let the Goodnight Man take her?

There was a long silence, broken by Steph. 'Which was worse, Berish? Being defeated by a maniac or falling in love with the only witness who'd seen his face? Think about it.'

'I should have protected her,' he repeated, like a stuck record.

'How long did you spend with her? A month? Do you think it's natural to throw away the rest of your life for so little?'

Berish said nothing.

Steph must have realised it was pointless. He stood up, crouched beside Hitch and stroked him. 'I was head of the Witness Protection Unit. I'm as responsible for what happened as you are.'

'That's why you buried yourself in Limbo.'

The captain let out a bitter laugh, got back on his feet, and took hold of the door handle, ready to go. 'Given that some of these missing persons are coming back, you think she will, too, don't you? Please let me hear it from your own lips that I'm wrong. Tell me you don't believe Sylvia is still alive.'

Berish held the captain's gaze, even though he wasn't sure how to reply. The silence became heavy. Steph wasn't giving up. It was the ringing of the phone that broke the tension.

Berish grabbed the receiver. 'Yes?'

'You're really going to love me for this.' It was the voice of the nameless hacker, with the noise of industrial machinery in the background. Berish wondered where he was calling from.

'Have you got something for me?' Berish was trying not to give anything away, because Steph was still looking at him from the door.

'Michael Ivanovič went to see a private doctor about a month ago, using a false name.'

'Are you sure it was him?'

'Listen to this. The doctor realises it's a gift from heaven. He'll be able to write a really impressive article for a medical journal about a case of *situs inversus*. So he starts asking lots of questions about Michael's heart condition. Michael realises what's going on and runs away. But the doctor doesn't give up and follows him home. Michael probably spots him, and the next day the unfortunate doctor's car goes up in flames, with the doctor inside. The police and the insurance company think there was a problem with the electrical wiring. The car went up in a flash, no way the driver could get out in time. Nobody bothered to take the investigation any further, firstly because these things do happen, and secondly because the doctor wasn't the kind of person to have enemies. So the thing was classified as an accident and the case was closed. But I took the trouble to read the notes on the doctor's laptop, and starting with the motive, I reconstructed the whole story.'

'Just a second.' Berish covered the mouthpiece with his hand and said to Steph, 'I promise I'll tell Mila about Sylvia, and I'll also do everything I can to keep her out of trouble.'

Steph appeared to take him at his word. 'Thanks,' he said, and left the room.

Once Steph had left, Berish went back to his phone conversation. 'Do you have an address?'

'Absolutely, my friend.'

The hacker gave it to him, and Berish wrote it down, hoping Michael Ivanovič still lived there. He was about to hang up and call Mila when the voice at the other end of the line stopped him.

'One more thing ... Ivanovič could have chosen a thousand different ways to kill the doctor. But there are a couple of things that should have made the police and insurance company suspicious.'

'Such as?'

'The accident report states that the locks on the burnt car were defective, but might have been tampered with. Plus, according to the pathologist, the state of the body suggested slow combustion, which doesn't quite tally with the idea of a quick fire. So I wouldn't put it past the murderer to have planned everything and to have been somewhere nearby, enjoying the show.'

Berish recalled the firebird in Stravinsky's ballet. 'Are you telling me this Michael Ivanovič is a pyromaniac?'

'I think our friend likes watching people burn.'

48

They met two blocks from Michael Ivanovič's address.

They had each made their own way there. Berish put Hitch on the back seat of the Hyundai and sat down next to Mila without asking her where she had been that afternoon, although he could see from the expression on her face that something was wrong.

'Are we sure he lives here?' she asked.

'That's what our informant said.'

'So how do we go about this?'

Berish checked the time. It was after eight. 'Unfortunately he may be at home.'

'Were you planning to search the place?'

'I don't know what I was planning, but maybe we should inform your friend Boris.'

Mila couldn't hold back a grimace of displeasure. 'Do you really want me to tell him how I got the information? Because he's sure to ask me.'

Berish hadn't thought of that. Calling Boris would mean revealing his source. How else would Mila know about Michael Ivanovič? 'You're right. But if we find out who his target is, we're going to have to tell someone.'

'I say let's think about that when the time comes.'

Berish nodded in agreement.

The two-storey apartment building was built in a circle around a rectangular hole filled with sewage that had once been a swimming pool.

Berish and Mila went in through the gate and headed straight for the back of the building. In order not to be seen, they would use the fire escape. Michael Ivanovič lived in Apartment 4B.

When they got to the foot of the stairs, Berish gave instructions to his dog. 'If anyone comes, bark. Got that, Hitch?'

Hovawarts were perfect guard dogs. So the animal sat politely, as if he had understood the command.

Both took their guns from their holsters.

'This isn't my usual weapon,' Mila said. 'I felt more comfortable with the one I lost in the fire at Kairus's nest. So I can't guarantee anything.'

Berish realised that this was a diplomatic way of reminding him how ineffective his aim had been when he had shot at Kairus inside that absurd maze in the redbrick house. He appreciated it, but the word 'fire' also reminded him of the last words the hacker had said about Michael Ivanovič.

I think our friend likes watching people burn.

He had mentioned this to Mila but hadn't told her how worrying he had found it. From his study of criminal anthropology, he knew that pyromania was the strongest indication of a sadistic personality.

And there was a special name for people like Ivanovič: fireworms. They were dangerous adversaries, because their aim wasn't just death, but destruction.

They reached Apartment 4B. There was no way of seeing inside. They looked at each other. Berish put his ear to the door, but the only sounds he could hear came from the neighbours' TVs – some had their windows open because of the heat.

With the risk of someone seeing them, they didn't have much time to decide. Berish nodded, and Mila crouched down to have a better view of the lock as she picked it.

Within a few seconds, the door was open.

Berish pushed the door and pointed the gun into the gloom inside. Behind him, Mila switched on her torch, lighting up a small dining room with a table in the middle strewn with old newspapers and empty bottles. Beyond the room was a long corridor. The apartment seemed deserted.

They walked in.

Berish took a few steps forward. Mila shut the door behind them. They stopped in the doorway of the living room and listened out for sounds.

'There doesn't seem to be anyone here,' Berish whispered, then added, as if it were necessary, 'But let's keep our guns out, anyway.'

'Can you smell it, too?' asked Mila.

Berish guessed she was referring to the strong artificial smell, something like floor cleaner. It was odd because the place didn't look all that clean. He shook his head, unable to figure out where the smell was coming from.

The main piece of furniture in the room was a brown sofa with torn filling. An old cathode-ray TV stood in a corner, and there was an empty dresser against the wall. Two chairs that didn't match and a small table made up the rest of the sparse furniture. There was a ceiling light with four arms, each with a frosted glass globe at the end of it.

The place looked like a temporary dwelling rather than somewhere that had really been lived in. It struck Berish immediately that this couldn't have been where Michael Ivanovič had lived over the past twenty years.

He moved here only recently, he thought. The place would serve as his lair until he had completed his mission, and then he would leave.

'Our friend didn't like the position of the sofa,' Mila said, shining her torch downwards.

Sure enough, Berish saw that one of the wooden legs was broken. 'Maybe he hid something under it.'

They both grabbed it by the arms and moved it aside, then pointed the torch at the floor, but there was nothing there.

Berish seemed disappointed.

'He probably did the same with the other furniture in the room,' Mila said, indicating the scratches on the wooden floor where the dresser had been moved. If Ivanovič was planning to be here for only a short time, why on earth had he moved the furniture around? To Berish, none of it added up.

To their right, a dirty curtain separated the living room from a small bathroom. Mila pulled it aside, to reveal a cracked toilet, an old ceramic sink covered in limescale, and a shower.

'The taps are missing,' Berish said, wondering if his anthropological studies could help him come up with a reason for this oddity.

'Let's go and see what's through there,' Mila said, breaking into his thoughts.

The last room was probably where Michael Ivanovič slept. The door was ajar, and Mila directed the beam of light through the gap.

'Look.'

Berish came up close to her arm, and looked in.

There was a map of the city pinned to the wall. And on it was an area circled in red.

'Do you think . . . ' Mila didn't need to complete the sentence: it was obvious the circle might mark the place where the killer had decided to strike. All they needed was confirmation. Mila took a step towards the room.

As Berish watched her advance with confidence, he realised that her move was too predictable. His mind had anticipated it because it was the expected thing to do.

Why had Michael Ivanovič left such an important clue in full view? Maybe he'd been so sure of himself that he never thought his hiding place would be discovered, but Berish didn't buy that. The answer came to him from anthropology.

In less than half a second, Berish put together a sequence of apparently insignificant data.

The smell of floor cleaner – the most widely available flammable liquid on the market. He had removed the bathroom taps – water extinguishes flames. He had moved the furniture around – forcing any possible intruder to go where he wanted them to. The map circled in red – an invitation to walk into the bedroom. The half-open door – the primer.

'Stop!'

Taken aback, Mila turned and looked at him.

Berish raised his eyes to the ceiling light.

He took the torch from Mila and pointed it upwards, revealing wires sticking out of the bulb sockets: the frosted glass globes were filled with an oily liquid.

'What is that?' Mila asked, moving out of the way.

'An incendiary device.'

With the torch, Berish followed the route of the wires, which ended at the bedroom door. He directed the beam along the side of the door and saw that one of the hinges was connected to a rudimentary contraption consisting of two electrodes and a low voltage battery, all held together with insulating tape. If Mila had opened the door, the circuit would have closed. There wouldn't have been an explosion, Berish knew that. Instead, a shower of liquid flame would have engulfed them, rapidly burning first their clothes, then their flesh.

It wouldn't only have been death, it would have been torture. Just the thing to delight a fireworm.

'Our Michael is clever,' Berish said, pondering the simplicity as well as the ingenuity of the trap.

Mila was still shaken. 'I should have been more careful.'

Berish just had to tear off one of the wires to defuse the device. They walked into the room.

When they were standing right in front of the map, they saw that the red circle marked a specific street.

'It isn't far. Just nine blocks from here.' But then Mila saw on Berish's face the same scepticism she herself was feeling. 'But what if Michael Ivanovič hasn't really left us a clue? What if this is just another lie to lure us into a trap?'

'Well, we'll find out when we get there.'

49

They knew they had come to the right place when they saw people out in the street.

Mila and Berish drew up in front of a six-storey apartment block. A fire alarm was ringing and the residents were in the process of evacuating the building. But there was no smoke.

They saw a police patrol car parked outside. The door on the driver's side was wide open and the flashing lights were on.

'A patrolman seems to have got here before us,' Mila said, getting out of her car. Then she spotted the doorman, who was helping people to leave the building. She and Berish went up to him, followed by Hitch. Mila showed him her badge.

'Where's the fire?' Mila asked, raising her voice to make herself heard over the alarm.

'I don't know exactly, but the smoke detectors indicate that it's an apartment on the fourth floor.'

'Who lives there?'

'A bigwig from the police department. He lives alone. His name's Gurevich.'

Hearing the name, Mila and Berish both went pale.

'What happened?' Berish asked.

'When the alarm went off, I immediately came out to help evacuate the building. But I think one of your colleagues is upstairs.'

'Is this the only entrance?'

'There's another one at the back.'

'So you haven't seen a stranger come out of the building . . .'

'No, but in all the confusion, I can't be sure.'

Berish looked at Mila. 'Call Klaus Boris and tell him to send a Special Forces team.'

She nodded. 'And what are we going to do?'

'We're going up.'

The sound of the fire alarm echoed down the stairwell, becoming ever more unbearable.

Berish motioned to Hitch to sit and wait for them. The dog obeyed and got ready to stand guard.

When they reached the landing, Mila saw that the door to Gurevich's apartment was ajar. She and Berish exchanged signals and took up position on either side of the door. They counted backwards symbolically, nodded three times, then Berish went in with his gun drawn, while Mila covered his back.

The apartment was in semi-darkness. From the entrance hall, nobody could be seen. They advanced a little way. There were no flames or smoke. But from the corridor ahead of them came a strong smell of burning. It wasn't the usual smell of a fire, Mila noticed. There was something else behind it, something pungent and pervasive. It took her a while to recognise it. It was the same smell that used to come off her skin in the days when she would press a hot iron to it to cause the pain she needed.

She saw Berish put his hand over his mouth, trying not to

retch. He, too, had understood. He gestured to her to indicate that they should move forward, which they did.

They were surrounded by period furniture and old paintings. A strong sense of the past lay over everything. The dark wallpaper and carpets added to the austere atmosphere.

The main corridor was like a passage in a museum. There was no time to wonder how a police inspector could afford to live in such luxury. They just had to keep moving.

They came to an open door. A shaft of light from inside the room ended at their feet. They looked around for anywhere the killer might be hiding, hoping this wasn't another trap. Then they repeated the ritual of counting backwards.

Once again, Berish was first over the threshold. Mila saw the look of horror on his face.

There were two bodies in there, close together.

The patrolman was lying on his back, his lifeless face turned towards them, the carpet beneath him soaked with the blood gushing from a wound to his throat.

Gurevich was unrecognisable. Foul-smelling smoke rose from his flesh. His eyes, which looked very white on his charred face, stared up at the ceiling. Mila was sure he was already dead, but then the pupils moved towards her, as if recognising her.

'Take care of the patrolman,' she said to Berish, shouting to be heard over the alarm. 'I'll see to Gurevich.'

She knelt down next to the inspector, unsure what to do to ease his pain. His clothes were stuck to his skin and formed a layer like white-hot lava. Nearby, a velvet curtain had been torn off its rail. The patrolman had probably used it to try and smother the flames before being attacked by Ivanovič. There was also the jerrycan Ivanovič had used to spread the flammable liquid.

Mila turned and looked at Berish, who was keeping an eye on the door but had bent over the patrolman and was listening to his chest in the hope of hearing a heartbeat. After a short while he stood up and shook his head.

'Gurevich is still alive,' Mila said.

'The police are on their way, and there's certain to be an ambulance, too.'

'We don't know if Ivanovič is still in the apartment, or in the building. He could be armed, seeing that he stabbed this poor fellow in the throat. We have to secure the premises.' Mila could see that Berish, too, was desperately trying to devise a plan.

'One of us has to go down and tell our people what's happened,' Berish said.

Just then, Gurevich grasped Mila's hand. 'He's in shock, you'd better go,' she said.

'I'll radio the operations room to put me through to the paramedics, so that I can inform them of his condition. Now don't take any risks, all right?'

Mila noticed that Berish's tone was oddly protective. For a moment, he reminded her of Steph. 'All right,' she said reassuringly.

Berish went back down the stairs, constantly looking behind him. The doorman had said the building had a back entrance, so it was quite likely that Michael Ivanovič had used it to make good his escape.

He found Hitch exactly where he had left him, as calm as ever.

As they went out through the front door, Berish saw the flashing lights of police cars approaching.

The police sirens and the fire alarm together created a din that made Berish especially agitated.

The first Federal Police car pulled up beside the crowd that had joined the residents and were now gawping at the scene. Three men in Special Forces uniforms got out, one of them a sergeant. Berish went up to him without any thought for the consequences.

'It happened on the fourth floor. One of our people is dead. Inspector Gurevich is seriously wounded and Officer Mila Vasquez is upstairs with him. The perpetrator's name is Michael Ivanovič, and he's sure to be armed. He may have escaped but I can't rule out the possibility that he's still in the building.' He realised that the sergeant had recognised him and was probably wondering what the pariah of the department was doing here. 'Tell your men to check among the crowd.' He indicated the small group of onlookers. 'The killer's a pyromaniac who enjoys watching the show, so he may still be nearby.'

'Yes, sir. An ambulance is on its way.' Then the sergeant went over to the other Special Forces men who were waiting in front of the building and gave them their orders in readiness to go up.

To keep out of their way, Berish went over to the car the patrolman had left unattended. He sat down in the driver's seat and grabbed the radio microphone. 'Headquarters, this is Special Agent Berish. Can you put me through to the paramedics who are on their way to Inspector Gurevich's home?'

'Very well, sir,' a female voice came over the loudspeaker. 'We're doing a radio link now.'

As he waited for the paramedics to come on the line, Berish tapped his index finger impatiently on the microphone and looked out through the windscreen. The crowd of neighbours and onlookers was slowly growing.

Where was Michael Ivanovič right now? Was he hiding among all these people, enjoying the smell Berish still had in his nostrils – smoke and human flesh – a smell he didn't think he would ever forget?

A male voice came over the radio. 'Ambulance crew 266. What's the situation? Over.'

'We have a man with burns. He's having difficulty breathing. It looks serious but he's still conscious. Over.'

'What's the cause of the burns? Over.'

'We think it's a mixture of chemicals. We're dealing with a case of arson. Over.' As Berish spoke, his eyes wandered to the rear-view mirror.

He saw Hitch moving about behind the car and heard his barking.

What with the alarm and the radio, he hadn't heard him before.

'Has the cause of the burns ceased? Over.'

But Berish ignored the paramedic, concentrating instead on what was happening at the rear of the car.

'Sir, did you understand the question? Over.'

'I'll call you back.'

He left the microphone on the seat, got out, and walked to the rear of the car. Hitch was growing even more agitated, and Berish saw that he was indicating the boot.

He's in there, he thought, Michael Ivanovič is hiding there to avoid capture. He couldn't have chosen a better place.

Berish glanced around in search of his colleagues but no one was looking in his direction. He realised he would have to act alone. He took out his gun and gripped it as tightly as he could. With his other hand, he reached out for the boot. With an abrupt action, he pressed the button to unlock the lid and simultaneously pointed the gun inside.

When the lid sprang open, a familiar smell greeted him, although the body from which it came wasn't as badly burnt as Gurevich.

He was naked and still conscious.

It wasn't Michael Ivanovič. Even though the man wasn't wearing his uniform, Berish remembered him as someone he'd seen having breakfast at the Chinese café.

In a flash, the sequence of events became clear, like a film being projected in his head. In the final scene of the film, he was bending over, trying to hear, perhaps too hastily, the heartbeat of the fatally wounded officer upstairs. But, quite apart from the deafening sound of the alarm, there was also the fact that he had pressed his ear to the wrong side of the chest. The left.

In *situs inversus*, the heart is on the right. He immediately looked up at the fourth floor of the building.

50

He had got up from the carpet the moment Gurevich had lost consciousness.

He had a strange smile on his face. He was holding a knife and was looking at Mila like she was trapped prey.

The scene playing out in front of Mila's eyes was surreal. Her mind had gone into a tailspin, but she still guessed the identity of this man who had risen from the dead.

Within a moment, everything was clear.

Michael Ivanovič had stopped the patrol car, neutralised the driver, and put on his uniform. Then he had turned up at Gurevich's door, a visit so late in the evening being less unusual in that guise. He had set fire to the inspector, but hadn't been able to escape from the building in time. When he had heard Mila and Berish arrive, he had stabbed himself in the throat with the knife – enough to lose blood and stage his own death.

The fake patrolman wiped his neck with his hand, confirming that it was only a surface wound. With his other hand, he threw the knife away and took an object from his pocket. It consisted of a small plastic bottle filled with orange liquid, from the lid of which sprouted two wires that ended in a box wrapped in black insulating tape.

Mila immediately realised it was another incendiary device.

She could shoot Ivanovič before he took another step, but she wasn't sure that was such a good idea. She didn't know if the device was activated by a button that he could press anyway before he collapsed on the floor.

Ivanovič was still smiling. 'Fire purifies the soul, did you know that?'

'Stop right there!' she yelled.

With an elegant gesture, like a discus thrower preparing the perfect throw, he reached back with his arm. Mila raised her gun and took aim. She was about to fire when a big white cloud rose behind Ivanovič, quickly engulfing him and moving towards her.

Through the chemical fog produced by the fire extinguisher, she recognised the dark forms of Special Forces officers. They were yelling excitedly, but moving in slow motion like ghosts, or like aliens that had come from another world to save her.

In less than a second, they had overpowered Michael Ivanovič and pinned him to the floor. Mila saw the surprise in his eyes as the officers immobilised him and took the dangerous toy from his hands.

Kairus

Exhibit 16-01-UJ/9

Fragment of the audio recording of the
interrogation on 28 September ████, at the
federal police department in ███████████.
Time: 17.42

Interrogator: *Where is she?*
Suspect: remains silent
Interrogator: *What happened last night?*
Suspect: remains silent
Interrogator: What's your involvement in the
  disappearance of Officer Mila Vasquez?

51

An obsession is the degeneration of a routine.

It is as if the mechanism of the mind, accustomed to repeating the same actions, suddenly jams and keeps repeating just one action *ad infinitum*, attributing an irreplaceable and almost vital significance to it.

In that word 'almost', though, lies the possibility of stopping the repetition and freeing the individual from the psychological slavery of his own fixation.

The day Simon Berish had come up with the definition, deriving it from his anthropological studies, he had also realised there would be no way out for him, and that he would continue to think about Sylvia for the rest of his life.

Love contaminates everything with memory, he often told himself. Love is like radiation.

So, whenever he touched something that belonged to the brief time they had been together – something she had used, handled, or merely brushed with her hand – the invisible negative energy contained in the object would radiate through his hand, climb up his arm, then go right down into his heart.

An hour before Sylvia walked into his life, Berish had been

peeling potatoes for dinner. He was going to cook some chicken. He wasn't much of a cook, but he got by.

It was a June afternoon and the light had changed in the city, forsaking the grey and deep yellow hues of May and veering now towards pink and blue. It was about twenty Celsius, like a subtle hint of summer, just mild enough not to worry about. Through the open kitchen window came the excited voices of children in a playground. The screeching of swallows faded in and out somewhere in the distance. The radio was on, tuned to a station broadcasting only old tunes – 'The Man I Love' by Billie Holiday, 'I Wish I Knew How It Would Feel To Be Free' by Nina Simone, 'It Don't Mean A Thing' by Duke Ellington, 'Moanin'' by Charles Mingus.

Dressed in jeans, a blue shirt with the sleeves rolled up, and a ridiculous straw-yellow apron with frills at the front, Simon Berish was moving between the table and the oven with the ease of a dancer. And, to top it all, he was whistling.

He was feeling strangely euphoric, and didn't know why.

He liked his job, and he liked his life. He was content. After two years in the army, he had realised that his natural next step would be to join the police. He had distinguished himself at the Academy, and had come a long way in a short time, reaching the rank of Special Agent much sooner than was common in the department. Being promoted to the Witness Protection Unit, under the command of Captain Stephanopoulos, was the icing on the cake of what had been an unforgettable year.

So he had every reason to be cheerful as he stood in the kitchen of that old apartment in a working-class neighbourhood. He deserved the aroma of roast chicken, he deserved Mingus and Ellington and Nina Simone and Billie Holiday. He would remember that moment for the rest of his life. Because an hour later everything would change. And all the things that had contented him before Sylvia would become a consolation prize.

He had rented the apartment a week earlier, using a fictitious name for the lease and taking the money he needed from the Unit's funds. He had been provided with a sum for expenses, as well as false papers and a medical insurance card.

The apartment was mostly furnished, but Simon had still moved in some furniture and ornaments from his own real home that morning, in order to attract the neighbours' attention to the new tenants in 37G.

The secret of passing unnoticed was to let people see you.

If he simply occupied the apartment, people would be sure to stick their noses in the business of the mysterious residents who had shown up out of the blue. The biggest risk in his work was gossip, which passed from mouth to mouth at the speed of light. So it was a good thing to keep a low profile.

Nobody spies on you, nobody takes an interest in you, if you're just like them.

Once he had unloaded the stuff from the van, he had flung open the windows and started to put everything in its place.

Having played the conscientious husband preparing the family nest, the only thing missing was the wife. There was just one drawback.

He had never seen her.

But he had read about her in the file Steph had given him. This wasn't his first assignment, but it was the first time he'd had to play the part of a husband. 'It'll be like one of those mail-order marriages, you know what I mean?' Steph had said, handing him a wedding ring – only gold-plated, though.

The apartment was on the ground floor. That might have seemed a vulnerable position, but he had chosen it deliberately to make sure they could get out easily if they had to. 'When you need to protect a witness, don't act the gunfighter,' Steph always said. 'Just grab their hand and run.'

When the doorbell rang, Simon stopped washing up, dried his hands on the apron and went to greet his new wife at the front door.

There, next to the entryphone, stood Joanna Shutton, as blonde as ever, giving him her usual brilliant smile. She was so attractive, Berish wondered why it was she couldn't find herself a man. Her male colleagues found her beauty daunting, and maybe that was why they'd started calling her 'the Judge'. Simon, though, always found her pleasant, as well as considering her highly capable.

Joanna greeted him like an old acquaintance, even patting him on the stomach and saying, 'You're looking well. Married life seems to agree with you.'

They laughed as if they had known each other all their lives.

Then Joanna said, 'I'd like to introduce my friend. I just picked her up at the station. She said she's been missing you these last few days. Take care of her.'

She stood aside to reveal a woman standing stiffly on the pavement, a slim woman in a blue jacket that was too large for her, her raven-black hair gathered in a plait. She was a holding a suitcase in one hand, its weight tilting her body slightly to one side, and her other hand was tightly closed to stop her wedding ring from slipping off her finger – they hadn't been able to find one her size.

She was looking around with a sad, lost expression on her face.

Simon went up to her with a big smile. She let him put his arms around her. He kissed her on the cheek and whispered in her ear, 'You must hug me or we won't be off to a good start.'

Saying nothing, Sylvia put down her case and did as she was told. But she did more than just return the hug: she made it last longer than necessary. He realised she didn't want to let go of him, and he sensed her fear as she clung to him with all her strength.

He knew at that moment that he would protect her above and beyond the call of duty.

Having made sure they didn't need anything else, Joanna left. Just before going out, though, she took Simon aside.

'She's unstable,' she said, referring to Sylvia. 'I don't think her nerves will hold out. She could blow your cover.'

'That won't happen.'

'It could have been worse,' she commented with typically feminine slyness. 'She is pretty, after all. Remember when Steph got me to "marry" that computer programmer with dandruff and glasses as thick as beer bottles? You're lucky.'

Simon was confused for a moment.

'Are you blushing?' Joanna asked, showing him no mercy.

'You'd like that, wouldn't you?' But then he grew serious. 'Do you think the Goodnight Man will come after her?'

'We don't even know he exists. Although – and I know I shouldn't say this – he does scare me.'

She was in earnest. Joanna Shutton always gave the impression of being the kind of police officer who was afraid of nothing. Or at least, the kind who would never admit it. But the things that were happening had shaken even her. It was the identikit of the Goodnight Man that had made them all nervous.

Those childlike features, those eternally still eyes, so deep they seemed alive.

They were trained police officers, the best detectives in the department. And the monster with the child's face was their perfect nemesis.

'I'm going off duty in an hour,' Joanna said as she left. 'But if you need anything, there's a new man on duty tonight. His name's Gurevich, I think he's all right.'

He and Sylvia barely touched each other on their first evening in the apartment.

He turned on the TV and kept the volume up to give the neighbours the impression the place was really being lived in – although neither of them bothered to watch it. She arranged the few things she had brought with her in the bedroom. She didn't close the door, but kept it ajar to make sure she could see him. Every now and again, he would walk past the door, just to let her know he was there and wouldn't let her out of his sight.

At one point, he found himself staring at her as she hung her clothes in the wardrobe. He didn't even realise he was doing it until she saw him and jumped slightly. He immediately moved away, feeling like an idiot.

Later, they had dinner: chicken and potatoes. It was nothing special, but she didn't make any comment. The only words they exchanged during the meal were requests to pass the bread or the mineral water.

At about ten, she went to her room, and Simon settled down on the sofa with a cushion and a blanket. He lay there with one arm behind his head, staring up at the ceiling, unable to sleep. He was thinking about her. He didn't know much about her, apart from what he had read in her file. He knew she was alone in the world, having grown up in an orphanage and then with a series of foster families. She had done lots of small jobs to make a living, but didn't seem to have ever had any ambition to do better for herself. Nobody loved her. Nobody had ever noticed her. Except for the suspicious character she had met in the place where one of the Goodnight Man's victims had last been seen.

'I didn't see him, he saw me. He smiled at me, and since then I haven't been able to forget him.'

Lying on the sofa, Simon reflected on the fact that until then, the case of the seven disappearances – dubbed 'the insomniacs' by the media – had existed only in the press and on the TV news. The only reason the Federal Police had launched an official investigation was to satisfy public opinion and not lose face.

The existence of an eyewitness, though, had been kept a secret. As had the identikit.

Stephanopoulos had managed to persuade his superiors to assign the investigation to the Witness Protection Unit. It wasn't the kind of case they usually dealt with, but the head of the department had readily agreed – anything to avoid the taint of failure.

At first, nobody had believed Sylvia. Only Steph was convinced it wasn't a deception to gain media attention. Having met her, Simon was equally sure she was telling the truth.

As he fantasised, he became aware of her standing motionless at the door of the living room. He turned and saw that she was in her nightdress. At first, he didn't understand what she wanted and was about to say something, but before he could do so she came towards him, and he shifted to make room for her, astonished by what was happening.

Sylvia lay down with her back to him, but resting her head on his arm. Simon lay his head back down on the cushion and relaxed.

'Thank you,' she said shyly.

Twenty years later, thinking about that first night on the sofa, Berish couldn't forget the warmth of Sylvia's body against his – that fragile body she had placed in his arms for him to take care of.

But maybe someone else had had more of an influence over her.

Would you like a new life?

Kairus's words to his victims over the phone had opened up a whole new dimension. One that Berish could never have imagined until a short time ago. The thought that there was a group of people who had passed through Room 317 of the Ambrus Hotel and were now ready to do anything for the preacher was a terrifying one, and not even what had happened today could chase it from his mind.

Gurevich's death had caused a major upheaval in the department, throwing as it had a new light on the man's private life.

The richly furnished apartment where he lived couldn't be accounted for by an inspector's salary. It was obvious he'd had another source of income.

Something had crossed Berish's mind, and he was sure it had crossed the minds of others who had set foot in the apartment after the killing – including Joanna Shutton. Something concerning a wad of banknotes given to a police officer twenty years earlier by a supergrass to help him escape the supervision of the Witness Protection Unit.

That was what Berish had been accused of, and he was still suffering the scorn and derision of his colleagues, even though there had never been any evidence that he had done anything wrong.

But the fact that Gurevich now looked as if he might have been the true culprit didn't mean Berish would be rehabilitated. On the contrary, it might mean the end of any hope of redemption.

While Michael Ivanovič was being grilled a few rooms away, Berish sat in his office with Hitch, waiting for his fate to be decided.

His superiors had to determine how to punish him for conducting an unauthorised investigation.

He didn't know if the Judge would use that as an excuse to ruin him once and for all, thereby avoiding any stain on the memory of a dead inspector. But that wasn't uppermost in his mind right now. What most concerned him was the army of shadows.

And the question of whether Sylvia was a part of it.

52

The room was shrouded in a soothing semi-darkness.

There were no windows and the walls were painted black. The furniture consisted of three rows of identical chairs, all facing in the same direction, like rows of seats in a cinema. But what was in front of them wasn't a screen but a one-way mirror.

On the other side of it, Klaus Boris was questioning Michael Ivanovič.

Mila was the only spectator.

The others preferred to sit comfortably at the computers in their own offices, following the scene via the closed circuit cameras that were covering it from different angles. Nobody used the room with the mirror any more.

That was why it was an ideal refuge.

Mila sat with her arms folded, staring at the glass. The interrogation room had fluorescent lights, a solid table in the middle and two chairs facing each other across it. On one sat Michael Ivanovič, handcuffed, while Boris roamed about the room like a cat stalking its prey. Boris was wearing an earpiece through which he was probably receiving instructions from the Judge.

Ivanovič – the red-headed, green-eyed 'fireworm' – was no

longer wearing the patrolman's uniform. They had given him a terrycloth T-shirt, tracksuit bottoms and, instead of shoes, slippers. In these clothes, he looked quite docile. But danger smouldered in him like embers beneath the ashes.

Mila saw the tattoos on his arms. They were unusual and disturbing.

There were no swastikas or upside-down crosses, no symbols of hatred and death, but a series of signs with a harmony of their own. They started at his wrists, went all the way up to his biceps, then disappeared beneath his T-shirt. There were similar marks on his handcuffed ankles.

They aren't tattoos, Mila thought. *I bet you did them yourself, because you like to feel fire on your skin.*

Ivanovič was more than a match for his interrogator.

'Do you have any idea the kind of trouble you're in?' Boris asked. In spite of being shut up in the room for three hours, he hadn't taken off his jacket or even loosened his tie. 'We can charge you with wounding the patrolman, murdering one of the heads of this department, maybe also murdering the doctor who wanted to write an article about you.'

It had been a long face-off, and they were moving to the final showdown, but Ivanovič was smiling to himself and arrogantly avoiding his interrogator's gaze.

'I'm glad you're enjoying yourself, but all it means, even in the best case scenario, is that you're going to rot in jail.'

'If you say so, sir.'

'Are you fucking me around, Michael?'

'No, sir. I didn't do anything.'

'No? Who was it, then?'

'There's a voice in my head that tells me what to do,' Ivanovič said in a calm monotone, as if deliberately reciting a script.

Boris leant towards him. 'Still on about those voices?'

'I'm telling the truth, sir. Why won't you believe me?' His tone was more insolent now.

'I'm not buying this crap, Michael. I've broken better people than you.'

'Really, sir?'

'Yes, really. And making up stories isn't going to help you.'

'As you wish, sir.'

Boris stared at him in silence. Then he decided enough was enough. He walked through the door into the room with the one-way mirror, where Mila was.

He switched off the speaker from the interrogation room.

'I need an explanation,' he said in a harsh tone, serving himself a glass of water from the cooler.

'All right.' Mila had known this moment would come, but she would have liked to avoid Boris's accusing look.

'When I came to see you in Steph's office in Limbo to ask you to be part of this investigation, I never imagined that one week later we'd be calling our friendship into question. And for what?'

'I know. I should have kept you informed.'

'Do you really think that's the only problem here?'

'You tell me.'

Boris took a sip of water, then gave a loud snort. 'I thought you trusted me.'

'You know me, you know how loyal I am. I would have come to you if I'd needed help, but I couldn't keep you constantly updated on what I was doing because you'd have put obstacles in my way or felt it your duty to report everything to the Judge. Let's be honest about this, Boris: you've become part of the system. I haven't and I never will.'

'So where did I go wrong, in your opinion? Go on, tell me . . . Thinking about my family? Caring about my salary and my career? In that case, yes, I plead guilty: I'm someone who follows the rules and obeys his superiors, whereas Mila Vasquez of course doesn't give a damn about these things.' He screwed up the cup and threw it angrily away. 'You say you respect me, you talk about loyalty, and then you go and put your trust in a man like Simon Berish.'

Klaus Boris was no different from his colleagues: when it came to passing judgment on other people, he followed the herd. Mila thought back to the moment when she had doubted Berish. What had thrown her was the mysterious envelope Berish had taken surreptitiously from his home and then given to the computer expert. She had tried telling herself it was none of her business, but that had done nothing to allay her suspicions. It wasn't until she had visited Gurevich's apartment that she had seen things clearly. And now she felt hurt by the way Boris was treating one of their colleagues, unwilling as he was to admit that the man might be innocent. 'Michael Ivanovič's motive for killing Gurevich was to show everyone that he was corrupt, and you're still talking about Simon Berish?'

The Hypothesis of Evil, Mila told herself: helping your fellow man by eliminating a hypocrite.

Boris seemed caught off guard. 'You don't know what you're talking about.'

'Show me you can still think for yourself, and that you won't become part of Joanna Shutton's attempt to cover up for her right-hand man just to save her own skin.' She could see her friend was hesitating. 'The Judge will sacrifice Berish and let people keep thinking he was the one who betrayed the department. He's going to be paying once again for something he didn't do.'

'You really want to talk about right and wrong? Then listen.' He took off his jacket and sat down on one of the chairs in the front row. 'None of Michael Ivanovič's victims are going to have justice.'

'What do you mean?'

Boris leant back in the chair. 'The Judge wanted us to apply the anti-terrorism protocol to Ivanovič. If it had been up to her, we'd have moved him to some secret prison and dragged a confession out of him by force.'

Shutton, it struck Mila, was quite prepared to use the terrorism angle to divert attention from the Gurevich scandal. 'And did the prosecutor agree?'

Boris shook his head at Mila's innocence. 'Don't you wonder why Ivanovič's lawyer wasn't present during his interrogation?'

Mila suddenly realised what was happening. 'The lawyer is doing a deal with the prosecutor.'

'And do you know what he's telling him right now? That his client is of unsound mind.'

Mila was horrified. 'Ivanovič planned Gurevich's murder in cold blood, he's tricked us all down the line: how can anyone say he's of unsound mind?'

Boris pointed at the one-way mirror, behind which Michael Ivanovič sat, still impassive, waiting for a fate he may already have planned. 'Did you hear what that psychopath said? He hears voices, he wants us to think he's a madman. His defence lawyer will maintain that Michael was abducted from his family when he was a child and has never recovered from the trauma. Plus, he suffers from a serious heart condition linked to his *situs inversus* and will never be able to stand prison. And of course he's a pyromaniac and a highly disturbed individual. Have I said enough?'

'And what do you think the prosecutor will do?'

'He'll say that until the prisoner's mental health has been assessed, we can't apply the anti-terrorism protocol, or even detain him like a normal suspect. Ivanovič will have to be transferred immediately to a psychiatric detention centre to be examined. If the doctors confirm the diagnosis, he'll serve his sentence in a special hospital which he could easily escape from one day.'

Mila was disheartened. 'A police officer has been killed. The prosecutor will never go against the department.'

'There's nothing we can do about it, I'm afraid.'

'If we lose Ivanovič, we'll never get to Kairus.' Mila played the Goodnight Man card, certain that Boris already knew all about it, including the fact that, twenty years earlier, the insomniacs case had been shelved with the Judge's complicity.

He hesitated, but was unable to reply.

'The news will come out sooner or later,' Mila persisted. 'Shutton has just one hope of saving her pretty designer arse, and that hope is in the hands of Michael Ivanovič. If we could get him to confess that somebody else put him up to it . . . '

'He's under no obligation to confirm the existence of a fictitious maniac even the police chose to ignore in the past.'

Kairus isn't a murderer because he has never killed, Mila told herself. *And he isn't a kidnapper if those who disappear come back. As far as the law's concerned, the Goodnight Man doesn't exist.*

Ivanovič turned to look in their direction. He couldn't see them through the mirror, but his eyes met Mila's anyway.

'They'll be coming to pick him up soon to take him to a secure facility,' Boris said in a disheartened tone. 'If we want him to give himself away, we need to use more complex tactics, set it up properly, with specific roles. We need to work on him psychologically. When I was an interrogator, before I was promoted, I learnt how to do that, so I know what I'm talking about. But we don't have time now.'

Mila turned to look at Boris. 'How long do we have left?'

'A couple of hours, maybe. Why?'

'You know, don't you, that we'll never again have an advantage like this over Kairus?'

'We can't use that. You'll just have to resign yourself.'

Mila paused, knowing that what she was about to suggest was risky. 'We should let him try.'

Boris didn't understand. 'Who are you talking about?'

'The man who's currently the best interrogator in the department.'

Boris got up from his chair. 'Don't even think about it.'

'We owe it to him.'

'What do you mean?'

'The chance to redeem his name. Berish is the best man for this, and you know it.'

Boris kept resisting, but Mila remembered what Berish had told her about the Hypothesis of Evil and about what preachers did.

They insinuated an idea.

Mila went closer to her old friend. 'I don't want this bastard to get off scot free. I don't want one of our people to have been wounded and the other to have died for nothing.' She put a hand on his shoulder.

Boris was surprised by the gesture. Mila hated physical contact.

'All right. But I'll tell you this right now, it isn't going to be easy to convince the Judge.'

53

'No way!'

The Judge's scream could be heard through the closed door of the office where the meeting with Klaus Boris was taking place.

'I won't allow him to make a fool of this department!'

'But what have we got to lose at this stage?'

'I don't care.'

Outside in the corridor, Mila kept her eyes on the floor in order not to embarrass the very man whose presence had unleashed this uproar. But Simon Berish simply stood, calmly leaning against the wall, arms folded. Nothing seemed to touch him. Mila envied his self-control.

'Why not let him try?' Boris was saying. 'We all know how well he's been doing with interrogations in the past few years.'

'I won't waste what little time we have left letting an amateur do anthropology experiments on Michael Ivanovič. Come up with another idea.'

Would her inspector friend bring up Gurevich's corruption in order to convince Shutton? Mila hoped he would. In the mean-time, Berish was still suspiciously calm in the face of the insinuations filtering out from the office. Mila went up to him. 'How can you stand it?' she asked.

Berish shrugged. 'You get used to it after a while.'

Mila summoned up her courage. 'I've got to ask – was it Gurevich who took that bribe?'

Berish immediately dampened her enthusiasm. 'How should I know what someone else did?'

'Incredible! You're still defending him.'

'I'm not going to take advantage of a man's death.'

Mila couldn't make up her mind if his attitude was brave or simply mad. 'I'm risking my reputation for you.'

'No one asked you to.'

'Can you at least tell me what happened?'

It was obvious he didn't want to, but he answered her all the same. 'I was assigned the surveillance of a criminal who'd decided to turn State's evidence on his associates. We were protecting him under a false name and had to keep an eye on him. Gurevich and I were both in charge.'

'Then why were you the only one they suspected when he escaped?'

'Because I was with him the night his son had an attack of appendicitis and he asked to go and see him in hospital. I'm not saying we'd become friends during the time I was forced to live with him, but I respected his decision to co-operate. It isn't easy for a man who's taken a particular path – whether it's right or wrong doesn't matter – to change everything, and risk his life in the process.'

'So what did you do?'

'I broke the rules and took him to hospital. So when he later escaped, they used that episode to maintain that we were in cahoots. The charge was dropped because they never found the money, but the mud stuck . . . and that's not so easy to get off.'

'I don't understand,' Mila said. 'Our colleagues had no right to judge you without proof.'

'Why should police officers care about the truth? They don't need a court of law to judge a colleague.'

Mila couldn't bear any more of his attitude. 'I don't understand how you can still be protecting the memory of Gurevich. You're innocent but you don't want people to know what really happened.'

'The dead can't defend themselves against accusations.'

'That's beside the point. I think it's just that – as you say – you're "used" to living like this. You actually enjoy it. Don't you have any self-respect? You use all the humiliation you suffer to be a martyr. Maybe that way you can lie to yourself and feel superior for letting other people bully you.'

Berish said nothing.

'We all fuck up, Berish. But that's no reason to let ourselves be persecuted the way you do.'

'True. That's why everyone tries to project a positive image of themselves, even if it isn't real. And the only person they confess their sins to is someone like me.' He drew closer to her. 'Do you know why I became the best interrogator in the department? These criminals don't know me, they don't know who I am, and yet when they look at me, they know I'm no different from them, that I, too, have something to hide. Whether that's true or not, it's my strength.'

'And you're proud of it?' She had decided to adopt the same harsh tone as Berish.

'Nobody's prepared to admit his own sins and get nothing in return, Mila. Not even you.'

She thought this over for a moment. 'Do you remember the tramp who hangs about near my house?'

'The one you take food to?'

333

'There's nothing altruistic in what I do. He's been there for at least a year and I'm only trying to gain his trust, because I want to flush him out, so that I can look him in the eyes and even talk to him. I don't have any feelings about him, I just want to find out if he's one of the residents of Limbo. I don't care if he's happy or not. We're only interested in other people's unhappiness when it reflects our own.'

'So what's your point?'

'My point is that I also play a part when I have to, but that doesn't mean I'm prepared to make compromises with myself.'

'And that's your sin, is it?' Berish replied in a tone of mock offence. 'Why don't you tell me about your daughter instead?'

Mila had to stop herself from turning to punch him.

But Berish stopped her from responding. 'At least I don't run away. I pay for my mistakes. But what about you? Who did you dump your daughter on in order to escape your responsibilities? Because it's obvious she doesn't exist for you, except when you decide she does.'

'What do you know about it?'

Their voices almost drowned out the animated discussion inside the office.

'So tell me, what's her favourite colour? What does she like doing? Does she have a doll she takes to bed with her on the nights you're not there?'

Those last words hit Mila with unexpected force.

What kind of mother would I be if I didn't know the name of my daughter's favourite doll?

'Yes, a red-headed doll called Miss,' she yelled in his face.

'Really? And how did you find that out? Did she tell you, or are you watching her in secret?'

Mila was taken aback. Berish realised that his words, which he had spoken just to hit back at her, were in fact the truth.

'I have to protect her,' she said by way of justification.

'Protect her from what?'

'From me.'

Berish was silent. He realised that the abuse he had been hurling at Mila was all down to the fact that he felt at a disadvantage, or maybe he was feeling the burden of all the years spent enduring endless humiliation. He hadn't been honest with her either. He still hadn't told her about Sylvia. But right now, all he wanted to do was tell her he was sorry.

It went quiet inside the office. The door opened. Boris was the first to come out. He didn't say a word. Then the Judge appeared.

She stared at Berish for a moment as if she didn't know him. Then she turned to Mila. 'All right, Officer Vasquez, your man is authorised.'

The news seemed to shake them both, putting an end to the argument they had been having.

The Judge walked away down the corridor, her stiletto heels echoing, leaving the usual trail of over-sweet perfume behind her.

Mila and Berish were a team again.

'You heard her, didn't you?' Klaus Boris said angrily to Mila. 'She called him "your man" because she wanted you to know that you're responsible. If anything goes wrong, the two of you will go down together, and there's nothing I can do about it.'

Berish wished Mila would turn to him, so that he could calm her with his eyes. But she didn't.

'I know,' she said.

Boris came and stood in front of Berish. 'We have about an hour left. Is there anything you need to interrogate Michael Ivanovič?'

Berish did not hesitate. 'Get him out of the interrogation room and take him to an office.'

54

The camera had been set up among stacks of files in a cupboard.

Berish insisted there was no point in hiding it: why not have it in full view on a tripod? But the Judge had refused to listen, reiterating that she was still in charge of the investigation.

In the room adjoining the office, Joanna Shutton sat in the front row, ready to enjoy the show on a TV monitor. Boris and Mila were a little way behind her. Mila was still shaken by the argument she and Berish had had in the corridor, but all the same she hoped he could pull this off.

Put an end to this nightmare, she encouraged him mentally.

At the moment, all you could see on the screen was Berish clearing the desk of anything Michael Ivanovič might use to attack him or harm himself. Berish spread a few documents on it to make sure it didn't look too empty, as well as a notepad, a couple of pencils, and a telephone placed a suitable distance from where Ivanovič would be sitting.

He had chosen an ordinary office because he didn't want to give the prisoner the sense that he was in a hostile environment.

Shortly afterwards, Michael Ivanovič came in, escorted by two officers holding him by the elbows.

He was dragging his feet because the cuffs around his ankles prevented him from moving easily. The two officers helped him to sit down and left the room. He was alone with Berish.

'Are you comfortable?' Berish asked.

Ivanovič's only response was to lean back in the chair and, with some difficulty because of the handcuffs on his wrists, prop his right elbow on the desk.

Berish didn't take the chair on the other side of the desk but sat down next to him. The hidden camera framed them both from the chest up.

'How's it going? Have they given you anything to eat and drink?'

'Oh, yes, they've all been very kind.'

'Good. I'm Special Agent Berish.' He held out his hand.

Ivanovič stared at it at first, then reached out awkwardly with his tattooed arms and shook it.

'It's all right if I call you Michael, isn't it?'

'Of course, that's my name.'

'I'm sure you've had just about all the questions you can take today, but I'm not going to lie to you, Michael. This is an interrogation.'

The prisoner nodded. 'I realise that.' He looked around. 'Are we being filmed?'

Berish pointed. 'The camera's among those files.'

Ivanovič lifted his arms and greeted it.

'Here we go,' Shutton cried in the next room. 'He's already made us look like idiots.'

Berish looked at his watch. 'You have a very good lawyer. In fifty minutes you'll be out of here. What do you want to talk about in the meantime?'

Ivanovič was amused, but played along. 'I don't know. You choose.'

Berish pretended to think about this. 'Vanishing for twenty

years can have its advantages. Being able to assume different identities, for instance: being who you like, or nobody at all. If you're nobody, you don't have to pay taxes. You know, when I was a child, disappearing was one of the things I most wanted to do. Second only to becoming invisible, so that I could spy on other people without being seen.'

Ivanovič smiled. He seemed vaguely intrigued.

'I'd have loved to disappear,' Berish went on. 'From one day to the next, without telling anyone. I'd have gone roaming in the woods, because in those days I loved camping. Then, a week or two later, I'd have come back. I was sure everyone would have been relieved to see me after all that anxiety. My mother would have cried, and even my father would have been moved. My grandmother would have made my favourite cake and we'd have had a party with all our relatives and neighbours. Even my cousins who lived in the north would have come down, although I hadn't seen them more than a couple of times since I was born. Everyone would have been there just for me.'

Ivanovič applauded softly.

Shutton didn't like that. 'What's he doing telling him about himself? It should be the other way round.'

Mila knew that Berish was trying to establish common ground. All the same, she glanced at her watch and prayed that he knew what he was doing. Five minutes had already gone by.

'Good story,' Ivanovič said. 'So what did you do?'

'You mean did I run away from home?'

Ivanovič nodded.

'Yes, I did.' Berish was serious now. 'And you know what happened? I wasn't away for anything like a week. Only a few hours, in fact. And when I decided I'd had enough and went home, there was nobody there to welcome me. They hadn't even noticed I was gone.'

Berish waited for Ivanovič to ponder these last words.

'But that's not how it was with you, was it, Michael? You were only six, far too young to run away from home.'

Ivanovič said nothing, but Mila noticed that something was changing in his face. Berish was provoking him.

He stood up and began pacing the room. 'A child is taken from a swing. No one sees a thing. Not even his mother, who's right there because the little park is just opposite her workplace. She always takes her son to that park, to play with the other children. But that day, Michael's alone and his mother is distracted because she's talking on the phone. For twenty years, no one knows what happened to the child. In fact, after all this time, people have forgotten about him. Only two people know the truth. One is little Michael, who's grown up in the meantime. The other one is the person who took him that day.' He stopped and looked Michael straight in the eyes. 'I won't ask you who it was. I don't suppose you'd tell me anyway. But maybe you could tell your mother. Wouldn't you like to see her again, Michael? The woman who brought you into this world, the woman who gave you life. Don't you think she has a right to know?'

Ivanovič said nothing.

'I know they've sent for her. She's out there now. I can have her come in. There's still time, if you like.'

It was a lie, but Ivanovič believed it, or at least seemed to. 'Why would she want to see me?'

Berish seemed to have found a way in. For the first time, Ivanovič was answering a question that concerned him personally. It was only a straw, but Berish clung to it. 'She's suffered a lot over the years. Don't you think it's time to relieve her of her guilt?'

'She's not my mother.'

Mila noticed the hint of annoyance in Ivanovič's tone. Berish had clearly scored a point.

'I understand,' Berish said. 'Never mind, then.'

Why was Berish breaking off the process in the middle when he had just managed to establish contact? Mila didn't understand.

'Do you mind if I smoke?' Without waiting for a reply, Berish took a packet of Marlboros and a lighter from his pocket. Mila had seen him borrow them from another officer a little while earlier. He simply put the things on the desk.

Ivanovič looked down at the lighter.

'That wasn't part of the agreement,' Joanna Shutton roared. 'He can't take a risk like that. I'm stopping the interrogation.'

'Wait,' Boris pleaded. 'Give him another minute. He knows what he's doing and I've never known him to fail.'

Berish was now walking up and down the room again with his hands in his pockets. Ivanovič pretended not to be interested but his eyes kept seeking out the lighter on the table – like a water diviner who, instead of water, responds to the call of fire.

'Do you like football, Michael?' Berish asked, for no apparent reason. 'I do.'

'Why do you ask?'

'I was just wondering what you've been doing for these past twenty years. You must have had a hobby of some kind. People usually have something they like to do to pass the time.'

'I'm different.'

'Yes, I'm aware of that. You're ... special.' Berish had emphasised the last word in an exaggerated way.

'Aren't you going to smoke that cigarette?'

'In a while,' Berish quickly replied, pretending to be concerned with something else – but maybe that was the result he was aiming at.

All the same, Mila began to worry. Ivanovič was longing for the sight of fire, and Berish was using the lighter as a means of pressure in order to obtain something from him. But whatever Berish had in mind, it wasn't working.

As if to confirm Mila's worries, Ivanovič took one of the pencils from the desk and began to doodle absent-mindedly on the notepad.

'In Inspector's Gurevich's apartment,' Berish resumed, 'you said something to Officer Vasquez that aroused my curiosity.' He seemed to be leaping from one subject to another without any apparent logic.

'I don't remember.'

'Don't worry, I'll refresh your memory . . . you asked her if she knew that fire purifies the soul.' Berish wrinkled his nose scornfully. 'Doesn't sound like much to me. Maybe it sounded great in your head, but I think it's a bit of a cliché.'

'I don't think so,' Ivanovič replied in a resentful tone.

Berish went to the packet of Marlboro, took one out, put it in his mouth and grabbed the lighter. He started passing it from one hand to the other, as if undecided whether or not to light it. Ivanovič followed these movements like a child fascinated by a juggler.

'What's he trying to do, hypnotise him?' the Judge said with a touch of contempt.

Mila could only hope that Berish still had the situation under control.

Berish lit the lighter and held up the flame between them. 'What's in the fire, Michael?'

A sinister smile appeared on Ivanovič's face. 'Whatever you want to see.'

'Who told you that? Kairus?'

Ivanovič's eyes were shining, but the gleam in them wasn't a reflection of the flame from the lighter. Rather, it was as if the fire came from inside him, from the depths of his soul. All the while, unconsciously, he kept doodling.

Berish took a folded sheet of paper from his jacket pocket. With a quick flick of his left wrist – like a magician – he opened it in front of Ivanovič's eyes. On it was the identikit of the Goodnight Man. He moved it closer to the lighter.

'What's he doing?' Shutton said. 'Two more minutes and I'm putting a stop to all this.'

Ivanovič's face was alive with excitement, like that of a child who can't wait to start a new game.

'What else did your master tell you?' Berish asked.

Ivanovič's mind seemed elsewhere, and his hand was shaking, causing the pencil to dig deep into the page of the notepad. 'That sometimes you need to go right down into hell to learn the truth about yourself.'

'And what's down there in hell, Michael?' Berish insisted.

'Are you superstitious, officer?'

'No, I'm not. Why do you ask?'

'Sometimes, if you know the name of the demon, all you have to do is say it out loud and he'll answer you.' The pencil moving on the paper was like a needle on a pressure gauge.

Why is Berish encouraging this madness? Mila was puzzled. Berish was giving Ivanovič the chance to frustrate all their efforts by giving credence to the idea that he was mentally ill. And their time was nearly up.

'Go in there and stop this nonsense,' the Judge ordered. 'I've seen enough.'

But Berish didn't give them time to intervene. He blew out the flame and took the Marlboro out of his mouth. The eagerness on Ivanovič's face vanished like a tamed fire.

Berish put the lighter back in his pocket and screwed up the paper with the identikit. 'All right, Michael. I think that's enough.'

*

Mila was lost for words. Joanna Shutton seemed determined to demand an account of what had happened.

Klaus Boris turned to Mila. 'I'm sorry.'

They all went into the office where the interrogation had taken place. Michael Ivanovič had already been taken back to his cell.

The Judge immediately laid into Berish, her voice echoing down the corridor. 'You're through, and not just in this case. I'm going to make personally sure you do no more damage. You're a failure, Berish. I don't know why we didn't just kick you out years ago when we had the chance.'

Mila noticed that Berish was letting her speak, as impassive as ever in the face of abuse. It suddenly struck her that this farce of an interrogation might have been revenge for the way they had treated him. Revenge on Gurevich, who had taken a bribe and let him get the blame for it. Revenge on Shutton, who was still protecting the guilty party even after his death, just to save her own skin. Revenge on the whole department and everything it represented. And Mila had helped Berish take his revenge, believing that all he would try to do was redeem his reputation.

Berish straightened his tie and made as if to leave the office, but Shutton, clearly unaccustomed to being ignored, barred his way. 'I haven't finished with you yet.'

Berish gently pushed her aside. 'Have you ever heard of the ideomotor effect?'

'What's that? Another of your anthropological discoveries?'

'Actually it comes from psychoanalysis. It's the process by which a mental image generates an involuntary movement.'

Shutton was about to say something, but the instinct that had helped her build her career stopped her.

'Everything the interrogator says or does,' Berish went on, 'provokes a particular action in the person under interrogation. That's why I showed him the fire.'

343

'Well?' Shutton asked stiffly.

'It's like when you're sitting at the table, chatting to someone, and instead of eating you're playing with the food on your plate and making shapes out of it. Or when you're on the phone and you grab a paper and pen and start doodling without realising it. Quite often, the things you draw don't mean anything, but sometimes they do. So, if I were you, I'd have a look right now at . . . '

He pointed to something behind them. Mila turned first, followed by Boris and the Judge. Silence fell over the room. They all stared at the same point on the desk.

The notepad on which Michael had been doodling earlier.

The drawing on the paper showed a rectangular four-storey building, with a row of skylights on the roof, a large front door and lots of windows.

Behind one of them was a human figure.

55

He would have liked to apologise to Mila.

But after the brief meeting in the office where the interrogation had taken place – while he was still enjoying his little
triumph over Joanna Shutton – he had lost sight of her. Maybe
she had returned to Limbo, or else gone home. Most likely, she
had left because she didn't want to speak to him.

What had possessed him to bring up Mila's daughter during
their argument in the corridor? It had been cruel of him, and he'd
had no right to do it.

But he was also convinced he'd hit a raw nerve. Why else
would she have revealed so many things about herself? Why tell
him about the tramp she gave food to, why reveal that she was
keeping an eye on her daughter from a distance? Why had Mila
confessed her sins?

Everybody wants to talk to Simon Berish, he remembered.

It was true for Mila, and it was also true for Michael Ivanovič.
Coming home to the apartment he shared with Hitch, Berish
kept hearing Michael's voice in his head.

What's in the fire, Michael?

Whatever you want to see.

Without switching on the light, Berish threw his keys on the table and collapsed on the sofa by the window. From outside came the cold, ghostly light of a street lamp. He loosened his tie and, using his heels, slipped off his shoes. Hitch lay down at his feet.

He had to call Mila. Apart from wanting to apologise to her, he had something to tell her. He hadn't been entirely honest with the others: the drawing on the notepad wasn't the only result of the interrogation.

The signs tattooed on Ivanovič's arms had given him an idea. They were the symbols of a special language – a language of fire – carved on his skin like hieroglyphics to be interpreted. And Berish had spoken to him in the same invisible jargon.

What else did your master tell you?

That sometimes you need to go right down into hell to learn the truth about yourself.

The man who had said those words wasn't the Michael Ivanovič who was trying to pass himself off as mad, Berish was certain of that.

And what's down there in hell, Michael?

Are you superstitious, officer?

It was this sudden, seemingly out of context question that had enlightened him. Michael had been trying to send him a message. But it was Kairus's voice that had spoken inside him.

No, I'm not. Why do you ask?

Sometimes, if you know the name of the demon, all you have to do is say it out loud and he'll answer you.

Berish was convinced that these words held the key to identifying the building Michael had drawn so absent-mindedly. The most important thing was to discover who that vague figure standing in one of the windows really was.

In the semi-darkness of his apartment, Berish became aware

of the sound of pouring rain. It was beating on everything, but only in his head. It should have washed away his thoughts, but instead it carried them with it.

And with the rain came a memory of the past.

The lights were off in the old apartment in the working-class neighbourhood. The thunderstorm had started about six, darkening the sky immediately. Sylvia had a high fever and Simon had to go out to buy antibiotics. Gurevich usually took care of such things – Joanna was right, the new man was good at his job. He did the shopping, paid the bills, and sometimes stayed for dinner. Berish passed him off as his younger brother who occasionally came to visit.

But this time, it was an emergency.

Simon felt it was his fault. He should have checked the medicine cabinet properly in advance, to avoid this kind of thing happening. There was gauze, plasters, aspirins, anti-inflammatories, but no antibiotics. It was risky leaving Sylvia alone: something he never did. But thanks to the thunderstorm, Gurevich was stuck in traffic and wouldn't be there for another couple of hours.

Sylvia had been delirious all afternoon. At first, Simon had made do with what he had in the house – a cool cloth for her forehead, and paracetamol. But that hadn't helped much, and she was getting worse.

So in the end, he left in his shirtsleeves, carrying an umbrella, and ran to the local pharmacy at the end of the block. He waited his turn at the counter, without taking his eyes off the window. Through it he had a partial view of the entrance to their building, although he wouldn't have been able to see anyone climbing in through the window. That was why he was so anxious.

He paid, grabbed the paper bag and ran home, without even

bothering to open the umbrella again. By the time he got inside, he was soaked through. He climbed the short flight of stairs with his heart in his mouth, fearing that all his worst nightmares were waiting for him just beyond the door. Once in the apartment, he went straight to the bedroom.

She wasn't there.

Instinctively, he reached for his gun. He was in too much of a panic to think clearly. He wanted to call out her name, but didn't. The rain outside was like an avalanche. He turned towards the living room, and that was when he saw her.

She was standing by the window, her nightdress stuck to her skin by sweat. She hadn't heard him come in because she had her back to him. She was holding the telephone receiver with both hands, as if it were very heavy.

She was on the phone to someone.

At first, Simon didn't grasp the significance of what was happening. Moving close to her, he realised that she wasn't speaking. She was listening.

'Who is it?' he said in alarm.

She gave a start and turned. Her forehead was damp, her eyes feverish, and she was shaking. 'It rang, but when I got up to answer there was no one there.'

As he gently took the receiver from her hands, he could hear a repeated engaged tone. He led her back to bed, thinking that the telephone call had been nothing but a fever dream.

Would you like a new life?

Was that what Sylvia had heard on the phone that night? Was it Kairus's voice penetrating the heart of a young woman who'd been badly treated by life? Was it the Goodnight Man coaxing her to go to Room 317 of the Ambrus Hotel and abandon herself to the shadows?

Now, many years later, sitting in the armchair in his apartment, Simon Berish found comfort again in an obsession that had returned, like an old friend, tapped him politely on the shoulder, and urged him not to ignore it.

And, in return, it offered him hope. A painful, senseless hope.

A few years earlier – after he had learned to live with Sylvia's disappearance – on the evening of an ordinary day in an ordinary week in an ordinary month, the phone had rung, and when he had answered he had heard the sound of a thunderstorm. His first instinct had been to look out of the window. It was only after seeing the moon shimmering in the sky that he had realised the rain was a long, long way away.

In the midst of the flood, he thought he heard breathing.

Then the line had gone dead, leaving him alone with a terrible question. A crawling sensation beneath his skin had told him that, yes, it was her. She had been trying to remind him of an evening of fever and pouring rain.

From then on, Berish had stopped resigning himself to the situation. The possibility that she was alive and well should have been a comfort to him. After all, at least one of his many prayers had been answered. Instead, it had brought a new question into his life.

Why didn't she stay with me?

In the semi-darkness of his apartment, with the light coming in from the street lamp, Berish suddenly felt tired. But at the same time he was close to seeing the whole picture.

What else did your master tell you?

That sometimes you need to go right down into hell to learn the truth about yourself.

And what's down there in hell, Michael?

Are you superstitious, officer?

No, I'm not. Why do you ask?

Sometimes, if you know the name of the demon, all you have to do is say it out loud and he'll answer you.

He'll answer you, Berish repeated. But when he had disappeared at the age of six, Michael Ivanovič was too young to know the demon's name. Too innocent to be asked if he wanted to change his life, too innocent even to want to. Too young to go to Room 317 of the Ambrus Hotel ...

Berish had a sudden insight. But he would have to wait until tomorrow to see if it worked out.

She's not my mother, Michael had said to him during the interrogation when he had brought up the subject. And he had been aware of a real resentment in those words – a palpable hatred. He couldn't figure out why Michael would want to say such a thing.

Only his real mother could know the reason.

Berish decided he would call Mila the following morning and tell her all about it. Then they would go together to check it out. And on the way there, he would find a way to apologise.

A pariah he might be, but he was sure that she at least would forgive him.

56

She had a sudden desire to see Alice.

Over the past few hours, Mila had become unexpectedly, and absurdly, anxious about losing her. She didn't know the reason for this anxiety, but there it was, for the first time.

That was why she was driving her Hyundai at top speed towards her mother's house. The urgency was different from the time when she had dashed there because of a stupid hallucination. She wanted to find Alice still awake. She wouldn't turn back, she wouldn't leave without seeing her. All she needed was a few minutes.

Mila had always felt unsuited to the role of mother. But after the argument with Berish and the encounter with Ivanovič, she had started to think her mistakes weren't beyond repair.

She's not my mother.

That was what Michael had said. But it wasn't the fault of the woman he now disowned that someone had taken him away when he was only six. Or maybe parents are always responsible for what happens to their children, simply because of the fact that they brought them into this dark, pitiless, irrational world where only evil seemed to make any sense.

As Mila drove, it wasn't the road, the cars, the houses that she saw in front of her. The windscreen had become a screen for memories. Her eyes projected images from a distant past onto the glass.

Without the evil that had been done seven years earlier, Alice wouldn't have been born. If a number of girls hadn't been abducted and killed, if some parents hadn't lost what they held dearest, Mila wouldn't have met Alice's future father. It was the Whisperer who had brought them together.

And made them a family.

He had been the creator, he had foreseen everything. They had fulfilled his plan. And Alice was born. Mila kept away from her partly in order to protect her, and partly because she didn't want to know if the Whisperer had cast his shadow over her daughter, too.

The Hypothesis of Evil also held true for her. Above all for her.

Is the lioness who kills the zebra's calves to feed her own cubs good or bad? Was the killing of innocent little girls, thanks to which Alice had been born, a positive or negative thing?

Because if Mila had agreed to be a mother – to be with her daughter, look after her, live like a normal family – she would have had to admit that the evil which had been done was the price to be paid for her happiness.

As luck would have it, Mila was unable to be happy. Her inability to feel empathy prevented her from knowing what she was missing. Alice, though, had every right to be happy with her life. It wasn't her fault. Even though Mila hadn't realised that before this afternoon, before the past week. And now she was hurrying to her to start making amends.

Tonight, watching her on a computer screen wasn't enough.

*

The lights were still on in the house. She walked up the path to the front door and took the key from under the pot of begonias.

Inside, there was a smell of biscuits.

Her mother emerged from the kitchen in an apron, her fingers sticky with dough. 'I wasn't expecting you, Mila,' she said, suspiciously.

'I'm not staying long.'

'Oh, do stay. I'm making chocolate shortbread. Alice has a school picnic tomorrow and has to get up early.'

'So she's already in bed.'

Ines could tell that Mila was upset. 'What's the matter?'

'It's about Alice's problem . . . I'm afraid it might be a form of autism.'

Now that Mila was at last expressing some concern for Alice, Ines felt it her duty to reassure her. 'She's fine.'

Mila gave a deep sigh. 'I hope you're right. If you are, then her lack of awareness of danger should decrease as she grows up. In any case, we just have to wait and see. In the meantime, we need to keep an eye on her. I don't want her going in for acrobatics on the roof, or setting the house on fire.'

'That won't happen.' Ines was trying to show confidence, even though both of them felt apprehensive. 'Why don't you look in on her? Maybe you could give her a kiss as she sleeps.'

Mila started towards Alice's bedroom, then turned and said, 'When Dad died and we were left on our own, how did you keep going?'

Ines wiped her hands on her apron and leaned back against the doorpost. 'I was young and inexperienced. Your father was much better than I was at giving you what you needed. I used to joke and tell him he should have been your mother.' She smiled for a moment, then grew sad. 'After he died, I found it hard to come to terms with the loss. I took to my bed. I couldn't provide for us, for you, and the grief I felt was the perfect alibi. Your father wasn't there any more, and I was no great shakes as a mother. You may not remember this, but there were days I could hardly get down the stairs.'

Mila did remember, but didn't say so.

'I knew it wasn't right for you to stay with me and bear the burden of all the memories in this empty house. Or sit and watch a mother who'd decided to bury herself alive.'

'Why didn't you give me away?'

'Because one morning, you came into my room and changed everything. You stood in front of my bed and said, "I don't care if you're sad. I'm hungry and I want my *bloody* breakfast".'

They both laughed. Ines never swore, liked to keep up appearances, and was always afraid of looking stupid. It sounded really strange to Mila to hear her say that word.

When they stopped laughing, Ines went to Mila and stroked her with the back of her flour-covered hand. 'I know you don't like to be touched. But please make an exception this time.'

Mila said nothing.

'I told you this because it'll happen to you, too. One of these days, Alice will surprise you with a word or a gesture. And you'll want to take her back and never leave her again. Until that happens, I'll keep her here. Let's say you're loaning her to me.'

They looked at each other. Mila would have liked to thank her for the story and the reassuring words, but there was no point. Ines already knew.

'There's a man,' she blurted out before she had even realised it. 'I haven't known him long, but ... ' She didn't finish the sentence.

'But he's made you think,' Ines said.

'His name is Simon and he's a police officer. I don't know, but I think maybe ... It's the first time in ages I've been so close to someone. Maybe the fact that we're working together makes it easier. But I think I trust him.' She paused for a moment. 'I've never trusted anyone before.'

Ines smiled. 'It's a good thing for you, maybe for Alice, too.'

Mila nodded in gratitude. 'I'll go and see her.'

Alice's room at the end of the corridor was shrouded in the amber-tinted semi-darkness that filtered through the shutters. Mila thought she was already asleep, but a few feet from the door she heard her voice and stopped dead.

She could see her clearly in the wardrobe mirror. Alice was sitting on the bed, talking to the red-headed doll.

'I love you, too,' she was saying. 'You'll see, we'll always be together.'

Mila was about to go in, maybe even give her a kiss – something she almost never did. But then she changed her mind.

Children who play by themselves are like sleepwalkers, and shouldn't be woken. The return to reality might be traumatic, and the spell of their innocence broken for ever.

So she stood there listening to the caring tone with which Alice was addressing her Miss. It certainly wasn't something the girl had learnt from her.

'I won't leave you alone. I'm not like my mummy. I'll always be with you.'

The words hit Mila like a punch in the chest. None of her self-inflicted wounds had ever caused her such pain. There was no blade in the world that could hurt her that much. Only her daughter's words had that destructive power.

'Goodnight, Miss.'

Mila saw Alice slip beneath the blankets with her doll and hold her tight. She stood paralysed, unable to breathe. The little girl had told the truth, plain and simple: her mother had abandoned her. But actually hearing her say it was different. She would have liked to cry if only she had known how. Her eyes stung, but no tears came.

When at last she managed to move, she retreated quickly as far as the front door and ran out, slamming the door behind her, without even saying goodbye to Ines, who was looking startled at her from the kitchen.

She parked the Hyundai where she shouldn't have – she didn't care – and walked quickly to her building, one thought in mind. There was a paper bag hidden under the bed. She had everything she needed in it.

Disinfectant, cotton wool, plasters and, most important of all, an unopened box of razor blades.

The giants on the billboard opposite followed her progress from above. The tramp looked up as she passed the alley, expecting something to eat, but Mila ignored him.

When she got to the front door of her building, her fingers were shaking so much she could barely hold the key to open it. She had to control herself. Her hand would have to be nice and steady when she held the blade. She climbed the stairs two at a time and reached the privacy of her apartment. The books filling the rooms fell silent – they no longer contained stories and characters, only blank pages. She turned on the light by her bed without even taking off her jacket. The one thing she wanted now was to cut herself. To feel what, over the past year, she had tried to replace with fear. To see the steel sink into the flesh of her inner thigh. To feel her skin tearing like a veil, the blood gushing out like hot balm.

To assuage pain with pain.

She leant down to get the bag out from under the mattress – a few more seconds and everything would be ready, and then she could forget Alice. This was where she had hidden it from herself a long time ago, when she had gone on this strange diet, deciding to abstain from her own blood.

She reached out for the bag. Stretching, she touched it with the tips of her fingers. An inch or two more, and she was able to grab it and pull it towards her. She tore it open.

But instead of the things she needed to harm herself, there was something else waiting for her.

Mila looked down at the strange object in her hand, not even asking herself how a brass knob with a key hanging from it had ended up here.

The key to Room 317 of the Ambrus Hotel.

57

Edith Piaf was singing '*Les amants d'un jour*'.

The foyer in its saffron-yellow semi-darkness was deserted. There were no guests about, the blind man in the check jacket wasn't sitting on the leather sofa, and there was no sign of the skinny porter with crew-cut grey hair, the gold ring in his left ear-lobe and the faded tattoos.

The music was the only inhabitant of the place, as poignant as a long-forgotten memory, as comforting as a lullaby.

Mila walked to the lift, pressed the button and waited.

When she reached the third floor, she walked down the long corridor, past the black varnished wooden doors, checking the room numbers until she came to the one she wanted.

Three figures in burnished metal. 317.

Mila took the brass knob from her jacket pocket. She turned the key in the keyhole. The door opened, letting the darkness out.

She crossed the threshold and reached for the light switch. The ceiling light above the bed came on. The tungsten elements in the old incandescent bulbs hissed, producing an opaque light.

The dark red wallpaper. The matching carpet on which the giant blue flowers seemed to float. The burgundy satin bedspread with the cigarette burns. The two bedside tables. On the grey marble top of the right hand one, next to a black telephone, and in line with the shadow on the wall left by a crucifix that had since been removed, there was something for her.

A gift from the Goodnight Man.

It's from darkness that I come, and to darkness that I must, from time to time, return.

A glass of water and two blue pills.

58

The mobile phone kept ringing but there was no answer.

Maybe she was still angry and didn't want to talk to him. It was understandable, Berish thought. He deserved it. He would have liked to drop by Limbo and clear things up – at this time of the morning, Mila was unlikely to be at home.

But he had woken up late, and only because Hitch was demanding to go out.

What was more serious was that he had fallen asleep, fully clothed, in the old armchair by the window. Now he had a sharp pain in the middle of his back, not to mention his neck muscles.

He couldn't recall sleeping so deeply for years. It was as if he had been hibernating. His uncomfortable position hadn't woken him or bothered him at all during the night. And he hadn't dreamed. It had been like one long journey from the moment he had closed his eyes to the moment he had woken up.

But even though he was aching all over, he felt full of energy now.

After a quick shower, he had changed his clothes, putting on a navy suit, and had a coffee. It was eleven o'clock on a brisk morning. The autumn air had finally replaced the dying summer. Berish filled Hitch's bowls with food and water. He couldn't take him along with him this time.

He called a taxi. He needed to check out the insight he had had the previous night before fatigue had overwhelmed him.

He would have liked Mila to be with him, but maybe she needed to let her anger cool off first. He wasn't sure how to behave towards her – he had only known her for a short time.

As soon as he showed up in Limbo with the result he was hoping to obtain within an hour at most, Mila would forget why they had argued in the first place. To tell the truth, Berish couldn't remember either. Maybe there hadn't even been a proper reason. Sometimes these things just happened.

The taxi drove up to the main entrance of the white apartment building. A flag fluttered in the middle of the lawn, the clatter of the rings securing it to the pole the only sound he heard as he got out of the car. He paid the driver and a few moments later walked in through the main entrance of the nursing home.

It was a nice place, deceptively so. Behind the main building was what amounted to a village, made up of white cottages with a cobalt blue finish.

They had indicated at reception the cottage where Michael Ivanovič's mother lived, and Berish walked along the inner paths of the complex, looking for the right door.

He knocked and got his badge ready as he waited. A few seconds went by, then the door was flung wide open.

The woman who greeted him was in a wheelchair. The badge immediately caught her eye. 'I've already told your colleagues everything,' she said indignantly before he could even open his mouth. 'Go away.'

'Wait, Mrs Ivanovič. This is important.' He had said the first thing that came into his mind, realising too late that he should have prepared an excuse.

'My son's a murderer, and I haven't seen him for twenty years. What can be more important than that?'

She was about to close the door again. But something had been set in motion, and Berish couldn't stop it now. He was sorry he didn't have Mila with him: she was more used to dealing with people. Too many years of trying to avoid the world and being avoided by it had made him incapable of interacting with other human beings – unless he was interrogating them.

'I spoke to your son yesterday. I think Michael wanted to send you a message . . .'

He was lying. In reality, Ivanovič had been all too clear on that point.

She's not my mother.

The door stopped an inch or two from his face. The woman reopened it slowly, and stared at him with an anxious desire to know.

She's looking for forgiveness and I can't give it to her, Berish thought as he entered the cottage.

Mrs Ivanovič wheeled herself to the opposite corner of the living room as Berish closed the door behind him.

'They came here last night and told me Michael had come back. And they told me what he'd done, without any concern for my feelings as his mother.'

She must have been fifty at most, but looked much older. Her hair had turned grey, and she wore it short, almost shaved. The place where she was living suited her. It was as functional as a hospital room and as basic as a prison cell.

'May I sit down?' Berish asked, pointing to a sofa covered in oilcloth.

Mrs Ivanovič made a gesture to tell him that he could.

Berish wasn't sure he had any words of comfort or sympathy to give her. He didn't think they would help anyway. There had been too much anger in the woman's voice.

'I've read the file on your son's disappearance,' he said. 'That scene in the park, with Michael being taken from a swing by someone you didn't even see, must still send shivers up your spine.'

'I wonder why you all think that,' the woman said. 'Do you really want to know what tortures me the most? If I'd turned round one second earlier, it wouldn't have happened. The phone booth I was calling from was just thirty feet away. A fraction of a second would have been enough – one less word in that damned conversation. They teach us to count minutes, hours, days, years . . . but nobody ever tells us the value of a second.'

That concession to sentimentality gave Berish hope that Mrs Ivanovič might yet open up. 'At the time, you and your husband were going through a divorce.'

'Yes. He'd found another woman.'

'Did your husband love Michael?'

'No,' she replied immediately. 'Now what's the message from my son?'

Berish picked up a magazine from a low table, took his pen out of the inside pocket of his jacket and began to reproduce, on a corner of the cover, the drawing Michael Ivanovič had done on the notepad during his interrogation.

'What are you doing to my magazine?'

'I'm sorry, there was no other way.'

He completed his copy of the four-storey rectangular building with the row of skylights on the roof, the large front door, and the human figure behind one of the many windows. Then he handed the result to Mrs Ivanovič.

She looked at the drawing for a moment, then gave it back to Berish. 'What's that supposed to be?'

'I was hoping you'd tell me.'

'I don't know what it is.'

Berish was sure she wasn't telling the truth. 'As he was drawing this, Michael said a lot of things that didn't seem to make much sense.'

'They say he may have gone mad. Seeing that he's going around killing people and setting them on fire, they're probably right.'

'In my opinion, he wants us to believe he's mad. When I asked him what was in the fire, he said, "Whatever you want to see". That made me think, and you know why?'

'No, but I'm sure you're going to tell me,' she said defiantly, making it quite clear that the wall she had built around herself over the years could not be breached.

Berish tried, anyway. 'We're so content with appearances that we don't look at what's inside the flame.' He paused and looked at her. 'The flame conceals something, Mrs Ivanovič.'

'And what's that?'

'The fact that we sometimes need to go right down into hell to learn the truth about ourselves,' he said, deliberately repeating the words Michael had used to him.

She opened her eyes wide, and for a moment Berish saw her son's expression reflected on her face.

'Do you know what's down there in hell, Mrs Ivanovič?'

'I live there every day.'

Berish nodded, as if taking this in. 'What did you do before . . . '

She looked down at her lifeless legs. 'I was a pathologist. Ironic, isn't it? For ten years I worked with dead bodies. People die all the time, and don't even know why. The things I've seen ... There are more devils in this life than there are in hell. You're a police officer, you know what I'm talking about.'

'Sometimes, if you know the name of the demon, all you have to do is say it out loud and he'll answer you,' Berish said, latching on to her words in order to quote Michael again.

She gave him a sidelong glance. 'What game are you playing, officer? Are you challenging God or the devil?'

'The devil can't be beaten.'

A thoughtful silence fell over the room. There was a weary expression in the woman's eyes.

'Are you superstitious, Mrs Ivanovič?'

'What kind of question is that?'

'I don't know,' Berish replied calmly. 'It's a question your son asked me, and I didn't know how to answer it. It was the last part of his message.'

'You've been making a fool of me. The things you've told me, that drawing ... They have nothing to do with me. What is it you really want?'

Berish stood up. With his big frame, he loomed over the woman, who retreated in her wheelchair. 'Before I came here this morning, I didn't actually think this had anything to do with you, but when you opened the door, I realised it did.'

'Go away,' she said, coldly.

'In a minute.' He wondered where to begin. 'Kairus entered his victims' lives through the telephone.'

'Who's Kairus?'

'Would you rather I called him the Goodnight Man? He was someone who made phone calls to people who were in despair and offered them something better. What puzzled me was how he managed to do that with Michael. He was only six, far too young to understand what could possibly be better for him. Which means he must have been kidnapped. But why take a risk like that when the others – the insomniacs – had gone to him of their own free will? He must have had a good reason.'

'You're talking nonsense,' the woman said.

But Berish kept looking straight at her. 'Michael has a congenital condition known as *situs inversus*, which causes serious heart problems.'

'So?'

'You and your husband were getting a divorce. Michael's father was about to start a new family and there probably wouldn't have been room in it for a sick child. But you wouldn't have been able to take care of him by yourself, would you? I assume you'd already had the first warning signs of the degenerative disease that eventually confined you to a wheelchair.'

Disconcerted now, she said nothing.

'Michael would have needed constant care. With no parents to look after him, he would have ended up in a home – because who would have wanted to adopt him with his condition? And the treatment he required was expensive. You'd studied medicine, you were only too well aware of what would have happened. Without the necessary financial resources, how many years would your child have survived?'

The woman began to cry softly.

'But one day, you get a phone call. You don't recognise the voice, but what the man at the other end says is quite sensible. He gains your trust, gives you a different outlook on things. He gives you hope. Even though you don't know who he is, he's the only friend you've had in ages. And what he asks you is this: "Would you like a new life . . . for your son?"'

Berish let the words hang in the air between them.

'So what did you do, Mrs Ivanovič? You did what you thought was best at the time, because you wanted Michael to have at least a chance. You took him to Room 317 of the Ambrus Hotel, you gave him the sleeping pill, and you waited for him to fall asleep. Then you left him on that bed and went away, knowing you'd never see him again. And you made up the story about the swing.'

Tears were now streaming down the woman's face.

'I'm truly sorry for you, Mrs Ivanovič,' Berish said, with all the compassion he was capable of. 'It must have been a terrible thing for a mother.'

'When you risk losing one thing,' she said through tightened lips, 'you can't accept it. But when you risk losing everything, you realise you actually have nothing to lose . . . I was hoping I'd die soon after that anyway. And yet I'm still here.'

Berish would have liked to leave. He felt that his presence had become intrusive. What could a man who'd never had children possibly know about a tragedy like that? And on top of everything else, he'd lied to justify being here.

She's not my mother.

Those contemptuous words kept echoing in his head. If only Michael knew what this woman had done for him, the sacrifice she'd made . . . But maybe he did know and that was why he condemned her. Whatever the case, Berish couldn't afford to feel too much pity because he didn't want to leave this place until he'd got all the answers he needed.

'As I said before,' he resumed, 'Kairus took a risk in choosing a child – because, as you know, people grow fond of missing children, they mentally adopt those whose pictures they see on milk cartons, and they don't give up easily . . . So if Kairus decided to go ahead anyway, and to leave behind a witness who could always change her mind and tell the police the whole story . . . then he must have had a good reason.'

The woman shook her head.

'What did he ask of you in return, Mrs Ivanovič?'

She looked down at the magazine and the drawing of the large rectangular apartment building. 'I didn't think he'd remember after all this time ... Do you see what this means, officer? My son hasn't forgotten me. This building is just opposite the park where I always used to take him.'

It was incredible. Everything had come full circle. The little park with the swing from which Michael had supposedly disappeared, his mother's anguish, the drawing he had done during the interrogation. Berish picked up the magazine on which he had copied that drawing and showed it to the woman again. 'And what is this place?'

'The morgue. I spent ten years of my life inside those walls when I was still a pathologist.'

Berish went to her and put his hand on her shoulder. 'It's not your fault Michael became a monster. But we can still stop the man who did this to him. What did Kairus ask you for, twenty years ago?'

'A body.'

59

He didn't think he could bear the tension.

He was nearly there. He just had to double-check. And he wanted to tell Mila, who must be there by now. If he could only see it through her eyes, he would confirm that it was all true.

Berish couldn't keep still on the seat of the taxi taking him to the department. Adrenalin was coursing through his veins. He had decided not to call Mila on her mobile: he needed to tell her the new information in person.

It had taken him twenty years. And now that he was close, he couldn't stop.

In the meantime, he was imagining a number of different scenarios. Some made sense, others didn't. But he was convinced that, in the end, every piece of the puzzle would fall into place.

The architect of the great deception – the Wizard, the Enchanter of Souls, the Goodnight Man, Kairus – was clever and unscrupulous.

But he could still beat him.

Berish asked the taxi driver to drop him in the square with the large fountain overlooked by Federal Police Headquarters.

The building's glass front reflected the early afternoon sun and the pale sky furrowed by the odd white cloud. Friday was well known to be the quietest day of the week. He had always wondered why. Maybe police and criminals alike needed a rest before a busy weekend. All the same, there seemed to be a lot of officers coming in and out of the building.

Joining the flow, Berish walked towards the main entrance.

As he did so, he noticed faces turning to look at him as he passed – like sunflowers searching for a ray of light, their eyes converged on him.

Colleagues who usually ignored him were now looking strangely at him. There was nothing special about those looks, except that their usual coldness had been replaced by surprise.

As the number of people staring at him in a suspicious manner increased, Berish instinctively slowed down, puzzled as to what was going on.

A voice behind him shouted something but he didn't realise at first who was being addressed. He looked round, as startled as everyone else.

'Stop right there, Berish!' came the voice again, and this time there could be no doubt.

Berish turned and saw Klaus Boris walking towards him, his arm outstretched. Was he really pointing a gun at him?

'Don't move!'

Berish just had time to put his hands up before other officers seized and handcuffed him.

60

In the interrogation room, silence was used as a means of torture.

But it was an invisible kind of cruelty. There was no law against it.

Simon Berish was in the same place that had hosted Michael Ivanovič only a few hours earlier. Unlike most other people who had been in this room, he knew why the white walls were covered in sound-absorbent material. The principle was that of an 'echoless' room, where sounds cannot penetrate. The body makes up for the lack of sound by creating artificial noises – tinnitus, ringing in the ears. In time, you're less and less able to distinguish reality from imagination.

A condition that, in the long term, can lead to madness.

But Berish knew they wouldn't leave him here that long. So he took advantage of the silence to do some thinking.

He kept wondering what they were going to accuse him of, but nothing came to mind. He sat waiting for someone to come and occupy the seat on the other side of the table and finally explain what was going on. In the meantime, he tried to look at ease – but not too much at ease – in order to present a neutral spectacle to the cameras trained on him from every angle. He was sure there was nobody behind the false mirror.

He was all too familiar with interrogation techniques, and knew that his colleagues would let him stew for a couple of hours before they put in an appearance. He just had to hold out. He wouldn't ask if he could have a glass of water or go to the toilet, because such requests were seen as signs that the suspect was weakening. And in a way, they were. If he was going to show them that he was blameless, he would have to subvert their plans.

A suspect who was either too nervous or too calm was almost certainly guilty. So was one who constantly asked why he'd been brought in. One who was too cold would confess immediately. A calm one was likely to get life imprisonment. The innocent ones did all these things at the same time, but weren't usually believed anyway. The secret lay in indifference.

Indifference threw them.

Some three hours had passed when the door at last opened and Klaus Boris and the Judge made their entrance, grim-faced and carrying folders.

'Special Agent Berish,' the Judge said, 'Inspector Boris and I have some questions to ask you.'

'If it's taken you so long to think of them, then it must be serious,' Berish said with an attempt at humour, even though he was already nervous.

'You have enough experience of interrogations to keep us here all night if you want to,' Boris said. 'So we're not going to play games with you, and I really hope you'll make things easy for us by deciding to co-operate straight away.'

'If you don't, Simon,' the Judge said, 'we'll have no choice but to terminate the session and hand all the papers over to the prosecutor. I can assure you we have enough for a charge.'

Berish laughed. 'I'm sorry, but why exactly are we here?'

'We know everything, but I want to give you the opportunity to defend yourself, or at least to explain.' Shutton pointed a finger at him. 'Where is she?'

Berish said nothing, partly because he had no idea what to say.

'What happened last night?'

Forgetting that he had actually slept like a log, Berish wondered if he really had done something the previous night. So he kept silent, in the hope of an epiphany.

The other two didn't take this well. Joanna Shutton moved to his right and leant in towards him until she was close to his ear. He could feel her warm breath and smell her over-sweet perfume, and both made him uncomfortable.

'What's your involvement in the disappearance of Officer Mila Vasquez?'

He froze. Not so much because the truth had at last been revealed, but because he didn't have an answer.

'Mila's disappeared?'

His anxiety was clearly genuine, and the other two exchanged glances.

'She was at her mother's house last night,' Boris said. 'When she left, she was clearly upset about something. Later, her mother called her at home, but she wasn't there. She hasn't been answering her mobile either.'

'I know,' Berish said. 'I tried this morning.'

'Maybe to give yourself an alibi,' the Judge said.

'An alibi for what?' he retorted angrily. 'Have you at least looked for her?'

They ignored him.

Boris came and sat down facing him. 'Tell me, Berish, how did you get back into the Kairus case?'

Berish summoned up all the patience he could. 'It was Mila Vasquez who approached me. I've been working with her since the night of the fire at the red-brick house.' Remembering Kairus's nest, he shuddered.

Shutton leaned on a corner of the table. 'You were there? Why didn't you show yourself? Why did you let Vasquez take sole responsibility for what happened?'

'Because Mila didn't want me involved.'

'And you expect us to believe you now?' She shook her head slowly. 'You attacked her that night in the red-brick house, didn't you?'

'What?' Berish said, taken aback.

'You took her gun and staged that attack.'

'There was someone in the house, someone who escaped. You saw that passage through the sewers.' He was starting to lose control, and he knew that wasn't good.

'Why get yourself all dirty in the sewers when you can use the front door?' Klaus Boris said.

'What on earth are you talking about?'

'Are you sure that if we search your apartment, we won't find Mila's gun?'

'Why are you going on about the gun? I don't understand.'

Shutton sighed. 'They finished inspecting the scene of the fire this morning. A human body can't withstand temperatures like that, nor can plastic or paper. But metal is another matter. Mila's gun wasn't among the metal objects recovered. So where is it?'

'You'll need to make up something a lot more substantial than that if you really want to pin any of this on me,' Berish said in an ironic tone. 'Otherwise, you'll have ruined a nice Friday for nothing.'

Once again, Shutton and Boris looked at each other. Berish had the unpleasant feeling that they really did have something up their sleeves. For the moment, they were playing with him, but when the time came they would show their hand.

'You're the one who paid the highest price in the insomniacs case,' Shutton said. 'I came out of it with my career intact, so did Gurevich and even Stephanopoulos. But you allowed yourself to get emotionally involved, you made one mistake after another, and you became the pariah of the department.'

'We both know what happened,' Berish said defiantly. 'And we know whose sins I paid for. You're just trying to find a way to keep me quiet.'

The Judge was unperturbed. 'I don't need your silence about Gurevich. And I don't need to play any tricks to incriminate you. The very fact that you weren't corrupt while someone else was is motive enough.'

Berish was really scared now, but he was determined not to show it. 'A motive for what?'

'It's hard to lose your colleagues' respect,' the Judge went on, feigning sympathy. 'To suffer their insults, to hear them bad-mouthing you. And not behind your back, but to your face. That hurts, especially when you know you're innocent.'

What was Shutton getting at? Berish didn't understand, but he could smell a rat.

'You have good reason to feel resentful. Maybe you think that one of these days you'll make everyone pay . . . '

'Are you insinuating that I'm behind everything? That I got all those missing persons to come back and start killing?'

'You convinced them because you knew what humiliation was, just as they did. The target of your resentment was Gurevich and, with him, the entire police force.' Shutton's tone was vehement now. 'A terrorist organisation needs an ideology and a plan. And there's no better combination than one that takes a body of the State as its target. You can destroy an institution with weapons, but you cause much more damage if you strike at its credibility. You've always had a grudge against the department.'

Berish couldn't believe his own ears. 'And what does all this have to do with Mila's disappearance?'

'She'd figured it all out,' Boris said. 'She was your pawn from the start. You lured her into the red-brick house.'

'No.'

The Judge looked sceptical. 'You manipulated Officer Vasquez by making her believe you were working with her, and at the same time making sure she said nothing to her superiors.'

'Think about it,' Boris said. 'This way you were in the best position to follow the investigation. You could stay on the sidelines while knowing everything that was going on.'

'But when Vasquez figured out what was really going on, you got rid of her.'

'What?'

'I even heard you arguing loudly in the corridor yesterday,' Boris said.

'An argument proves nothing.'

'You're right: it isn't evidence,' the Judge said calmly. 'But a witness who saw you take her from her apartment last night is.'

Berish's first thought was that it wasn't true. They were bluffing. 'And who is that witness?' he asked.

'Captain Stephanopoulos.'

61

They don't have anything.

He was still in the interrogation room and kept telling himself that Shutton and Boris had cobbled together that kidnapping charge just to see if he would fall for it. But why Steph, of all people? Why would Steph do something like that to him?

For a moment, he was afraid they hadn't told him the truth about Mila. Maybe something terrible had happened to her. But what reassured him was the thought that it would have been more convenient for them to accuse him straight out of ... He didn't want to say the word 'murder', even to himself. He had been going around in circles for a while now, unable to face up to the problem.

But for now he had rather more urgent demands. He needed to have a drink and go to the toilet. His strategy of feigned indifference clearly wasn't working, seeing that they were still keeping him here.

By now, the prosecutor should already have formulated the charge, he thought. *And I should have been transferred to a cell.*

What time was it, anyway? They'd confiscated his watch along with his gun and badge when they arrested him, and there were no clocks in interrogation rooms: the idea was to confuse the suspect, make him lose all sense of time. But he calculated that it must be after eight in the evening.

And to think that the day had got off to such a good start! His visit to Michael Ivanovič's mother might have provided him with the key to solving the case – the paradox was that now he couldn't use it. For a moment, he thought of suggesting a deal to the Judge and Boris but what could he ask for in return? They would never let him go.

And there was no guarantee they would believe him.

His only hope was to suggest to Shutton that she stood to gain something by it. He knew her well enough to know that she would agree to anything just to shift blame for what Gurevich had done away from herself. But for that to happen, Joanna had to be made to seem like the real winner in this game – the person who had finally solved the mystery of Kairus and the insomniacs after twenty years. Berish was sure the media already had an inkling of what was going on. They wouldn't be able to keep things secret for much longer.

Suddenly, the door of the interrogation room opened, and he immediately straightened up on his chair. His enemies were back, it seemed. And so he suppressed his thirst and his need to urinate and prepared for a second round, praying that he would be able to hold out for as long as possible.

But the man who came in, keeping his back to him, was wearing a navy blue tracksuit with the Federal Police insignia and a small hat with the brim pulled down over his eyes. Within seconds, Berish's senses were on the alert: anyone needing to camouflage himself that way couldn't possibly have friendly intentions.

Berish stood up, unable to do anything else. The man turned. It was Stephanopoulos.

*

The captain closed the door behind him. Berish stared at him in bewilderment.

'We don't have much time,' Steph said, taking off the hat.

'What are you doing here? Aren't you the one who pinned this on me?'

'That's right,' he readily admitted. 'I'm sorry, but I had to.'

Berish couldn't believe his ears. He felt anger rising within him. 'Had to?'

'Listen.' Steph took him by the shoulders. 'They'd decided to frame you even before Mila disappeared. You fitted perfectly: the police officer with a grudge who sets himself up as the leader of a terrorist organisation. They wouldn't have had to mention to the press what happened twenty years ago, except for the part about you and Sylvia to prove how untrustworthy you were.'

'But you gave them the evidence they needed.'

'Yes, but when I retract it, the charge will collapse and they'll have a lot of explaining to do to the media.'

Berish thought this over. It was a good plan. As long as Steph was willing to retract. Just then, he remembered the cameras trained on them.

'They're watching us right now, and you've just admitted—'

'Don't worry. They're all in a meeting with the Judge, and anyway, before coming I shut off the CCTV. Let's come to the second reason I'm here.'

Berish no longer knew what to expect.

There was a hint of anxiety in Steph's eyes. 'When they find out what really happened, they'll stop looking for her.'

'What? What are you talking about?'

'As you know, in a missing persons case, thirty-six hours have to pass from when the subject was last seen before they initiate a search. For a police officer, the interval is shorter, just twenty-four hours, but even that's too long for her.'

379

'I don't follow.'

'After Mila's mother reported her missing this morning, they went to check her apartment. Her Hyundai is still parked outside the building. There's no sign of forced entry, but that doesn't mean anything. She'd left her mobile, her keys and even the spare gun she'd been carrying since she lost her service pistol in the fire.'

Berish was starting to understand. 'If they think there's been a crime, they wouldn't have to wait a day. That's why you accused me of kidnapping her – to speed up the search.'

'To give her a chance,' Steph said. 'You were already in the shit. They were about to bring a terrorism charge against you anyway.'

Berish looked closely at his former superior. 'You think this is her, don't you? You think she's gone missing of her own free will.'

Steph sighed. 'I don't know. It's possible someone abducted her then took her things back to her apartment to make it look as if she'd run away. But I've told you before: Mila tends to go to extremes. I don't know if it's a self-destructive streak, but she's attracted to danger like a moth to a flame.'

Berish tried to think things through. 'According to Shutton and Boris, she was upset when she left her mother's house last night.'

It must have had something do with the child. Something had been simmering inside her for ages, and last night's visit had triggered it off. Berish remembered Mrs Ivanovič's words: 'When you risk losing one thing, you can't accept it. But when you risk losing everything, you realise you actually have nothing to lose.'

It was that difference between 'one thing' and 'everything', Berish realised, that Kairus exploited.

'I think Mila wanted to see with her own eyes what's in the darkness,' Steph said. 'But there's nothing in the darkness except the darkness.'

Berish felt he had to make a decision. There was no time to lose. 'I know who Kairus is,' he said.

For a moment, the captain was rendered speechless. He turned as pale as if he were about to have a heart attack.

'I can't tell you more now,' Berish went on. 'You must help me get out of here.'

Steph thought for a moment. 'All right.'

He left and returned a few minutes later with Berish's badge and a pair of handcuffs. Berish hadn't asked to have his gun back. In a manhunt, it usually made a difference if the fugitive was unarmed, and he had no intention of giving his colleagues an extra excuse to shoot him.

'What are you going to do with the badge?' Steph asked.

'I need it to get in somewhere,' Berish said, slipping his wrists into the handcuffs.

Steph took him by the arm and they went out into the corridor.

The officers who were standing guard looked at them in astonishment, but Steph, confident of his rank, was unperturbed. He even ordered one of them to help him escort the prisoner to the toilet.

Since Berish hadn't asked to go before, it sounded like a plausible request.

They walked down the corridor, keeping their eyes open, hoping Klaus Boris or one of Shutton's acolytes didn't suddenly appear. When they reached the toilets reserved for prisoners, Steph kept straight on.

'Where are you going, sir?' the escort asked.

Steph turned and glared at him. 'Until his guilt has been established, I'm not going to let one of our men piss in the prisoners' toilet.'

And so they kept walking towards the police toilets, where

there were no bars on the windows. When they got there, Steph left the escort to stand guard outside, and went in with Berish.

'I'll wait five minutes before I raise the alarm,' he said, pointing to the window. 'That'll give you time to get to Limbo. From there, there's a door that leads to the back of the building.' He handed him the office keys and those to his apartment and his Volkswagen. 'It's parked near the Chinese café.'

'Could you go to my apartment and get Hitch?' Berish said. 'He's been on his own for hours, poor thing. He'll be thirsty and he needs a walk.'

'Don't worry. I'll go straight away.'

'Thanks.'

'Don't thank me. I got you into this mess.' He removed the handcuffs from Berish, then put his little hat back on. 'Find Kairus, and then find Mila.'

62

Sitting in the dark, Berish listened to the sirens in the distance.

They were looking for him – hunting him down. It wasn't safe to stay in Steph's apartment. His colleagues would be sure to check here, too. Not immediately, though. They were too busy looking for him in other places. All the same, this apartment was bound to be on their itinerary, especially since the captain had practically let the prisoner escape from under his nose.

Of course, they would wonder why the key witness had decided to go to the interrogation room to see the man he had accused. They would probably smell a rat and give him the third degree. But even if they threatened him, Steph wouldn't talk.

For the moment, Berish still had a slight head start.

He was sitting upright, staring straight ahead, his hands in his lap, with his badge under one of the palms.

It wasn't just a simple ID, but the key to entering the kingdom of the dead.

Berish checked the time. It was after midnight. He stood up. He could go.

*

He parked Steph's Volkswagen and sat in it for a moment looking out.

A rectangular four-storey building, with a row of skylights on the roof. A big main door and lots of windows. But, unlike Michael Ivanovič's drawing, there was no human figure behind any of them.

He knew, though, that the man he was seeking was inside.

The state mortuary was a squat concrete monolith in the middle of nowhere. But the main part of the building was underground.

Sometimes you need to go right down into hell to learn the truth about yourself.

In fact, Kairus's young disciple was right. What Berish was interested in was the bottommost level of the basement.

He walked to the entrance. Beside it was a small lodge where a watchman sat engrossed in a TV show. The audience's laughter and applause echoed through the foyer.

Berish knocked on the glass partition. The watchman, who was obviously not expecting a visitor at this hour, gave a start. 'What do you want?'

Berish showed him his badge. 'I'm here to identify a body.'

'Can't you come back in the morning?'

Berish just stared at him without saying a word. It only took a few seconds of this treatment for the watchman to sit up and take notice.

He phoned his colleague in the basement to inform him that a visitor was on his way down.

Room 13 was where the sleepers were kept.

As the steel lift slowly descended to the basement, Berish wondered why they had chosen that number.

Are you superstitious, officer? Michael Ivanovič had asked him.

People who built hotels or skyscrapers usually skipped the number thirteen. Here, though, there was no point.

No, I'm not superstitious, Berish thought. *And neither are the dead, because there can't be anything more unlucky than dying.*

The lift came to a halt with a pneumatic hiss and, after what seemed like an interminable pause, the doors opened wide to reveal a red-faced attendant waiting for him.

Behind the man was a long corridor.

Berish had expected to see white tiled walls and sterile fluorescent lighting, intended to give visitors the illusion of being in a large space, even though it was so many feet underground, and to counteract the sense of claustrophobia. In fact, the walls were green, and there were orange lights at regular intervals along the skirting board.

'The colours prevent panic attacks,' the attendant said, handing him a light blue gown that matched his own uniform.

Berish put it on, and they started walking.

'The corpses on this floor are mainly homeless people and illegal immigrants,' the attendant said. 'No ID, no family, so when they kick the bucket they end up down here. They're all in Rooms one to nine. Rooms ten and eleven are for people who pay their taxes and watch football matches on TV, just like you and me, but suddenly drop dead of a heart attack on the metro one morning. One of the other passengers pretends to help them, instead of which they grab their wallet, and *voilà*, the trick has worked: the man or woman vanishes for ever. Sometimes, though, it's just a question of bureaucracy: a member of staff messes up the paperwork, and the relatives who come in to identify the body are shown another body entirely. It's as if you aren't dead and they're still looking for you.'

The man was clearly trying to impress him, Berish realised. But he chose to ignore that.

'Then there are the suicide or accident cases: Room twelve. Sometimes the corpse is in such a bad state, you can't believe it was ever a person. Anyway, the law requires the same treatment for all of them: they have to stay in the cold chamber for at least eighteen months. Then, if nobody claims or identifies the body, and the police have no intention of reopening the investigation, authorisation is given to dispose of it by cremation.' He had quoted the rules from memory.

Precisely, Berish thought. *But for some, things turned out differently*.

'And then there are those in Room thirteen,' the attendant said, almost as if reading his mind.

He was referring to the nameless victims of unsolved murders.

'In cases of murder, the law states that the body constitutes evidence until such time as the identity of the victim has been confirmed. You can't sentence a murderer if you can't prove that the person he murdered actually existed. In the absence of a name, the body is the only proof of that existence. That's why there's no time limit to how long it can be kept. It's one of those odd legal technicalities that lawyers like so much.'

Until such time as the criminal act that had caused the death was determined, the body could neither be destroyed nor be allowed to decompose naturally. But Berish knew that without that legal paradox, he wouldn't be here tonight.

'We call them the sleepers.'

Unknown men, women and children whose killers hadn't yet been identified. They had been waiting for years for someone to turn up and deliver them from the curse of resembling the living. And, just as in some kind of macabre fairy tale, for that to happen all you needed to do was say the magic word.

Their name.

The room that housed them – Room 13 – was the last one at the far end of the corridor.

They came to a metal door, and the attendant fussed with a bunch of keys until he had found the right one. Opening the door let out a gust of foul air. Hell didn't smell of sulphur, Berish noted, it smelt of disinfectant and formaldehyde.

As soon as he stepped into the darkness, a row of yellow ceiling lights came on, triggered by sensors. In the middle of the room stood an autopsy table, and the high walls were lined with dozens of drawers.

A steel beehive.

'You must sign in, it's the rule,' the attendant said, holding out a register. It struck Berish as a cruel joke to have to write down his name in a room like this. Your name is the first thing you learn about yourself after you come into this world, he thought. When you're only a few months old you recognise its sound and know it refers to you. As you grow up, your name tells you who you are. It's the first thing other people ask of you. You can lie, you can invent a new one, but you always know what the real one is and you can never forget it. When you die, what remains behind isn't your body, or your voice, but your name. Whatever you've done will sooner or later be undone. But your name will be what you're remembered by. Without a name you can't be remembered.

A man without a name isn't a man, Berish concluded, as he distractedly signed the register.

'Which one are you interested in?' the attendant asked, starting to grow restless.

At last, Berish opened his mouth. 'The one that's been here the longest.'

AHF-93-K999.

The drawer with that label was third from the bottom on the left hand wall. The attendant janitor pointed it out to the visitor.

'Of all the bodies down here, that one doesn't even have the most original story. One Saturday afternoon, some kids were playing football in the park. The ball went into the bushes, and that's where they found him. He'd been shot in the head. There was no ID on him, and no keys. His face was still perfectly recognisable, but nobody called the emergency numbers to ask about him, nobody filed a missing person report. Until they find his killer, which may never happen, the only evidence of the crime is the actual body. That's why the court ruled that it should be kept until the case was solved and justice was done.' He paused for a moment. 'It's been years now, but he's still here.'

Twenty years, Berish thought.

The attendant had probably told him the story because, spending so much time down here, he probably didn't get much of a chance to talk to real, live people. But Berish already knew the story: he had heard it from Michael Ivanovič's mother that very morning.

What the attendant couldn't possibly have imagined was that the secret held behind those few inches of steel went beyond a mere name. Berish had made this night trip to the morgue because of a far more important mystery, one for which too many people had died.

The body was the solution.

'Open it up,' he said. 'I want to see him.'

The attendant did as he was told. He activated the air valve to open the drawer and waited.

The sleeper was about to be reawakened.

The drawer slid backwards on its hinges. Beneath that plastic sheet was the price Michael Ivanovič's mother had had to pay the Goodnight Man.

The body.

The attendant uncovered the face. It was still young, even though twenty years had passed. That's the only privilege of death, Berish thought: you can't grow older.

Compared to the identikit based on Sylvia's description, Kairus hadn't in fact aged at all.

Berish would have liked to linger over the fact that this face had been his obsession for such a long time. Or on the fact that the enemy had tricked them, making them chase after a dead man, while the preacher continued to circulate undisturbed among them.

But what he was really thinking was how ironic it was that he should find the Goodnight Man right here, among the sleepers.

He also couldn't help thinking that he had come to a dead end. What little he had thought he knew about the case up until now, or which had been revealed to him by others in the past few days, could have been a lie.

He didn't know, and now there was no way of checking.

And that meant there was no way of finding Sylvia – or of discovering what had happened to Mila.

'So who is he?' the attendant asked impatiently. 'What's his name?'

Berish stared at him. 'I'm sorry, I don't know.' He turned away, ready to go back up the surface. He felt weary all of a sudden, his legs barely able to carry him.

The attendant pulled the sheet back over the face. The unknown man was still *AHF-93-K999*.

Sometimes, if you know the name of the demon, all you have to do is say his name out loud and he'll answer.

But, as Berish had just learnt, the demon's secret was that he actually had no name. There was nothing for him to do now except leave.

Behind him, the attendant pushed the drawer back in and the door clanged shut – for how much longer, no one knew. 'That's what the other man said.'

Berish stopped in his tracks. 'I'm sorry?'

The attendant shrugged. 'The police officer who was here a few days ago. He didn't recognise him either.'

For a moment, Berish couldn't speak. The words stuck in his throat. 'Who was it?' he asked at last.

The attendant showed him the register he had made him sign earlier. 'The name's right here, on the page before yours.'

63

The man who was currently their most wanted returned to Federal Police Headquarters.

It was two in the morning, but the department seemed as frenetic as if it were midday. What nobody could have imagined, though, was that Simon Berish would be stupid enough to come back here.

He parked the Volkswagen in a side street and walked to the back door he had used to make good his escape, a few hours earlier, and which led straight to Limbo.

He crossed the threshold into the Waiting Room, and thousands of eyes stared at him. Surrounded by all these missing persons, he felt like an intruder, guilty of being alive – or at least of knowing that he wasn't dead.

His footsteps echoed through the rooms, announcing his presence, but he didn't care.

He was certain that, even this late at night, someone was waiting for him.

He heard Hitch barking – he had probably recognised his master. He was tied up outside the office door. Berish stroked him reassuringly, then untied him, but motioned to him to sit and wait.

The door was ajar. Inside, the light was on and a shadowy figure was visible.

'Come in,' said a man's voice.

Berish pushed the door with the palm of his hand, and it slowly opened. Captain Stephanopoulos was sitting at his desk, still wearing the navy blue tracksuit with the Federal Police insignia he had worn that afternoon. His glasses were perched on the tip of his nose. He was writing.

'Take a seat. I've nearly finished.'

Berish did as he was told. He sat down in front of the desk and waited for Steph to finish.

After a moment or two, the captain put his pen down and looked at him. 'Forgive me, but it was important.' Calmly, he removed his glasses. 'What can I do for you?'

'We've been chasing a ghost.'

'So you found the body.' Steph seemed pleased with himself, but his smile struck a false note on his pale face.

'The first time Mila came to see me at the Chinese café, I told her Kairus didn't exist, that he was just an illusion. I was right.' Berish paused for a moment. 'It was you who made those people disappear. But twenty years ago, the media and the public nearly screwed everything up by linking the first seven missing persons – the ones we innocently called the insomniacs.'

'I wasn't very experienced then,' Steph admitted regretfully. 'I got better later.'

'You had to divert the investigation before you were found out. There was only one way: to accuse someone else. Then you would let some time go by, and the disappearances would start again. But this time without anything standing in your way.'

'I see you've done your homework.'

'Twenty years ago, you contacted Michael Ivanovič's mother, who worked at the morgue as a pathologist. You told her you would save her son's life, give him a new family and the medical care he needed ... You persuaded her just as you persuaded Sylvia.'

Steph put his hands together under his chin as a sign of approval.

'But in the case of Michael's mother you asked for something in return. A nameless corpse. All she had to do was wait for the right opportunity, which came along soon enough. An unidentified body, found by chance in a park by some kids playing football. Nobody would notice – dead bodies come and go in a morgue, and the police have more important cases to deal with than the murder of some poor nameless fellow with a bullet in his head. The date of death on the pathologist's report didn't matter. Mrs Ivanovič would change it anyway, moving the death forward by a month.' Berish paused. 'The poor man couldn't be "officially" dead yet, could he? He had to wait for thirty days so you had enough time to put your plan into action ... That's how you created Kairus. Mrs Ivanovič took a photograph of his face while it was still in one piece, and you showed it to Sylvia and instructed her on what to tell the police.'

'That was a good story about Kairus smiling at her in order to be remembered, don't you think?' Steph said smugly. 'I surprised even myself when I thought of that touch.'

'When Sylvia came forward, we placed her under protection. But it wouldn't be for long. Because for everything to work, you had to make the witness disappear, too.'

'That's right.'

'The proof that Kairus had taken her was the lock of Sylvia's hair that was sent to the department a few days later.'

'With the date of his death brought forward, the body in the

393

morgue could be shown to have still been alive on the day the witness was abducted. Nobody would see the trick.' Steph smiled. 'If anyone insisted on searching for the Goodnight Man, I would see to it that all he found was that unidentified body. Case closed.'

'Chance death of the culprit: a stroke of luck. A gift from the gods. Incredible as it might seem, that false truth would put an end to the investigation without leaving any trail.' Berish suddenly felt like an accomplice. 'But that wasn't necessary. The investigation was shelved before that happened. Thanks to me, Joanna and Gurevich. And you, as our chief, simply had to agree. If anyone – me, for instance – had persisted with the case, that nameless corpse in Room thirteen would still have been there waiting for him.'

Steph clapped three times, slowly, as if approving every word. 'There's still one thing you haven't asked me. And I'm sure you're going to.'

To satisfy his demand, Berish asked, 'Why?'

Steph's lip was quivering, but he seemed pleased to be asked all the same. 'Because the people I was helping to disappear were very unhappy. Life had denied them any joy, any shred of dignity. Take the first one – André García, who'd had to quit the army because he was a homosexual. Or Diana Müller, forced to pay for the sins of the woman who had given birth to her. Roger Valin, who had to take care of his mother for as long as she lived. And Nadia Niverman? She would never have had the courage to run away from that violent husband of hers. Not to mention Eric Vincenti, a police officer tormented day after day, right there in front of my eyes, in this very office, by the missing persons cases he couldn't solve. They all deserved a second chance.'

'You used the resources and expertise of the Witness Protection Unit to put your absurd plan into operation. You had access to money and documents for creating false identities, the same resources we used to give new lives to those who co-operated with the law.'

'Criminals,' Steph said. 'People who didn't deserve our help.' He was making an effort to keep calm, but beads of sweat had formed on his forehead.

'How did you manage to persuade them over the phone?' Berish asked.

'They needed me. They didn't know it, but they'd been waiting for me all their lives. The proof of that is the fact that they trusted me even though they never saw me. I told them that if they really wanted a drastic change, they had to go to Room 317 of the Ambrus Hotel, lie down on the bed and take a sleeping pill – a one-way ticket to the unknown.'

'Or to hell.'

'Then I'd arrive and take them away using the goods lift. I'd save them from their wretched lives, and sometimes from themselves too.'

'And more recently you had Eric Vincenti to help you.'

Steph smiled. 'I chose him on purpose. I was getting old.'

'But what happened when they woke up?' Berish was unable to keep the bitterness out of his voice.

Steph shook his head in disappointment. 'Don't you understand? I gave them new lives. They could start over again. How many of us are granted an opportunity like that?'

Berish knew there was something twisted in the captain's psyche. 'When did you lose touch with reality, Steph? When did you stop distinguishing what's true from what isn't?'

The captain's lip quivered again.

'And why me?' Berish asked, almost imploringly, although he hated himself for it.

'You're thinking about Sylvia . . . ' Steph leant towards him and looked him straight in the eyes. 'You're no different from any other police officer. You didn't really care about the girl, you only cared about the way she made you feel. Did it ever occur to you that you might not have been the right man for her?'

'You're wrong,' Berish retorted.

'One lesson I've learnt in all the years I've worked in the department is that no one really cares about the victims – not the police, not the media, not the public. In the long run, everyone only ever remembers the names of the criminals, and the victims are forgotten. Limbo is the proof that I'm right.' He was getting carried away now, and raising his voice. 'You're interested in catching the monster, condemning the monster in your courts of law ... That's why, for all your sakes, I created Kairus.' He laughed. 'Kairus was our neighbours' cat when I was a child. That's where I got the name from.'

Berish felt betrayed.

'And I made him your obsession,' Steph went on. 'He's been keeping you alive all these years.'

'I've been keeping *him* alive!' Berish banged his fist on the desk. 'He took my life from me in order to have his own.' He paused, and tried to calm down. 'In fact, it's you who stole my life, because you're Kairus.'

Steph seemed amused. 'You don't know what you're talking about.'

'The Hypothesis of Evil,' Berish said.

'What?'

'Doing evil for a good end. With the risk that the good can turn into evil.'

'I saved them! I never hurt anybody.'

Berish stared at him. 'Yes, you did. You kept an eye on those missing persons of yours. Maybe it made you feel good about your work. It made you feel like a benefactor. But when you started to realise they weren't happy with the new lives you'd given them, you persuaded them to come back and take revenge on everything and everyone. You're the preacher.'

'No, that's not true,' Steph said, alarmed by Berish's accusation. 'The Goodnight Man really exists.' Steph's eyes were wide open, like those of a man overcome by terror. 'It was us. By chasing after him all these years, we summoned him. And in the end he appeared.'

'What you're saying doesn't make any sense. You're mad.'

Steph reached across the desk and grabbed Berish's arm. 'That's why I went to the morgue a few days ago. I had to make sure Kairus was still in that drawer and hadn't woken up and walked out of his own accord. As his creator, I had to look him in the face after all these years.'

Berish pulled his arm away. 'Stop it, Steph. You're the one who brought Mila and me together.'

But Steph wasn't listening any more. 'I can't stop him. There's nothing else I can do.' He sat back in his chair, his hands in his lap.

'Yes, there is. Tell me where she is.'

Steph's eyes suddenly returned to Berish.

Berish saw him pull a gun out from under his desk and place it under his own chin. The noise of the shot coincided with his last words.

'Find her.'

Steph's head fell forward onto the desk, scattering the papers that were on it about the room. Berish leapt to his feet.

He could hear Hitch barking outside the door. He went around the desk, lifted Steph's lifeless body, rested it back in the chair, and gently closed his eyes.

Realising that his own hands were stained with blood, he took a step back. This was partly his fault. The sweat on Steph's forehead, his pallor, his quivering lip had all been signs that he was about to do something crazy, but Berish had been unable to interpret them.

As he tried to make some sense of what had happened, his eyes were drawn to the gun Steph had used to kill himself, which was lying next to him.

He read what was engraved on the side of the handle. A serial number and the initials of the police officer it had belonged to.

M.E.V.

María Elena Vasquez, he said to himself. This was the weapon Mila had lost in the red-brick house before the fire. Berish couldn't believe it: it was Steph who'd been there that night, in Kairus's nest, and who'd run away, dodging his bullets. If only he'd aimed more carefully, this whole thing would have been over ages ago.

But Berish also realised something else. That he was fucked.

The Judge and Klaus Boris believed he had taken that damned gun, and now they would also blame him for Steph's death. They would accuse him of eliminating the witness who had identified him. And getting rid of the weapon wouldn't be enough: a ballistics report would establish that it was Mila's . . .

He had forgotten about Mila for a while, but now the thought of her hit him hard.

Steph's death wiped out any hope of finding her.

Berish stood there motionless for a long time, looking at the scene. Everything in the room accused him of murder. He had got his answer, but at what cost? He had no idea what would happen now to him or to Mila.

Impossible as it might seem, he had to keep a clear head. Otherwise, he might as well give himself up immediately. If there was any chance at all of getting out of this situation, he had to find it, and now. *Afterwards* was a word that didn't exist, *afterwards* was a word that meant nothing.

First and foremost, he had to go over what had happened in this office from the moment he had come in. That was the only way to find the weak spots in the crime scene that might help his defence.

He went back to the moment he had opened the door. Steph had invited him in, but he was already sitting down ... writing.

Maybe he'd been writing a suicide note.

Berish hurriedly looked through the papers scattered on the floor. He had no way of knowing what the note contained – he hadn't been paying attention, damn it. Frantically he picked up one paper after another, then cast them aside. Then a particular sheet drew his attention because of its unsteady, rushed hand-writing: that of a man who has already made up his mind to end it all. Berish didn't know whether it was setting him on the right track or not, but he had only one option.

Find her ... Steph had said as he died.

And what was written on that sheet of paper was an address.

64

The town was about a hundred and twenty miles from the city.

To get there, he used Steph's Volkswagen. Taking a train or a bus would have been equally risky in his situation. He didn't use the motorway, but chose secondary roads and avoided two road blocks.

Using a dead man's car – especially when you were about to be accused of his murder – wasn't a great idea. But Berish had no choice. He had driven all night, calculating – or rather hoping against hope – that Steph's body wouldn't be found for another couple of hours.

Before leaving the city, he had dropped Hitch at a kennel, explaining that it was an emergency. He hadn't felt up to taking him along, since he had no idea what he would find and didn't want anything to happen to his one and only friend.

His fear might turn out to be unfounded but Berish had been prone to a strange paranoia lately. The people he loved had a tendency to vanish from his life. First Sylvia, then Mila. He hadn't been able to stop thinking about Mila as he drove. He couldn't rid himself of the idea that he was partly responsible for what had happened to her.

But what exactly *had* happened to her?

The impossibility of finding an answer made him take ever more risks. Like driving to an unknown address in a small town he had never been to before.

It was about six on Saturday morning when the first houses came into view. The streets were deserted, except for the odd person jogging or walking his dog. The office workers' cars were neatly parked in the driveways.

Following a map he had bought at a service station, he reached the area where the address was situated – a quiet neighbourhood on the other side of town. Until recently, it must have been in the middle of the countryside.

The house number he was looking for corresponded to a two-storey white house with a sloping roof and a well-tended garden. He parked at the kerb, and, without getting out of the car, tried to see through the windows.

The house didn't look like a lair or a prison. It looked like the home of people who were reasonably well-off. People who saved in order to send their children to university, he thought. People with families.

But that might just be a façade.

It was quite possible the preacher's followers were inside, keeping Mila prisoner. Maybe in a little while he'd see Eric Vincenti, his colleague from Limbo, come out through the front door, and he would know that he was on the right track. For the moment, though, he had to stay in the car and wait. There was no point letting his anxiety get the better of him and going to take a look. What could he do anyway? He was unarmed.

He was in serious danger and he was alone.

The army of shadows was all around him, everywhere and

nowhere. Behind every individual, an invisible multitude was concealed. That was what his enemy was: a single evil soul with many faces. But there was nothing supernatural about any of this, Berish remembered. There was always a rational explanation. That was why he thought he could still win.

He had been too long without sleep, and it was beginning to tell. His back was aching, the muscles tight with stress. For a moment, he leant his arms on the steering wheel and felt an unexpected relief. The nervous tension faded, and his eyelids started to droop because of the warmth inside the car. Without realising it, he was falling asleep.

He closed his eyes, forgetting everything. All it took was a second, and a shot of adrenalin jolted him back to reality, in time to see a woman in a dressing gown walking back into the house after coming out to pick up the newspaper from the driveway.

He had last seen Sylvia one evening at the end of June. It was only after she had disappeared that he had realised he didn't even have a photograph of her. So for twenty years, the only image he had of her was the one he kept in his memory.

How hard he'd tried not to forget even the tiniest wrinkle on that face! How many times the memory of her had threatened to slip away along with the past! How upset he had been the day he realised he could no longer remember her voice!

That June evening – the one he would always think of as 'the last'– they had dined on the terrace, oblivious of the danger. Like a married couple.

Anybody seeing them would have thought of them as the young couple from 37G. No one suspected they were a police officer and the witness he was protecting. But maybe that was because they were really in love.

When that feeling had come to the surface – after their first kiss – he should have begged off the assignment without hesitation. He knew how dangerous getting involved emotionally might be for both of them. Instead, he had remained. He had decided for the two of them, and he hadn't been honest.

But he had realised it too late. What opened his eyes was what happened on the morning after that fateful last evening.

Before falling asleep, they had made love. She had surrendered herself to him, sinking her head into his bare shoulder, breathing his skin.

At dawn, still hungering for her smell, he reached out between the sheets to touch her. But she was already up. Then he looked for her lingering warmth on the bed linen and the pillow.

But all he felt was coldness.

At the time, that feeling, which would stay with him for many years, simply alarmed him. He leapt out of bed, wrapping the sheet around him. He looked for her everywhere in the apartment, but deep down he already knew the truth.

The first thing he did when panic finally gripped him was to go to the bathroom and throw up – not the kind of thing expected of an experienced police officer. Then, when he lifted his head from the sink, he had seen something on the shelf under the mirror.

The bottle of sleeping pills that made everything clear.

Twenty years later, on a very similar morning, Berish felt the same need to vomit.

Find her . . . But Stephanopoulos hadn't been referring to Mila. Berish knew that now.

He was scared, even though he thought he was ready. Every time he had allowed himself to imagine the possibility of finding her, his fantasy had only taken him as far as the precise moment when he saw her again. What happened afterwards was a mystery, and he would have to solve that mystery for himself.

He got out of the car and, heedless of everything, walked towards the front door.

65

When Sylvia opened the door, she was exactly as he remembered her.

Even her raven-black plait was still the same, only slightly greyer.

She pulled her dressing gown tighter around her. It took her a few seconds to work out who this man standing there was. 'Oh, my God!' she suddenly said.

Berish took her in his arms without knowing exactly what to do. Since her, he hadn't had much physical contact with anyone. He was angry, disappointed, embittered. But the negative feelings gradually faded, leaving behind a pleasant warmth, as though some silent force in the universe had worked to put things right.

Sylvia detached herself from him and looked at him again, smiling incredulously. But her happy expression quickly turned to fear. 'Are you injured?'

Looking down, Berish realised that his hands were caked with blood, as were his clothes. He had forgotten how dirty he had got trying to help Steph.

'It's not mine,' he said quickly. 'I'll explain.'

She glanced around, then took his arm and gently drew him into the house.

She had helped him out of his jacket, sat him down on the sofa, and was now wiping the blood from his neck with a wet sponge.

Berish was surprised by this intimate gesture, but let her do it. 'I have to get away from here. They're looking for me. I can't stay.'

'You're not going anywhere,' she replied, gently but firmly.

He humoured her, and for a moment he felt at home. But this was not his home. There were framed photographs on the furniture and walls that testified to that. They showed a different Sylvia. A cheerful Sylvia. Berish felt a sense of inadequacy and unease: he had never made her laugh like that.

With her in the photographs was a little boy, who later became a young man. The whole history of that transformation was there in front of Berish. The face was strangely familiar. He thought of the child they could have had together.

But what tortured him was the face you couldn't see in these photographs, the face of the person who had taken them.

Sylvia saw his eyes searching the room. 'Isn't my boy handsome?'

'You must be very proud of him.'

'Yes, I am,' she said, pleased. 'He's just a child in that one. But now he's all grown up. You should see him. It's enough to make me feel old and out of date.'

'Isn't he likely to come back any minute? What if he finds me here?'

He was about to get up, but she put a hand gently on his shoulder to stop him. 'Don't worry. He's been gone for a while now, he says he wants to "experience things for himself".' She frowned. 'Well, who am I to stop him? That's what children are like. One day they're asking you for chocolate, the next they're demanding their independence.'

When Sylvia had opened the door to him earlier, Berish had feared that Steph – the preacher – had approached her, too, and persuaded her to commit a murder as payback for the good he had done her twenty years earlier. But maybe he hadn't even tried it with her, because in her case his plan had worked perfectly. There was no trace of disappointment in this house, no resentment that he could have played on.

Looking away from Sylvia, Berish asked the question he'd been longing to ask. 'I was wondering who took these photos of you and your son. I mean, do you have a husband, a partner?'

She gave an amused grin. 'There isn't any man in my life.'

He didn't want to show it, but her answer made him happy. But then he felt ashamed of himself for being so selfish: Sylvia had always been alone in the world and deserved to have a family more than anyone.

'What have you been doing for the past twenty years?' He was hoping for an answer that would give some meaning to the time he had spent waiting for her.

Sylvia came straight out with it. 'Forgetting. It isn't easy, you know. It takes determination and tenacity. When you knew me, I was an unhappy young woman. I never knew my parents. I spent most of my childhood in institutions. No one had ever really taken care of me.' She lowered her eyes as if to apologise for what she had just said. 'Of course, I'm not talking about what happened between us.'

'I'm quite the opposite. I've spent all this time trying to remember everything about you. But the details kept fading, and there was nothing I could do about it.'

'I'm sorry, Simon. I'm sorry you got into trouble twenty years ago because of me. But after all, you were a police officer.'

'Trouble?' He was astounded. 'I loved you, Sylvia.'

From the expression on her face, he could see it hadn't been the same for her.

He had been deluding himself for twenty years. He felt like an idiot for not realising it sooner.

'You couldn't have saved me from my sadness,' she said, trying to console him. 'Only I could do that.'

Sylvia's words reminded him of the story Mila had told him about the tramp who lived near her house, the one she always left food for.

I want to flush him out, so that I can look him in the eyes ... I don't have any feelings about him, I just want to find out if he's one of the residents of Limbo ...

I don't care if he's happy or not. We're only interested in other people's unhappiness when it reflects our own ...

In those few sentences she had summed up her total lack of empathy.

Berish suddenly realised he wasn't all that different from Mila. He had never really asked himself how Sylvia felt. He had taken it for granted that she was happy because he was.

We always expect to get something in return for our feelings, and when that doesn't happen we feel betrayed – Berish realised all this in just a few seconds.

'You don't need to justify yourself,' he said to Sylvia, caressing her. 'Someone offered you a new life, and you took it.'

'I lied to get it.' She was referring to her false testimony that led to the identikit of Kairus. 'Worst of all, I lied to you.'

'What matters is that you're all right.'

'Do you mean that?' She had tears in her eyes.

Berish took her hand. 'Yes, I do.'

Sylvia smiled gratefully. 'I'll go and make you a coffee and see if I can find you a clean shirt. One of my son's should fit you. You just relax. I'll be right back.'

Berish watched her get up and leave the room with the sponge she had used to clean him up. He hadn't asked her what her son's name was and she hadn't told him. But maybe it was better that way. That part of Sylvia's life didn't belong to him.

He realised that for years he had studied anthropology in order to understand people, but that he had neglected the fact that you couldn't analyse human behaviour without taking feelings into account. Every act, however insignificant, was dictated by one emotion or other. It had taken just a short chat with Sylvia for him to understand what might have happened to Mila.

Klaus Boris said she had been upset when she left her mother's house.

Up until this moment, Berish hadn't given any weight to that remark. Now, though, he had a feeling that something must have happened to hurt Mila the evening before she disappeared.

Something connected with her daughter.

He recalled that, after discovering that Kairus was a preacher, she had wanted to abandon the investigation – she was afraid of the similarities between this case and that of the Whisperer case, and that there might be repercussions for the little girl.

If something really had happened between her and her daughter, then there was only one place she could go.

The place which for many – including Sylvia – had represented the solution to their unhappiness. The place where, as Steph had said, Mila could get a one-way ticket to the unknown.

'How could I have been so thoughtless?' Without realising it, Berish had spoken that thought out loud.

He saw Sylvia standing by the door, holding a clean shirt. He was sure she had heard him.

'Why won't you tell me why they're looking for you?' she asked, her face clouding over.

'It's a long story, and I don't want to get you involved. That's why I'm going to leave now and let you carry on with your life. Nobody will connect me with you or your son, I promise.'

'At least get some sleep, you look tired. Why don't you lie down on the sofa? I'll get you a blanket.'

'No,' he said. And this time he was sure. 'I got my answer, and that was what I wanted the most. I have to go now. There's someone who needs me.'

66

Once more he stepped through the revolving door into the strange atmosphere of the Ambrus Hotel.

Berish had the impression he hadn't simply walked into a hotel. Yet again, it was like crossing the border into a parallel world – a poor imitation of the known world, made by a treacherous god. He wouldn't have been surprised to discover, for example, that gravity didn't work here, or that you could walk on the walls.

Hitch probably felt something similar, because he seemed nervous. Berish had taken him out of the kennel because he needed his sense of smell. Seeing his master again, Hitch had leapt for joy.

'Hey, you can't bring that animal in here,' the porter said indignantly, emerging through the red velvet curtain behind the reception desk.

Berish noticed that he was dressed like the first time – jeans and black T-shirt – but could have sworn that, compared to then, the tattoos on his arms were less faded, the crew-cut hair less grey. He felt as if he had travelled back in time, and was now seeing the same porter, only younger.

But these were false perceptions, the result of constant anxiety and of the need to give a meaning – even an absurd one – to what had happened within these walls over the years.

There was a kind of energy field in this place, the residue of all the clandestine encounters that had taken place here, the thousands of people who had passed through these rooms – people who had either simply slept here or given vent to their baser instincts. Afterwards, the beds were always remade, the sheets and towels washed, the carpet cleaned, but the invisible traces of that primitive humanity remained.

The porter tried to cover those traces with the voice of Edith Piaf – but in vain.

Ignoring the reprimand about his dog, Berish walked to the desk, past the blind black man who sat, impassive as ever, on the threadbare sofa.

'Do you remember me?'

The porter looked at him for a moment. 'Hi,' he said, as if in confirmation.

'I need to know if the lady friend who was with me the last time I came has been back recently.'

The porter thought this over for a while, then pursed his lips and shook his head. 'Haven't seen her.'

Berish tried to figure out if he was telling the truth or not. From the way Hitch was running about nervously, trying to attract attention, he knew her scent must be in the air.

Mila had been here.

But Berish had no proof of that, and he couldn't accuse the porter of lying. 'Has anybody booked Room 317 in the past few days?'

'Business hasn't been too good.' He pointed to the rack behind him. 'As you can see, the key's still there.'

Calmly, Berish leant across the counter and grabbed him by his T-shirt.

'Hey!' the man protested. 'I don't know what goes on in the rooms, and I don't even check who comes in and out of that door. I'm the only porter, even at night. I sit back there in my hole, and only come out when someone wants a key – in this place, people pay cash, and they pay in advance.'

Berish let go of him. 'The first time I came here, you mentioned a murder that took place in Room 317 thirty years ago . . .'

The porter didn't seem too happy to be reminded of that story. It was as if it made him uncomfortable.

'I wasn't here thirty years ago, so there's not much I can tell you.'

'Tell me anyway. I'm curious.'

His eyes glazed over. 'My friend, around here curiosity has a price.'

Getting the message, Berish put his hand in his pocket and took out a banknote.

The porter slipped it under the counter. 'A woman was stabbed to death. Twenty-eight wounds. As far as I know, the killer was never caught. But there was a witness, her little daughter, who managed to escape by hiding under the bed.'

Berish would have liked to ask if that was all there was to it. He'd been expecting a clue, something to suggest a specific link between Stephanopoulos and Room 317. Instead of which, the gut feeling he had had the first time he had come here was still valid.

The preacher had chosen the room for tactical purposes. The most requested and least suspected room, perfectly situated next to the goods lift.

If Mila really had been back to the Ambrus Hotel – and he was sure now that she had – and Steph had helped her disappear, it was because she had wanted to.

She had reached her breaking point. She would never come back.

There was no one left who could clear Berish. They would pin Steph's murder on him, and that was all they needed to blame him for everything else.

A culprit who was alive and well was more exciting news than a preacher who was dead and buried.

The captain was right. No one cares about the victims. They all want the monster.

And Berish was ready.

67

Sunset was draining the last light from the valley.

Berish was sitting on a bench in the park, stroking his dog and admiring the view. They had spent all afternoon strolling around and were both tired now.

Hitch could sense that they would soon be parted, and that this silent visit to his favourite spot was actually a farewell. He was resting his muzzle on Berish's lap and was looking up at him intensely with his brown, incredibly human, eyes.

Berish had got him when he was still a puppy, straight from the breeder. He still remembered Hitch's first night in his apartment – the makeshift barrier to stop him leaving the room, the ball he had bought along with the dog food to encourage him to play, the puppy's lively curiosity about his new sur- roundings, and his desperate wailing when his new master went to bed.

That first time, Berish had been unable to resist, even though the breeder had told him that would happen and that he had to ignore it if he wanted the puppy to get used to being alone. After an hour or so of yelping and whining, he had got out of bed and gone to comfort him. He had sat down on the floor, let Hitch settle between his crossed legs, and stroked him until they had both fallen asleep on the floor.

He had got Hitch because he was convinced that dogs didn't judge you. For a pariah like him, Hitch was the perfect friend. Over time, he had changed his opinion. Dogs could be better judges than anyone, but what they couldn't do – fortunately for humans – was speak.

Berish had already made up his mind to hand himself in, but he wanted to enjoy his dog's company and this lethargic freedom for a little while longer – because he knew that a man stops being free, not when they put handcuffs on him, but the moment they start hunting him down.

Just a few hours from now, he would be in an interrogation room again, with someone he hoped with all his heart he could confess his sins to – even though the only sins his colleagues wanted to hear about were the ones he hadn't committed.

First, though, he had one last thing to do. He owed it to his only friend. And to a little girl.

A fleeting regret went through him and faded with the last drop of sunlight. A dark sea had spread across the valley. The shadows were moving towards him like high tide.

Berish decided it was time to go.

When Mila's mother opened the door, she recognised the face of the fugitive she had just seen on the television news.

'I'm sorry,' Berish said immediately, not knowing what else to say. 'I'm not here to hurt you and I don't know where your daughter is, I swear.'

She peered at him, trying to recover from the fright he had given her. 'They've told me some terrible things about you.'

For a moment, Berish thought she was going to slam the door in his face and call the police. But she didn't.

'The last thing Mila told me the evening before she disappeared was that she trusted you.'

'And do you trust your daughter?' Berish asked, without holding out much hope.

She nodded. 'Yes, I do. Because Mila knows the darkness.'

Berish looked around. 'This won't take long. I've already made up my mind to give myself up as soon as I leave here.'

'I think it's the right thing to do. At least you'll have a chance to defend yourself.'

That won't happen, Berish would have liked to say. But he kept silent.

'I'm Ines.' She held out her hand.

Berish shook it. 'If you don't have any objection, I have a present for your granddaughter.'

He moved aside to reveal Hitch.

Ines looked surprised. 'I've been thinking of getting her a dog. I'd have done it to stop her brooding about her mother's disappearance.'

She let them both in and closed the door.

'He's docile and very obedient,' Berish said.

'Why don't you tell Alice yourself? This hasn't been a good day for her. She fell in the park while running.'

'That kind of thing happens to children.'

'Oh, but didn't Mila tell you? Alice has no awareness of danger.'

'No, she never told me that.'

'Maybe because she thinks of herself as a danger to her own daughter.'

Hearing these words, Berish suddenly understood a lot about Mila.

'If you'd like to talk to Alice, she's in her room.'

*

She walked him there, and stood in the doorway, watching, as Berish advanced into the room. Alice was sitting on the rug in her nightdress. She had a big coloured plaster on her knee.

She was having a tea party. All her dolls had been invited. But pride of place was reserved for the red-headed doll.

'Hello, Alice.'

The girl turned distractedly to see who the man was who had just called her by name. 'Hello,' she said, then looked at the dog standing behind the visitor.

'I'm Simon, and this is Hitch.'

'Hello, Hitch.' Alice accepted the name as if were a small gift.

Hearing his name, the dog barked.

'May we sit with you?'

Alice thought for a moment. 'All right.'

Berish sat down on the floor and Hitch immediately crouched next to them.

'Do you like tea?' Alice asked.

'Very much.'

'Would you like a cup?'

'I'd love one.'

She poured him some of the imaginary drink and handed it to him.

Berish held the cup in mid-air, trying to summon up the strength to speak. 'I'm a friend of your mummy's.'

Alice made no comment on this. It was as if she were trying to shield herself from a painful subject.

'Mila told me about you, and I was curious to see you. That's why I'm here.'

Alice pointed to the cup. 'Aren't you drinking?'

Berish raised it to his lips, a pang in his heart. 'Your mummy will be back soon.' He made that promise without knowing if he was telling the truth or a lie.

'Miss says she's never coming back.'

Berish didn't understand at first. Then he remembered that 'Miss' was Alice's name for her favourite doll. Mila had told him that during their argument, the last time they had spoken.

I provoked her, he thought.

So tell me, what's her favourite colour? What does she like doing? Does she have a doll she takes to bed with her on the nights you're not there?

Yes, a red-headed doll called Miss.

'Your mummy can't do without you,' Berish told Alice, praying that his prophecy would come true.

'Miss says she doesn't love me.'

'Well, she's wrong,' he replied, perhaps a little too vehemently, provoking a surly look from Alice. 'I mean . . . Miss doesn't know that, she can't.'

'Okay.' It was as if Alice were making a mental note of it.

Berish wanted to say more, but he didn't know her well enough. 'The day she comes back, you'll go to the playground together. Or to the cinema to see one of those cartoons children like so much. And you'll eat popcorn, if you like.' He realised how clumsy his attempts were when all Alice did was nod – children have all the wisdom of the world, and sometimes they humour grown-ups as we might humour mad people.

Growing up, Berish had lost that precious common sense and turned into yet another of the stupid people who populate the earth. That was why he decided that enough was enough. He was about to get up when Alice stopped him.

'Won't you come with us?'

The question threw Berish. 'I need to go away for a while, so I'd like to ask you a favour.'

Alice looked at him and waited.

'They don't allow dogs where I'm going ... So, if you'd like to, you could look after Hitch.'

Alice opened her mouth wide in astonishment. 'Really?'

Actually, the question was directed at her grandmother, who was still standing by the door, her arms folded, and who responded by nodding. Alice picked up her favourite doll and handed it to Berish.

'I'm sure they allow dolls where you're going, so she can stay with you and keep you company.'

He didn't know what to say. 'I'll take care of her, I promise. And I swear Miss will be happy with me, too.'

Alice seemed taken aback. 'Her name isn't Miss.'

'Isn't it?'

'No. Miss isn't a doll. She's a person.'

A baleful shudder went through Berish, and he felt a lump in his throat. He took her by the shoulders and made her look him in the face. 'Listen to me, Alice. Who is this person you're talking about?'

For a moment, she seemed puzzled by his question. Then, as if it were the most natural thing in the world: 'Miss is the Goodnight Lady. She always comes and says goodnight to me.'

Hearing this female version of one of Kairus's names froze the blood in Berish's veins. 'Alice, this is very important,' he said. 'You are telling me the truth, aren't you?'

She nodded solemnly.

When you're a child, Berish thought, *your room seems like the least safe place in the world. It's the place where you're forced to sleep alone, at night, in the dark. The wardrobe is where monsters hide and there's always something menacing lurking under the bed.*

But Alice had no awareness of danger, he remembered ...

Maybe that was why her mother watched her from a distance.

In spite of the terror he felt, Berish knew what he had to do.

68

The lights in Mila's small apartment were all out, apart from the light from the computer, reflected on Berish's face. On the screen were images taken at night in Alice's room. Around Berish, there were hundreds of books, stacked up like fortresses.

Searching in the laptop's memory for recordings of the previous few nights, he had found the one from two days earlier – the night Mila had disappeared.

He saw Mila's reflection in the wardrobe mirror as she stood motionless in the corridor. She was listening. The words about to be uttered were probably the ones that had upset her.

Alice was sitting on the bed, speaking softly.

'I love you, too,' she was saying. 'You'll see, we'll always be together.'

But she wasn't talking to the red-headed doll she held in her arms.

There was someone standing in a corner, hiding. A shadowy figure darker than the surrounding darkness. Berish had to move closer to the screen to make it out.

'I won't leave you alone. I'm not like my mummy. I'll always be with you.'

Berish couldn't believe it. He felt an icy blade of fear sink into his back.

'Goodnight, Miss,' Alice said as she got into bed. At that same moment, Mila ran away.

That was when the shadow detached itself from the wall, took a step forward, and stroked the child's hair.

Miss is the Goodnight Lady. She always comes and says goodnight to me.

She didn't know she was being filmed. That was why the action of lifting her head to the camera was totally spontaneous.

69

A dark house shrouded in silence.

Simon Berish was just a dark shape against the glass of the back door, which he had carefully closed behind him.

He was sorry he had left Mila's gun in Steph's office and was now completely unarmed.

But Sylvia probably didn't expect visitors at three in the morning. Maybe she was sure she had already won. It was also possible that she was always on the alert. He couldn't be certain.

He couldn't be certain of anything any more.

The light from the street lamps filtered into the rooms like white fog. Berish took advantage of it to see his way as he walked slowly through the small dining room, his steps barely louder than a whisper, his ears tensed to catch any new sound.

The first thing he did when he reached the corridor was to turn towards the living room. There was the sofa where she had lovingly wiped off Steph's blood. He could still feel the caress of her hand on his neck – an invisible, sacrilegious stigma.

He walked towards the stairs. He had to find out where Sylvia was – he assumed she would be asleep at this hour. He went up one step at a time. The wood creaked beneath his feet. The stairs seemed to go on for ever.

When he reached the landing, he stopped to look at the framed photographs on the walls, illuminated by the greyish moonlight. That morning, Sylvia had told him about her son.

Isn't my boy handsome?

And here they were. At the fairground, on a beach, behind a birthday cake. To an attentive eye, their smiles seemed insincere. They weren't so much showing them as wearing them.

And the boy, growing next to his mother as if by magic, again seemed familiar to Berish. But this time Berish recognised him: Michael Ivanovič.

She's not my mother.

He hadn't understood what Michael had meant by those words during his interrogation, but now it all became clear. He had wondered who Steph had entrusted the six-year-old to after picking him up from Room 317 of the Ambrus Hotel. Now he knew. He had promised him to his precious witness. And Sylvia had accepted the pact in return for that gift.

She had raised him, moulding him according to the precepts of the cult. Then she had sent him back to carry out his deadly mission. She knew that if they caught him, he would never betray her.

This was yet another manifestation of the Hypothesis of Evil. The good that turns to evil then back to good and then back to evil again – in an inexorable cycle of life and death.

The pieces were falling into place. But, as he had that morning, Berish wondered who had taken those pictures.

Then he spotted in the background of one of the pictures the nose of a car he knew.

Steph's Volkswagen.

That was the confirmation he had been seeking.

Two preachers.

A man and a woman. He never imagined that the Goodnight Man had a twofold soul – good and evil.

Find her . . .

Steph's last words. Referring to Sylvia. Or rather, to Kairus, Berish corrected himself.

It was us. By chasing after him all these years, we summoned him. And in the end he appeared. That was what Steph had said. And Berish had assumed it was his madness speaking.

But now there was no time to linger on the implications of his discovery. The doors opening onto the corridor were all open. Berish began inspecting the rooms one by one. When he got to the last one, he realised it was the master bedroom.

He leant forward, expecting to find Sylvia fast asleep. He was already thinking of ways of neutralising her.

But the bed was untouched.

He stopped to think. It was pointless wondering where she was. She could be anywhere. But he was convinced that the house hadn't yet revealed all its secrets.

He went back to the corridor, intending to continue searching downstairs. But his professional instincts told him not to neglect anything.

As he turned to go back downstairs, with his back to the only window, he noticed a thin shadow gently swaying on the wall opposite. Like a pendulum.

He looked up and saw, above his head, a rope hanging from the ceiling.

He reached out to grab it and pulled it down. The trapdoor slid on its hinges and a ladder unrolled in front of him. Like the tongue in a giant's mouth. Like a footbridge leading to another world.

Berish climbed up into the attic.

*

As his head came up through the floor, he breathed in dust and the smell of spent candles. A dormer window cast a beam of icy light that formed a white pool in the middle of the large room.

Around him on the walls were hundreds of photographs.

The effect was similar to the Waiting Room in Limbo. But the faces staring at him from the walls were those of the people who had disappeared from Room 317 of the Ambrus Hotel.

Living people who don't know they're alive. And dead people who can't die.

They were as sad as old ghosts, as tired as people who have too many memories to forget.

Beyond that collection of faces, Berish recognised the form lying on a camp bed. He did not need to ask himself who it was. He ran to her and took her hand.

'Mila,' he said softly.

No reaction. He put his ear against her mouth, hoping to hear her breathing or feel it on his skin. But he was too nervous and couldn't work out if she was still alive. He listened to her heart.

There was a beat, although a weak one.

He would have liked to thank God. But then he saw the state she was in: wearing nothing but her underwear, her hair soaked with sweat, her knickers yellow with urine, her lips cracked from thirst. The scars on her skin were old, but her bare arms were covered in new bruises that were deep and purulent.

Drugs administered intravenously, he thought. They had induced a coma-like sleep.

Just like the man she had loved – Berish knew the story and recognised the grim synchronicity of it all. Before he had sunk into his own sick state of unconsciousness, that man had given her Alice.

But the same thing wouldn't happen to Mila, Berish vowed to himself even before he vowed it to her.

Heedless of any danger that might be lurking in the house, he took her in his arms. He had to get her out of here. She weighed very little. When he turned, he saw Sylvia. She was watching him.

'I can give you a hand if you like,' she said.

These words – normal, sensible, wise – sent more of a shudder through him than any threat might have done. There was no madness in her expression, no malevolence in her voice.

'Seriously,' she insisted, 'I'll help you take her away.'

'Don't come near her,' Berish said coldly.

She wasn't armed, and was still wearing the same dressing gown. After twenty years, she had deceived him again.

With Mila in his arms, Berish moved forward, urged on by all the missing persons on the walls. As he came close to Sylvia, he thought for a moment that she was going to bar his way. They looked at each other like two people trying to learn to recognise one another. Then she stood aside.

He climbed down the ladder, taking care not to lose his balance. He knew she was still watching him. But he ignored her. He retraced his steps all the way to the ground floor. He could hear Sylvia's footsteps behind his, following him at a distance, like a child.

The monster seemed so fragile, and so human.

Before he went out through the front door, he turned to her and a question rose to his lips.

'How many of you are there?'

Sylvia smiled. 'We're an army of shadows.'

As he crossed the threshold, he was blinded by the flashing lights of the police cars that had pulled up in front of the house. But there was no hostility in them.

He saw Klaus Boris come towards him with an alarmed look

on his face. 'How is she?' he asked, referring to Mila.

'She needs help, now.'

The paramedics came up behind Boris with a stretcher. A male nurse relieved Berish of the weight of Mila's unconscious body. He stroked her face as he let go of her. She was put in an ambulance, which set off with sirens blaring.

He followed it with his eyes as he walked down the street.

'Thanks for the phone call,' Boris said.

But Berish didn't even hear him. Just as he didn't see his colleagues handcuff Sylvia and take her silently away. All that Simon Berish – the pariah – wanted to do was disappear.

Room 317 of the Ambrus Hotel

Exhibit 2121-CLLT/6

Transcript of the recording, 23.21 hours on 29
February ███████

Subject: telephone call to the emergency
number at ███████████████ made by the night
porter of the Ambrus Hotel. Switchboard
operator: Officer Clive Irving.

N.B. This call is thirty years earlier than
the present events.

Operator: Police, how may I help you?
Porter:(agitated voice) I'm calling from the
  Ambrus Hotel. I'm the night porter here. A
  woman has died in one of our rooms.
Operator: What's the cause of death?
Porter: Her body is covered in cuts. She's
  been murdered.
Operator: Who did it?
Porter: I have no idea.
Operator: All right, sir. Could the
  perpetrator still be in the hotel?
Porter: . . .

Operator: Sir, did you hear my question?

Porter: Yes, I heard it.

Operator: Then can you give me an answer?

Porter: There was a little girl in the room. She was the one who unlocked the door when we rushed up there after hearing the screams.

Operator: You haven't answered my question.

Porter: Listen, I don't mean any disrespect . . . but did you understand what I just told you? Room 317 was locked from the inside when we arrived.

Operator: I understand. I'll send a patrol car straight away.

End of recording.

70

He had bought her flowers.

After ten days in intensive care, spent struggling between life and death, and another ten days recovering in hospital, Mila was about to be discharged.

Berish didn't want to miss that. He had visited her almost every day. At night he had stood looking through the window of the intensive care unit, watching for the slightest change in her sleeping body. He had been present when the doctors had woken her from the pharmacological coma that had followed the one induced by the powerful drugs administered during her brief captivity. Mila had been in serious danger because those drugs had slowed down her breathing and, deprived of oxygen, she had been slowly dying.

But the doctors had managed to save her. Tests had shown that the early-stage hypoxia had not caused too much damage.

Mila had some motor difficulties – especially in one leg. But other than that, she seemed quite well.

Once she was out of the coma and had left intensive care, Berish had visited less often. He had been anxious to avoid the parade of city dignitaries and department bigwigs who had flocked to the bedside of the new heroine of the media.

The Kairus story had caused an enormous stir.

The only one not to gain anything from it was Berish. But at least the fact that he was still an embarrassment to the Federal Police meant that he was left alone and wasn't displayed to the media like a trained puppet.

Being a pariah had its advantages after all.

Some things, though, had changed. At the Chinese café, none of his colleagues bothered him any more. A couple of days earlier, one of them had actually said hello to him. These were trifling things, of course. Even though the blame lay with Gurevich, he knew he would never be fully rehabilitated in their eyes. But now he could at least come into the café knowing they would let him have his breakfast in peace.

As he walked to the main entrance of the hospital with a bunch of gladioli in his hand, he felt ridiculous. He had let the florist convince him, but he wasn't so sure now that it was the right gift for Mila. There wasn't anything particularly feminine about her. It wasn't that she was masculine, but there was something wild and untamed in her. That was what attracted him to her.

When he got to the sliding door, he noticed a large receptacle in the middle of the smokers' area and dumped the bunch of flowers in it.

Then he went in.

A private room had been set aside for Mila in a wing under police surveillance. There seemed to be something going on. A number of officers stood in the corridor. They had just escorted someone to the room.

Berish recognised Klaus Boris, who had called him at home the night before to summon him here and was now coming towards him with a friendly expression on his face and holding out his hand.

'How is she today?' Berish asked, returning the handshake.

'A lot better than yesterday. And she'll be even better tomorrow.'

Berish pointed to the door. 'Shall we go in?'

'This time I haven't been invited to the party.' Boris handed him a yellow folder. 'Seems like you're the only man who has. Good luck.'

'There are a few things we still have to check out,' Joanna Shutton was saying. She was sitting on one of the two single beds with her legs crossed, showing off her silk stockings. The room was already pervaded with the smell of her Chanel No. 5.

Mila was on the other bed, but she wasn't lying down any more. Her face was pale and there were dark rings under her eyes. She was wearing her hooded top, but hadn't yet put her shoes on. Her feet swung beneath her, not touching the floor. She was sitting, but keeping her balance with her arms. A crutch was propped next to her. A bag with her things stood ready to go home with her.

'Come in, Simon.'

The Judge's tone was intimate, just like the old days, when they were friends.

Berish advanced into the middle of the room with the yellow folder in his hand. Mila gave him a silent smile. She was the one who had requested this meeting. Berish hoped it was a good idea.

'I was just telling her about the latest developments,' Joanna Shutton said. 'Roger Valin, Eric Vincenti and André García are still at large. We suspect they're being sheltered by other members of the cult.'

Berish was pleased to hear that the upper echelons of the department had abandoned that stupid terrorism idea.

'As we know, Nadia Niverman and Diana Müller are dead,' Shutton went on. 'Michael Ivanovič is in a psychiatric hospital and has been declared insane. And last but not least, the female preacher we know as "Sylvia" is in jail and has withdrawn into total silence.'

Berish saw a hint of anxiety on Mila's face.

'At least you now have an idea of how many other missing persons have joined the cult,' she ventured.

'Yes,' the Judge said, 'thanks to the photographs on the walls of the attic where they kept you prisoner.'

Mila nodded.

'But there are still plenty of unanswered questions.' Shutton looked at Berish, as if handing over to him.

'So it's true, Steph killed himself.' Mila still found it hard to believe.

Berish knew how she felt. 'He did it right in front of me. I think he wanted to clear his conscience. Steph knew he was partly responsible for what Sylvia had done. But he found it easier to simply write an address on a sheet of paper, and give me the solution to the mystery that way, than admit his own guilt.'

'So there really were two of them ...' For a moment, Mila seemed overwhelmed, barely able to believe any of it.

Joanna took advantage of the pause to exchange a rapid, knowing glance with Berish, then looked at her watch. 'I have a meeting with Mayor Roche in forty minutes, so I have to go. If you don't mind, Officer Vasquez, Berish will finish the story and answer all your questions.' The Judge held out her hand with its showy rings and polished nails. 'Get well, dear. We need you.'

As she went out, Shutton avoided meeting Berish's eyes again. The door closed. They were alone.

It was only now that Mila noticed the yellow folder Berish was carrying. 'What's that?'

'All right,' he said, almost solemnly, sitting down next to her. 'Let's start from the beginning ...'

71

'Do you remember me telling you about the Hypothesis of Evil?'

'That good and evil aren't separate, but coexist and can even get blurred.'

'Precisely. The factor representing good in this story is Stephanopoulos. As you already know, twenty years ago the captain decided to use the resources of the Witness Protection Unit to help people disappear. They were people he thought deserved a second chance in life. In his judgement, the solution to their problems was to start from scratch. His idea was to give them a new identity, enough money to start over, and the opportunity to live in a place where no one knew what they had done before.'

'Steph was a good man,' Mila said, as if the slightest doubt cast on him hurt her.

'He thought of himself as a benefactor, but he also had a distorted vision of reality, and that got worse over time.' Berish didn't want to say that Steph had probably gone mad, although it was what he meant. 'In the end, I think he became the victim of something bigger than him. In fact, when he realised that something wasn't working in the system he'd created, he made no attempt to come forward and tell the truth. He let people like

Valin or Vincenti murder with impunity. The only thing Steph did to stop things getting even more out of hand was to bring the two of us together by pointing you in my direction.'

Mila sighed, as if admitting that he was right. 'He wanted us to solve the case because he wasn't sure himself what was really going on.'

'To be on the safe side, he followed us to Kairus's nest. When we spotted him, he started the fire to erase his tracks.'

Mila asked him, first with her eyes, then verbally, 'What was it that Steph didn't foresee all those years ago?'

'The dark element that crept into his philanthropic project. Once again, the Hypothesis of Evil.' Berish paused for a moment 'Two preachers: one working for good, the other for evil. And the evil factor in the story is Sylvia.' He still found it hard to speak her name. 'Steph chooses her as the key witness to confirm the existence of Kairus in order to throw the investigation off track. He has enough confidence in her to entrust little Michael to her. But Sylvia isn't what she seems. Quite apart from raising her adopted son as a pyromaniac, she used the people Steph had helped to disappear. She was his shadow, she operated behind his back, and he didn't even notice. She got in touch with these people and persuaded them to join the cult because – and this was Steph's real mistake – it wasn't enough to offer a second chance to people who weren't used to living, people who had been badly treated by life. Predictably, they couldn't handle the new situation, they were full of resentment and hatred. For them, change had turned out to be a painful illusion.'

'So Sylvia became their leader,' Mila said. 'It was as if Steph had recruited them for her. She and Steph were bound together from the start. But how did they meet?'

Berish took a deep breath. 'Room 317 of the Ambrus Hotel.'

Mila raised an eyebrow sceptically.

'The first time we went there, the porter mentioned a crime that took place thirty years ago. We didn't take it into account because it happened ten years before the insomniacs started to go missing. That was our mistake.'

'What happened in Room 317 ten years before Kairus?' Mila asked after a moment's hesitation.

'A murder.' Berish was trying hard not to show how disturbing he found the story. 'The hotel had only opened a few days earlier. One night a woman was stabbed to death. What really created a sensation was that her daughter saw the murder. She only stayed alive because she hid under the bed.'

'Sylvia.' She said it almost automatically.

Berish nodded. 'Since she could identify the killer, the little girl was immediately handed over to the Witness Protection Unit. It was Steph who dealt with her.'

Mila seemed shaken by the revelation. 'Did they ever find the killer?'

'No, never,' Berish said. 'But that isn't all. There's something that doesn't quite add up. People heard the woman scream, but by the time help arrived, they found the room locked from the inside.'

'Could it have been the daughter who . . . ' She didn't complete the question.

'Who knows? Maybe she just closed the door when the killer ran out, because she was afraid he might come back and kill her – fear can make us do all kinds of things. The police certainly thought she was innocent. Among other things, the murder weapon was never found, and according to the pathologist, the wounds were so deep, it was unlikely that a ten-year-old girl would have been strong enough to inflict them.'

That seemed to be all, but Mila could tell from Berish's

expression that there was something else he wanted to say but that he was too afraid to do so. 'There's more, isn't there?'

'Yes,' he admitted with a sigh, and handed her the yellow folder.

Mila stared at it, reluctant to open it.

'It's all right, take your time,' Berish said.

At last she opened the folder. It contained a single photograph.

'It was taken at the scene of the crime,' he said.

Mila recognised Room 317 – the dark red wallpaper, the matching carpet with the huge blue flowers. The bed looked just the way she remembered it. There was a crucifix on the wall and a Bible on one of the bedside tables. What was missing was the faded aura the place now had. At the time the photograph was taken, very few guests had walked on that carpet or slept in those sheets, so everything looked new and untouched. In the doorway stood some of the hotel staff: a black porter in a uniform with white and burgundy stripes, and two chambermaids in starched caps and spotless white aprons. There was an atmosphere of decorum. The Ambrus Hotel hadn't yet become a place for illicit encounters.

As Berish had said, it was a crime scene, so there were police officers and forensics people going about their work. The victim was lying on the bed, covered in a blood-soaked sheet. In the background, a girl who looked about ten clung in tears to a policewoman who was taking her out of the room. The girl must have been Sylvia. Next to them, a young Steph seemed to be telling his female colleague to take good care of her.

Mila kept looking at the picture. Everyone seemed either busy performing a task, or stricken with horror at the sight of the body on the bed.

Only one man was looking at the camera.

He was in a corner of the room – and of the photograph –

holding a brass knob from which hung the key to Room 317. He was wearing a dark red uniform – the uniform of a hotel porter. There was a smile on his face. The man, who seemed to be posing for the shot, was the Whisperer.

Mila couldn't take her eyes off him.

Berish took her hand. 'Why did you go to the Ambrus Hotel? Why did you take the sleeping pill that had been left for you on the bedside table?'

Mila looked up. 'Because it's from the darkness that I come. And to the darkness that I must, from time to time, return.'

'What does that mean, Mila? I don't understand.'

She stared at him. 'What's there to understand? *He* knows. Because he knows me.'

Berish guessed that she was referring to the Whisperer.

'He knew I'd do it because the call is always too strong, the temptation too painful to resist.' She paused. 'And if you can't understand that ... '

She didn't finish the sentence but Berish knew what she was trying to say. He could never get close to her if he didn't understand why she was always drawn to the unknown.

But then, as if to console him, Mila went on, 'I met him only once, seven years ago. The only words he said to me marked me deeply. It was a kind of prophecy. Or maybe it was just a shot in the dark.' Mila closed the folder. 'He's no different from other human beings. He eats, he sleeps, he has the same needs as anyone else. He has his weaknesses, too, and he can die. We just have to catch him. The rest is just a pointless, wicked fantasy.'

These final remarks brought Berish some relief. 'Do you really remember nothing about those days you spent in Sylvia's attic?'

'I told you, I was asleep all the time,' Mila replied with a smile, handing him back the yellow folder. 'I'm fine. All I want to do is go and see my daughter.'

Berish nodded. He was about to leave the room.

'Simon,' she said, stopping him.

He turned.

'Thank you.'

22 October

Her mother was coming home.

To welcome her appropriately, her grandmother had insisted she wear her prettiest dress, the blue velvet one, with her shiny shoes. But Alice didn't like that dress. It rode up to her waist when she sat down and she was always having to pull it down. Plus, she couldn't play in it because Ines kept telling her not to get it dirty.

Wearing that dress was a sure-fire way to get told off.

Her grandmother said it was a special day: Mila had been through a rough time, and they had to be nice to her. Alice had agreed to play her part, never imagining it would involve drastic changes – nobody had told her about it, nobody had consulted her. Ines had simply packed a little bag for her and told her she was moving to her mother's house because Mila wanted to spend some time with her.

For the moment, she could only take three toys with her. It had been hard to choose, because the red-headed doll – her favourite, returned to her – obviously had to be one of the three, so it was all the others she had to decide among and she didn't want to be unfair to any of them.

How would they be able to sleep without her in that room in her grandmother's house? And would she feel lonely without them?

Luckily, there was Hitch. The policeman named Simon hadn't wanted him back even though he hadn't in the end gone to the place where they didn't allow dogs, as he'd told her he would. He came to see him every day and they would all go out to the park together. Alice knew her friend would go back to his real master sooner or later, but she hoped she could keep him a little while longer.

Simon said Hitch would stay with her and teach her to understand danger and to assess the risk in things. When she had learnt that, then he would take the dog back.

She liked Simon. What she liked most about him was the way he talked to her. He never told her what to do, but waited for her to work it out for herself.

Adults are never patient, Alice thought. But Simon was different. He had even asked her about Miss. But when he asked questions, he never looked at her as if she had done something wrong.

Alice had told him that Miss was able to get into the house thanks to the key hidden in the garden under the pot of begonias.

It had all started because of the red-headed doll.

She had taken it to school, hidden in her rucksack. The teacher didn't want them to bring toys to class, but for Alice the doll wasn't a toy but her best friend – and that was a different thing entirely.

But then something awful had happened.

During the day, Alice had been so busy that she had forgotten all about her. By the end of classes, when the school bus had taken her back home, the red-headed doll had disappeared.

Alice was in a panic, and didn't know what to do. She couldn't even tell her grandmother, who would be sure to punish her. She thought of giving Mila a photograph of the doll because Ines had told her that her mummy looked for people who were missing, and so she was sure she could find her doll.

But her mother didn't come that evening. And Alice found it hard to get to sleep, wondering where her dear friend could possibly be – scared and alone, out there in the cold.

At some point during that restless night, she had a felt a hand on her forehead. At first, she thought her prayers had been answered and Mila had come to her. But then she had opened her eyes and seen another woman sitting on her bed. She was always being told off for not being aware of danger, but this time there was nothing to be afraid of, because the stranger was holding her red-headed friend in her arms.

She had come to give her back her doll.

'What's your name?' Alice had asked her.

'I don't have a name.'

And so she had simply started calling her 'Miss'.

Having returned something that Alice thought she had lost for ever, the woman had asked her if she would like her to come back and see her every now and then. Alice had said yes. She didn't come every night, only occasionally. She'd ask her about school, about the games she played. She was always nice. Alice felt a little bad at first, because she was breaking one of her grandmother's rules: never talk to strangers. But if Miss came to her house, then she couldn't be a stranger.

Simon had agreed with her about that. That was why Alice trusted him.

But there was another secret she would have liked to tell him.

She had made Miss a promise, with her hand on her heart. It had happened the last time she came to see her. And everyone knew you couldn't break promises made with your hand on your heart. A school friend had told her that his older cousin knew a boy who had broken a solemn oath and had then suddenly disappeared for ever. No one knew what had happened to him and his parents were still looking for him.

Alice didn't want to disappear for ever. And only Miss could release her from her promise.

But when Mila came back from the hospital and took her to her apartment, she was tempted to tell her everything. Then her mother hugged her, which was something she never did. And as she held her, Alice didn't feel any warmth coming from her body. That was strange. It wasn't like when her grandmother hugged her. There was something . . . wrong.

Then Mila showed her around her new home. It was full of books, so many books you could hardly move – there were even books in the toilet.

That evening, they had dinner together. Her mother had made pasta with meatballs. It wasn't actually very good, but Alice didn't say anything. Hitch wolfed it all down. Mila was behaving differently from usual – for example she stood by the bathroom door and watched Alice as she cleaned her teeth. Then the dog settled in an armchair and she and Mila went to bed. The mattress was too narrow for the two of them and the pillows weren't as comfortable as she liked. They switched off the light and lay there in silence. Alice knew her mummy was still awake. Little by little, she moved closer to her. Then Mila reached out and pulled Alice towards her.

This time, the feeling wasn't wrong.

Alice crouched on top of her. Mila started stroking her long ash-blonde hair. Slowly, the action came to a stop. From the rhythm of her breathing, Alice knew her mummy was falling asleep. But she herself couldn't get to sleep yet. Mila moved and said something. She must have been dreaming. Alice thought again about the secret Miss had confided in her.

There's a special person who wants to meet you.
Who?
Someone who can make all your wishes come true.
Any wish?
Any wish at all.

She wasn't sure it was true, although she wanted to believe it. There was only one way to find out the truth. She had to follow the instructions the Goodnight Lady had made her learn by heart. So she slipped out of her mother's arms and walked barefoot across the cold floor to the window.

Outside, directly facing her on the building opposite, was a huge billboard with a couple of smiling giants. But then she lowered her eyes and saw him. Miss was right. He was waiting for her. He was there, looking straight up at her window. Dust whirled in the wind between the walls of the alleyway. A scrap of paper was dancing around his legs, like a ghost child demanding attention.

Alice raised her hand and waved at him.

The tramp smiled back.

Exhibit 2573-KL/777

██████████████ Prison
Penitentiary District N. 45

Report of the Director, Dr Jonathan Stern
25 October
For the attention of Chief Prosecutor Bertrand
Owen

Subject: CONFIDENTIAL

Dear Mr Owen,
In reply to your request for regular
information regarding prisoner GZ-997/11, I
wish to inform you that Sylvia is still in
solitary confinement. She does not communicate
with the prison staff and spends most of her
day sleeping. She does not exhibit any
behaviour contrary to the rules and does not
make any requests.
   However, I must bring it to your attention

that in the past few days she has acquired a somewhat unusual habit.

She constantly cleans and washes everything she touches, picks up the hairs she sheds on the pillow or in the sink, and cleans the dishes and the toilet every time she uses them.

In other circumstances, we would be tempted to suspect that this unusual fastidiousness is intended to prevent us from obtaining organic material in order to extract her DNA.

But having already performed genetic tests, without finding a match, we have yet to find an explanation for this unusual behaviour.

I cannot refrain from pointing out the remarkable similarity to another prisoner who, many years ago, was involved in what is now known as the Whisperer case.

I hope I have answered your query fully, and will keep you informed of further developments.

Yours sincerely

Dr Jonathan Stern
Director

Author's Note

We have all wanted to disappear at least once in our lives.

When things get too much for us, we may think the solution is to go to the station and get on a train at random – maybe just to escape for a few hours, on a sunny Tuesday morning in winter. If we've ever done it, we'll never talk about it. But we'll never forget that liberating feeling when we switched off our mobile phone and forgot all about the internet, breaking free of the shackles of technology and trusting to fate to take us where it wanted.

A novel about missing persons returning had been an obsession of mine for a long time. I would even go so far as to say that it was the origin of the character of Mila Vasquez.

Before I began writing, I interviewed police officers, private detectives and journalists. But above all, I talked to the friends and relatives of those who chose the darkness – or were chosen by it.

In all these encounters, however, I always had the feeling that I was exploring only part of the phenomenon: the part that is in the light. The other part invariably remained unknown.

*

My obsession with missing persons would have remained unresolved if one of them had not contacted me one day.

After *The Whisperer* was published, I received an email from a man who claimed to have 'erased' his previous existence and started a completely new one – with a different identity and a whole new set of relationships.

I had no way of checking if what he told me was true or a cleverly concocted piece of deception. But we began a correspondence, in the course of which I learnt a series of truths – all well-argued – that fascinated me to such an extent that a story began to form in my mind.

This unknown man described in great detail how to bring to fruition what may start as only a fantasy. The only time he departed from strict anonymity was to tell me his nationality – Italian – and the name of his cat: Kairus.

At the end of our brief exchange of emails, I realised that the only way to really understand what it meant to vanish into thin air . . . was to vanish myself.

My escape, though, lasted barely a few weeks, the time I needed to bring my novel into focus. Obviously, those closest to me were informed, and I never really cut the umbilical cord connecting me to my previous life. But I did switch off my mobile phone and temporarily abandoned my email addresses and social network profiles. Suddenly, I found myself in a parallel world.

For obvious reasons, my experiment was a fairly mild one, partly because I was constantly aware that my time as a missing person would come to an end. I did discover, though, that disappearing doesn't always mean liberation: the darkness beckons to you at first, then wins you over, and only lets you go on its own terms.

When I returned home, family and friends asked me where I had been. I always replied with the short version of the truth: visiting morgues.

They know now that the slightly longer answer is this book.

Whenever the question of disappearances comes up, the same statistics are always trotted out. But there is no point listing figures here, or reiterating that an average of twenty-one people out of every million disappear every day – that data has appeared in newspapers before now.

What nobody points out is that it is impossible to say how many missing persons there are around us at any given moment. In the streets, on the buses, as we do our shopping. We look at them, but we just don't know.

But they too, hidden behind their false identities, are looking at us.

That is why my most heartfelt gratitude goes to the anonymous author of the emails that brought all this home to me – whether he was a real missing person or not – as well as to his cat Kairus. Wherever you are and whatever you are doing, I hope for you that it was worth it.

Donato Carrisi

Acknowledgements

Stefano Mauri, my publisher. For his esteem and friendship. Because respect for the readers depends on trusting the writer.

Fabrizio Cocco. For his constant and indispensable presence. I am indebted to his dark wit and his talent.

Giuseppe Strazzeri, Valentina Fortichiari, Elena Pavanetto, Cristina Foschini, Giuseppe Somenzi, Graziella Cerutti. Their invaluable passion transforms my stories into books.

Deborah Kaufmann. Because Paris is also now partly my home.

Vito, Ottavio, Michele. True friends always show you the way.

Alessandro, for the future. Achille, for the beginning. Maria Giovanna Luini, for the present.

My sister Chiara, my parents, my family.

Elisabetta. The words belong to her.

In particular, Luigi Bernabò, my agent. A model of style – in life and in writing. For his strength, his tenacity, his affection.

My sources:

Officer 'Massimo' of Police Headquarters in Rome, who years ago inspired the character of Mila Vasquez. 'I look for them everywhere. I'm always looking for them' are his words, and they perfectly sum up the torment he goes through. The silence of missing persons is his curse.

Byron J. Jones, known as 'Mister Nobodies'. He is the man who helps people to disappear, a genuine escape artist.

Jean-Luc Venieri, who led me through the obscure temples of anthropology and explained how, like criminology, it could become a useful investigative tool.

Professor Michele Distante, author of the article *The cult and the figure of the preacher*.

All proceeds due to me from sales of the Greek translation of this novel will remain in Greece and will be donated to Boroume (www.boroume.gr), which provides meals to those in need. At such a difficult time in the history of that great country, I cannot forget the debt that human civilisation owes her culture. If, for example, thousands of years ago, the Greeks had not coined and given meaning to words like 'hypothesis' and 'anthropology', I would not have been able to tell the story you have just read.

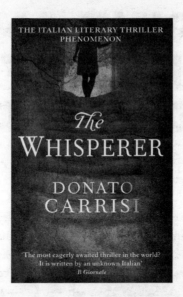

THE ITALIAN LITERARY THRILLER
PHENOMENON

The
WHISPERER

DONATO
CARRISI

'The most eagerly awaited thriller in the world?
It is written by an unknown Italian'
Il Giornale

Six severed arms are discovered buried in a forest clearing.
They are arranged in a mysterious circle, and appear to belong
to missing girls between the ages of eight and thirteen.
But the rest of the bodies are nowhere to be found.

Criminologist Goran Gavila is given the case.
A dishevelled, instinctively rebellious man, he is forced to
work with young female police officer Mila Vasquez. Lithe,
boyish, answering to no one, Mila has a reputation as a specialist
in missing children. She also has a tragic history of her own that
has left her damaged, unable to feel or to relate to others.

Theirs is a fiery but strangely affecting working relationship –
and as they uncover more secrets about the dark secrets in
the forest, their lives are increasingly in each other's hands ...

*

'Gripping, multi-layered and difficult to put down,
this is a top class literary thriller' *Choice*

CRIME AND THRILLER FAN?

CHECK OUT THECRIMEVAULT.COM

The online home of
exceptional crime fiction

KEEP YOURSELF
IN SUSPENSE

Sign up to our newsletter for regular recommendations,
competitions and exclusives at www.thecrimevault.com/connect

Follow us on twitter for all the latest news @TheCrimeVault